Dora got to her feet and wriggled the dress over her head.

Only a moment after she'd dunked the whole thing in the fountain, however, she heard a man's voice utter a foul swear word behind her.

"What *are* you doing, you mad little twit?"

Dora glanced behind her and saw the Lord Sorcier standing just behind the bench she'd just vacated. His finery was every bit as pristine and untouched as it had been at the beginning of the evening, except that he had now loosened his neck cloth a bit. His golden eyes raked her up and down, clearly aghast.

"I would have thought the situation was self-evident," Dora told him calmly. "Does a man of your formidable knowledge really require the concept of laundry to be explained to him?"

By Olivia Atwater

REGENCY FAERIE TALES
Half a Soul
Ten Thousand Stitches
Longshadow

HALF a SOUL

Regency Faerie Tales: Book One

OLIVIA ATWATER

orbitbooks.net

Copyright © 2020 by Olivia Atwater
The Lord Sorcier copyright © 2020 by Olivia Atwater
Excerpt from *Ten Thousand Stitches* copyright © 2020 by Olivia Atwater

Cover images by Shutterstock

Orbit
Hachette Book Group
1290 Avenue of the Americas
New York, NY 10104
orbitbooks.net

First Orbit Paperback Edition: June 2022
Simultaneously published in Great Britain by Orbit
First Orbit eBook Edition: April 2022
Originally published by Starwatch Press in 2020

Orbit is an imprint of Hachette Book Group.
The Orbit name and logo are trademarks of Little, Brown Book Group Limited.

The publisher is not responsible for websites (or their content) that are not owned by the publisher.

The Hachette Speakers Bureau provides a wide range of authors for speaking events. To find out more, go to www.hachettespeakersbureau.com or call (866) 376-6591.

Library of Congress Control Number: 2021952843

ISBNs: 9780316462709 (trade paperback), 9780316462808 (ebook)

Printed in Canada

MRQ

6   2023

Dramatis Personae

Theodora Eloisa Charity Ettings – the previous Lord Lockheed's daughter and ward of the current Lord Lockheed; only possesses half a soul; goes by Dora

Vanessa Ettings – Lord Lockheed's daughter; Dora's younger cousin; prize of the marriage market

Frances Ettings – Lady Lockheed; Dora's aunt and guardian; a meddling hen

Lady Hayworth – the countess of Hayworth; a friend of Auntie Frances; another meddling hen

Elias Wilder – the uncouth Lord Sorcier and court magician of England; performs three impossible things before breakfast each day

Mr Albert Lowe – Lord Carroway's third son; a charitable physician and war veteran; the only man in London who enjoys the Lord Sorcier's company

Lord Carroway – the viscount of Carroway; Albert's father

Lady Carroway – the viscountess of Carroway; Albert's mother

Miss Henrietta Jennings – ex-governess, spinster and chaperone; companion to Lady Hayworth's daughter

George Ricks – workhouse master of the Cleveland Street Workhouse

Mrs Martha Dun – a merchant's widow; runs an orphanage sponsored by Lady Carroway and the Lord Sorcier

Mr Edward Lowe – Lord Carroway's oldest son; Albert's older brother; an exceedingly eligible bachelor

Abigail – a child afflicted by the sleeping plague

Lord Hollowvale – faerie nobility; the marquess of Hollowvale; fascinated with English propriety; in possession of half of Dora's soul and several very fine coats

Lady Mourningwood – a faerie baroness and dour chaperone

Lord Blackthorn – a faerie viscount and English enthusiast

Prologue

Theodora Eloisa Charity Ettings was a very long name for a very small girl. This, her aunt liked to say, was probably why she was such a handful – by the time one had fully shouted the words "Theodora Eloisa Charity Ettings, you get back here this instant!" said ten-year-old girl was almost always long gone.

Today, Theodora Eloisa Charity Ettings – who generally preferred the name Dora – was busily escaping her adult captors, with the goal of making her way to the wild woods behind Lockheed Manor. These woods were full of fantastic trees to climb and fast-flowing muddy creeks with which to dirty her skirt hem, all of which sounded much more interesting than sitting down to learn embroidery with her cousin Vanessa.

Auntie Frances's shouts faded behind Dora as she darted through the tree line, giggling to herself. Strands of her curly, reddish-gold hair caught among the branches, tugging their way free from her neatly coiffed bun. Dora tripped over her pristine white skirts, catching herself just in time to avoid a fall – but the toe of her slipper ground the fabric of her hem into the dirt, staining both shoe and dress. Later, Dora's aunt would be furious and her punishment severe . . . but for now, Dora was free, and she had every intention of taking advantage while she could.

There was a particularly good tree for climbing just across the creek, near the blackbird's nest she'd found last time. Dora hadn't got very far up the tree before getting stuck, but she'd ruminated on the problem for more than two weeks now, and she was sure she would be able to climb much higher this time if she set her mind to it.

Just as Dora had settled onto the banks of the creek to pull off her slippers, however, an elegant male voice spoke from behind her.

"Oh, little girl," it sighed. "How like your mother you look."

Dora turned her head curiously, wiggling her bare toes in the cold water before her. The man behind her had appeared quite out of nowhere – and surely there had to be magic involved, because his long white coat was unstained by his surroundings, and his eyes were the fairest shade of pale blue that she had ever seen before. Being an imaginative little girl, Dora was not surprised to note that his ears were very gently pointed at the tips, but she *was* very surprised to see that he was wearing at least four jackets of different cut and colour, all layered carelessly atop one another.

"I don't look a thing like my mother, Goodman Elf," Dora informed him matter-of-factly – as though tall, handsome elves addressed her every day of her life. "Auntie Frances says that Mother's hair was lighter than mine, and that she had brown eyes instead of green."

The elfin man gave Dora a kind smile. "You humans always miss the most important details," he said. "It's not your fault, of course. But your mother's soul and yours are of the same bright thread. I spotted the resemblance in an instant."

Dora pursed her lips consideringly. "Oh," she said. "I suppose that makes sense. Well – were you one of Mother's friends, Goodman Elf?"

"Alas," the elf told her, "I was not. Once, she may have called me such – but she later changed her mind in a manner most abrupt." His unnatural blue eyes fixed upon Dora, and she felt a strange shiver go through her. "You have also been very impolite, firstborn child of Georgina Ettings," he said. "I am no 'Goodman Elf'. Indeed, you should address me as 'Your Lordship' or 'Lord Hollowvale', for I am the marquess of that realm. You can tell that I am important, for I am wearing many expensive jackets."

Dora narrowed her eyes at the elf. At first, it had been quite a delight to meet a real-life faerie – but she was now beginning to suspect that she would be much happier crossing the creek and climbing her tree. "I had no way of knowing your title," Dora sniffed. "And I have never heard of Hollowvale, anyway. If it's a real place, then it is far outside His Majesty's domain, and therefore of no consequence here."

Those pale blue eyes blazed with ice. The water at Dora's feet grew even more chilly than before, and she pulled her toes up out of the creek in a hurry.

"Do you not know what happens to impolite young children who wander in the woods, firstborn child of Georgina Ettings?" Lord Hollowvale asked Dora in a quiet, dangerous voice.

Dora backed her way slowly towards the creek. "You said you weren't my mother's friend," she told the elf warily. "I have no cause to be polite to strange men who sneak up on me, Lord Hollowvale."

The elf's pale hand flashed forward like a serpent, grasping Dora by the neck. She let out a strangled cry, reaching up to claw at his hand with her fingernails – but he was much stronger than he appeared, and there was a cold, inhuman fury to his grip.

"Georgina Ettings promised me her firstborn child," Lord Hollowvale told Dora in his chilly voice. "And I shall take my due. I expect that you shall be much more polite once I have taken your soul, little girl."

Dora tore at his hand, thrashing and writhing in fear. But as the elf spoke, a strange coldness ran through her body, wiping away the sharpest edges of her terror. Her protests slowed, and her mind began to wander strangely. An elf had snatched her from the creek, it was true – but the danger that he posed seemed less pressing and more dreamlike than before. Surely this problem would pass, and Dora would soon continue on her way to the tree she was after.

Lord Hollowvale let out a sudden cry of pain, however, and he dropped her to the ground.

Behind him, Dora's golden-haired cousin Vanessa stumbled back, with a pair of bloody iron scissors in her hand and a horrified expression on her pretty features. *Oh dear*, Dora thought to herself distantly. *But Vanessa is so sweet and obedient. How could she stab a marquess with her embroidery scissors?*

"Dora!" Vanessa gasped fearfully. She stumbled across the mud towards her cousin, helping her up from the ground. "Please, Dora, let's run, we *must!*"

Lord Hollowvale staggered to his feet, clutching at the back of his leg. Vanessa had given him a terrible gash along the back of his calf, such that he had to limp towards them. Deep crimson blood stained his fine white coat, and his face twisted with terrible anger. "This girl's soul is mine by right!" he hissed. "You will give her to me this instant!"

Vanessa turned upon the faerie, holding her bloody scissors before her with a stricken expression. "I do not want to hurt you," she said. "But you shall not touch my cousin, not for *any* reason."

Lord Hollowvale jerked back from the scissors. Fear briefly clouded his face as he glanced down at them – a strange circumstance, since the scissors were only slightly bigger than Vanessa's tiny fist, and their eyes were decorated with cheerful little roses. Vanessa drew Dora slowly around the faerie and back towards the manor, keeping her scissors squarely between herself and the marquess.

"As you wish, niece of Georgina Ettings," the elf spat finally. "I have full half of my payment. May you make good use of the other!"

And then – even as they watched, with their eyes fixed directly upon his form – he disappeared into thin air.

"Oh, Dora," Vanessa sobbed, as soon as the elf had gone. "Are you all right? Has that awful elf done something to you? I was so afraid. I only meant to scold you back to lessons, but he was right there, and I had my scissors in my apron—"

"Why are you so upset?" Dora asked her curiously. She knit her brow at her cousin. "Why, it's over and done with now. You can come and climb my tree with me if you like."

Vanessa looked at her, bewildered. "Are you *not* upset?" she asked fearfully. "He was very terrible, Dora, and all of that *blood* . . ."

Dora smiled pleasantly at her cousin, though she felt as she did that something important was missing from behind the expression – something that had been there only minutes ago. "I suppose I *should* be upset," she said. "A normal person would be, wouldn't they? But perhaps I will be upset later, after I have thought on it."

Vanessa insisted that they return to the manor immediately. Dora went with her, though she still had a fondness for the tree across the creek. As Vanessa wept relating the story to Auntie Frances, it slowly began to dawn on Dora that she was not acting as she normally ought to act. All of her emotions had dulled to a distant sort of fancy – as though she were observing herself in a dream.

Auntie Frances gave them both the most horrified look, as Vanessa recounted the elf's words. "*Quiet!*" she begged Vanessa. "Quiet, both of you. You mustn't say a word of this to anyone else, do you understand? Do not even speak of it to your father, Vanessa!"

Vanessa gave Auntie Frances a teary, wide-eyed look. "Why ever not?" she asked. "That elf has *done* something to Dora, I know he has! We must find someone who can fix her!"

Auntie Frances snatched at her daughter's arm, dragging her

forward. She got down on one knee and lowered her voice fearfully. "Dora is faerie-cursed," Auntie Frances said. "Look at her eyes! One of them has lost its colour! Perhaps the entire rest of this family is cursed with her, if it's true what her foolish mother did. If anyone were to find out, we would be driven off the land!"

Dora's aunt made them both swear not to breathe a word to anyone else. Dora found this perfectly agreeable. In fact, she felt no distress about the situation at all, except for a faint bit of worry, easily ignored. It was rather like a fly, buzzing distantly about in the corner – she knew it was there when she bothered to pay attention to it, but in the greater scheme of things, it really didn't signify at all.

Vanessa promised only with the greatest reluctance. When they went to bed that night, she crawled beneath the covers with Dora and held her tightly.

They slept with the iron pair of scissors just beneath the pillows.

Chapter One

ir Albus Balfour was nattering on about his family's horses again.

Now, to be clear, Dora *liked* horses. She didn't mind the occasional discussion on the subject of equine family trees. But Sir Albus had the most singular way of draining all normal sustenance from a conversation with his monotonous voice and his insistence on drawing out the first syllable in the word *pure*bred. By Dora's admittedly distracted count, in fact, Sir Albus had used the word *pure*bred nearly a hundred times since she and Vanessa had first arrived at Lady Walcote's dratted garden party.

Poor Vanessa. She had finally come out into society at eighteen years old – and already she found herself surrounded by suitors of the worst sort. Her luscious golden hair, her fair, unfreckled complexion and her utterly sweet demeanour had so far attracted every scoundrel, gambler and toothless old man within the county. Surely Dora's lovely cousin would be equally attractive to far better suitors . . . but Dora greatly suspected that such men were out in London, if they were to be found anywhere at all.

At nineteen – very nearly pushing twenty! – Dora was on the verge of being considered a spinster, though she had supposedly entered society alongside her cousin. In reality, Dora knew that Vanessa had only put off her own debut for so long in order to keep her company. No one in the family was under any illusions as to Dora's attractiveness to potential suitors, with her one strange eye and her bizarre demeanour.

"Have you ever wondered what might happen if we bred a horse with a dolphin, Sir Albus?" Dora interrupted distantly.

"I— What?" The older fellow blinked, caught off his stride by the unexpected question. His salt-and-pepper moustache twitched, and the wrinkles at the corners of his eyes deepened, perplexed. "No, I cannot say that I have, Miss Ettings. The two simply do not mix." He seemed at a loss that he even had to explain the second part. Sir Albus turned his attention instantly back towards Vanessa. "Now, as I was saying, the mare was *pure*bred, but she wasn't to be of any use unless we could find an equally impressive stud—"

Vanessa winced imperceptibly at the repetition of the word *pure*bred. Aha. So she *had* noticed the awful pattern.

Dora interrupted again.

"—but do you think such a union would produce a dolphin's head and a horse's end, or do you think it would be the other way around?" she asked Sir Albus in a bemused tone.

Sir Albus shot Dora a venomous look. "Now see here," he began.

"Oh, what a fun thought!" Vanessa said, with desperate cheer. "You do always come up with the most wonderful games, Dora!" Vanessa looped her arm through Dora's, squeezing at her elbow a bit more firmly than was necessary, then turned her eyes back towards Sir Albus. "Might we inquire as to your expert opinion, sir?" she asked. "Which would it be, do you think?"

Sir Albus flailed at this, flustered out of his rhythm. He had only one script, Dora observed idly, and absolutely no imagination with which to deviate from it. "I . . . I could not possibly answer such an absurd question!" he managed. "The very idea! It's impossible!"

"Oh, but I'm sure that the Lord Sorcier would know," Dora

observed to Vanessa. Her thoughts meandered slowly away from the subject, and on to other matters. "I hear the new court magician is quite talented. He defeated Napoleon's Lord Sorcier at Vitoria, you know. He does at least three impossible things before breakfast, the way I hear it told. Certainly, *he* could tell us which end would be which."

Vanessa blinked at that for some reason, as though Dora had revealed a great secret to her instead of a bit of idle gossip. "Well," Vanessa said slowly, "the Lord Sorcier is almost certainly in London, far away from here. And I wonder if he would lower himself to answering such a question, even if it *were* the sort of impossible thing he could accomplish." Vanessa cleared her throat and turned her eyes to the rest of the garden party. "But perhaps there are some here with a less *impossible* grasp of magic who might offer their expert opinion instead?"

Sir Albus's moustache was all but vibrating now, as he failed to suppress his outrage at the conversation's turn away from him and his prized horses. "Young lady!" he sputtered towards Dora. "That is *quite* enough! If you wish to discuss flights of fancy, then please do so somewhere far afield from us. We are having a serious, adult conversation!"

The man's vehemence was such that a drop of spittle hit Dora along the cheek. She blinked at him slowly. Sir Albus was red-faced and shaking with upset, leaning towards her in a vaguely threatening manner. Dimly, Dora knew she *ought* to be afraid of him – any other lady might have cringed back from such a violent outpouring of passion. But whatever impulse normally made ladies wither and faint in the face of frightening things had been lost on its way to her conscious mind for years on end now.

"Sir!" Vanessa managed in a shocked, trembling voice. "You must not address my cousin in such a way. Such behaviour is absolutely beyond the pale!"

Dora glanced towards her cousin, considering the way that

her lip trembled and her hands clutched together. Quietly, she tried to mirror the gestures. Her aunt had begged her to act *normal* at this party, after all.

For a moment, as Dora turned her trembling lip back towards Sir Albus, a chastised look crossed his eyes. "I . . . I do apologise," he said stiffly. But Dora noticed that he addressed the apology to Vanessa, and not to her.

"Apologise for what?" Dora murmured absently. "For impacting your chances with my cousin, or for acting the boor?"

Sir Albus widened his eyes in shocked fury.

Oh, Dora thought with a sigh. *That was not the sort of thing that normal, frightened women say, I suppose.*

"Your apology is accepted!" Vanessa blurted out quickly. She pushed to her feet as she spoke, dragging Dora firmly away by the arm. "But I . . . I'm afraid I must go and regain my composure, sir. We shall have to discuss this further at another time."

Vanessa charged for the house with as much ladylike delicacy as she could muster while hauling her older cousin behind her.

"I've fumbled things again, haven't I?" Dora asked her softly. A distant pang of distress clenched at her heart. Acute problems rarely seemed to trouble Dora the way that they should, but emotions born of longer, wearier issues still hung upon her like a shroud. *Vanessa should be married by now*, Dora thought. *She would be married if not for me.* It was an old idea by now, and it never failed to sadden her.

"Oh no, you haven't at all!" Vanessa reassured her cousin as they slipped inside the house. "You've saved me again, Dora. Perhaps you were a bit pert, but I don't know if I could have stood to listen to him say that word even one more time!"

"What, *pure*bred?" Dora asked, with a faint curve of her lips.

Vanessa shuddered. "Oh, please don't," she said. "It's just awful. I'll never be able to listen to anyone talk about horses again without hearing it that way."

Dora smiled gently back at her. Though Dora's soul was

numb and distant, her cousin's presence remained a warm and steady light beside her. Vanessa was like a glowing lantern in the dark, or a comforting fire in the hearth. Dora had no joy of her own – though she knew the sense of contentment, or a kind of pleasant peace. But when Vanessa was happy, Dora sometimes swore she could feel it rubbing off on her, seeping into the holes where her own happiness had once been torn away and lighting a little lantern of her own.

"I don't think you would have enjoyed marrying him anyway," Dora told Vanessa. "Though I'll be sad if I've scared away some other man you would have liked more."

Vanessa sighed heavily. "I don't intend to marry and leave you all alone, Dora," she said quietly. "I really worry that Mother might turn you out entirely if I wasn't there to insist otherwise." Her lips turned down into a troubled frown that was still somehow prettier than any smile had ever looked on Dora's face. "But if I *must* marry, I should hope that it would be a man who didn't mind you coming to live with me."

"That is a very difficult thing to ask," Dora chided Vanessa, though the words touched gently at that warm, ember glow within her. "Few men will wish to share their new wife with some mad cousin who wears embroidery scissors around her neck."

Vanessa's eyes glanced towards the top of Dora's dress. They both knew of the little leather sheath that pressed against her breast, still carrying those iron scissors. It had been Vanessa's idea. *Lord Hollowvale fears those scissors*, she had said, *so you should have them on you always, in case he comes for you and I am not around to stab him in his other leg.*

Vanessa pursed her lips. "Well!" she said. "I suppose I shall have to be difficult, then. For the only way I shall ever be parted from you, Dora, is if you become mad with love and desert me for some wonderful husband of your own." Her eyes brightened at the thought. "Wouldn't it be wonderful if we fell in love at the same time? I could go to your wedding, then, and you could come to mine!"

Dora smiled placidly at her cousin. *No one is ever going to marry me*, she thought. But she didn't say it aloud. The thought was barely a nuisance – rather like that fly in the corner – but Vanessa was always so horrified when Dora said common sense things like that. Dora didn't like upsetting Vanessa, so she kept the thought to herself. "That would be very nice," she said instead.

Vanessa chewed at her lower lip, and Dora wondered whether her cousin had somehow guessed her thoughts.

". . . either way," Vanessa said finally, "neither of us shall find a proper husband in the country, I think. Mother has been bothering me to go to London for the Season, you know. I believe I want to go, Dora – but only if you swear you will come with me."

Dora blinked at her cousin slowly. *Auntie Frances will not like that at all*, she thought. But Vanessa, for all of her lovely grace and charm and good behaviour, always did seem to get her way with her stern-eyed mother.

On the one hand, Dora thought, she was quite certain that she would be just as much a hindrance to Vanessa's marriage prospects in London as she was here in the country. But on the other hand, there were bound to be any number of Sir Albuses hunting about London's ballrooms as well, just waiting to pounce on her poor, good-natured cousin. And as much of a terror as Vanessa was to faerie gentry, she really was as meek as a mouse when it came to normal human beings.

"I suppose I must come with you, then," Dora agreed. "If only so you needn't talk of horses ever again."

Vanessa smiled winsomely at her. "You are my hero, Dora," she said.

That lantern light within Dora glowed a tiny bit brighter at the words. "But you were mine first," she replied. "So I must certainly repay the debt."

Vanessa took her by the arm again – and soon Dora's thoughts had wandered well away from London, and far afield from things like purebred horses and impossible court magicians.

～⌒∽⌒∽～

Auntie Frances was *not* pleased at the idea of Dora accompanying her cousin to London. "She'll require dresses!" was the woman's very first protest, as they discussed the matter over tea. "It will be far too expensive to dress two of you! I am sure that Lord Lockheed will not approve the money."

"She can wear my old dresses," Vanessa replied cheerfully, as though she'd already thought this through. "You always did like the pink muslin, didn't you, Dora?" Dora, for her part, merely nodded along obligingly and sipped at her teacup.

"She'll drive away your suitors!" Auntie Frances sputtered next. "What with her *strangeness*—"

"Mother!" Vanessa protested, with a glance at Dora. "Must you speak so awfully? And right in front of her as well!"

Auntie Frances frowned darkly. "She doesn't *care*, Vanessa," she said shortly. "Look at her. Getting that girl to feel anything at all is an exercise in futility. She may as well be a doll you carry around with you for comfort."

Dora sipped at her tea again, unfazed. The words failed to prick at her in the way that they should have. She wasn't upset or offended or tempted to weep. There was a small part of her, however – very deep down – that added the comment to a longstanding pile of other, similar comments. That pile gave her a faint sinking feeling which she never could quite shake. Sometimes, she would find herself taking it out and examining it in the middle of the night, for no particular reason she could discern.

Vanessa, however, was quite visibly crushed. Her eyes filled up with tears. "You can't mean that, Mother," she said. "Oh, *please* take it back! I shan't be able to forgive you if you won't!"

Auntie Frances stiffened her posture at her daughter's obvious misery. A weary resignation flickered across her features. "Yes, *fine*," she sighed, though she didn't look at Dora as she said it. "That comment was somewhat over the line." She pulled out her lace handkerchief and handed it over to her daughter. "Do you really wish to go to London, Dora?" she asked. It was clear from her tone that she expected to hear some vague, noncommittal answer.

"I do," Dora told her serenely. Auntie Frances frowned sharply at that and glanced towards her.

Because Vanessa wants me there, Dora thought. *And I don't want to leave her.* But she thought that this elaboration might complicate the point, and so she kept it to herself.

Auntie Frances said that she would think on the matter. Dora suspected that this was her way of delaying the conversation and hoping that Vanessa would change her mind.

But Vanessa Ettings always did get her way eventually.

Thus it was that they soon took off for London, all three of them. Lord Lockheed, always distant and more consumed with his affairs than with his daughter, did not deign to accompany them – but Auntie Frances had pulled strings through her sister's husband to secure them a place to stay with the Countess of Hayworth, who was possessed of a residence within London and only too pleased to have guests. Since Vanessa had declared her interest so belatedly, they had to wait for the roads to clear of mud – by the time they left Lockheed for London, it was already late March, with only a month or two left in the Season.

After so much fuss, the carriage into London was not at all how Dora might have imagined it. Even in her usual detached state, she couldn't help but notice the stench as they entered the city proper. It was a rude mixture of sweat, urine and other things, all packed together in too close a space. Auntie Frances and Vanessa reacted much more visibly; Auntie Frances pulled out her handkerchief and pressed it over her mouth, while Vanessa knit her brow and craned her head to look outside the carriage. Dora followed Vanessa's lead, glancing over her cousin's shoulder to see out the window.

There were so very *many* people. It was one thing to be told that London was well-populated, and another thing entirely to see it with one's own eyes. All those people running back and forth in the street got into each other's way, and they all seemed somewhat cross with one another. Often, their driver had to yell at someone crossing in front of their carriage, shaking his fist and threatening to run them down.

The noise would have been startling, if Dora were capable of being startled. It settled into her bones more readily than anything else had ever done, however – the biggest fly yet in the corner of the room. Dora found herself frowning at the chaos.

Thankfully, both the hubbub and the awful scents died down as their carriage crossed further into the city, onto wider, calmer avenues. The jumble of buildings that passed them slowly became more elegant and refined, and the suffocating press of people thinned out. Eventually, their carriage driver stopped them in front of a tall, terraced townhouse and stepped down to open the doors for them.

The front door of the townhouse opened just as Dora was stepping down after her cousin and her aunt. A maid and a footman both exited, followed by a thin, steel-haired woman in a dignified rose and beige gown. The two servants swept past, already helping to unload their things, while the older woman stepped out with a smile and took Auntie Frances's hands in hers.

"My dear Lady Lockheed!" the older woman declared. "What a pleasure it is to host you and your daughter. It has been an age since my last daughter was married off, you know, and I've had little excuse to make the rounds since then. I cannot wait to show you all around London!"

Auntie Frances smiled back with unexpected warmth, though there was a hint of nervousness behind the expression. "The pleasure is all ours, of course, Lady Hayworth," she said. "It's ever so gracious of you to allow us your time and attention." Auntie Frances turned back towards Vanessa, who had already dropped into a polite curtsy – this, despite the fact that they were all certainly stiff and miserable from the journey. "This is my daughter, Vanessa."

"It's so delightful to meet you, Lady Hayworth," Vanessa said, with the utmost sincerity in her tone. It was one of Vanessa's charms, Dora thought, that she was always able to find *something* to be truly delighted about.

"Oh, how lovely you are, my dear!" the countess cried. "You remind me already of my youngest. You can be sure we shall be fighting off more suitors than we can handle in no time!" Lady Hayworth's eyes swept briefly over Dora, but then continued past her. Dora was wearing a dark, sturdy dress which must have made her appear as a very fine lady's maid, rather than as a member of the family. Lady Hayworth turned back towards the townhouse, beckoning them forward. "You must be awfully tired from the road," she said. "Please come inside, and we shall set a table—"

"This is my cousin, Theodora!" Vanessa blurted out. She reached out to grab Dora's arm, as though to make sure no one could mistake the subject of her introduction. The countess turned with a slight frown. Her gaze settled back upon Dora – and then upon her eyes. Lady Hayworth's warm manner cooled to a faint wariness as she took in the mismatched colours there.

"I see," the countess said. "My apologies. Lady Lockheed did mention that you might be bringing another cousin, but I fear that I quite forgot."

Dora suspected that Auntie Frances might have downplayed the possibility, in the hopes that Vanessa might change her mind before they left. But Lady Hayworth was quick to adjust, even if she didn't quite pause to finish the formal introduction.

Still, Lady Hayworth led them into a comfortable sitting room, where a maid brought them biscuits and hot tea while they waited for supper to finish being prepared. The countess and Auntie Frances talked for quite some time, gossiping about upcoming parties and the eligible bachelors who were known to be attending them. Dora found herself distracted by the sight of a tiny ladybird crawling across the knee of her gown. She was just thinking that she ought to sneak it outside before one of the maids noticed it, when Vanessa spoke and broke her out of her musings.

"And which parties will the Lord Sorcier be attending?" Dora's cousin asked the countess.

Lady Hayworth blinked, caught off-guard by the inquiry. "The Lord Sorcier?" she asked, as though she wasn't certain she'd heard Vanessa correctly. When Vanessa nodded emphatically, the countess frowned. "I admit, I do not know offhand," she said. "But whatever romantic notions you may have taken up about him, I fear that he will not be a suitable match for you, my dear."

"Why ever not?" Vanessa asked innocently over her tea. "He's quite young for the position of court magician, I hear, and very handsome as well. And is he not a hero of the war?" Dora heard a subtle, misleading note in her cousin's voice, however, and she studied Vanessa's face carefully, trying to pick apart what she was up to.

"That much is true," Lady Hayworth admitted. "But Lord Elias Wilder is really *barely* a lord. The Prince Regent insisted on giving him the French courtesy title, of course, with all those silly privileges that the French give their own court magicians. Technically, the Lord Sorcier may even sit in on the House of Lords. But his blood is common, and his manners are exceptionally uncouth. I have had the misfortune of encountering him on several occasions now. He has the face of an angel, and the tongue of some foul . . . *dockworker*."

Dora found it amusing that the countess apparently considered dockworkers to be an appropriate foil for angels. She was briefly distracted by the notion that hell might be full of legions and legions of dockworkers, rather than devils.

"He does sound terribly unsuitable," Vanessa said reluctantly, regaining Dora's attention. "But please, if you don't mind – I would love to meet the Lord Sorcier at least once. I've heard such stories about him, and I would be crushed to leave London without even seeing him."

The countess tutted mildly. "I suppose we shall see," she said. "But for the very first thing, I have a wish to see you at Lady Carroway's ball. She has *many* fine and suitable sons, and you could do worse than entering London society at one of her parties . . ."

The subject meandered once again, until they were brought into dinner. They met Lord Hayworth that evening in passing, though he seemed quite busy with his own affairs, and less than interested in his wife's social doings. Once or twice, Dora thought to ask Vanessa about her interest in the Lord Sorcier, but her cousin kept demurring and changing the subject of conversation, and she eventually decided it was best to drop the matter while within current company.

Dora next thought that she would wait to ask until they were off to bed . . . but directly after dinner, she was swept away by a maid and given a hot bath, then bundled into a very lovely feather-down bed a few rooms down from her cousin.

Tomorrow, Dora thought distantly, while she stared at the foreign ceiling with interest. *I am sure we'll speak tomorrow.*

Quietly, she pulled the iron scissors from the sheath around her neck and tucked them beneath her pillow. As she drifted off to sleep, she dreamed of angels on the London docks, filing up and down the pier and hustling crates of tea onto ships.

Chapter Two

*F*or many days, Dora had no opportunity at all to speak to her cousin.

In fact, when she woke in her room the next day, she had to search out a maid to be told that Lady Hayworth and Auntie Frances had gone out shopping for accessories with Vanessa. Partway through the day, someone sent word that they would be unaccountably delayed, as they had been invited to dinner at the residence of one of Lady Hayworth's friends. After a day of ambling uncertainly about the townhouse, Dora finally went back to bed early, hoping that the next day might offer more fortuitous circumstances.

When Dora next woke, she was advised that Vanessa was getting her gown adjusted at the last moment, on Lady Hayworth's recommendation. This being the second day in a growing pattern, Dora did not waste any more time sitting at windows drinking tea. Instead, she asked where she might find something to read. She was directed towards a single bookcase within a small library, where were the sorts of books that ladies ought to read. Here she found a tattered, type-printed novel tucked away in the corner – perhaps a guilty pleasure for one of Lady Hayworth's absent daughters – and spent a few hours reading. The subject matter would have been quite shocking, if she had been the sort to shock, but it was an entertaining novel all the same.

The third day, Dora decided that it was time she went outside – and so she did. She put on her most reasonable dress and walked right out the front door and into the street. If the servants thought there was something odd about her walking out alone, they must have been convinced that there were some mitigating circumstances to which they were not privy, because no one tried to stop her. Then again, since Dora had no sense of fear, she was quite good at projecting a mild, distracted sort of confidence.

There were a few servants coming and going along the street. Dora picked out a distracted-looking maid who was currently carrying freshly laundered sheets. She sped up her pace and plucked at the woman's sleeve.

"Excuse me," Dora said. "There are iced desserts in London, aren't there?"

The maid turned towards her with a blink. "Er," she said. "Yes." She frowned at Dora's attire, clearly attempting to suss out whether she was someone to be respected. The maid must have decided to err on the side of caution, because she added, "The ladies like to eat fruit ices at Gunter's, on Berkeley Square."

Dora smiled at her. "Thank you very kindly," she said. "Could you tell me which way it is to Berkeley Square?"

Many streets and many strange conversations later, Dora found herself wandering a more mercantile part of London, with shops on every side. She meandered through a few of them, appreciating the sheer spectacle of so many fine goods in one place. More than once, she lost track of her original intent and had to ask directions again. By the time she made it to Berkeley Square, however, a dangerous rumble had started up in the sky, and cold raindrops had begun to pitter-patter against her skin.

Dora spent a few extra moments looking up at the clouds, shielding her eyes from the rain. Those clouds were dark and roiling, and she found herself staring at them with an awed fascination.

Nearby, a young lady squealed beneath her bonnet, rushing

through the rain for the nearest overhang. Dora looked after her and remembered belatedly that she was trying to act as normal as possible while in London, in order to help Vanessa's chances of finding a suitor.

Slowly, Dora backed her way beneath the closest overhang, and through the door of a nearby shop.

A bell rang softly as the door opened, announcing her presence. Dora glanced around curiously, taking in her surroundings. The shop was small but prestigious – many bookshelves lined the walls, filled to the brim with expensive-looking leather tomes. All of the books had the look of something handwritten, rather than cheaply printed. A wood and glass counter showed a handful of illuminated scrolls on display. An ancient silvered mirror hung behind that counter. In it, Dora saw a beautiful ballroom alight with hundreds of candles. The distant sound of violins played in her ears, and she leaned across the counter to take a closer look.

There was a Dora in the mirror as well – but this Dora was wearing the pink muslin gown that Vanessa had given her, and her hair was coiled up into a rusted red bun. There was a string of very fine pearls wound about her neck that she didn't immediately recognise. An ominous crimson stain had spread across the front of the gown, beneath the pearls. As Dora lifted her hand to her own chest, she saw dark red dripping down the tips of her fingers.

As she watched, a tall man stepped up behind her. His messy, white-blond hair and pale skin flickered in the unearthly candlelight; his eyes were a peculiar molten reddish-gold that danced along with the flames. He was dressed in full evening attire: a fine white jacket and a silver waistcoat. His neck cloth was subtly loosened, however, and the smile on his handsome face held a faintly devilish edge to it.

"Don't drip on the books, dear," he said in her ear. His voice was soft and low. He drawled his words with the slightest bit of a northern accent, so that they curled down faintly at the end. Dora found herself so entranced by the sight and sound of him that it took her a spare moment to process his words.

The mirror Dora wasn't the only one dripping everywhere. As Dora glanced down, she saw that she was soaked in very real water from the rain outside.

"Oh my," she said, turning around to face him. "I *haven't* dripped on any books, have I?"

The man behind her was not wearing evening attire – he was wearing a casually buttoned brown jacket and a white neck cloth in a simple knot – but in all other respects, he looked quite like the man in the mirror. His eyes were even stranger and more arresting up close, so that Dora ended up staring up into them, appreciating the way that they danced with some faint inner light.

He blinked very slowly and languidly as she looked up at him. "I don't believe you have," he said. If Dora wasn't mistaken, in fact, he was briefly put out by the fact that she hadn't jumped into the air and screamed when he'd sneaked up on her.

Dora glanced back towards the mirror – but the image of the ballroom was gone. The surface had gone dull and black now, and it reflected absolutely nothing.

"Did you see something of interest in there?" asked the man next to her.

"I suppose I did, now that I think on it," Dora mused. The sight of the ballroom hadn't struck her as particularly unusual at the time, but now that she'd been asked to consider it directly, she could see where it wasn't the sort of thing one normally saw in mirrors.

Presently, however, Dora became aware that there was another patron behind one of the freestanding bookshelves, watching them intently. Brown-haired and slightly shorter than the man in front of her, he would have been quite handsome in a more normal manner, were it not for the speckling of scars along his right cheek. Still, he was neatly dressed for the day in a stiff coat and sturdy Hessians, and he had a smile that seemed to make those scars disappear beneath its warmth.

"Now where did this young lady appear from?" the brown-haired man chuckled. "You didn't summon her, did you, Elias?"

The fair-haired man, Elias, shot the other man the sort of withering look that only good friends could manage without risking a duel. "If I were going to bother with a summoning, Albert," he said, "I'm quite sure I could think of better things to call upon than some half-drenched maid."

The brown-haired man, Albert, only gave him another rueful smile. "If you were a gentleman, Elias," he said, "you would offer her your coat. I'm sure the lady must be quite chilled."

Elias glanced away from both Dora and his friend, his inquiry about the mirror suddenly forgotten. "You are perhaps the only man who might accuse me of being a gentleman without being turned into a frog," he told Albert acidly. "Take back that awful insult, before I think of an alternative animal."

Albert ignored Elias and shrugged off his own coat, offering it out to Dora. "On my friend's behalf," he told her politely. "Since he is grumpy today."

Dora took the coat from Albert, more out of automatic politeness than anything else. But as she did, her eyes caught on his hand. What she had at first taken for some sort of glove on his right hand was in fact nothing of the sort. It was instead a hand made entirely of *silver*, which moved with all the fluidity of a normal human appendage. A momentary glance was enough to assure her that Albert's left hand was quite normal by comparison. Dora returned her gaze to the silver right hand with an openly curious look, forgetting about the coat that she still clutched.

Albert looked down at his hand and shot her a half-smile. "The Lord Sorcier's work," he explained. "I lost my real hand, and much of my arm, to shrapnel, I'm afraid. But this one is quite something, isn't it?"

The Lord Sorcier, Dora thought. *Elias Wilder.* She flicked her eyes back towards the fair-haired man. If she wasn't mistaken, he seemed mildly embarrassed by the subject of conversation, though he quickly hid the emotion behind a bored affectation.

"I'm quite sure it's impolite to stare at cripples," Elias told Dora in a droll tone.

"I don't mind," Albert said cheerfully. "Besides which, I'm quite sure it's even worse to *call* a man a cripple, Elias."

The Lord Sorcier scoffed at this, but soon fell silent. A moment later, a short, wiry man bustled out from the back room, carrying a full stack of books. "Just as you asked!" said the shorter man, as he set the books down on the counter. "Everything I could find on the various humours. Some of these were *quite* difficult to track down."

The Lord Sorcier reached out to open the front cover of the book on top of the stack. Inside, Dora saw a set of diagrams marked up with scribbled, handwritten notes. She leaned curiously around the man's elbow, conscious not to let her hair drip onto the pages. The notes, she saw, were all in some very formal sort of French which she couldn't immediately puzzle out. Given time, she was certain she could put together a translation—

"You know," Elias said conversationally, "the last woman to come so close to me caught her hair on fire. It was a dreadful mess. I'm quite sure she still has a scar."

Dora glanced up at him. Elias was watching her with an arched eyebrow, which confused her. His tone suggested that he was trying to be friendly, but if she wasn't mistaken, his expression was one of faint disgust – *oh.*

I'm acting strangely again, Dora thought. She backed away from him quickly.

"My apologies," Dora said. "I was very curious about your book."

"You were very curious?" Elias repeated in that low, sonorous voice. He added a soft laugh, which *also* seemed friendly, but now Dora wasn't quite sure whether she ought to take it as such. "Well then. That makes it all better. Was there anything else you were curious about, while we're at it? Shall I take off my trousers and let you take my measure?"

Dora knit her brow. "Take your measure?" she asked. "What ought I to be measuring, sir?"

Albert sighed heavily and reached out to snatch the jacket that still dangled from Dora's fingers. He tucked it around her shoulders. "Do ignore him," he said. "I always do, when he gets this way."

The man behind the counter groaned, and Dora saw that his face had gone red. "Oh, please don't do this in my shop, Lord Sorcier," he begged Elias. "Perhaps *your* reputation can't possibly get any worse, but you know I have a business to run!"

Dora considered the fair-haired man next to her more closely, exerting herself so that she might focus on him. This was indeed the Lord Sorcier, then? The man she'd heard so much about? The one that Dora had accidentally inspired Vanessa to go chasing after for a fleeting glimpse?

He was indeed quite handsome, she had to admit. Even in half dress, the Lord Sorcier was resplendently wild, with his wind-tossed hair and his arresting golden eyes. Only once before had Dora seen such an ethereal visage – and that had belonged to a cruel and noble faerie.

It was a shame, she thought, that so many beautiful things were also so ugly on the inside.

The Lord Sorcier straightened, looking down upon Dora with an expression that she *did* know very well. It was the same one her aunt had used on her many times before – the one that said she was too foolish even to understand when she was being insulted. "It's quite all right, John," Elias addressed the man behind the counter. "The little chit is nearly as dull as a Sunday morning service. You can come and find me if she ever realises what I meant."

"*Elias*," Albert warned his friend reprovingly.

Dora tilted her head at Elias, considering. "I'm not certain what I did to insult you, my lord," she said. "Have I offended you somehow, or am I simply conveniently placed while you are otherwise upset?"

Her even, curious tone made the Lord Sorcier frown. Dora was certain that she had reacted incorrectly this time, but she didn't care. She had little effort to spare for making unpleasant men more comfortable.

". . . women who don't understand personal boundaries always offend me," Elias said finally. "Dim-witted people offend me even further."

"Oh dear," Dora said mildly. "That must be very difficult indeed."

Already, the fair-haired man had begun to turn away from her – but he glanced back at that. "Pardon?" he asked. "What must be difficult, exactly?"

Dora smiled at him politely. "Being offended at yourself so very often," she said. "That seems a sad way to live, my lord."

Albert guffawed. "Oh," he said. "She's got you there, hasn't she?"

Both of the Lord Sorcier's eyebrows rose at Dora this time. For a moment, she wondered whether she had angered the man so much that he might turn *her* into a frog. But as the moment passed, he merely shook his head in irritation and turned to Albert.

"This first book is in some sort of confounding French," Elias said to his friend. "You'll have to read it for me."

Albert stepped forward to glance at the book. "Medieval French, it seems," he said. "It's not all *that* different, Elias. Your French is just abominable."

"Yes, well," Elias muttered. "We weren't all raised in a household with highbrow French tutors, Albert. My French expertise remains limited to asking after a warm meal or a whorehouse. I suppose my profanities are still quite sharp as well."

Albert gave Elias another reproving look, but it was clear that the Lord Sorcier had no intention of censoring himself in front of Dora. Similarly, it was probably becoming clear that Dora was not prone to having vapours over the conversation. "Is this why you really brought me today?" Albert asked. "I have offered more than once to *teach* you better French, Elias. One might realistically expect the Lord Sorcier to know the language of alchemy and *sorcery*."

Elias waved his hand dismissively. "I haven't the time to learn," he said. "Besides which, I have *you*."

Albert shook his head but said no more on the subject. He glanced towards Dora. "I've just realised," he said. "I quite forgot our introductions, on top of everything else. I am Mr Albert Lowe. This is Lord Elias Wilder. He's charmed to meet you, I assure you."

Dora smiled at Albert. "I am Theodora Ettings," she said. "But you may call me Dora if you like, Mr Lowe. If we are being politely dishonest with one another, then you may assure the Lord Sorcier that I am charmed to meet him too. But in all truth, I *am* charmed to make *your* acquaintance."

"You see, Albert?" Elias said. "That is exactly the problem. Now you have charmed the young lady, and you shall not be rid of her. You even gave her your jacket. Once her mama finds out, you'll be before an altar before the week is through."

"That is quite impossible," Dora told Elias offhandedly. "My mama is dead. My father as well." She said it only because she expected it might take him aback, and she was pleased to see that it did. "My aunt might perhaps pursue the poor gentleman, but only on my cousin's behalf." Dora smiled back towards Albert. "My cousin *is* quite pretty. But I shall only introduce her to you if it pleases you."

Albert blinked at that. Perhaps, Dora thought, she was not

supposed to be quite so direct about attempting to find her cousin a suitor? But he seemed very kind, and he *was* a mister at the very least.

"I shall . . . take it into consideration," Albert said finally, with a humorous glint in his eyes. "My mother, Lady Carroway, will be hosting a birthday ball for my older brother. I would be pleased to have her send you and your cousin an invitation. I have insisted that Elias attend, you see, and I cannot think of any other woman who might converse with him at length without fleeing the premises."

"I am not coming," Elias interjected crossly – but Albert ignored him.

Aha, Dora thought, dimly pleased by this development. Albert must have been one of Lady Carroway's quite suitable sons. This meant that the countess would approve of him, which only made the whole idea even better.

"I believe that my cousin will be coming to Lady Carroway's ball already," Dora said. "But if I am to be frank, you may need to ensure I have an invitation as well. Our hostess has been quite determined to forget me." Albert raised his eyebrows at that, and Dora frowned. "Perhaps I should not have said that aloud," she admitted. "You will be kind enough not to repeat it, Mr Lowe? I would hate to cause a scandal, for the sake of my cousin."

Albert pressed his silver hand to his chest. "I do so swear it," he said solemnly. "And I shall insist that Mother send you your very own invitation, Dora."

"I am not coming, Albert," Elias repeated emphatically. "You shall be stuck entertaining the two ladies on your own, I warn you."

When Albert ignored him again, he let out a sharp breath and snapped his fingers in the air. The books on the counter floated up next to him.

"You may put the books on the Treasury's account," Elias

informed the shopkeeper, who had been politely trying to ignore their conversation so far, "as they are necessary to my duties."

The shopkeeper nodded with only the slightest wince. The Prince Regent was not particularly well-known for paying his bills on time.

Elias turned for the shop's exit, and the floating books trailed along behind him as he left. Rain parted neatly around him and his books, as though it had run into the surface of a perfectly invisible parasol.

Albert shot Dora a rueful glance. "I expect that is meant to be my cue to leave," he said. "I suppose I must go translate another magical book, for the sake of king and country." He frowned at the jacket around her shoulders. "You may keep that until the ball if you like. I would hate for you to catch a chill."

Dora shook her head and slid the jacket off her shoulders, offering it back out to Albert. She had a hunch that it would cause her trouble to go home with it. "Thank you for the offer," she said, "but please do take it back. I barely feel the cold, in any case."

Albert took the jacket back reluctantly and gave her a bow. "Until the ball then," he said. "It was a pleasure."

Dora watched after Albert as he headed out to rejoin the Lord Sorcier. *I do hope Vanessa doesn't intend to try and marry the Lord Sorcier,* she thought. *Albert seems much kinder. I shall have to dissuade her as soon as I am able.*

"You have my deepest apologies, miss," the man behind the counter said with a sigh, interrupting her thoughts. "A man in my business really cannot turn away the Lord Sorcier, you understand, however abhorrent his behaviour."

"Oh yes," Dora said distractedly. "Of course, I understand."

"Please, allow me to help you," he said, by way of changing the subject. "Was there something in particular for which you were looking?"

Dora turned back towards him, pursing her lips. *I do believe this is a magic shop*, she thought. *How fortunate.* "Perhaps there is," she said. "I'm afraid I only have a bit of pin money. But if you happened to have a book of faerie peerage on your shelves, I would be most obliged."

Chapter Three

*D*ora returned to the countess's townhouse shortly afterwards, well before dark. If anyone had noticed her strange
departure, no one thought it relevant enough to mention. The
next day, however, she was budged from bed by a maid, who
told her that she was expected at breakfast with the family.

"Dora, my dear," Auntie Frances said, as she entered the room.
"The countess has received a most peculiar letter. Lady Carroway
has personally begged your presence at her ball, along with that
of your cousin. I'm quite certain that she must have mixed you
up with someone else, given that you have no connection of
which I'm aware, but I thought I might ask if you knew anything
about this."

The countess and Vanessa were both sitting at the table along
with Auntie Frances. For her part, Vanessa looked somewhat
miserable, though she was wearing a brand-new gown in the
latest style, and her hair was put up with a number of beautiful
opalescent butterfly pins. Vanessa's face brightened as she looked
over at Dora's entrance, however, and she hurried to pull out
the chair directly next to her.

"Oh yes," Dora said, since she expected that any sort of lie
would eventually come undone anyway. "I met her son, Mr
Albert Lowe, in a shop on Berkeley Square. He was ever so
polite. I offered to introduce Vanessa to him, since Lady

Hayworth had been speaking of how suitable Lady Carroway's sons were."

Auntie Frances blinked at Dora as she walked over to take her seat next to Vanessa. That Dora had dared to venture out on her own, without any sort of proper escort, seemed to vex and astound her. But Auntie Frances could not possibly deny the usefulness of having such a personal invitation, and so she carefully limited her reply. "I was not aware that you had gone out, Dora," she said. "I am sure you know that you shouldn't have done that. But since you have done, it seems that we shall need to dress you up appropriately for Lady Carroway's ball."

"I'm quite fine with the pink muslin," Dora assured her aunt. "No one in London has ever seen it before, and it fits me very well."

"Yes, well." Auntie Frances cleared her throat. "We shall at least see that it is taken in for you more nicely. Perhaps we can sneak you into the shop today, in spite of the short notice."

Lady Hayworth frowned lightly at Dora. "Did you say Mr Albert Lowe?" she asked. "Oh dear. Yes, I can see how Lady Carroway would be enthused at your interest. I'm afraid that Albert is the *least* suitable of her sons, and she has been having trouble finding him a wife."

"Is he?" Dora asked, knitting her brow. "I cannot imagine why. He served against Napoleon with the Lord Sorcier, I'm told, and he is very charming."

The countess sighed. "Yes dear," she said patiently. "But he is not a *whole* man. He is missing an arm, for goodness' sake. You cannot have failed to notice." She narrowed her eyes in thought. "Still," she continued slowly. "I hear that Albert is a physician, which is more respectable than can be said of most third sons. And this is fortunate in its own way. It was Dora who received the personal invitation, so we shall have her set her cap for Albert. Lady Carroway will be pleasantly inclined towards the family after that, I am sure, and we can aim to snare her oldest son for Vanessa." Lady Hayworth beamed at this bit of logic. "Why, you could be a viscountess, Vanessa, and the *next* Lady Carroway. Wouldn't that be lovely?"

Vanessa set her lips into an unhappy line. But she was not prone to disobeying authority figures, and so she nodded silently rather than contradicting the countess. She glanced over at Dora from beneath her eyelashes. "You said that Mr Albert Lowe served with the Lord Sorcier?" Vanessa murmured. "I shall have to see if he is inclined to arrange a meeting."

Dora frowned vaguely at that. "I have met the Lord Sorcier," she told her cousin. "He was there with Albert that day. Lady Hayworth is right, Vanessa – Lord Elias Wilder is quite terrible. You must forget him, please."

For once, Auntie Frances nodded her head in agreement with Dora. "You see, Vanessa?" she said. "If even Dora can feel distaste for the man, then he is to be avoided. Please put the thought from your head. We have a chance to position you well with the next Lord Carroway, so focus your attentions on that instead."

Vanessa narrowed her eyes down at her plate. "Yes, Mama," she said obediently. But again, Dora got the distinct feeling that her cousin had not listened to any of them, and that she had some sort of plan in mind regardless.

"Well!" Lady Hayworth said. "This is a fine turn indeed, but it means that we shall have to redouble our efforts. Finish your food quickly. I expect I shall have to bully our way into an appointment to fix up Dora's dress."

Auntie Frances smiled at Lady Hayworth, and Dora swore that she could see the stars in her eyes as she did. It was clear that Auntie Frances thought the world of the countess. "We are so very lucky to have you on our side, Lady Hayworth," she said. "I do not like to imagine what we would have done without you."

Dora looked down at her food. It occurred to her only belatedly that the countess and her aunt had decided she ought to marry Albert, and never once consulted her on the matter. She wasn't entirely certain how to feel about that.

He is quite kind, Dora thought. *Though I only met him briefly. And it is a terrible shame that so many mamas and their daughters have been avoiding him only because of his arm.*

But the idea that Dora was to be pawned off on Albert distressed her in a very vague manner. It did not seem right that he should be used in some scheme to snare his older brother. Besides which, Dora was quite certain that she did not have the capacity to properly feel love for *anyone*, and a man as sweet as Albert did deserve to be loved.

"Are you upset, Dora?" Vanessa whispered over to her. Obvious concern laced her voice. It was rare for Dora to feel anything at all deeply enough to show it on her face.

"My stomach is off," Dora lied to her in a soft murmur. She didn't wish for Vanessa to worry too badly. "I did promise to introduce you to Albert. Please don't let them make me a liar."

Vanessa reached out to squeeze her cousin's hand beneath the table. "I would love for you to introduce us," she assured Dora. "I promise, I will make sure to speak with him."

This comforted Dora somewhat, so she squeezed Vanessa's hand back.

True to her word, the countess swept them all away to the dress shop directly after breakfast. The poor dressmaker was clearly already overwhelmed, but the countess must have been an important woman indeed, for she managed somehow to browbeat her way into an appointment nonetheless. After one of the tailors had stuck a few dozen pins into Dora's gown, they left it behind them for picking up later, and went down to Gunter's for some of those ices which Dora had been so interested to try.

By the time they were done with ices, Vanessa's back had straightened, and there was a strange new steel in her posture. Vanessa engaged with Auntie Frances and Lady Hayworth with a deceptive enthusiasm, asking questions about how she ought to approach Lady Carroway's sons, and what she might do to charm the lady herself. But Dora greatly suspected that they had not heard the last of Vanessa's insistent interest in the Lord Sorcier, and she quietly vowed to herself to corner the awful man and keep him well away from Vanessa, in the unlikely event that he *did* end up at Lady Carroway's ball.

A few days later, once Dora's dress had been returned, she found herself subjected to the most intense party preparations she had ever experienced. The countess was determined that Vanessa's first official appearance in London should be exceptional, and so all four of them spent the entire day getting dressed. Dora found she had to whisper requests to the servants to bring her and Vanessa snacks, as they were both so monopolised that they couldn't get away.

When she was finally released from captivity and shown to a mirror, Dora found herself briefly arrested by the sight there. The pink muslin now hugged her as though it had been made for her; at Lady Hayworth's direction, the dressmaker had lowered its neckline ever so slightly so that it was just this side of daring. The countess had also deigned to lend Dora some proper pearls, which seemed to lengthen the line of her neck. The maids had pulled her hair into a rusted red bun, leaving only a few delicate curls to frame either side of her face.

But while the sight was a bit more appealing than usual, it was not this that gave Dora pause. In fact, there was a vague worry niggling at the back of her mind, and it took her a long moment to put her finger on just what it was.

I look like I did in the mirror at the magic shop, Dora thought. *Except that I think I was bleeding terribly in that reflection.*

Dora felt a moment of regret that she hadn't asked the shop

owner just what sort of spell was on the mirror. But as Lady Hayworth rushed them all into a carriage outside, the thought soon darted away again, just as it had done at the shop.

"Lady Carroway favours what topics of discussion again?" Auntie Frances quizzed her daughter, as the carriage took off for the ball.

"Embroidery and charitable works," Vanessa answered dutifully. "And above all else, her children, of course."

Auntie Frances beamed at Vanessa approvingly, before turning her attention to Dora. "And what must you do before the end of the evening?" she asked leadingly.

"I must dance with Albert twice," Dora replied distantly. "As he will feel obliged to come calling upon me if I do."

"Very good," Auntie Frances said. Dora couldn't help but feel a moment of pleasure at the rare praise, in spite of her continued discomfort with the idea.

"Do be sure that Lady Carroway *sees* you dancing with Albert," the countess told Dora. "It will put her in a most favourable mood towards Vanessa and your aunt."

"I am not quite certain how I can force Lady Carroway to watch me dance," Dora mused aloud. "But I shall do my best, I suppose."

"Dora!" Auntie Frances said reprovingly. "Don't be pert. Lady Hayworth has been awfully kind to you for that sort of attitude."

Dora thought to point out that Lady Hayworth had barely spoken to her at all since they'd arrived in London – but thankfully, her instincts told her just in time that this would be a poor idea. She nodded instead. "My apologies, Lady Hayworth," she said. "I am simply very anxious to ensure that things go well for Vanessa."

"You are forgiven, dear," said the countess. "But do watch your tone better once we enter the party. The *ton* can be merciless about those sorts of mistakes."

I should probably keep my mouth mostly shut in that case, Dora thought to herself.

They arrived at Carroway House just after sunset. Normally, the countess said, they would have waited just a bit longer in order to be fashionably late, but since they'd been so personally invited, Lady Hayworth thought to take advantage of the early sparseness to visit Lady Carroway and her sons. Everyone knew that the countess herself was eager to socialise more, after all.

As they were announced into the ballroom, Dora was struck by an uncanny sense of déjà vu. A great many candles glowed along the walls, flickering across the space. A quartet had started up some music, and already two young ladies were dancing together on the floor, though the hostess had yet to officially open the ball. All in all, the image could have been plucked straight from the mirror in the magic shop.

This does not bode well for the state of my dress, Dora thought. *And for my health as well, I suppose.*

Lady Carroway was already crossing the floor towards them, with Albert on her arm. She was a short woman, with the same brown hair and kind eyes as her son, and Dora thought that the smile on her face must have been more than simply polite as she approached their gathering. Albert, for his part, was looking particularly dashing in an emerald-green waistcoat and the same tall Hessians as before. He was wearing gloves this evening, so that the silver of his hand was covered.

"Lady Hayworth!" exclaimed Albert's mother, releasing his arm long enough to take the countess's gloved hands in her own. "It has been too long. I'm so glad that you were able to attend."

Lady Hayworth exuded a polite warmth in return, though Dora thought that it didn't quite reach her eyes. "You know I simply couldn't stay away," she said. "And Dora was so insistent that she wished to come. You had hoped to meet her, I believe? This is Miss Theodora Ettings. She is the previous Lord Lockheed's only daughter."

Dora thought that "insistent" was probably an overstatement of her enthusiasm towards the ball, but she tried to force some awkward cheer into her smile as Lady Carroway turned her attention towards her. Albert's mother glanced almost immediately at Dora's mismatched eyes, and her brow knit lightly. But she made no comment on the obvious strangeness. "What a pleasure to meet you, Miss Ettings," she said. "Albert has spoken very highly of you. I hope we shall get the chance to speak further as the evening goes on."

This was all very positive news as far as Auntie Frances and the countess were concerned. Dora rummaged up another smile. "I'm very flattered, Lady Carroway," she said. "I shall try to live up to his praise." She glanced at Albert, and added, "You weren't *too* complimentary, I hope, or I shall have an impossible task ahead of me."

Albert laughed and took Dora's hand to bow over it. "I will measure my compliments in the future, Miss Ettings," he said. "You are looking very lovely this evening. I hope you will do me the honour of saving me a dance."

This was obviously only polite of him, given that he had ensured her invitation in the first place, but Dora knew that his words had only encouraged everyone around them to believe that they were somehow well matched. The lines in his mother's forehead smoothed away as she saw this exchange, and Dora suspected that she might already be making marital plans in the back of her head. She wondered if Albert was at all aware of the trap into which he had wandered.

"I would like nothing better than to save you a dance," Dora assured Albert. "In fact, you may have your pick of dances, if you like." It was a bit forward of her, but she hoped that it would convince her aunt and the countess that she was showing a proper interest in him. "Please," she added, "allow me to introduce my cousin, Vanessa Ettings." This was also cheeky of her, but since Albert had already implied that he was willing to be introduced, it was barely permissible. "Vanessa, this is Mr Albert Lowe. I shall increase my praise towards him and say that he is handsome, polite *and* charming since he has apparently been setting high standards for me while my back has been turned." Dora smiled serenely at Albert. "Turnabout is fair play, Mr Lowe."

"I give you your point, Miss Ettings," Albert told her. He turned now to bow over Vanessa's hand. "It is a pleasure to meet you, Miss Vanessa," he said. "I would be most obliged if you would save a dance for me as well."

Vanessa gave Albert a radiant smile of her own. The sincerity of the expression only added to her considerable beauty, and as Dora looked at her, she thought that her cousin must surely be the loveliest woman in all of London. "Dora has not exaggerated in the least, for her part," Vanessa said. "How lovely to meet you, Mr Lowe. I look forward to dancing with you."

The countess introduced Auntie Frances, and within moments she had smoothly redirected the conversation towards Vanessa, enfolding her into conversation with Lady Carroway. As the others talked, Albert offered out his arm to Dora.

"The Lord Sorcier has attended in the end, despite his protests," he said. "I will admit, I had to threaten to withhold my translation skills in return for his presence. I must go and confront him now, and I would appreciate a trustworthy companion at my back as I do so. Might I steal you from your family?"

Dora took the proffered arm. "You might do, yes," she said. "I take it the Lord Sorcier is still grumpy?"

"He is almost always grumpy," Albert admitted. "But if one can endure his profane behaviour, he is also quite a fascinating conversationalist. He has been a most loyal friend to me, and so I am determined to see him acclimatised to polite society in return."

Dora pursed her lips as they headed away from the others. "May I be so bold as to ask *why*?" she said. "It seems to me that the Lord Sorcier has no love for polite society, and that it has none for him in return. Is there something you hope for him to gain from all of this effort?"

Albert considered this for a moment. "I appreciate the directness," he said, "so I will speak directly in return. Elias is a terribly unhappy man. He wraps himself up in very serious matters, and rarely gives himself the opportunity to rest and enjoy himself. I don't by any means expect that he shall suddenly fall in love with society balls. But perhaps a delicious meal and a dance or two shall do his heart good and blunt the worst of his miseries."

Dora nodded at this, taking it in. "Then I will do my best to engage him," she said, "if only for your sake. But I cannot promise that such engagement shall remain polite, if he is in his usual form."

Albert smiled at this. "I trust you to handle him at your discretion, Miss Ettings," he said. "And thank you. I take this as a favour."

They were well out of earshot of the others, and so Dora thought to warn Albert about the sordid plans involving him and his oldest brother – but before she could do so, they came in sight of Elias, who was settled into a side chair with a painfully bored expression on his face. He was wearing the same white jacket and silver waistcoat that Dora had seen in the magic shop's mirror, and this distracted her uncomfortably as she thought again of the crimson stain that might soon be found upon her dress.

"Elias," Albert greeted him as they headed closer. "I see you have already driven away Lord Ferring. I think that must be record time for you." Albert released Dora's arm and gestured towards her. "I have brought you a greater challenge."

Elias arched one white-blond eyebrow. "I see that," he drawled. "And what is it you wish for me to *do* with your dog, Albert? Shall I take it outside for a walk? Need I fetch it some treats from the table?"

Dora tilted her head at him. "You could try and teach me to speak," she said. "But I fear that my diction is already better than yours, Lord Sorcier."

Albert laughed, already sounding pleased. "I thought that you might take Miss Ettings for the first dance," he said. "As soon as my mother decides to start things off."

Elias narrowed his eyes at both of them. "I am not fond of this conspiracy," he informed them. "One of you at a time is already bad enough. Two is quite intolerable."

Dora turned innocently towards Albert. "*Le sorcier insinue que nous serions intolérables,*" she observed. "*Quelle ironie.*"

Albert shot her a delighted look. "*Mais il a raison, non?*" he replied. "*Si nous parlons français, ce n'est que pour le contrarier.*"

"Oh, that is beyond enough!" Elias fumed. "If you are going to insult me, at least have the decency to do it in the king's tongue! Why did we even fight a war with the French if not to keep them out of England?"

"Insult you?" Dora asked. "Why, we were doing nothing of the sort. I seem to have committed a faux pas, speaking in a language which eludes you. You have my deepest apologies, Lord Sorcier." She drew out the French of his adopted title with a perfectly sanguine expression.

Elias opened his mouth, no doubt ready to shoot off a *scathing* reply. But before he could do so, Lady Carroway got up to call the ball to attention, announcing the first dance. Albert looked meaningfully at the Lord Sorcier. "Be *reasonably* kind to Miss Ettings," he told Elias, "and I shall see about your book first thing tomorrow morning."

The Lord Sorcier hissed in an irritated breath. But he shoved to his feet and offered one gloved hand out towards Dora. "I would like the record to state that I am doing this only under great duress," he told them both.

"You may note it on my dance card later, if you like," Dora told him. She took his hand, feeling odd as she did so. It was quite rare that Dora had any dance partner at all, though men did sometimes ask her out of pity. For all that the Lord Sorcier was clearly displeased at the notion, his hand was warm, and he was appropriately gentle with his touch. He smoothed the obvious scowl away from his features as they headed out onto the floor, and for a moment, Dora daydreamed that she was dancing with a handsome young man who *wanted* to be there with her.

Elias glanced down at her as they began, keeping his expression cool. This close, his golden eyes were even more arresting, and Dora found herself staring. "Does this amuse you, Miss Ettings?" he asked acidly. His tone rather spoiled the daydream, and she brought herself back to the present.

"I am rarely amused," Dora told him honestly. "But I do enjoy dancing. And you are not terrible at it. I thought that you might make yourself so on purpose."

"I have no particular wish to insult Albert or his family," Elias said dryly, "however much he may try my patience, at times. I will admit, I thought for a moment about treading on your toes, but I have decided against it."

"How gentlemanly of you," Dora said. His eyes narrowed, and she smiled absently. "Ah yes, you hate being called a gentleman. Since you have spared my toes, I will refrain from saying it again. It seems only fair."

Elias made a soft *hm*. "I despise parties," he said, "but I understand the concept of armistice. I doubt I shall send you away weeping in any case, no matter how outrageously I try. Let us speak of something marginally interesting, then."

Dora nodded to herself. "I have just the thing," she said. "Our conversation was interrupted before, at the shop. I was about to tell you what I saw in the mirror. As it happens, I saw us both exactly as we are now, in our evening best. But I think that I was covered in blood, and that seems to me to be a sort of bad omen at best."

Elias missed a step, and Dora blinked. He turned towards her with wide eyes. "And you've only just now thought to bring up this little detail?" he demanded. "So calmly, too? Are you attempting to play a joke on me, Miss Ettings?"

Dora winced. *I should have sounded more distressed*, she thought. The image in the mirror *did* trouble her. In fact, it set within her a certain awful, creeping dread. But it seemed that Dora was incapable of expressing that dread in a believable fashion. "I am distressed," she assured Elias. "But I am doing my best to stay calm. I assume by your reaction that I should indeed be worried?"

"That mirror is a scrying tool," Elias told her. "It shows all manner of things if you are in the right frame of mind. Had you told me that day of what you'd seen, I would have advised you that it could be either something of worry or nothing at all. But since the greater part of your vision has now come to pass, it is more likely than not that you caught a glimpse of the future."

Dora frowned dimly. "Yes," she said. "That is very distressing. I don't suppose you know of any way to avoid such a future?"

"Divination is a very imprecise art," Elias said with a scowl. "But it would be remiss of me not to try, obviously. Do you know where it was that you were injured?"

Dora lifted her hand to her chest, just where the ugly stain had been, and his scowl deepened. *That is not a good sign*, she thought.

The song ended, and Elias began to head off the floor, clutching her arm tightly. Someone tapped on Dora's shoulder though, and she turned to see Albert standing behind them.

"It's only fair that I should rescue you from Elias for a moment," Albert told her. "May I have the next dance, Miss Ettings?"

Dora opened her mouth to respond – but Elias cut her off. "You may not," he told Albert curtly. "I need to go discuss matters with the lady."

Albert shot him a surprised look. "I see," he said. "But in that case, you're best served staying on the dance floor, Elias. She'll otherwise be obliged to dance with any other man who asks."

A dim, distant horror flickered at the back of Dora's mind. *Two dances with the same woman shows interest*, she thought. *People will expect the Lord Sorcier to come calling on me.* "Oh," Dora said, but the words came out far milder than she intended. "No, I don't think—"

"Fine," Elias snapped, ignoring her. He turned back towards the dance floor. "What silly little rules," he muttered to himself. "*Obliged* to dance, really?"

"This is a very bad idea," Dora informed him. But there was a spark in his manner now, and it occurred to her that the hint of something more magical, mysterious and dangerous must have appealed to the Lord Sorcier's sensibilities far more than a normal society ball.

"Nonsense," Elias said. "You're unlikely to find anyone else at this party more suited to solving your impending doom, Miss Ettings. Now, can you remember anything else from the image in the mirror? Any little detail at all?"

"I was distracted by the man who came up behind me, I'm afraid," Dora said. "That was you, by the way. Just so I'm clear."

The Lord Sorcier's eyes narrowed in thought. "Well, what sort of dangers might one run into at a party like this?" he speculated. "There are knives about, I suppose. Duels sometimes happen, once people get far enough into their cups. Is there anyone who dislikes you enough to harm you so gravely, Miss Ettings?"

Dora shook her head at him. "Not that I know of," she said. "Though . . ."

Elias leaned forward. "Though?" he prompted her.

Dora pondered the matter of her longstanding curse. It did not seem wise to bring that up with the Lord Sorcier, but her first instinct had earlier been that this must have something to do with Lord Hollowvale, and it was probably even *less* wise to ignore that possibility. "There is a man back in Lockheed who wishes me ill," she told him. "I have a pair of scissors with me, which he fears. But those scissors might also be used against me, I suppose."

Elias blinked at her. "I will admit," he said, "you are proving to be far more interesting than I first assumed, Miss Ettings." Dora walked herself past him as the dance's steps dictated, and caught sight of Vanessa nearby, staring at her curiously. Dora's cousin was holding what looked like a glass of deep red punch. "Retire from dancing for the evening and stay close. If anyone asks, you may tell them I have mauled your toes—"

"No," Dora told Elias suddenly. "Wait. I believe I've mistaken something, my lord." She met his eyes again squarely. "If you would be kind enough to fetch me a glass of that punch, it would be of immense help to me."

Elias now looked utterly bewildered. At first, Dora thought he might refuse and accuse her of playing a trick on him again. But as this second dance came to a close, he turned them both off the floor, and he humoured her request by heading for the side table where the punch sat out.

As Elias made his way back with a glass of punch, Dora waited patiently, considering the situation. She wasn't sure just what to expect, or even when to expect it – but surely enough, just as the Lord Sorcier had come within a few steps of her, another gentleman jarred his elbow by mistake. Elias whirled with such sudden violence that several people nearby gasped and staggered back; as he did, the punch splashed forward, spilling all across the front of Dora's dress.

Elias had raised his arm against the other man – to do what, Dora wasn't sure – but he caught himself just in time and froze in place with his hand partially extended. His pulse hammered against his throat, and Dora thought for a moment that there was a strange fear in his golden eyes. Elias took a deep breath and drew himself up. "Be careful where you're moving," he hissed at the man next to him.

"Oh, Dora!" Vanessa had already hurried over, aghast. "Oh no, your dress!"

Elias turned back to look at Dora. As he saw the red stain on her dress, a flicker of consternation crossed his face. But Dora only smiled at him. "Thank you very much, Lord Sorcier," she told him. "I am much relieved."

Vanessa gave her a curious look – but Dora's cousin was used to far stranger things from her. "Dora?" she murmured. "What on earth is going on?"

"Nothing awful," Dora assured her. "But please stay back from me. I would hate to stain you too." She nodded towards Elias and began to nudge her way through the crowd. "Excuse me," she said. "Pardon me. Can anyone tell me where I might wash up?"

Chapter Four

$\mathcal{D}$ora spent some time in the retiring room scrubbing at her dress, but it became clear in a hurry that the tools available to her were insufficient for saving the muslin. This caused a faint disappointment in her. She was pleased to be alive and unharmed, of course, but the dress had been very pretty, and it was the first one she had ever owned that had been tailored to fit her properly.

Rather than return to the party in her obviously ruined gown, Dora slipped her way out one of the side doors into a back garden. She was sure that Auntie Frances would be upset with her for failing to dance with Albert, but she couldn't imagine that the man's kindness extended so far as to walk onto the dance floor with a woman covered in punch.

There was a very lovely fountain in the middle of the garden – it looked like a blossoming flower capped with a very fine pineapple. Dora settled herself onto a bench to watch it, musing on the near future. Lady Carroway had wanted to speak to her, but that also seemed unlikely in her current state. Perhaps it was for the best if she wanted to avoid pinning down poor Albert at the altar. But then, Dora had hoped to use the conversation to extol Vanessa's virtues instead.

She frowned vaguely at the fountain in front of her. *That is a lot of water*, she thought. *Enough to soak my dress properly. Perhaps I could scrub out the worst before the party is through.*

Dora got to her feet and wriggled the dress over her head. Only a moment after she'd dunked the whole thing in the fountain, however, she heard a man's voice utter a foul swear word behind her.

"What *are* you doing, you mad little twit?"

Dora glanced behind her and saw the Lord Sorcier standing just behind the bench she'd just vacated. His finery was every bit as pristine and untouched as it had been at the beginning of the evening, except that he had now loosened his neck cloth a bit. His golden eyes raked her up and down, clearly aghast.

"I would have thought the situation was self-evident," Dora told him calmly. "Does a man of your formidable knowledge really require the concept of laundry to be explained to him?"

Elias pinched at the bridge of his nose with his fingers, sucking in a breath. "My dear Miss Ettings," he said slowly. "You are standing in a viscount's back garden in your unmentionables, washing your dress in a fountain. Have you truly no concept of the strangeness of your situation?"

Dora paused, looking down at her dress where it soaked beneath her hands. *Oh*, she thought. *He's probably correct.*

"No wonder your cousin is so desperate," Elias muttered. "If you keep behaving in this way, you'll be ruined within the week."

Dora turned towards him fully at that, concerned. "What about my cousin?" she asked. "Is something wrong with her?"

Elias groaned softly. "Please put your dress back on, Miss Ettings," he said. "I am not unused to the female figure, but I would prefer not to be caught in a scandal that might tarnish Albert's mother. I am sure that I would never hear the end of it."

Dora sighed and pulled the dress back out of the fountain, squeezing the water from it where she could. Out of the corner of her eye, she saw the Lord Sorcier pull a finely polished wooden wand from his jacket. He flicked it once, and the dress jerked itself from her hands, rolling itself into a tight ball. Pink- and red-tinged water dripped from its folds onto the grass. When it had straightened again in her hands, Dora saw that the dress was now both perfectly dry and devoid of all colour. There was no remaining trace of the punch stain – though the pink muslin was now unmistakably a *white* muslin.

"Oh," Dora said. "That is very kind of you, my lord. Thank you." She tugged the dress back over her head. It took more than a bit of effort to make it lay correctly without a maid's help – but within a few moments, she was at least presentable again.

"I played a part in wrecking the dress in the first place," Elias said with a hint of annoyance.

"In a way, I think that you were fated to wreck the dress," Dora told him helpfully. "Perhaps we should both blame the mirror instead."

Elias scowled. "This is why I hate divination," he muttered. His eyes flickered towards the leather sheath that still dangled over Dora's chest, with the two finger loops of her embroidery scissors sticking out of it. "Your . . . *scissors* are still visible," Elias murmured at her. He sounded half-perplexed by the idea, as though he were trying to decide whether scissors ought to be considered scandalous or not.

"Oh." Dora glanced down and tucked the scissors down the front of her stays once more. For some reason, this seemed to relax the magician. He stowed his wand and gestured towards the bench.

"Sit," Elias told her. "I need to have a proper look at you, now that I know what afflicts you."

Dora sat down on the bench obediently, giving him a curious look. "*Do* you know what afflicts me?" she asked. "I wonder."

Elias came around the bench to stand in front of her. His golden eyes studied her in a penetrating manner, as though he were examining her beneath the surface of her skin. Dora closed her arms over her chest, distantly uncomfortable beneath his gaze in a way that she had not been before, even while dressed in her underthings.

"Your cousin tells me that you are faerie-cursed," Elias said finally. "I will admit, I avoid the Fair Folk as much as possible, and I have never seen someone who was faerie-cursed before. Still . . . I should have seen that there was something off about you."

Dora frowned. Vanessa's interest in the Lord Sorcier suddenly made an awful amount of sense. *The moment I was gone from the room, she must have cornered him and spilled everything*, Dora thought. "Vanessa should not have told you that," she said. "Our whole family might be ruined if it were to get out."

"I have no interest in ruining your family," Elias replied absently. He continued to study Dora with a focused consideration. "I have *much* interest in investigating the strange and unnatural."

The words "strange" and "unnatural" added themselves to the small pile of miseries at the back of Dora's mind. But she forced herself to straighten and put down her arms. "Will you swear it then?" she asked him. "You'll swear not to tell anyone else what's happened to me?"

"Oaths are dangerous to a magician, and I do not make them lightly," Elias told her. "So I will not swear to that. But I *will* swear that I currently have no intention of bringing you harm. That shall have to suffice." His gaze came to rest on her face, and his lips turned down into a frown. "Your eyes were not always different colours, I assume? The grey one drained of colour after the elf got hold of you?"

Dora looked away. "Yes," she said. "That's correct."

"I have had reason to study the spiritual humours lately," Elias told her. "I wonder if the elf might have drained you of one of them." He reached up to rub at his chin. "Would it be fair to say that your emotions and cognitive abilities are out of balance, Miss Ettings?"

Dora nodded slowly. She was still uncomfortable with the idea of trusting the Lord Sorcier with such a terrible secret – but now that Vanessa had revealed her situation, the only reasonable thing left to do was probably to humour him. "I do not feel things the way that others do," Dora said. "There is little difference between my dreams and my reality. I can sometimes exert myself to act more normally, but it is difficult, and I do not think I ever get it quite right."

Elias nodded thoughtfully. "I have not seen you scared or angry even once," he said. "You didn't so much as flinch when I came up behind you in the magic shop." He narrowed his eyes at her. "But you know when you *ought* to be scared or angry, don't you? You responded tartly when I called you a dog. There must be some shred of real emotion left to you, even if it is deeply buried."

Dora considered that logically. ". . . there is, I think," she said with faint surprise. "I have often thought that I am capable of . . . of emotions with a long tail. I am not sure if that makes sense. I do not feel the shock of fear, but I can feel dread – I was scared of the image in the mirror after thinking on it for a while. And while you do not enrage me, per se, I am vexed when I think of the way that you treat others."

Elias smiled sharply at that. "Alas," he said. "Such long-tailed vexation will not drive you away – so it is rather useless to me." He stepped back from her again. "Have you felt happiness at all, Miss Ettings? Even the sort with a long tail?"

Dora settled her chin into her hand. "I don't know what happiness ought to feel like any more," she said. "It is the most elusive feeling of all, I think. But . . . I feel at peace when I am near Vanessa. She is like a warm lantern to me. I think it must be because she loves me so obviously. When I am around her, I do not need to pretend to be something I am not."

Elias tapped at his cheek thoughtfully. "How intriguing," he murmured. "Well! This shall require more investigation than I can manage in a single night. I shall have to arrange more time with you somehow, and not too far apart from my actual duties." He shook his head. "I shall have to think on it further. In the meantime, do at least try to keep all your clothing on, Miss Ettings. My specialities lie in the sorcerous arts and *not* in extracting young ladies from scandal."

Dora got back to her feet and retrieved her gloves from the bench where she'd left them. "I do not mean to do scandalous things," she told him. "But I will try harder to keep my head about me." She nodded politely. "I appreciate your engagement in my troubles, Lord Sorcier. I hope you do not go to too much trouble on my behalf."

"I go to exactly as much trouble as I like," Elias told her with another wry half-smile. "And none but the Prince Regent can force me to do otherwise, I assure you." He paused. "Sometimes even he has his difficulties."

Dora pulled her gloves onto her hands. "I will thank you, nonetheless," she said. "But I must excuse myself. Lady Carroway expressed that she would like to speak to me tonight, and I cannot avoid her without being terribly rude."

Elias stepped neatly out of her way as she headed back into the party.

At least, Dora thought as she sneaked her way back towards the ballroom, *Vanessa is not interested in marrying the Lord Sorcier after all*. But the idea had now struck her that perhaps Vanessa had actually dragged them all to London only to find a cure for Dora, and that bothered her as well.

Soon, Dora knew, she was going to have to corner her cousin and demand an explanation.

It didn't take much searching to find Vanessa in the ballroom. Dora's cousin had gathered a respectable crowd of both men and women around her. Vanessa was so generous with her attention and approval that this often happened, as people discovered in her a genuinely interested listener and slowly flocked to tell her their favourite party stories. Already, the older women showed signs of doting on her, and the eligible men began to size up their chances with her.

As Dora approached, however, Vanessa's eyes caught on her, and she moved to make room for her cousin. "Dora!" she said. "Your dress! How did you get it so clean?" Her brow knit as she noted the subtle change in colour. Few people in the room would probably remember the difference between the light pink dress Dora had worn before and the white one that she wore now – but since it had been Vanessa's own dress, she was bound to spot the oddity.

"The stain wasn't quite so bad after all," Dora told her. "Though it did take some work." She ventured onward before Vanessa could ask further questions. "There are so many people here," Dora said. "I've never been quite so overwhelmed before. I was hoping you might join me for a moment on the balcony?"

Vanessa nodded and turned instantly to give her apologies to those closest to her. At least one man who had been hovering with the clear intent to ask for a dance stepped back awkwardly to let her pass. Vanessa took Dora by the arm, and the two of them headed towards the balcony.

"Normally, you must worry when you leave *me* alone," Dora told her cousin in a quiet voice, as they crossed the room. "But see – I left you for only a moment, and you have spilled our family's worst secret to the Lord Sorcier. What were you thinking, Vanessa?"

Vanessa frowned. "I was thinking that if anyone might be able to cure you, Dora, it would be the magician who does three impossible things before breakfast," she retorted. "And I was right, wasn't I? He said that he would investigate the matter."

"It was very careless of you," Dora replied calmly. "Now tell me the truth, Vanessa – are you really here to find a husband, or did you simply come to London to find the Lord Sorcier?"

Vanessa bit her lower lip, and Dora sighed. *Just as I thought.*

They exited onto the balcony, and Vanessa carefully closed the door behind them. "I offered to marry the Lord Sorcier if he could fix you," she admitted when the door had closed. "I know it isn't much of an offer for a man of his position, but I hadn't much else to propose, and I fear I panicked somewhat."

Dora shook her head in disappointment. "I warned you what an awful man he was," she said. "Please tell me he didn't accept your offer?"

Vanessa had the good grace to look embarrassed at this. "He did not," she admitted. "He said that if he wanted something pretty to place on his mantle, he could buy something much less expensive than a wife. But he *did* say that he would try to cure you anyway, Dora, and that's what matters."

"It is not what matters," Dora informed her. "For we are now in London, and Auntie Frances and the countess are on the warpath. If I do not miss my mark, you shall have a husband soon whether you want one or not, Vanessa. You had best start thinking about what sort of husband you'd like, before they choose one *for* you."

Vanessa clasped her hands behind her, looking down at the ground. "I greatly dislike the way they talk about tricking some man into marrying me," she sighed. "Is it naive of me that I thought I might simply meet someone agreeable and then ask whether they found *me* agreeable?"

"Very naive," Dora confirmed. "Auntie Frances has always said that you ought to be a princess. I am surprised that she is willing to entertain even something so low as a viscount-in-waiting, given her aspirations."

Vanessa winced. "I'm quite sure that I've danced with every one of Lady Carroway's sons by now," she said. "There is not a thing wrong with any of them, except that I cannot yet remember which face goes with which name."

"Except for Albert, of course," Dora supplied.

"Except for Albert," Vanessa agreed readily. "Do you know, I think he must be his mother's favourite? She smiled the brightest when he danced with her, and she keeps returning to check on him."

Dora didn't say the thing that she was thinking. *Albert is her favourite because he is broken. She feels she must make up for that with extra love, the same way that Vanessa feels for me.*

And that, Dora thought, was why Vanessa would always remember Albert, even if she didn't recall his brothers. There was an odd defensiveness to her affections, such that they skewed towards those who hadn't enough affection already. It was an admirable quality, as long as it was measured.

"Well," Dora said. "I must speak with Lady Carroway, and I should probably dance with Albert at least once. But I intend to warn him about the old hens' plan. I'll tell him it was none of your idea, at least."

Vanessa's expression fell into a worrisome conflict. She picked at her. "Do you . . . not *like* Albert, Dora?" she asked.

Dora blinked. "Of course I like him," she said. "I meant all of the things that I said about him. But I am faerie-cursed, and I should not be marrying anyone." Vanessa opened her mouth to protest, but Dora shushed her. "If nothing else," she said, "Lord Hollowvale might come back for me. I will not put anyone else between that faerie and me, and you cannot convince me such a thing would be either reasonable or kind. Perhaps if I am ever cured, I shall think on the possibility."

"The Lord Sorcier will cure you, then," Vanessa said stubbornly. "And you will marry whomever you like."

Dora leaned over to kiss her cousin's cheek. "And you will remind me of this moment, I am certain." She turned to open the door back into the ballroom. "Decide on your husband-to-be soon, Vanessa," Dora said. "We will need plenty of time to scheme against the hens if you are to marry someone that you *like*."

Vanessa smiled at that. "I will redouble my efforts," she promised.

Dora slipped back inside and went in search of a dance partner.

~ᴇ⌒ᴏ⌒ᴏ~

Albert found Dora in short order – mainly, she suspected, because neither of them was otherwise engaged on the dance floor. As he approached, she took a moment to appreciate their similarities. *I am odd*, Dora thought. *And Albert is odd. And everyone is aware, on some level.* The thought made her feel as though they were secret comrades, just waiting to exchange information about the doings of all those other, more normal partygoers.

"You must have made quite the impression, Miss Ettings," Albert observed, as he came within speaking distance. He looked quite pleased. "I never would have guessed I'd see the day that Elias engaged in unforced dancing."

"You shouldn't be so impressed," Dora told him. "I cheated outright. I gave him a magical riddle to solve."

Albert chuckled. "Cheating or no cheating," he said, "it was an unprecedented event. The Lord Sorcier has fled back to his research for the evening, but I daresay he might have actually enjoyed himself first." He extended his hand. "Might I have the dance he stole from me earlier? If you are not too tired, that is."

Dora took Albert's hand obligingly. "I am not too tired," she assured him. As they headed for the dance floor, she considered him curiously. "Are you aware of the grand conspiracy going on behind your back, Mr Lowe?"

Albert raised an eyebrow at her. "You may need to be more specific," he said. "These parties are a veritable hotbed of gossip and conspiracy."

Dora nodded at that. "Of course," she said. "I am referring

to the three matrons who have decided that you and I ought to get married, for varying reasons of their own."

Albert laughed again. "I am missing an arm, Miss Ettings," he told her, "not my eyes or ears. My mother is already exceptionally wroth with Elias for trying to steal you from me – her words, not mine. I told her that he was working under the severe handicap of his personality, and that she shouldn't begrudge him the attempt."

Dora gave Albert a bemused look. "I am sure the Lord Sorcier would be horrified at the supposition," she said. "In either case, I simply thought to let you know. I have no intention of marrying at the moment, so it's rather a moot point."

Albert raised his other eyebrow at that. "You haven't?" he asked. "How strange. I thought marriage was why most eligible young ladies came to parties like these. Certainly, everyone isn't here just to celebrate Edward's birthday."

Dora shook her head. "It would be most unwise for anyone to marry me right now," she said. "Though the Lord Sorcier has kindly offered to help me with my predicament. Perhaps he shall even solve it, if he is as genius as I hear."

Albert had knit his brow as Dora spoke – but at this, the lines on his forehead smoothed away and he seemed quite pleased again. "There is no problem, then," he said. "For Elias *is* quite genius. And he is feeling very charitable towards you for some reason, which I think to be a fine thing." A satisfied smile crossed his face. "Don't worry, Miss Ettings – I shall be sure to dash my mother's hopes before the night is through. I shall instead set my sights on the most unattainable lady I can find, and they will all soon leave me be out of pity."

Dora smiled at that. "How very clever," she said. "I wish I could take notes, but my own strategies must be more underhanded. It is far harder to foil these plots when you are a woman. If the hens suspect I am making myself unattractive to suitors, they might simply auction me off to whoever bothers to bid."

Albert considered this seriously. "How troublesome," he said. "Well . . . let me think a moment. Perhaps I can be clever again." He led her past another couple as he turned the matter over in his mind. Then: "Ah. Yes, I have it. I shall simply bully Elias into calling upon you tomorrow. The mothers of the *ton* may consider him distasteful, but I cannot think of any man that might be foolish enough to bid against him, as it were."

Dora shook her head. "I cannot imagine he will like that," she said. "We truly do not get on, Mr Lowe, whatever you may think."

The music spun to an end, and Albert bowed to Dora. He took her arm to lead her off the floor, and she thought she saw a sparkle of mischief in his eyes. "I believe that you get on just fine," Albert said. "But it hardly matters. If Elias intends to speak more with you, then he will need an excuse. Why not use this one? It will solve your problems neatly, after all."

"I will not argue with your logic," Dora said. "Only with your confidence. But I shall give you nearly half odds, since you have surprised me more than once tonight."

"Indeed," Albert told her, with a twitch of his lips. "Be up on time tomorrow, Miss Ettings. Elias is an early riser." Albert led Dora back to her table, where Auntie Frances and Vanessa were already seated. "Thank you for your indulgence, Lady Lockheed," he said. "I believe I have returned your charge with toes unharmed."

Auntie Frances waved a hand generously. "I do not worry at all to leave my Dora in your care, Mr Lowe," she said. "You are, after all, such a perfect gentleman." Dora's aunt glanced towards her meaningfully. "You do not have any other dances on your card right now, dear? You could keep dancing if you liked." The words were clearly meant for Albert, but even Auntie Frances wasn't bullish enough to shove Dora back at him directly.

Albert's eyes alighted on Vanessa, however, and he offered out his hand to her. "Miss Vanessa," he said. "Might I dare to ask another dance of you?"

Vanessa blinked at him. Auntie Frances widened her eyes just next to her daughter, and Dora imagined that she could hear the sound of all her aunt's intricate plans shattering against the floor.

Vanessa would have accepted the dance regardless, of course. But even if she had not been inclined to accept, she could hardly turn down Albert without seeming impolite. His family would snub her badly if she did, and gossip would follow on top of that.

"I would love another dance," Vanessa told him warmly. "Thank you for asking, Mr Lowe."

An unattainable lady indeed, Dora thought, as she watched them walk out to dance. She wondered if Albert was aware of the full implications of what he'd done. He was, after all, so very clever.

"What have you *done?*" Auntie Frances hissed to her, aghast. "How hard can it be to hold one man's attention, Dora?"

Dora tilted her head at her. "Why, it isn't what I have or haven't done," she said. "Vanessa is simply too lovely tonight, I think. Can you really blame Mr Lowe for his interest?"

Auntie Frances floundered at that, unable to search out a suitable reply. Certainly, she wasn't about to deny her daughter's popularity.

But Dora *did* feel bad for Lady Carroway, who watched this dance with such a sad and knowing expression on her face. She was, after all, only guilty of hoping that her son might have finally found a woman of mutual interest. And now, he had gone and thrown away that chance in order to pursue a woman with far too many other prospects.

Still, Albert's mother found the opportunity to approach their table. And from the look on her face, Dora suspected that the lady still harboured some determination to foil her son's foolishness.

"Miss Ettings," Lady Carroway greeted her. "I am so glad

that the Lord Sorcier's clumsiness did not result in your absence entirely tonight." Her eyes narrowed as she spoke Elias's title, and Dora had to hide a bemused smile. "I was hoping to discuss your love of charity work before you left."

Dora blinked. "My love of charity work?" she echoed. Auntie Frances pinched at her leg beneath the table, and she forced herself to nod. "Of course," she corrected herself. "I hadn't realised that was common knowledge." It was as close to an outright lie as Dora had ever uttered, but there was simply no getting around the matter with Auntie Frances watching her like a hawk.

"Lady Hayworth mentioned it in passing," Albert's mother said. There was an oddly satisfied smile on her face now. "She said that you were hoping to find further opportunities for charity while in London. If I may suggest, my son Albert often lends his services to those in need. I am sure that he could take you with him sometime soon – with a proper chaperone, of course."

Oh dear, Dora thought. *Clearly, Albert gets his cleverness from his mother.*

"That is such a generous offer, Lady Carroway," Auntie Frances observed brightly. "We would be delighted to help with any necessary arrangements."

Dora had the distinct impression that the two mothers had communicated something silently between them, just over her head. "That sounds simply lovely, Lady Carroway, thank you," Dora said, because she was expected to say it. "Though, I would hate to impose upon Mr Lowe while he is doing his work." Her eyes tracked Albert and Vanessa as they danced.

"There is no imposition involved," Lady Carroway assured Dora. "Albert has mentioned more than once how he could use an assistant. Why, the arrangement couldn't be more perfect."

Dora gave up. *Good luck with this one, Mr Lowe*, she thought at Albert.

"Why then, it's settled," Auntie Frances said. "And what a fortuitous turn of events, Lady Carroway!"

Fortune, Dora thought, had far less to do with the matter than did three particular meddling hens.

Vanessa gave Dora a curious look when she returned – but they hadn't the chance for another clandestine conversation before she was swept away by another prospective suitor. Instead, Dora found herself sitting out the rest of the dances, lending her consideration to the brand-new predicament in which she had found herself.

Chapter Five

*T*heir small party left the ball late, but there was a sense of grim triumph in the carriage on the way back to Lady Hayworth's townhouse. The night hadn't been the unqualified success that Auntie Frances and the countess had wanted, but Dora could see that they were both quite pleased with themselves for adjusting to such unexpected difficulties. The two of them discussed how best to make use of Dora's access to Albert, even as she dozed on Vanessa's shoulder.

Dora was still very sleepy when they arrived back at the townhouse, and she fell into bed almost immediately as a consequence. It did not even enter her mind to ask that she be woken early – but she *was* awoken, and somewhat before what some would term to be a decent hour for the morning after such a ball.

"Dora!" Vanessa hissed her name, shaking her awake. "Dora, you must wake up! The Lord Sorcier has come to call. He says he wishes to see you, but the butler is doing his very best to turn him away."

Dora yawned slowly awake, pushing herself up and rubbing at her eyes. "Oh dear," she said. "I don't think that will end very well." She levered herself off the bed and went searching for her stockings. "You will have to help me dress in a hurry."

She wasted little time, pulling on her cotton morning dress

and heading for the stairs. A familiar voice filtered up from below.

". . . too early to call?" Elias asked, his tone terse and annoyed. "The sun has been out for hours now. The rest of the civilised world is awake and doing useful things. You're up and answering doors yourself, by God – I'm sure the lady can find her way out of bed without unduly straining herself."

Dora could only imagine the poor butler's consternation. He'd probably been instructed to force the Lord Sorcier to leave by any means necessary, but the man was unlikely to be cowed by simple pleasantries – which were, Dora assumed, the only weapon of note in the servant's arsenal.

"In fact," the butler stammered, "the lady is not at home."

"Oh, is she not?" Elias asked. His voice dripped with sardonic disbelief. "I see. No matter, then. I must be off shortly to investigate a plague, but I'll return directly after I am finished with that, if the lady is *not at home*."

A horrified silence ensued, as the butler considered the possibility of a plague-touched Lord Sorcier returning to the house later that afternoon.

"Perhaps you should check again with the lady of the house, and see if Miss Ettings might yet be found," Elias said dryly. "She could check beneath the furniture, in case the lady is hiding."

Dora headed further down the stairs. The doorway came into view, and she saw Elias leaning against the frame, looming over the butler in a subtly ominous manner. The Lord Sorcier was clearly dressed down for the duties he'd just mentioned, clad mostly in black and brown. His neck cloth was barely tied. Had Dora the ability to feel embarrassed, she might have felt it in that moment. *I am not sure whether I should be embarrassed for him or embarrassed for myself*, she thought. *This is by far the least respectful call of which I have ever heard.*

"Oh!" Dora said. She pitched her voice audibly as she

approached. "I didn't realise you would be paying a visit this morning, my Lord Sorcier."

Elias glanced over towards her with a grim scowl. "Miraculous!" he declared. "The lady has appeared from thin air." He narrowed his eyes at her. "Were you in fact hiding beneath the furniture, Miss Ettings?"

Dora smiled serenely at him. "Beneath the sofa," she told him. "But now, here I am. How might I be of assistance?"

The scowl on Elias's face deepened. A hint of amusement floated across Dora's mind, as she realised he was steeling himself to say something most unpleasant. "I was hoping to continue our discussion from last evening," Elias said. "Waiting for another of those frivolous affairs in order to speak to you did not suit me."

Dora took a few steps closer to the doorway, clasping her hands in front of herself. "I see," she said. "You are a busy man, it seems, and I am very flattered." And then, because she could not stop a strange, teasing impulse that had bubbled up within her, she added, "You should have sent flowers, however."

Elias stared at her. Slowly, a kind of murderous intent flickered up behind his golden eyes. "Pardon?" he said, enunciating each syllable distinctly. "I am not certain that I heard you correctly, Miss Ettings."

"My apologies," Dora told him. "I am told that I mumble on occasion. I said that you should have first sent flowers with your calling card, and then come to call . . . perhaps tomorrow, during the proper hours. That is the way of things. Mr Lowe told me that you are not always aware of societal expectations, and so I thought you might appreciate plain speaking."

Elias drew himself up with a long, steadying breath. Dora wondered for a moment whether he might lose what little composure he had gathered. But after that moment, he controlled himself and forced a sardonic smile. "I see," he said. "You will have to forgive my ineptness, Miss Ettings. I am obliged to you for your advice."

Dora did not really mean to drive Elias off, however, given that he *had* come for her benefit. Since the butler was still staring at him aghast, and not looking in Dora's direction, she gave Elias a very stately, serious sort of wink. "I would hate to inconvenience you, however," she continued, "since you are already at the door. I hope that the countess will not despise me if I invite you in for some tea. I shall have to ask her, you understand, since I am currently her guest."

"Of course," Elias said dryly. He settled himself back against the door frame. "I will wait ever so patiently."

Dora ventured further inside the house, inquiring for Lady Hayworth. The countess was not hard to find – she was in a dour sort of mood, as she had been informed of the Lord Sorcier's presence at her door not a few minutes prior.

"The Lord Sorcier is calling, my Lady Hayworth," Dora told her innocently, as though she had no idea that the woman was already aware. "I suppose I must invite him in for tea?"

Lady Hayworth gave Dora an incredulous look. "Surely you didn't *speak* to him, Miss Ettings!" she said.

"Should I not have done?" Dora asked her. "My apologies. I was not certain what else to do."

The countess pinched at her nose. "We shall not be rid of him now," she murmured. "This is terrible. And his *manners*! I ought to turn him away regardless." Still, the man's reputation earned him a moment of hesitation, even from the formidable Lady Hayworth. "Yes, fine," she sighed. "Bring him in for tea. If we are fortunate, he shall become bored with you in short order – but it hardly matters, as long as you pursue Mr Lowe's charity work with enthusiasm."

Dora nodded dutifully. "I will see if I can dissuade the Lord Sorcier's interest," she said. "I will be most unobliging with him." This, Dora thought, might incline the countess to overlook any lapses in politeness between them.

Lady Hayworth nodded and drew herself up. "I shall have

to chaperone," she said. "Do not worry, Dora. I am capable of handling a scoundrel like the Lord Sorcier."

I am not certain that you are, Dora thought to herself as they headed into the morning room and called for a servant to let Elias inside. *But I do look forward to seeing you try.*

That said, it *was* most problematic that the countess decided to sit so near Dora. The woman was very nearly hovering over her, as Elias entered the morning room with another broad scowl resplendent on his delicate features. "Lady Hayworth," he said shortly, by way of greeting. "How little you have changed since our last interactions."

The countess smiled evenly. "And you as well, my Lord Sorcier," she said. "Though one might have expected you would improve your manners given enough exposure to the *beau monde.*"

The French term made Elias narrow his eyes, and Dora wondered whether the countess had learned of his abominable French. "I cross myself against the day that I might become a pleasant-mannered man, Lady Hayworth," Elias responded acidly. "Pleasant-mannered people are simply the worst sort of people. *Decent* people become properly angry when presented with miserable injustice, but pleasant-mannered people never do."

The countess arched one cool eyebrow. "We could of course entertain your proclivity towards crass political discourse, Lord Sorcier," she said. "But I was under the impression that you had come today for a *somewhat* less miserable purpose."

Elias blinked and glanced towards Dora. "Yes," he said. "Well." He cleared his throat. "The lady and I have matters to discuss. But I see from your posture that you shall be hovering over us the entire time."

Given the blunt atmosphere in the room, the countess didn't bother to disagree. "The young lady is under my roof, and I shall therefore see that she is properly chaperoned," she replied.

Elias narrowed his eyes at Lady Hayworth. He stalked towards the chair that was closest to Dora and settled himself into it. "On the matter of divination," he said to Dora as though they might pick right back up where he had left off the evening previous. "I have dug a bit deeper into it, much as it has never been my preference."

"Oh?" Dora asked him. "That is so kind of you. You didn't have to go to such lengths to satisfy my fleeting curiosity." Dora was not actually certain just *why* the Lord Sorcier thought that divination was relevant to her situation, but she thought it best nevertheless to give him an excuse for the discussion.

"Indeed," Elias said. "It was even less enthusing than I remembered it to be. But it has its applications." Dora saw for the first time that he had brought a leather bag with him, of the sort that a physician might carry. Elias opened the bag to extract a small silver hand mirror, which he offered out to her. "This is something akin to the mirror which you saw in John's magic shop. The enchantments are actually quite simple, since they rely primarily on the capability of the person looking into the mirror."

Dora took the mirror with a blink. "I wouldn't know what capabilities I might have in that regard," she said. "Certainly, I am not a magician, my Lord Sorcier."

Elias settled back into his chair with a considering look. "Nevertheless," he said. "I have humoured you, Miss Ettings. Now, humour me in return. What do you see when you look into that mirror?"

Dora glanced down at the reflection in the mirror's surface. At first, she saw only herself – her rust-coloured hair was some-what mussed since she had prepared herself so hurriedly, and a few unfortunate freckles showed upon her nose. But in due time, the reflection faded to a yawning black, and Dora tilted her head at the mirror in her hands.

"You are not casting some sort of wicked spell on the girl,

Lord Sorcier?" Lady Hayworth asked suspiciously. Her voice sounded suddenly far away, as though she were speaking from a distance.

"If I were, Lady Hayworth, to tell you so would make me an outright ninny," Elias drawled. He sounded equally distant, and his low, melodious voice wavered strangely, as though it were a tuning fork. "But if you had even an ounce of magical knowledge, you would know that I hardly require a mirror in order to ensorcell a fragile young lady. In fact, I could do so from afar, as long as I possessed something that belonged to her."

The black expanse within the mirror pulled back slowly. The Lord Sorcier's face appeared within it – but Dora knew instantly that there was something different about him. There was a real and terrible fear on his handsome features, and his forehead was smeared with dried blood. Seeing that, Dora felt suddenly silly for ever having mistaken punch for blood – the real thing was much different to behold, and far more dreadful.

Elias was standing with several other men upon the foot of a bridge. He was wearing a uniform, Dora thought, and it looked as though it had not been washed for some time. Still, his wild white-blond hair stood out among the other men, and the bright fire that danced between his fingers commanded attention. The men around him fired muskets, so that she couldn't tell the difference between the smoke of the guns and the smoke of the flames. The Lord Sorcier had no musket – nor indeed did he require one, given the far more deadly weapon in his hands.

". . . if I were a black magician, that is," Elias said distantly, and his tone seemed hard now. "But I am not, Lady Hayworth. And if you intend to accuse me of such, you had best be prepared to repeat your words before the Prince Regent. It is primarily the court magician who stands between England and the dark arts. I cannot fulfil that duty if there are whispers that I abuse my magic."

Dirt flew, and a sudden chaos came upon the line of men. At first, Dora lost sight of Elias entirely – but then she found him on the ground, thrown violently back by some concussive force. The fire in his hands had winked away, and far more blood now stained his uniform.

His mouth was open, and his face was agonised. It took Dora a moment to realise that he was screaming, since she heard no hint of the actual sound.

"I will retract that much, Lord Sorcier," Lady Hayworth murmured reluctantly. "None in this household will gainsay your loyalty to England. Your lack of couth, on the other hand, is a matter of open record."

Dora stared at the thrashing figure of the Lord Sorcier, unable to reconcile the sight with the man who had handed her the mirror. The chaos of the entire scene afflicted her badly; she knew that it would haunt her far more terribly than even the pile of miserable words she kept at the bottom of her mind. *Is this the war?* Dora thought. *This must be what the soldiers were doing off in France not so very long ago.*

"Fortunately," Elias said lightly, "lack of couth has not yet been named a crime. Though I am sure Lord Hayworth might bring it up when the House of Lords next convenes. You should suggest it to him."

Another soldier staggered towards the Lord Sorcier, clearly off-kilter himself. As he collapsed to his knees before Elias, Dora recognised Albert's brown hair and currently dirty features.

Men closed in around them in a tight panic. Dora saw them all shouting things, but she couldn't tell the nature of their words. Albert, still dazed and bleeding himself, tore back the Lord Sorcier's uniform. Beneath, Dora saw two hideous-looking injuries – one on Elias's right arm, and one at his shoulder. The blood was awful – but far worse was the way in which Elias's pale skin seemed to burn. It was this burning, Dora thought, that made him scream so painfully. But it surely could not have helped matters when Albert went digging into those injuries with his surgeon's knife.

I ought to be sick, watching this, Dora thought to herself. But for once, she was glad to be devoid of most emotion. The awful scene in the mirror might well haunt her nightmares, but at least it did not make her shiver or cry.

Albert pried loose a bloody, jagged-looking piece of shrapnel from the injury in Elias's shoulder. As he tossed it aside, the burning there lessened and faded away. The second jagged bit of metal was much harder to dig out, and Dora greatly wished that she could look away. But there was the peculiar sense that she wasn't even properly in her body, and so she didn't know quite how to turn her head.

Albert dug and dug, and the Lord Sorcier's eyes rolled back in his head. He seemed in danger of fainting – but as Albert retrieved the other bit of shrapnel, he slapped the Lord Sorcier's cheek and murmured something to him which forced the other man to focus.

Men fell around them – some merely injured, some glassy-eyed with death. But others reached down to haul Elias to his feet . . . and Dora was discomfited to see that hellish fire reappear between his hands.

Mercifully, the mirror now went black – the vision snapped away before she could see the results of his magical handiwork.

"Miss Ettings?" Elias asked. Dora glanced up at him sharply. It seemed wrong to her, suddenly, that he seemed so clean and relatively relaxed. But *was* he relaxed? Dora remembered now the way that he had jumped at that small brush across his shoulder at the party. The confusion on his face, she realised, had been a distant cousin to the frightful fear he'd worn upon the battlefield.

Elias frowned at her. "You *have* seen something, then," he said. There was a note of triumph in his voice which suggested he had confirmed some sort of theory.

"I did," Dora agreed. A faint nausea churned in her stomach – but as usual, it failed to make its way into her voice. "I believe that I saw Mr Lowe save your life."

The Lord Sorcier's eyes widened a fraction at that, and Dora knew then that he had not anticipated she might see such an awful scene. "That is . . . interesting," Elias said slowly. He looked genuinely troubled. "You have my apologies. That was . . . an unfortunate day."

Dora chewed at her lip. She wanted to ask all manner of questions about what she'd seen, but she knew that the countess was listening intently to every word they spoke. If Lady Hayworth thought that Elias was showing her such things, she would probably toss him out that instant. "I saw the past, then," Dora observed, moving delicately past his apology. "How novel. I didn't realise that was possible."

"Possible," Elias agreed. "But very unlikely. That is twice now that you have seen something, which means that the first time was not a fluke. You are particularly prone to divinations, Miss Ettings."

"How preposterous," Lady Hayworth muttered. "Miss Ettings is not a magician, my lord. We surely would have noticed by now."

"I agree," said Elias. "She is not. But the spell on this mirror was my doing, and not hers. Miss Ettings has merely the mindset necessary to reliably divine." He smiled sharply. "Some itinerant dreamers are capable of divination, given the proper circumstances. Those who stumble into faerie often see fantastic visions as well, while they are on the other side. I surmise that setting even a single foot in faerie might offer such sights . . . though obviously, as Miss Ettings is sitting with us in this tearoom, she is simply an unusually accomplished daydreamer."

Dora frowned at Elias. He had clearly added the latter part about daydreamers for the benefit of Lady Hayworth. It was Dora's connection to faerie that concerned the Lord Sorcier.

One foot in faerie, she thought. But what did that mean? Both of Dora's feet were quite firmly settled in England right now, on the floor of the morning room in Lady Hayworth's townhouse.

"One hopes you did not come here to insult the young lady," the countess said archly.

"I did not," Elias replied – and now he sounded thoughtful. He rose to his feet, and Dora realised that he had left his tea untouched. "In fact," he said. "I believe that I shall call upon her again." Elias fixed his strange golden eyes upon Dora, and she found herself tempted for the very first time to look away. Still, she forced herself to hold his gaze. "The lot of you do love to ride in Hyde Park, don't you?" he continued. "I am busy for today and tomorrow, but I will bring a carriage for you at half past four, two days from now."

Lady Hayworth sniffed. "You seem quite certain you will be received, Lord Sorcier," she said. "Miss Ettings already has other plans. She cannot be expected to rearrange her schedule for you on a whim."

Elias frowned at Dora, and she sighed. "I am . . . busy, Lord Sorcier," Dora said. It certainly wouldn't do to call the countess a liar in her own home. "If you leave your card, of course, I will see you when I may."

Lady Hayworth smiled approvingly at Dora as she said this. Dora's words came with the clear implication that she would not be seeing the Lord Sorcier again at all.

You cannot be too thick to understand this, Dora thought at Elias, annoyed. *The countess is right here next to me. I cannot just accept.* She held his eyes, willing him to understand.

Elias shrugged. "I see," he said. "Clearly, I should know better than to knock at such a well-mannered door." He nodded towards Dora. "I will see you when you may, then, Miss Ettings."

Dora closed her eyes with a sigh.

So much for that, she thought glumly. *The Lord Sorcier has better things to do than to argue with the countess in order to investigate my curse. Vanessa will be terribly disappointed.*

"Lord Sorcier," Lady Hayworth said. "Your mirror."

Dora opened her eyes again. Elias had not so much as paused on his way out of the morning room. "I hardly need it," he replied. "Miss Ettings may keep it, if she so wishes."

Lady Hayworth made as though to object – it was certainly not proper for the Lord Sorcier to be giving Dora *gifts* – but he was gone before the countess could make her case.

"You must get rid of that thing immediately," Lady Hayworth said to Dora with a frown. "You cannot be accepting magical trinkets from that man. The rumours!"

Dora clutched the mirror closer, trying to think quickly. "I should not have insulted the Lord Sorcier by turning him down," she said. "He has left the mirror on purpose, Lady Hayworth. If I discard it, I will have seven years of terrible luck, I am sure."

The countess scowled at that, but Dora saw that she had reconsidered. "What a thoroughly unpleasant man," Lady Hayworth muttered. "Well! Hide it in a dresser somewhere, and do not take it out. We are the only two people who know that you have it, and neither of us shall tell anyone that you accepted it."

Dora nodded, relaxing slightly. "I will go and put it up now," she said. "Thank you for your help, Lady Hayworth. I am not certain that I could have handled him on my own."

This compliment assuaged the countess, such that she waved Dora off to her room.

Upstairs, Dora set herself on the edge of her bed and stared into the mirror. For just a second, she thought she could see those black depths again – but they slipped away from her when she next blinked, and only the silver backing of the mirror remained.

Dora stowed the mirror in her dresser, wondering whether

the Lord Sorcier had indeed caught her meaning. Surely, Dora thought, he would not have left the mirror if he had not.

The image of his bloody, agonised face floated back to her as she stood awkwardly in front of the dresser.

Dimly, she noted that her hands were shaking.

That has not happened before, Dora thought. *How curious.*

In a few more minutes, however, the shaking stopped . . . and, as was the usual way of things, Dora found her attention diverted once again as she realised that she hadn't yet had any of the delightful-looking biscuits downstairs.

Chapter Six

Vanessa was desperate to know just what it was the Lord Sorcier had talked about with Dora – in fact, she sneaked into Dora's room that evening after dinner and refused to leave until she'd been given every small detail.

"One foot in faerie?" Vanessa puzzled afterwards. "But what could he mean by that?"

"I would be only too pleased to ask him, if I could manage to speak with him," Dora sighed. "But the countess is determined to keep him away from me, and even while he *was* here, she was keenly listening to every word. I would not be surprised if he now gave up this whole charade and never bothered with me again."

Vanessa frowned at that. "I don't believe that will happen," she said. "I have done my due diligence on the Lord Sorcier, and if there is one thing everyone can agree upon, it is that he is even more stubborn when he feels he is being thwarted. Perhaps this is a good thing, Dora – if the countess makes everything very difficult for him, then he shall not lose interest in your curse." Vanessa smiled at a stray thought. "Perhaps he might even marry you! He did come courting today, after all."

"That much was an outright sham, Vanessa," Dora said. "And I would not recommend that you set your heart on such a silly thought."

Dora pushed Vanessa out of the room after that, forcing her to bed. Her cousin had received more than one set of flowers today, which meant that she was likely to start receiving suitors any day now. It wouldn't do for her to be rumpled and tired-looking when they arrived.

Dora was just preparing for bed herself . . . but before she could put her head to the pillow, she found herself pulling the Lord Sorcier's mirror from the dresser, holding it before her as she settled on the edge of her bed again.

The memory of the awful scene she had witnessed earlier that day still gave her a faint sense of nausea. But the Lord Sorcier had implied that there was a connection, however tenuous, between Dora's curse and the things that she saw in the mirror. She knew it would only benefit her if she could manage to bring on those visions more reliably.

The mirror's silvered back remained stubbornly visible, however, no matter how much she tried to force it into that dull blackness.

Dora chewed at her lip. *I saw the future once, and then the past*, she thought. *Both times, it was something to do with the Lord Sorcier, even if he was only present.*

Perhaps, Dora thought, she ought to focus on trying to see something more to do with *him*.

Even as she had the thought, the silvered back of the mirror rippled like a pond. Dora focused her thoughts on the Lord Sorcier – she imagined him standing before her as he had done earlier in the day, with his wild hair and golden eyes and care-less manner of dress.

Blackness encroached upon the mirror's back. Slowly – ever so slowly – the figure of the Lord Sorcier solidified, becoming more real than before. He was sitting at a writing desk, looking over one of the tomes he had bought from the magic shop by the light of a candle. His jacket and his neck cloth were gone, however, and his waistcoat was unbuttoned. Had Dora been capable of the emotion, she might have been mortified to see him in such a state of undress. Even so, she couldn't help but stare.

"Ah, there you are," Elias said briskly. He still had his eyes upon the book in front of him, and it took Dora a moment to realise that he was *addressing* her. "I was beginning to think I'd need to send you step-by-step instructions, Miss Ettings."

"Step-by-step instructions *would* have been nice," Dora said. She paused, realising that she had just managed to speak. That had never been the case before in one of her visions. "May I ask what on earth is going on?"

Elias turned in his chair. "Visions of the past and future are unpredictable at best," he said. "But one may scry distant lands or distant people with better reliability. I normally protect myself against such intrusions, but the mirror that you hold may bypass those protections if I please it to. It was a tricky bit of magic, if I do say so myself."

Dora frowned distractedly. "Then you are at home right now?" she asked. She glanced down at herself and saw that she was wearing only her nightgown. This was, in many respects, far worse than being caught by the Lord Sorcier in her stays and underthings – but he did not seem the least bit fazed, and so Dora decided that she shouldn't be fazed either.

"I am at home," Elias agreed. "It has been a very long and very awful day, I might add. I will be glad to divert my attention to something less hideous for a brief time." He closed the book on the desk and leaned back in his chair to consider her. "I will admit," he said, "I was worried that you might be scared away from further scrying after what you saw today. I must apologise again for that."

Dora knit her brow. The words were utterly sincere. But of all things, the Lord Sorcier had finally chosen to apologise to her when she didn't require an apology. "I do not know why you should apologise," she told him. "It was a true thing that I saw, for all that it was ugly. I am sure that it pained you far more to live through it than it pained me to watch it." She glanced away from him, unable now to look him in the eyes. "I am glad to have seen it, for all that it disturbed me. I realise now how awfully I misconceived the war. I had the notion that it was all men in bright uniforms and neat lines simply being brave all the time. I must instead apologise to you for my own wretched silliness."

A long silence extended between them. Eventually, Dora looked back up at the Lord Sorcier and found that he was studying her with a strange look in his eyes. ". . . you were not silly," he said finally. "You had no way to know. Pleasant-mannered men will not tell you of that side of the war because it is distressing. Pleasant-mannered women, like the countess, will not hear of it in their presence. As a result, the ugly parts are largely not thought about by those who did not cross the channel." A bitter weariness flickered across his face. "I cannot help but feel that if we had fewer pleasant-mannered people, then perhaps there would also be fewer of these hideous wars."

This gave Dora a distant sense of shame for some reason. Just now, in perfect privacy with the Lord Sorcier, she thought she might understand how he had come to be the way that he was. That shame slowly morphed into a dull sadness, which she thought she might examine more deeply at a later date.

Elias cleared his throat, and Dora returned her attention to him directly. "I have a theory on your condition, Miss Ettings," he told her, by way of changing the subject.

Dora blinked. A hint of something unfamiliar swam through her chest. It wasn't . . . happiness, per se. It was lighter than most emotions, however, and she decided that it might be some flavour of hope. "I am very pleased to hear it," she told him. Then, because she was sure that her voice had not communicated her feelings on the matter clearly enough, she added, "Truly. I fear my abilities of expression are not adequate to the task of thanking you properly."

Elias smiled at that. For once, it was not a bitter or sardonic smile. It was soft, and perhaps relieved. The expression utterly changed his mien, and Dora thought in that moment that he was really very beautiful. "You may not be so grateful when I tell you my theory," Elias said. "For I am still working out exactly what to do about it."

"Nevertheless," Dora said. "To have a theory at all is more than I ever expected."

Elias nodded slowly. "Well," he said. "As strange as it may sound, I believe that part of you *is* in faerie, Miss Ettings. Whichever part of you the faerie stole, he took it back with him to his lands on the other side. That missing part of you must still endure there, for you are unerringly capable of divination when given the proper instrument. I might even go so far as to say you could see such things in a normal mirror, if you strained yourself."

Dora considered this. "Then I would need to steal that part of myself *back* from him?" she asked. "That is your concern — that I would need to walk into faerie."

Elias shook his head at her incredulously. "You will not be walking into faerie, Miss Ettings," he said. "What a ridiculous idea. If anything, *I* would be walking into faerie." He frowned deeply at that, then added, "But since I avoid the place at all costs, we shall name that only as a last, most desperate resort."

"I could not ask you to do something so dangerous, my lord," Dora agreed. "I would not even think of it, in fact."

Elias raised an eyebrow at Dora. "I insist on 'my lord' only when I am intent on bullying someone," he told her. "You may call me Elias, at least in private. It's shorter, and it doesn't make my stomach churn."

Dora knew that she ought to be flustered at this. Whatever the Lord Sorcier thought, the use of Christian names between men and women was a scandal in and of itself. But the embarrassment she should have felt was absent, and she saw no reason to deny his request if it might keep him feeling charitable towards her.

"As you wish, er . . . *Elias.*" Dora had to force herself to say the name aloud. This time, there *was* a flicker of embarrassment, but it was quickly gone again. "I suppose that you should call me Dora then, out of simple fairness."

"Hm." Elias considered this. "Dora. That's a nice, straightforward name. I assume the more lengthy version is bizarre and unwieldy?"

Dora sighed. *He was so much more pleasant for a time*, she thought. "My full name is Theodora Eloisa—"

"Oh, dear lord, don't tell it all to me now!" Elias snapped. At Dora's confused look, he added, "You should never tell your full name to a magician. Nor to a faerie, for that matter. It gives them power over you."

Dora pursed her lips. "In truth," she told him, "I am already far too deep within your power for it to matter. You know the secret that could ruin my family, and you are the best chance I have at any sort of cure. A name is a small thing compared to those."

Elias frowned at that, clearly unable to find a logical reply. "I suppose you're correct," he said finally. "But I don't wish to own your name, Miss Ettings."

A smile flickered across her lips. "You are supposed to call me Dora," she reminded Elias.

This *did* fluster him, but only because she had caught him out on his own request. "Yes, fine," Elias muttered. "*Dora.*"

Her smile settled in more deeply at that. "Might I ask, *Elias*, if you know exactly what it is the Marquess of Hollowvale stole from me?"

Elias raised an eyebrow at the name, but he did not comment on it directly. "I have my suspicions," he said. "But they are difficult to prove, one way or another."

Dora nodded. "Then perhaps you could tell me what it is that you suspect?" she offered.

Elias rubbed at his chin. "I *suspect* that the faerie has stolen much more than just your humours," he said. "It is possible that he has taken half of your entire soul." He paused. "Likely, the faerie meant to take the whole thing, but you told me that he was distracted from the task. I have heard of faeries stealing souls before – though that is before my time – but I think that a faerie stealing only *half* a soul must be without precedent. If I am correct, then your case is probably the first."

Dora sighed. "Oh dear," she said. "That must mean that it will be difficult to solve."

"Almost certainly," Elias agreed. But there was a keen light to his eyes as he said it that made Dora suspect he considered this a good thing. *Vanessa did say that he enjoys difficult things*, she remembered.

"Well . . ." Dora said slowly. "If you cannot steal back my soul directly, then I am not entirely certain of the possibilities that remain."

"Oh, plenty," Elias said distractedly. "We might try stealing it back from afar. We might even try regrowing it – this has never happened before, so who knows what might be possible? I will have to continue researching and thinking on it, but I will let you know when I have something new to try."

Dora glanced past Elias at the book on his writing desk. "You have other things to worry about, of course," she said. "Are you truly investigating a plague?"

The darkness she had seen in him before returned abruptly, settling upon him like a heavy cloak, and Dora found that she regretted the words. "I am," Elias said. "But it's none of your concern." Dora felt the finality in his voice, and she knew that he had finished with their conversation. "You should go to bed, Miss . . . Dora."

"I would, Elias," Dora told him evenly. "But I have no idea just yet how to *stop* scrying."

That earned a slight twitch of his mouth, at least. "You'll want to focus on yourself, and not on me," Elias said. "Think on your actual surroundings and the real sensations that you feel."

Dora tried to do as he asked. She turned her attention inward; she tried to imagine the hardness of the mirror in her hand and the feel of the soft bed beneath her. But her mind wandered inattentively away, and she found herself soon wondering instead what a faerie like Lord Hollowvale might see when they looked at her, if she was indeed missing half her soul. Would the strands of her soul be ragged and torn? Perhaps they would simply be dull and colourless, like her other eye—

"Dora," Elias said dryly. "You are still here."

Dora blinked. "Oh," she said. "I'm very sorry. I'm afraid that focusing on myself is actually quite difficult."

Elias shook his head. "I see. Well . . . for the meantime, at least, I suppose I can offer you a push." He raised one hand, and Dora felt a kind of tug at her chest. He shooed at her with his fingers . . .

. . . and she found herself sitting back on her bed at the townhouse, staring down into a silver-backed mirror.

Chapter Seven

*ora was roused from bed the next day bright and early. One of the maids began getting her ready as though she were supposed to go out somewhere, but the servant either could not or would not tell her where it was she was going. At least, Dora thought, she was wearing one of her more practical dresses, and she was allowed to don the sturdier set of half-boots she had brought with her from the country, rather than those awkward pattens.

For just a moment, Dora found herself wondering whether Elias had shown up and bullied his way past the countess again. The idea of spending the morning with him sparked a vague interest in her that she could not quite pin down.

That spark withered disappointingly, however, when Dora came downstairs to find Albert in the morning room with Auntie Frances and the countess, and another woman that she did not immediately recognise. Albert was himself dressed in very practical clothing, and he had his physician's bag with him. He was chatting very amiably with the two hens and the third woman, but Dora could not help hearing the note of impatience in his voice as she entered the room.

". . . absolutely not fit for a lady," Albert was saying. "I have argued the matter with my mother at length now, but she refuses to understand how different this is from her own charity work."

"Your concern is most touching," Auntie Frances replied with a polite smile. "But you will find that our dear Dora is unusually resilient. Her affection for those in need is so strong that it allows her to persevere where other ladies might wither."

This lie was so outrageous that Dora nearly laughed. But she cleared her throat delicately instead, clasping her hands in front of her. "How lovely to see you, Mr Lowe," she said. "To what do we owe the pleasure?"

Albert shot her a rueful look. "Miss Ettings," he greeted her. "My mother informs me that you are most eager to help me in my charity work today." Dora could tell from Albert's tone that he knew very well just *who* had been so eager to arrange this whole thing, and that it had not, in fact, been her. "I thought I might try one last time to argue against such an idea. I am slated to go somewhere very unpleasant today."

Dora smiled apologetically. "I am not bothered by unpleasantness," she said, since Auntie Frances and the countess were watching her like a hawk. "I will do my best not to be a nuisance to your work."

Albert sighed heavily. "I will not further impede this arrangement, then," he said, "lest my mother cook up something even more far-fetched." He got to his feet and offered out an arm to Dora, who took it obligingly.

"Miss Henrietta Jennings will be accompanying you as a chaperone," the countess said, and Dora looked over at the third woman, who had been keeping very silent until now. "I am afraid that Lady Lockheed and I are otherwise engaged today, but Miss Jennings was my daughter's governess at one time, and she will be a fine substitute in our absence."

Miss Jennings – a neatly kept brunette in her thirties – did not look terribly pleased by this arrangement. But she rose to her feet as well and inclined her head towards Albert and Dora. "I am sure that there is nothing to worry about while Miss Ettings is engaged in charity work," she said. "But I shall be about for the sake of propriety."

Albert took a deep breath at that. The poor man was already being forced to look after *one* woman while doing his work. He was probably wondering whether he would be able to do anything of use at all while watching after *two* women.

"I see," he said finally. "Well. Let us be off, then. I have much to accomplish and only so much daylight left to me."

Albert turned with Dora to head for the front door – but Auntie Frances kept her back for just a moment, encouraging Albert to go ahead. When Dora gave her a curious look, Auntie Frances smiled down at her in a motherly fashion.

"We have discussed the matter with Miss Jennings," Auntie Frances said. "She will be very obliging with you and Mr Lowe, Dora. You should have plenty of opportunity to catch his interest in whatever way you choose."

Dora blinked at her slowly. "Auntie Frances," she said, "are you implying that I should openly flirt with Mr Lowe?" Perhaps such a thing should not have surprised her. Auntie Frances was less concerned with maintaining Dora's reputation than she was in snaring poor Albert and gaining Lady Carroway's favour for Vanessa, after all.

"You will be helping Mr Lowe directly," Auntie Frances told Dora. "I am not sure what all that entails – but you could certainly be forgiven for brushing his hand or leaning in closely to him if it were for a noble, charitable cause. This situation is really quite a boon, Dora, and you must take full advantage while you can."

Dora resisted the urge to sigh openly. "Of course, Auntie Frances," she said. This day was looking to be steadily worse for Albert by the moment, and Dora noted to herself that she ought to apologise to him the first instant that she could manage it.

When Dora did rejoin Albert and Miss Jennings at the front door, she saw that Albert had brought an unmarked carriage with him. The driver was an older man with a stiff posture, a balding pate and a very impressive, steel-grey moustache. Dora could not help but notice that this driver had a flintlock prominently displayed on him, as though to pre-emptively warn away troublemakers. He shot Albert a bemused look as the two ladies stepped into the carriage.

"I am glad that you have dressed practically, at least," Albert observed to Dora, as the three of them settled into the carriage. "But I confess, I am not sure what to do with you. I *have* mentioned need for an assistant, but I will be tending to the sick and injured, and almost all of that will require dirtying your hands. Some of it will be very distressing indeed."

Dora shrugged. "Auntie Frances was being truthful when she said that I have a very solid constitution," she told Albert. "You may offer me what work would be useful. I promise to tell you if it would distress me overmuch."

Albert frowned at that, but Dora suspected that he was genuinely considering her words as the carriage carried on. For her part, Dora hoped that Albert might take the words to heart. She was not prone to being upset, after all, and it would make her feel better about the foolish arrangement if she could at least offer Albert some semblance of real help in the process.

When the carriage finally came to a stop, Albert handed scarves to both Dora and Miss Jennings, advising that they wrap the cloth around their noses and mouths, and he soon did the same for himself. "There will be plenty of bile about," he told them. "Be sure to stay as clean as possible while we are here."

Here turned out to be an imposing prison-like building which Albert informed them to be the Cleveland Street Workhouse – a place of last resort for the poor and injured and indigent. As they entered, Dora was relieved to have the scarf over her nose, for the smell was absolutely abominable; there was upon the air some damp, acrid scent of lye, which stung at her lungs, mixed with more than a hint of offal. Poor Miss Jennings looked about to faint – Dora slipped an arm through hers, just in case, and she felt the ex-governess lean slightly upon her.

Dora had heard only general things about the workhouses, but she had never before had occasion to enter one herself. The general dining room, not far from the entrance hall, was currently packed to distraction with men, women and children in various states of misery. Certain of the men were obviously dreadfully ill or missing limbs; the women were tired and forlorn, and some of the children had too few fingers. Even if there hadn't been that awful lye on the air, they all would have still had trouble breathing, given the cramped confines and the sheer number of people about.

Though they were in a kind of dining hall, there was currently no food about. Instead, most of the people had taken up places at the table or against the walls. All of them had rough hemp rope in their laps, which they were pulling apart strand by strand. The work was miserable-looking; many of the workers were bleeding from their hands, but they had long since ceased to notice their injury.

The inmates of the workhouse – for they were clearly inmates and not benevolent charity cases, as Dora had heard it told – all showed at least some interest in their group's entrance. A few of them seemed to recognise Albert, for he got nods and murmurs in his direction. Soon, one of the inmates rose to his feet and disappeared down a hallway; he returned with a tall, pinched-looking fellow in somewhat better clothing, who shook Albert's hand and led them out of the madness towards a different wing of the facility. This area, though dark and dank, at least seemed somewhat quieter since most of its inhabitants were stretched out weakly, two and three to each bed against the walls.

"We have some coughing, some vomiting, some simple lack of vigour," observed the pinched-looking man. Albert had introduced him to the ladies as George Ricks, the workhouse master, though Albert's aloof tone of voice suggested to Dora that he did not much like the man. "There is one new pregnant woman, unfortunately."

"Unfortunately?" Albert asked, as he approached one of the beds. "Why is that particularly unfortunate?"

The workhouse master gave Albert a long-suffering sort of look. "Newborns can hardly do useful work to earn their keep," he said. "It'll be nothing but a drain on us as soon as it is born."

"How terrible for you," Dora said evenly, before she could stop herself. Albert shot her a sideways glance, but she saw a mute, frustrated agreement behind his normally warm eyes.

George Ricks looked down at her condescendingly. "I didn't realise you'd be bringing ladies with you," he told Albert. "They're far too soft for this business. Nothing but trouble, mark my words." Before any of them could respond, he added, "I have other things to tend to. You can call in one of the inmate nurses if you like."

As he left the room, Dora stepped closer to Albert, watching him as he opened his leather physician's bag. He peeled away his gloves, tucking them into the bag; this revealed the silver glint of his right hand, which was very fascinating to look at. "I must admit, I now aspire to be troublesome," Dora told him. "That unpleasant man truly begs to be caused trouble."

Miss Jennings sniffed beneath the scarf she wore about her face. "Soft indeed!" she said. "I'd like to see that man try to run a proper nursery and then call women *soft*. This sickroom is a terrible mess."

It was the first time the woman had evinced anything other than polite greetings or neutral murmurs of agreement in their presence so far. Dora found herself pleased by the hint of contrariness in her character. "It is, isn't it?" Dora said. "I am sure that we can do *something* about it, though there is little to be done for the lack of space. The bedding certainly requires changing."

Miss Jennings turned to Albert. "There must be a laundry in this place," she observed. "I can smell the lye, even from here."

Albert nodded, and Dora saw pleasant surprise growing upon his face. "This workhouse handles local laundry for a fee," he said. "The laundry is downstairs in a basement area. The smell creeps up from there, I'm afraid."

Albert directed Miss Jennings to one of the inmate nurses – an older woman named Susan, who had a distracted gaze and shaking hands. The two of them headed downstairs to fetch some fresh sheets, and Dora realised shortly thereafter that Miss Jennings had neatly accomplished Auntie Frances's request and left Dora quite alone with Albert in the process.

"I am very sorry for all of this," Dora told him promptly, as Albert began inspecting the patients one by one. Occasionally, he would ask her to help a patient to a sitting position, or to hold his bag while he worked. "I will do my best not to be a bother. But I should also warn you that Miss Jennings is supposed to give me a wide berth so that I might touch your hand and seduce you, or something silly like that."

Albert shook his head incredulously. "This all seems very ridiculous," he told her. "I was aware on some level just how far society mothers are willing to go to snare husbands for their daughters . . . but sending you to a workhouse, Miss Ettings? Have your guardians no appreciation for your safety?"

Dora glanced around herself idly. "I do not know if they truly appreciate the conditions here," she said. "Pleasant-mannered people do not speak of ugly things, after all."

Albert shot Dora a surprised look, and she realised that she had more or less repeated something that Elias had said to her. "I nearly forgot that you had seen Elias yesterday," Albert said as if reading her mind. "He must have made his usual sort of impression."

Dora considered that. "I believe that he did," she said. "Though I begin to think that he made a very different sort of impression upon the countess than he did upon me." She frowned to herself. "I did not realise you had saved his life during the war. It makes sense, of course, given your relationship. That is why he made you that arm, isn't it?"

Albert glanced instinctively down at his right hand. It was utterly smooth – nearly normal-looking, but for its unnatural material. "I suspect so," he said. "But Elias will claim that he did it in case I should need to perform surgery on him again. He does not like to admit to generous impulses." Albert looked back up at Dora, and she saw surprise in his eyes. "That I saved his life is not common knowledge. Did Elias tell you that himself?"

Dora shifted on her feet. "He did . . . in a way," she said slowly. "More by accident than anything." She did not enjoy the idea of explaining to Albert how personally she had witnessed his past. "It's the war that he's angry about, isn't it? All of that awfulness, and the fact that people refuse to speak of it?"

Albert took a deep breath. Now, he really did look uncomfortable. "Elias is angry about a great number of things," he said. "And I am sure that he would tell you about all of them at length if you were to ask him. But he holds onto that anger in a way that is both highly productive and terribly miserable." He chose his next words very carefully. "I think that Elias has been angry now for so long that he is scared to let it go – I think he is scared that it would make him too complacent, and he might become all of those things which he so despises in others."

Dora nodded slowly. She had not known the Lord Sorcier as long as Albert had, but this sounded very accurate. "I find that awfully sad," she murmured, and she could not help but glance at Albert's silver hand again. *Someone who cared enough to create something like that doesn't deserve to be forever unhappy*, Dora thought.

When Dora looked up, she saw that Albert's eyes were crinkled, and she thought he might be smiling at her from beneath his scarf. "I think you must be one of the only other people in the world who finds it so, Miss Ettings," Albert said. "Elias is so very good at convincing people to despise him."

Dora smiled faintly back at him. "I have been contrary since

I was very young," she said. "The moment that it became clear to me how much the Lord Sorcier wanted me to hate him, I think I must have become determined to do the opposite."

Albert laughed. "He has never had a handle on you, Miss Ettings," he said. "Not since the moment he met you. I will admit, I have a contrary nature of my own – I love to watch him struggle with you. It's as entertaining a show as anything I've ever seen."

Dora raised her eyebrows at him. "You hide your contrariness well, Mr Lowe," she said. "I am impressed."

Albert became absorbed in his work again shortly thereafter. Miss Jennings and Susan came and went more than once while Dora walked with him, pulling down sheets and replacing them with fresh ones. Occasionally, Dora caught Miss Jennings glancing her way, but it was clear that the former governess was being quite casual in her duties as chaperone. Once, Dora pressed her hand to Albert's shoulder while Miss Jennings watched, just in case the chaperone was supposed to report back to Auntie Frances and the countess on Dora's efforts.

After a time, Albert and Dora came to a boy with a great gash on his leg, which was bleeding sluggishly beneath a cloth. Albert gently pulled the cloth away, while Dora held the boy's hand and pulled down her scarf to smile encouragingly at him.

"My name is Dora," she told him. "What is yours?"

The boy's eyes glanced warily towards his leg, but he forced them back to Dora in short order, trying not to seem afraid. "Roger, m'lady," he mumbled. The words sounded clumsy, and Dora suspected he wasn't often prone to such politeness.

"I am sorry that you're hurt, Roger," Dora told him. "You are being very brave so far, though. I'm quite impressed." This made Roger straighten slightly in place, and Dora was surprised to feel a distant hint of pride herself. She was really barely a lady, and most men tended to give her strange or pitying glances as soon as they saw her mismatched eyes. But Roger had no concept that Dora might be anything but utterly respectable, and his odd need to impress her made the smile on her face somewhat more genuine.

Nearby, Albert winced at the sight of the injury. "This will need stitches," he said. He looked towards Dora hesitantly. "Are you up to helping with that?"

Roger blanched at the suggestion, and Dora tightened her hand on his reassuringly. "I can perform all manner of different stitches," Dora informed Albert. "But I have never tried to stitch up skin before. I am willing to try it, I suppose."

Albert blinked at her. "I was *certainly* not suggesting you should stitch him up yourself!" he said, aghast. "I only hoped for you to hold the skin together for me while I did the deed." He paused, then added, "That is bad enough, I realise."

Dora nodded. "I can do that," she assured him. "Please don't worry yourself on my account."

Albert insisted that they wash their hands in hot water first – Dora asked him why and was bemused at his honest reply: *I haven't the first idea*, he said, *but another surgeon recommended it to me, and it seems to work well enough.* This, Dora thought, was a refreshing thing to hear. She could not think of any other gentleman who had ever admitted to her that he did not know something.

Poor Roger nearly fainted when he saw Albert pull out that wicked-looking needle. Dora tried to console him, but he was already wiggling around in discomfort. "You'll need to hold still," Albert told him, gently but firmly.

The gash on the boy's leg was objectively awful to look at. Dora inwardly blessed the missing half of her soul for once, as she reached down to pinch at the bloody edges of the gash with her fingers. Roger let out a soft whimper as Albert began to sew him up, and Dora became aware that other inmates were watching them with fascination. *How awful*, she thought. *Though I suppose they must have little else of interest to watch.*

Thankfully, Albert was quick about his work. He tied off the stitches and wiped down the injury. "This should suffice for now," he told Roger. "But if it starts to smell or if it becomes even more painful, you should tell the workhouse master to fetch me right away."

"He won't fetch you," Roger said wryly. "It'd be troublesome on him."

Albert sighed. "I'll come and visit again soon, then," he said. "Just to check."

As they went on, Dora frowned at Albert from beneath her scarf. "You learned surgery during the war, Mr Lowe," she said slowly. "But I was told that you're a physician now."

Albert shook his head ruefully at that for some reason. "I prefer surgery," he said. "I know my physician's credentials are considered more respectable – but truly, Miss Ettings, proper physicians have the *strangest* medical ideas. Their obsession with bleeding confuses me terribly. I have never known bleeding to *improve* a patient . . . though I suppose it certainly quiets them." He considered this very seriously, and then added, "On that note, I might prescribe bleeding for Elias one of these days. But only because he could sometimes use quieting."

Dora snorted, but did not otherwise respond.

Their rounds went on, even into other rooms. Dora soon realised that there were *multiple* sick rooms. In fact, it seemed that there were almost more sick and injured people here than there were healthy ones. None of them were in very good condition, and Dora felt a moment of empathy for Miss Jennings, who had taken on a task of even greater enormity than she knew.

In the very corner of one of these rooms was a peculiar sight. A single bed had been set aside, where a little girl was curled up fast asleep. The other beds had been pulled away from the corner, and Dora could not help but notice that the other inmates had refused to share that bed in particular.

Albert stared at that bed, and there came such a wary look

on his face that Dora knew he had some knowledge of what was going on. "How long has it been since she woke up?" Albert asked one of the men nearby.

"Not since two days ago," the inmate replied, and he made a fearful cross over his chest. "Will you be takin' her out of here, then? She's got no mother to stop you, doctor, an' it'd be a great relief."

Dora took a step towards the bed, but Albert reached out to stop her. "Go and fetch the workhouse master, please," Albert asked the man.

As soon as he had gone, Dora turned towards Albert. "What is going on?" she asked.

A bleak expression crossed Albert's features. "A sleeping plague," he said. "The victims fall asleep and simply never wake. I've been encountering it all over the place in the workhouses. We don't yet know how it spreads, but the children are particularly prone to it for some reason."

"We?" Dora repeated.

Albert pinched at the bridge of his nose. "Elias and I," he said. "I'll need to send for him. He thinks that the plague has a magical component to it, and I cannot say that I disagree. It's certainly beyond any treatment I've tried so far."

Dora looked back towards the little girl in the bed. She was not a very *pretty* little girl. Her hair was lank, oily and straw-like, and there were pockmarks on her little face. But this was awful in and of itself, and Dora found herself with a hard knot in her stomach as she contemplated the fact that no mother would even miss her.

"Why is she here?" Dora asked Albert quietly. She wanted to ask more than that. She wanted to ask: why was it so awful here? What sort of people could allow a little girl to fall asleep in that condition at all? Was there no one with a heart that might find that girl a clean and proper bed of her own, away from all this hideousness?

"I don't know," Albert said. Though he was only answering the obvious question, there was an awful weariness in his voice that suggested he had asked all of the *rest* of those questions of himself many times already.

Dora stared bleakly at the sleeping girl. And though she could not feel things very keenly, she thought perhaps a tiny sliver of the Lord Sorcier's bitter anger might have infected her, deep down.

Chapter Eight

*I*t took Elias barely an hour to arrive at the workhouse, once the message had been sent off to him. He swept into the sickroom like an unexpected storm, with his hair unkempt and his golden eyes flashing. He was back in half-dress, with his practical brown and black clothing and his loosened neck cloth. He did not wear a scarf around his mouth, but the acrid air did not seem to bother him.

Albert barely had to gesture towards the bed in the back corner – it was perfectly clear just where the other inmates had shoved the girl.

"How long has she been sleeping?" Elias asked brusquely. He had not yet noticed Dora, she thought, given his focus on the matter at hand.

"Perhaps two days, according to the others," Albert replied.

"That's slightly earlier than we've found them before," Elias said. He pulled a paper cigarette from his jacket and pressed it between his lips. As he gestured with his other hand, fire flickered up between his fingers, lighting the end of the cigarette.

Dora watched intently with her brow furrowed. She had not seen the Lord Sorcier indulging in this habit before, and he had certainly never smelled to her of tobacco. But this seemed to be a practical matter rather than a pleasurable one – as Elias exhaled a veil of smoke, it drifted unnaturally about the room, darting into corners like a cat. Where it passed, it left a faint silver glow, which faded slowly away again.

The smoke curled about the sick room, lingering at least a little bit upon every inch. The inmates watched it pass with varying levels of fear and fascination. Some jerked back from it as it touched them – but the silver glow found them all regardless, before inevitably disappearing once again.

Eventually, the smoke dissipated entirely, and Elias frowned. He snuffed the cigarette with his fingers. "Not a trace of black magic," he said tightly. "Nothing that tobacco might show, anyway. I had hoped we might find a hint of it this close to the start of the illness."

Dora sidestepped from where she was so that she could see past Elias again. "What does that mean?" she asked him.

Elias startled at the question. His golden eyes fixed upon Dora, and he looked suddenly perplexed. "What *are* you doing here, Miss Ettings?" he asked.

"That is a bit of a story," Dora admitted. "But you thought the plague might be magical in nature. Does this mean that it isn't?"

Elias narrowed his eyes. "It means," he said, "that *if* magic is indeed involved, then it is of the sort that deals an injury and then departs. But if that's so, then it fails to explain why the plague sometimes spreads." The inmates began to murmur at that, and Elias glanced around at them. "To other *children*," he emphasised darkly. And then, as though to demonstrate, he crossed the last bit of space between him and the bed and pulled back the threadbare covers to lift the little girl into his arms.

Albert stepped aside, and Dora realised that Elias meant to simply take the girl with him. She began to follow him without being entirely conscious of it. "Where will you be going?" she asked.

Elias turned his head, and again Dora saw a flicker of confusion cross his face – as though he'd nearly forgotten she was there. "Elsewhere," he said. "Somewhere I can investigate further, in peace."

Dora dropped her eyes to the little girl in Elias's arms. She was small and light enough that he had her nearly upright, with her cheek pressed against his shoulder. She did not look like a feverish, suffering patient so much as a listless puppet with cut strings.

"I would like to come with you," Dora said.

Elias frowned. "Why?" he asked. His tone was more distracted than confrontational, and Dora thought he must have really desired an answer.

Dora thought on it for another moment. But whatever instinct had prompted her to ask was like a lily pad floating on the water without any sort of root. It *existed*, but it had no discernible cause. "I don't know," she said finally.

Albert gave Dora a strange look at this. But Elias accepted the answer with a nod, aware as he was of her condition. "If you like, then," the Lord Sorcier said. "But I am not Albert. I will not be coddling you."

"I am well enough aware of your nature not to expect as much," Dora said dryly. She looked towards Albert. "You will not be upset if I desert you, I expect," she said. "Given that you did not want me here in the first place."

Albert coloured at the direct observation. "I will not stop you, certainly," he replied. "But I would like to retract my earlier worries, Miss Ettings. You have indeed been of practical help today, and I would not decline if you wished to accompany me again." He frowned. "Though you may need to bring your much-absent chaperone if you wish to go with Elias. Where has she wandered off to now?"

"Miss Jennings is ahead of us by one room, I believe," Dora said absently. "I suppose I will fetch her." She went to do so, and found Miss Jennings arguing with a recalcitrant patient, who had accused her of wanting to steal his bedding.

"We will be leaving," Dora told her. "The Lord Sorcier is removing a sick child from the premises." Then, on afterthought, she added, "Mr Lowe has suggested that we should accompany him." This was an outright lie, but Dora hoped that Albert would not grudge her the escape, given that she had apparently been somewhat useful that day.

Miss Jennings glared at the old man in the bed. "*Someone* shall need to pry your dirty sheets from you," she informed him. "But it seems that it shall not be me." She turned on her heel and took Dora by the arm. "It is already early afternoon, unless I miss my mark," Miss Jennings said. "We will need to have you home well before dark, Miss Ettings."

"Yes, of course," Dora said. Miss Jennings had not reacted badly to the mention of the Lord Sorcier, which Dora supposed to mean that Auntie Frances and the countess had not mentioned their aversion to the man. That, at least, was a helpful oversight.

The two of them had to walk quickly to catch up with Elias, who had started for a hired hackney outside. Miss Jennings eyed the small car with a frown.

"That will be an unsuitably close fit for all of us," the ex-governess noted.

Elias glanced back towards her with a look of distaste. "Your chaperone, I presume?" he asked Dora, who nodded minutely. He shrugged at Miss Jennings. "You can always walk, if you prefer," Elias said. He gave an address to the driver and stepped up into the cab. Dora got in after him, which necessitated that Miss Jennings hurry to follow suit.

The cab did not take them too terribly far. It came to a stop only a few minutes later, outside a small, run-down building located within the Strand. This one had at least a tiny garden in the front, and even a few bright flowers. Elias paused at the front door, still holding onto his sleeping charge, so Dora knocked at it for him.

An older, matronly-looking woman in a dress and apron

answered in short order. She seemed so unsurprised to see the Lord Sorcier that she didn't even bother with a greeting. Instead, her dark eyes glanced down at the little girl, and she sighed. "Oh no," she said. "Another one?"

"I presume the upstairs room is still free, Mrs Dun?" Elias said, by way of reply.

"It is," she said softly. Her eyes glanced past him, towards Dora and Miss Jennings, and she frowned in surprise. Clearly, Mrs Dun was not used to the Lord Sorcier coming with company. Still, she said nothing as the two of them followed him inside.

The building was light and airy, with many open windows. Dora thought it might have been some well-to-do merchant's house once upon a time. Now, however, she could see children peeking out at them through bedroom doors as they passed. It was hard to see much of them, as they stayed carefully out of sight, but they did not seem dirty or miserable like the children in the workhouse had been. Mrs Dun stopped to shoo these children gently back, closing the doors as they went. She led Elias up the stairs towards a remote sort of room that had been marked in paint with a red X.

Dora might have expected something ominous to be beyond that door – but as Mrs Dun opened it for them, she was surprised to see that it was simply a small, relatively pleasant bedroom. It had another broad, sunny window and two child-sized beds, both currently empty.

Elias carried the little girl over to one of those beds. Mrs Dun pulled down the covers, and he laid the girl very gently down.

Dora watched this with a peculiar feeling in her chest. Everything had begun to feel very dizzy and uncertain ever since she'd swallowed down that fragment of confusing anger. But it occurred to her as she watched Elias tuck the little girl into bed that she had been furiously wishing that someone might come along and put the girl somewhere nicer at least. And now, Dora thought, someone *had*.

There was an unmistakable look of grief and frustration on the Lord Sorcier's face as he looked down at that bed. Dora felt a dull pain in her heart as she watched him.

"What can I do?" Dora asked, before she could think better of it.

Elias glanced her way. The fire in his eyes was now tired and subdued, but he considered her question regardless. "I must take a bit of time to prepare," he said. "But she does not look terribly comfortable. You might help Mrs Dun clean her up and find her something less filthy to wear while I am busy."

Elias left the room, and it was then only Dora, Mrs Dun and Miss Jennings crowded into the small space.

"The gentleman could have at least taken the time to make introductions," Miss Jennings murmured with a crinkle of her nose.

"Do not call him a gentleman," Dora told her automatically. "He really does not like it."

Mrs Dun smiled at Dora as she said the words. The matronly woman inclined her head towards them both. "I am Mrs Martha Dun," she told them. "I run this house on behalf of the charitable ladies' board. It is normally an orphanage, but the Lord Sorcier had need of a place to isolate these patients. Since he supplies such a sizeable portion of our funds, I did not see the harm in obliging him."

Dora blinked. "He has never mentioned anything of the sort before," she said. For some reason, the revelation mixed that pain in her heart with a strange, fluttery feeling. *Albert did say that Elias hates admitting to charitable impulses*, she thought.

Mrs Dun's smile turned wry. "That does not surprise me in the least," was all that she said.

Dora introduced herself and Miss Jennings to Mrs Dun. At that point, they turned themselves to the task of cleaning up the sleeping girl – who, in lieu of another name, Dora decided to call *Jane*. The task might have been unwieldy with only one or two of them, but three was just enough to make much lighter work of it. The workhouse had not been clean at all, and from the way that Mrs Dun handled Jane's old clothes, Dora suspected that the woman might intend to burn them whole. They wiped the little girl down and put her into a simple, clean cotton shift instead.

Jane's straw-like hair was such a matted mess when they got down to it that Mrs Dun sighed and declared that they would have to cut the bulk of it off. At this point, poor Miss Jennings was beginning to visibly flag – she had been doing so much running about at the workhouse that now her hands had started to tremble. Dora took pity on the poor woman, who had been told after all that she was merely to be a chaperone today, and asked if Mrs Dun might take Miss Jennings down for some tea. "I have my own scissors," Dora told them both. "I keep them quite sharp, for reasons of my own. I can see to Jane's hair."

Miss Jennings accepted this suggestion with great relief, and the two of them descended the stairs, leaving Dora alone with the girl. She pulled free the scissors that Vanessa had given her so long ago and began to cut away at the worst of the tangles.

Elias knocked politely at the door partway through, and Dora called him inside. As he came to stand behind her, she felt his gaze keen upon her back.

"What *are* you feeling, Dora?" Elias asked quietly. "Have you thought on it?"

Dora blinked down at the scissors in her hand. "It's quite a mess," she said softly. "Back in the workhouse, there was a moment where . . . I was so deeply furious. The kind with a long tail, Elias. It is still making me nauseous. If I were normal, I think that I might want to yell at someone, or cry. But those things don't come naturally to me, and they do not give me any relief."

Silence fell between them. Dora felt a knot in her throat, and she tried to swallow it down. "I was very relieved when you brought her here," she said. "But I am still frustrated. Why *are* the workhouses like that? I thought they were a matter of charity."

A hand came down on Dora's shoulder and squeezed. "*This* place is a matter of charity," Elias said. "The workhouses are a matter of sweeping undesirable things from sight."

Tears pricked at Dora's eyes – but they were only the surface of that very deep well of misery that lingered inside her. "That George Ricks man," she said. "I think he really hated all those people he takes care of. It was like he didn't even see them. I didn't know that it was possible to be so callous."

Elias tugged Dora gently around to face him. He slid his arm around her shoulders entirely, and Dora found herself pressed against his chest, much as Jane had been before. He was very warm up close, and he had the sweet scent of myrrh on his clothing, beneath the hint of tobacco smoke from earlier.

Dora could not remember ever having been so sick with anger before. But she had been sad or tired sometimes, and Vanessa often held her when this was the case, until her lantern warmth could banish those dull feelings. There was a lantern warmth to Elias too, Dora realised now. It was hotter, and not as soft as Vanessa's, but it was somehow even more comforting because of that. Dora knew that he was angry too, and it relieved her to know that there was even one other person in the world who found such things obviously intolerable.

"There is such a thing as evil in this world," Elias told her quietly. "It does not help to look away from it. It does not even help necessarily to look *at* it." His fingers brushed through her hair, and she shivered. "But sometimes, when you cannot force the world to come to its senses, you must settle only for wiping away some of the small evils in front of you."

Those few, inadequate tears soaked into his waistcoat. Dora nodded dully – but much as she wanted to pull away and let Elias do his work, she found she couldn't bring herself to move. There was a unique comfort in leaning against him like this, and she knew that she would probably never have that comfort again once she stopped.

They lingered like that for a few minutes. And maybe Dora was imagining it, but she thought that perhaps Elias was thinking something similar – that he gained some small comfort from holding onto her, and that it would be difficult for him to set that comfort aside.

There was another knock at the door, however, and this made Elias tense and press Dora away from him. His now ungloved hand brushed hers, which made Dora's heart turn queerly in her chest – but he then let out a surprised hiss of pain, and she saw that he had touched the scissors by mistake. Dora blinked and set aside the scissors, reaching down to take his hand in hers. "Are you all right?" she asked. "I forgot that I had these out. Please say that I haven't cut you?"

Mrs Dun came inside, and Dora became dimly aware of the impropriety of the situation. Not only had they been in the room *alone* together, but Dora had ruined Elias's attempt to salvage her dignity by taking up his hand and *touching* him. But surely, she thought, a practical woman like Mrs Dun must have some understanding if Elias were *injured*.

Elias tugged his hand back stiffly. But Dora saw before he did that there was no blood of which to speak – only a small, angry red burn in the shape of the edge of her scissors.

"I'm fine," Elias said stiltedly, covering his hand. "Only surprised."

Mrs Dun looked between the two of them. For a moment, Dora worried that the woman might say something about their closeness – but she smiled pleasantly instead and smoothed the matter over as though nothing obviously untoward were going on. "Miss Jennings mentioned that neither she nor Miss Ettings have had aught to eat for a while now," the woman said. "I have some light pickings if you would like to fix that, Miss Ettings."

Dora nodded. "I am nearly done with Jane's hair," she said. "I will come down afterwards."

"Jane?" Elias asked. "Is that her name?"

Dora avoided his eyes. "It is what I have called her for now," she said, "since we cannot know her real name until she wakes up."

Elias winced at that for some reason. But whatever he was thinking, he didn't say it out loud. Dora turned her attention back to Jane's hair, making somewhat quicker work of it than she had first intended. As Mrs Dun waited politely, hovering just outside the doorway, Dora murmured to Elias, "Are faeries and magicians both afraid of scissors, then?"

Elias watched the wall with a stoic sort of expression, rather than look at her as she spoke. "Iron," he corrected her quietly. "It is bane to faeries, and anathema to all magic. I would appreciate it if you did not speak of it again, Miss Ettings."

Dora narrowed her eyes. She dropped her tone even further with her next sentence. "And that is why your magic failed upon the battlefield, isn't it?" she asked. "You were pierced with iron. You could not use it again until Mr Lowe pulled the shards from your body."

"It is not common knowledge," Elias said in a low voice. "Please do not spread it about, Dora."

Dora nodded seriously. "I cannot think why I should do so," she told him. "You are keeping my secrets. I shall keep yours as well." As the last of Jane's matted hair fell away beneath her scissors, she turned to face him directly. "But are magicians *burned* by iron, Elias?"

His golden eyes shuttered at that, and Dora was certain that a brand-new wariness had blossomed in his manner.

"I will not press the matter," she said. "I know that you have work to do."

Elias nodded shortly, and she rose back to her feet, walking past him for the hallway.

Mrs Dun, Dora discovered, had found far more than just light pickings. She had put herself to the trouble of making them a proper lunch, and as Dora ate, she found that she was actually quite hungry. Afterwards, Dora dared to go back upstairs to check on the Lord Sorcier's progress, but since the door was closed, she found herself too worried to knock and possibly disturb him, so she came downstairs again and visited Mrs Dun and some of the other children.

There were eighteen children in the house, she came to learn, excluding Jane – all of them had been taken from the workhouses and relocated, and many were patients whom Albert had treated at one time. Mrs Dun, whom Dora learned to be a widow, had the running of the house, and the sheer extent of her duties sounded exhausting. For much of the time, she was responsible for cooking, cleaning and educating all eighteen children, though some of the older ones had learned to help her. The children clearly adored her, however, and Dora could not help but favourably compare Mrs Dun's stern but loving manner to the awful hardness that she had seen in George Ricks.

Miss Jennings, though weary, was instantly at ease with the children in a way that Dora was not. The ex-governess smiled at them and humoured their stories, occasionally reaching out to absently fix a shirt collar or wipe a cheek.

Eventually, Elias reappeared at the foot of the stairs with an annoyed frown on his face. "You, Miss Ettings!" he barked.

Dora blinked over at him.

"You have a tolerable understanding of French, I believe?" he asked.

"Yes, tolerable," Dora agreed.

Elias gestured towards the stairs. "I'll need your opinion on a translation."

Dora rose to her feet and headed over to join him. To her mild disappointment, Miss Jennings followed her this time.

Upstairs, Elias settled Dora in front of one of those medieval

French tomes, whereupon she struggled through a translation of the qualities of the phlegmatic humour. After she had read it to him multiple times, the Lord Sorcier nodded and pulled out his wooden wand, passing it over Jane. Nothing in particular happened that Dora could see, and Elias frowned in consternation.

"Were you expecting something in particular, my lord?" Miss Jennings asked curiously. The ex-governess, it seemed, was not immune to the novelty of watching a magician work.

"If we are dealing with an imbalance of humours, then phlegm seems to be the most likely culprit," Elias said slowly, as though thinking aloud. "According to these scholars, too much of it should lead to sleepiness. And if phlegm is associated with water, as they say, then I should be able to dowse its overabundance. But she has a child's tiny share of phlegm, it seems, and not an overabundance at all." Elias turned towards the two of them. "Might I compare to one of the two of you? Miss Ettings –" He paused and shook his head, and Dora thought that he must have remembered too late that she was also unlikely to have a normal set of humours. "Miss Jennings," he corrected himself. "If you would."

The ex-governess agreed, with the sort of smile that suggested she would be telling the story of her examination by the Lord Sorcier for the next few weeks at least. Elias passed his wand before her – and this time, it seemed to waver in his hand this way and that, as though pulled along on an invisible tide.

This did not seem to please him, of course, since it had put him back to square one – Miss Jennings had even more phlegm than Jane did, and the ex-governess was still quite wide awake. Elias let out a violent sigh and closed the book in front of Dora. "Not the humours, then!" he said crossly. "How useless." Elias waved them away. "I will be at this all night. Unless the two of you intend to sleep in the other bed, you will wish to take your leave soon."

"That does not sound so terrible," Dora observed. Miss Jennings shot her a bewildered look, however, and Dora realised that she had said something strange again. "I was . . . attempting a joke," Dora offered. "Please forgive me." She still wasn't quite sure which part of the suggestion was so unbelievable, without any hint to go on, but Miss Jennings had seemed so *instantly* astonished that Dora supposed it was something to do with her chaperone's duties.

"We'll take our leave, then," Miss Jennings informed Elias. She took Dora's arm, and the two of them headed for the door. Dora could not help but glance back over her shoulder as they left, however.

The last thing she saw before leaving was the tense, frustrated figure of the Lord Sorcier settling into a chair to theorise anew.

Chapter Nine

*A*untie Frances was at home when Dora returned with Miss Jennings. She was instantly eager to hear all about how Dora's day had gone and whether she had successfully caught Albert's attention. Dora found that she was feeling less patient with this nonsense than usual, given the things she had seen that afternoon – but her aunt could not tell the difference between Dora's normal distraction and her current shortness, which played in her favour for once. Dora mentioned Albert's assertion that she would be welcome to join him in his work again, which pleased her aunt well enough that she only frowned a little bit at the addendum that Dora had spent part of the afternoon helping the Lord Sorcier instead of Albert.

Vanessa, it turned out, was at a private dinner party that evening, and so Dora took her dinner in her room and stared at her dresser with a great temptation. Somehow, she managed to hold herself off for another hour yet before she went to retrieve the mirror there.

Dora's mind was so intent upon Elias that it did not take her long to solidify the sight of him in her imagination. A vision of him swam before her, now sitting in a chair next to Jane's bed with an awful, tired-looking expression on his face.

Since Elias had felt her presence before, Dora had to assume that he knew already of her intrusion. Still, there was a long silence before she could figure out just what to say.

"Things are not going well," Dora observed evenly. The idea pressed upon her more heavily than she could properly express.

"I have spent all of this time trying to formulate theories and tests for when we found another victim," Elias said wearily. "I thought certainly that this time one of my ideas would work. But I have tried everything on my list, and I am out of ideas once again."

There was a grim finality to that statement that Dora very much did not like.

"But you have time," she said slowly. "You have found the victim much sooner, you said. And Jane does not seem to be feverish or suffering."

Elias closed his eyes. "It is difficult to keep alive someone who cannot eat or drink on their own," he said. "Mrs Dun will do her best. But I cannot in good conscience raise your hopes."

Dora settled onto the other empty bed nearby. It had no weight and no real feeling beneath her fingers. But it was so easy for her to forget what real things felt like that it hardly made a difference, she decided, if she were awake or dreaming or scrying.

She *was* upset, of course. The hopelessness on Elias's face came with a melancholy realisation that even this small, specific attempt to fix things likely would not come to fruition. But Elias, Dora thought, had both the long-tailed emotions and the acute ones, and she could not imagine how much more wretched this whole business must have made him feel.

Jane, she thought, had not been the first victim to lie in this room. Mrs Dun had told them that Elias had brought more than one child here to try and understand their condition. He had given each child a soft, quiet bed and a bit of sunlight – but he had failed, each time, to stop their inevitable deterioration as they slept away the last of their lives.

Dora reached out towards Elias's hand on the arm of the

chair. Her fingers met some sort of resistance as she touched him, but there was an odd numbness to the sensation that suggested neither of them could feel it much at all. She held on, still, for lack of anything better to offer.

Elias curled his fingers around hers, though it was rather like grasping for the hand of a ghost.

I wish that I was here again in person, Dora thought.

"You will be at this until the end, then," she said, breaking the bleak silence that had descended. "You will be here, or searching for more books, or researching new ideas?"

Elias nodded slowly. "I will not give up and leave her be," he murmured.

Dora tried to squeeze his hand – but she knew that the gesture had done nothing from his lack of reply. "You are the best person to try, of course," she said. "But perhaps while you are trying your magic, Mr Lowe and I can search for answers by other means. Have all of the afflicted children so far come from the workhouses?"

Elias frowned at that. Dora saw him fighting against the glazed defeat in his eyes. "They have," he said slowly. "But that is not necessarily significant. Albert sees the workhouses often, which is how he came upon this plague. It is quite possible that if he more often saw the countryside, he might have brought the first cases to me from there."

Dora thought on this. "Either way," she said, "you have never seen an adult with this strange disease. If we speak to the children at the workhouses and watch them closely, perhaps we might find a commonality between the ones who fall prey. If the plague is magical, as you suspect, then they must all come into contact with its source at *some* point."

Elias took in a deep breath. Some of the awful malaise cleared from his posture, and Dora's own helplessness retreated as she realised she had been the cause. "That is . . . quite a good idea," he said. "I would be obliged to both of you if you might pursue it further." He turned to look at her and his golden eyes flickered with uncertainty. "I fear that I will be unable to research your curse for a time, however, now that there is another victim. I am sorry, Dora."

Dora shook her head clearly. "What good would it do to have all of my feelings again, if I must use them only to look on all this misery?" she asked. "I would rather see this done before you spend another moment on me. My troubles are not pressing."

Elias managed a small, wry smile at that. "Do you know, Dora," he murmured. "I have known many human beings with a full soul to their name who do not have half so much compassion or practicality as you. On a poor day, I might assume this to be a kind of indictment of the human soul. But today, I believe that you might simply have an overabundance of both qualities." He met Dora's eyes, and she felt his warmth seep into her soul, like a balm around its ragged edges. "In short, though I am terrible at saying it . . . I am glad that you are here."

The gratitude in his face gave Dora pause. It was yet another expression that she had not ever expected to see upon the Lord Sorcier. How different she found him in that moment from the man who had first tried to startle her in the magic shop on Berkeley Square! Yet it was not the man himself who had changed so much as her perspective on him. Elias was still disagreeable to all proper society and politeness. But as Dora inspected herself, she found that he had claimed a warm spot in her heart that she normally did not lease to anyone but her fondest cousin. That Elias seemed to have found a similar fondness for her, even for an instant, started up again those distant, confusing flutterings for which she yet had no name.

"I think you are a good person, Elias," Dora told him, by way of reply. In public, she might have censored the thought, but doing so took an uncommon effort for her, and she had started to find that effort to be pleasantly unnecessary around him. "And whether we should succeed this time or not, I think that Jane is lucky to have your effort." Dora glanced towards the girl in the bed and was reminded of the undercurrent of dread that still played beneath the surface of her mind, thinking of how little time she might have left. "If you require any more translations, and Mr Lowe is otherwise engaged," she added, "I hope that you will let me know."

An odd confusion played about the magician's features as she spoke. Dora wasn't quite sure of the cause – in fact, she thought that she had spoken rather *too* bluntly, so that her meaning could not possibly be mistaken.

Elias smoothed his face again, however, and he returned to his more usual sardonic smile. "I am sure that I will take you up on your offer," he informed Dora. "Though it may require me to bypass the dragons which guard you. I will be sure to set aside my dragon-slaying accoutrements in preparation."

Dora stayed with Elias for a while longer, sitting in companionable silence while he continued to consider his options. The hour grew quite late, in fact, before she blinked and found herself slumped over in bed, with her cheek upon the mirror and her thoughts in disarray.

⁓⦿⁓

When Dora roused herself, she was pleased to find that she had a rare breakfast alone with Vanessa, since she had slept through the first half of it. Unfortunately, Vanessa had heard of Dora's brush with the Lord Sorcier the day before, and she was most eager for news on his progress. When Dora told Vanessa that the Lord Sorcier had no intention of pursuing her cure for the meantime, her cousin was aghast.

"But he must!" Vanessa cried, and Dora had to shush her before she drew the wrong sort of attention. Vanessa lowered her tone reluctantly, but her expression was distressed. "If he will not cure you, then I cannot think who will, Dora. And what shall we do when the London Season is over, and you must go back to Lockheed?"

Dora shook her head at her cousin. "You misunderstand, Vanessa," she said. "I will not be pursuing my cure for the meantime either. There are more important matters afoot, and I cannot in good conscience look away from them."

Dora tried to relate the horrible things she had seen in the workhouse, and her concern for Jane, who even now weakened by the hour. But to Dora's surprise, Vanessa did not seem to be listening to her as closely as she might have expected. Instead, her fair cousin's face grew distant and worried, and Dora suspected that Vanessa was even now attempting to concoct some new plan to salvage her soul.

"Vanessa!" Dora said finally. "Are you not listening? There are people suffering much greater awfulness than me."

"Oh, Dora!" Vanessa replied, with tears in her eyes. "There have *always* been people suffering more greatly than you, I am sure. But you are my cousin, and I love you best. Is it so wrong of me to put you first, after all the years you've borne this hardship?"

Dora blinked at her. It was exactly the sort of heartfelt speech she might have expected of Vanessa. But for once, the subject gave her uncomfortable pause.

"Vanessa," she said, "I have always held your sweetness and generosity in the highest of esteem. I am beyond surprised – nay, *disappointed* – to hear you suggest that I should leave a little girl to die in favour of my own needs."

Vanessa faltered at this. Dora saw the struggle on her cousin's face as she attempted to reconcile her impulses. Vanessa pressed a hand to her mouth and briefly ceased to speak.

For the first time, Dora saw her cousin in a different light. Her love and generosity were still profound, of course – but these feelings of hers were also quite simple and childish in a way. Vanessa loved fiercely and protectively, and she always did prefer to champion those she thought abandoned. But never, Dora realised, had her cousin ever exhibited love or even pity for anyone that she had not seen with her very own eyes.

The discovery of this lacking in her cousin made Dora terribly uneasy. For so many years, she had considered Vanessa to be the perfect model of a lady – the epitome of everything to which Dora ought to aspire herself, once she regained her full faculties. But now, for all that Vanessa was quite lovely in so many respects, Dora had found an unpleasant quality in her that dashed that perfect image from her mind.

"This is what you want, then, Dora?" Vanessa asked softly.

Dora frowned at her. "It is what you ought to want as well," she said, though some part of her knew that she was being churlish in her insistence.

Vanessa looked down. "I would like to change my nature," she said quietly, "if only because I hate so much to disappoint you, Dora. But I cannot truthfully pretend to prefer this course of action, except on your behalf. I *will* support it, if only because I have rarely seen you even this much upset."

Dora pressed her lips together. There was a terrible, disconnected feeling in her that she could not remember ever feeling before. Until now, she had always been of a mind with Vanessa on all the things she thought most important. To lose that feeling was almost as terrible a grief as if she'd lost Vanessa herself.

"Come with me," Dora said to her cousin.

Vanessa blinked uncertainly at this. "Come with you?" she asked. "What . . . to the workhouses, Dora? But I am not as stalwart as you are – they would surely give me vapours! And besides which, Auntie Frances and the countess would never allow it."

Dora narrowed her eyes at her cousin. "Nevertheless," she said, "we have always been honest with one another, Vanessa. And much as I love you, I cannot help but think that it will always disappoint me to think on this conversation of ours unless you later come with me to see the workhouses with your own two eyes." She paused, then added, "If you can engineer your way to London in order to find the Lord Sorcier, my dear cousin, I believe that you can find your way now to a workhouse with me."

Vanessa hesitated again on this. Dora could see her cousin's mind turning with anguish upon the idea.

Dora stood from the breakfast table and inclined her head. "I have been as truthful as I might," she said. "If you care for what little remains of my heart, I believe that you will find your way clear to my request."

As Dora made her way back out into the hallway, she heard a knock at the front door, not very distant from her. The butler murmured to someone, and the door closed again.

"What is this?" Auntie Frances exclaimed loudly. "What new devilry is upon us *now*?"

Dora altered her path towards the front entryway, where her aunt currently stared down the butler. The servant had in his arms a fresh delivery of roses – but they were no roses that Dora had ever seen before, and she suspected that they were unlikely to be seen by anyone again. One half of the flowers had petals of an unearthly emerald-green, which seemed to glow with their own whimsical sort of light. The other half were airy and insubstantial – and as she marvelled at them, Dora realised that they were crafted entirely from a silvery-grey smoke which seemed to waver in the drafty air of the townhouse.

The flowers were, she thought, the exact colour of her eyes.

Auntie Frances turned towards Dora with wide eyes. "This is spite!" she quavered. "The magician has some unreasonable grudge against this family! I cannot think what we have done to deserve such ire!"

Dora tilted her head, bemused. "I hardly think that he would send such lovely flowers out of spite, Auntie Frances," she said. "Though . . . since I did taunt him on the matter of flowers, I can see his perverse nature leading him to send them *now*." Inwardly, Dora began to suspect the flowers as a sort of apology for the delay of her cure, but she did not say this aloud.

"He does his best to thwart your attachment to his so-called friend at every turn," Auntie Frances moaned, as though she hadn't heard a word. "What a horrible, nasty man! He cannot intend to marry you, so why would he press this suit of his except to embarrass us all?"

Dora glanced down at that. She knew, of course, that Elias had only taken up the silly matter of courting her in order to protect both Dora and Albert from the old hens' designs. But to hear it said aloud – that he could not *possibly* intend to marry her – left a hollow sort of feeling inside her.

Why should the truth distress me? Dora wondered. *I was pleased to have an excuse not to marry this Season. That Elias continues the charade is generous of him given how frantically busy he currently is.*

"Nevertheless," Dora told her aunt, "it is not good to throw away magical gifts." Dora said this mainly because she saw that Auntie Frances was considering the flowers with the utmost distaste, and the idea of losing them bothered Dora greatly. "Please do not fan his spite, Auntie Frances. He is very busy, and it must at some point disappear if we do not antagonise him further."

Auntie Frances sighed heavily and shook her head at the butler. "Oh!" she said. "Go and hide them somewhere! My nerves cannot bear the sight of them any longer."

Her aunt departed the front entry with haste – but Dora hurried towards the butler as she exited. "I will put them away," she assured him.

Dora took the flowers up to her room and placed them on the dresser, above the drawer where she'd hidden the mirror. They were truly very pretty, she thought – though they must have been only a moment's work for someone of the Lord

Sorcier's prodigious talent. Dora found herself staring at them for longer than she ought. Eventually, her eyes caught upon a calling card, nestled among the flowers. She tugged it free and looked down at it.

Lord Elias Wilder, the card said in messy cursive handwriting. And though the name was no surprise, Dora felt warm and vaguely confused while looking down at it. The name was ever so slightly crooked, and she found herself wondering whether Elias had written the card with his own hand. It seemed the sort of thing that he would do. Auntie Frances probably would have considered it another insult, but Dora's mind lingered pleasantly on the idea for some reason.

Imagine, said a small voice at the back of her mind, *if only these flowers were meant sincerely.*

It was a bewildering thought. Dora was not sure just where it had come from. She had never been exceptionally fond of flowers, nor dreamed of having them sent to her. But *these* flowers were very agreeable to her, and it was particularly strange to wish that they were hers even at the same time that she already *owned* them.

I have far more important matters to attend to than flowers, Dora reminded herself, much as she had reminded Vanessa.

She forced herself to abandon her useless staring upon them, and left them on the dresser behind her.

Chapter Ten

Albert must have talked to Elias – because he showed up for Dora the next few days running, much to the hens' delight. Albert was not terribly pleased to give them reason to hope for wedding bells, but both he and Dora were cognisant of their short deadline, and so he bore their excitement with classic English stoicism. He brought Dora to each of the workhouses where they'd found cases of the plague before, so that they might question the inmates.

Dora had held some stray hope that perhaps the Cleveland Street Workhouse was some nightmarish exception, and that the other workhouses would be better, but she was soon forced to discard this notion. The other workhouses were equally awful in their own ways, all cramped and miserable and full of illness. The inmates of these workhouses were not all set to the task of unwinding hemp rope; some were out in the yards breaking rocks, while many of the women and children were fervently engaged in spinning and sewing, their exhaustion plain upon their faces.

Though Miss Jennings was of course forced to come along, she was an unexpected boon to the whole endeavour – Dora was only so good at holding children's attention, but the ex-governess had a way of snapping them into well-mannered behaviour as Dora asked them questions. Afterward, Dora was positive she'd seen the woman slipping treats to the most obedient children for their troubles.

There was certainly a general uneasiness surrounding the plague – and plenty of speculation about its origins. Dora swiftly began to realise that there was more guessing and superstition available than hard facts. Many of the children to whom she spoke had their own rituals and precautions which they swore worked to protect them from being infected, each one wildly different from the others.

"Perhaps there is something to the posies?" Miss Jennings observed, as they headed back towards Albert's place in the sickroom. The ex-governess had taken almost as much of an interest in the endeavour as Dora had done; she had even brought along a small journal and some charcoal with which to take notes.

"Perhaps," Dora said dubiously. "At least we have written it down. If there is truly some protective magical merit to the flower, then I suppose the Lord Sorcier will know it." She shook her head. "The only thing all the children can agree upon is that the workhouse master has been casting the evil eye on those he finds distasteful. And while I am sure Master Thomas is just as terrible as Master Ricks, I find myself doubtful that *all* of the workhouse masters who have had sick children are secret magicians."

"I have written it down as well," Miss Jennings said stubbornly. "We are not experts, Miss Ettings, and so we do not know what is relevant."

"You seem very intent upon our work, Miss Jennings," Dora observed. "I am glad of it, but I will admit to being surprised. I am sure that you could have stationed yourself in a corner somewhere and had tea all day, given how little your employers actually wish for you to watch me."

Miss Jennings flushed at that, and Dora realised that the ex-governess had probably only been encouraged to lax diligence through hints and implications, rather than open language. Nevertheless, the chaperone composed herself. "I do not do nothing very well, I am afraid," Miss Jennings said. "I will admit, it stings my sense of virtue to be paid to *avoid* chaperoning. But a woman in my position cannot be picky for money, Miss Ettings, and I am being paid unnaturally well to look the other way for you." She glanced down guiltily at the journal in her hands. "I have always loved children, of course. But I suppose I have applied myself to the matter in part to assuage my conscience."

Dora gave her a quizzical look. "And what position are you in, Miss Jennings?" she asked curiously.

The ex-governess shot her a surprised look. "Well . . . I am a spinster, Miss Ettings," she said. "I have little in the way of wealth or connections, other than what Lady Hayworth and her daughter generously offer me." Her eyes grew troubled. "I am technically of a rank with you, you know. My father was a baron. But he had four daughters, and I never did manage to marry before he died. I was lucky to be offered a position as governess. Lady Hayworth's daughter has kept me on at her new home as a companion, but I can tell that her husband dislikes having me around."

Dora knit her brow. "Perhaps I shall be a governess too, then," she said before she could think better of it.

Miss Jennings gave her a stricken look. "Oh, surely not!" she said. "Please do not imagine it, Miss Ettings. It is not so fine a job as you must be thinking, and you can be turned out at any time. Once or twice, when the lady was upset with me, I thought that I must certainly end up somewhere just like this." She shook her head. "Mr Lowe is a fine man. I can tell that he is not your preference, but you *must* consider your future, Miss Ettings. You have a brief chance to win him over, and you must surely take it."

Dora frowned. *I should not have suggested my lack of interest*, she thought. *I hope Miss Jennings does not tattle on me.*

As they rejoined Albert, he admitted that he'd had little luck with his own careful interrogations. Dora had expected that they would move on to another workhouse to keep trying, but she was surprised when Albert ordered their carriage to return to the townhouse.

"Is something the matter?" she asked.

Albert gave her a surprised look. "No, nothing," he said. "My mother has insisted that your household join us for a private dinner tonight. Were you not told?"

Dora shook her head. "I was not," she said. "Though I suppose someone might have mentioned it and I did not pay close enough attention. That does sometimes happen."

"Do prepare yourself, Miss Ettings," Albert said sympathetically. "I expect that my mother shall insist on further conversation with you. If you find yourself overwhelmed, you can turn the subject to flower arranging – she cannot stand it, but she will not want to treat you impolitely. It could buy you a moment's breath."

Dora smiled at him. "That is uncommonly helpful advice, Mr Lowe," she said. "I will do my best to endure, but it is good to know."

Surely enough, as soon as they returned to the townhouse, Dora was swiftly dragged into her room and assaulted by the maids. She didn't have much that was proper to wear to a dinner with a viscountess, so she was forced to wear the white muslin for a second time. This did not particularly bother Dora herself, though Auntie Frances moaned about it for a good few minutes on their way to Carroway House. The countess was forced to send her regrets due to a headache, though she was pleased enough to see them on their way.

Vanessa, of course, was utterly resplendent. She had acquired a soft blue dress which suited her hair and complexion very well. Had Dora been on better terms with her cousin, she would have thought that Vanessa looked well enough to be a bride on her wedding day – but that hint of unease had yet to disappear, and Dora suspected that it would not go away until Vanessa had gone with her to one of the workhouses.

It was strange being welcomed to Carroway House without any sort of crowd surrounding them. The hallways felt empty in comparison to their last visit, and they were led into a far smaller room for their dinner.

Lady Carroway rose to greet them, offering many enthused greetings and kisses on the cheek to the ladies among their party. Lord Carroway himself and his two eldest sons were present, along with Albert, and the group was introduced all around. Dora did not miss the fact that she was seated directly next to Albert and his mother near the foot of the table. Vanessa had been seated closer to the head, just next to Auntie Frances and across from Albert's two older brothers, which must have delighted Dora's aunt.

"Oh, please do tell me how your work with my son has been going, Miss Ettings," Lady Carroway asked Dora, not very long after the soup had been brought out. "I hear the two of you have been awfully busy."

Albert coughed lightly into his hand. "I do not think that is a subject fit for dinner, Mother," he warned quietly.

Lady Carroway waved him off. "We are near the foot of the table," she said. "I am sure we can keep our voices down so as not to disturb anyone else."

Dora frowned at this, forcing herself to focus on the moment at hand. *I must somehow stick to proper subjects*, she thought. "We have . . . been to many of the workhouses now," she said slowly. "They are to be pitied, Lady Carroway, for certain. The children, in particular."

"Oh yes," Lady Carroway agreed sympathetically. "I am always so worried about the children. Our charity group runs an orphanage, you know, and I think it must be the most important of our work."

"I know," Dora told her, and this time she felt a genuine bit of warmth towards the woman. "I have been to the orphanage. And it is very important work. Would that all of the children in the workhouses were so well cared for, Lady Carroway."

Lady Carroway smiled at that. "Perhaps when you are married, Miss Ettings, you may see to sponsoring your own orphanage," she suggested. "That would be a very worthy endeavour. I would be pleased to help you." Albert's mother could not help but glance at him as she said this, and he hunched his shoulders very slightly beneath her gaze.

"That is very generous of you, my lady," Dora said. It was not difficult for her to keep a neutral tone, of course, but she thought that Albert looked most uncomfortable now, and so she changed the subject. "Perhaps I will fill the orphanage with flowers," she added. "I do love flowers. I think that I would fill the place with fresh lavender when I could get it. Do you have a favourite flower, Lady Carroway?"

Albert's mother winced minutely, but she kept her smile stubbornly in place. "Oh, I . . . I often cannot choose," she said. "Lavender does sound nice."

"Chrysanthemums have an even sweeter smell, though, I find," Dora continued. "Oh. Now I cannot seem to choose either. Do you think that I could put the two together, or would that be silly?"

Albert perked up slightly now, with a grin playing about his mouth. "But are the two even in season together, Miss Ettings?" he asked. "I confess, I do not know enough about flowers to say."

Lady Carroway shot her son a dirty look, but Dora pretended not to notice. "Oh dear, Mr Lowe," Dora said. "I believe you're right. Chrysanthemums blossom later in the year than lavender. Now I really must choose one or the other, and I do not like to choose."

Albert's mother looked desperate now to change the subject

again. But before she could interject to do so, a footman stepped into the dining room and cleared his throat. "Lord Elias Wilder for Mr Albert Lowe," the servant informed them.

Lady Carroway's mouth dropped. "What, in the middle of dinner?" she demanded. "Why on earth would you let him in, Chalmers? You must tell him we are already entertaining!"

"The warmth of your welcome remains unparalleled, Lady Carroway," Elias said dryly. He had already swept past the footman into the dining room. Elias was dressed much the same as he had been when Dora had last seen him – and though his clothing was clean, Dora could not help but notice how drawn and tired his face appeared.

"Your business surely must wait," Lady Carroway told Elias, with a narrow-eyed gaze.

"Nonsense!" This interjection came from the head of the table, where Lord Carroway currently sat. He got to his feet and crossed towards Elias. "I have told Chalmers that the Lord Sorcier is always welcome in our home, dear," Lord Carroway addressed his wife. "He has done our family enough service that he should never be treated as a stranger."

Elias bowed his head slightly towards the viscount in acknowledgement. "I will surely wear out that welcome any day now," he said. "But if you are mad enough to accept me, then I shall not protest."

Lord Carroway chuckled warmly at this and clasped Elias by the arm. "Come, come," he said. "Have a seat at the table, magician."

Elias shook his head. "I am in the middle of business," he said. "I require Albert's help—"

"But you have that look about you," Lord Carroway observed. "You have had your head in your books and forgotten to eat, haven't you? Lady Carroway would have *my* head if you left without something in your stomach."

Albert's mother narrowed her eyes at that. She had surely

been meaning to protest that they hadn't set a place at the table, that they hadn't prepared for an extra guest, that it was all a terrible inconvenience upon her – but she didn't dare to contradict her husband in mixed company. Rather, she stayed silent, unwilling to voice her sentiments one way or another.

"Please have a seat by all means," Lord Carroway said. "Once we've eaten, perhaps you and Albert may retire to a study. Chalmers! Go tell someone to set an extra place at the table for the Lord Sorcier."

Elias arched a weary brow. "As you wish, Lord Carroway," he said. "But I would beg you to put me next to Albert so I may at least begin discussion with him."

"Alas," Lord Carroway said. "I would have had you next to me, to hear more of your miserable politics." The viscount's broad smile suggested that he did not think anything miserable of Elias at all, which Dora found quite fascinating. "But yes. If I am stealing you from your work, I suppose that you may sit where you will."

This meant, of course, that Elias would be much closer to Lady Carroway's side of the table – a circumstance which did not seem to delight the hostess. As Elias turned to search out Albert, however, he saw for the first time that Dora was present. Their eyes met, and Dora thought for just a moment that she saw the Lord Sorcier's lips twitch in something dangerously close to a smile.

"Well!" Elias said. "How convenient. Two French linguists at once. I will sit between you, then, and solicit two opinions at once."

Lady Carroway could not possibly have appeared more miserable at this turn of events. She looked towards Albert, silently begging her son to say something. But Albert seemed only too delighted to oblige; he rose to his feet and moved his chair further down to make room.

One of the servants returned to set Elias's place; no sooner had the magician settled himself than he glanced towards Dora. "Miss Ettings," he greeted her. "How fine you look this evening. The dress does seem familiar, though, doesn't it?"

Dora smiled at him. From anyone else, the comment would have been an insult – and surely most of their company must have interpreted it as such. But since Elias had scoured the dress of colour himself, she suspected it was a friendly rejoinder instead. "Lord Sorcier," she acknowledged him. "I fear you do not look so fine yourself; one suspects you have not slept enough. And your clothing also seems familiar. One suspects that you have slept *in* it."

Elias laughed. There was an odd delight to it that Dora had not heard before. "I am not fit to spar with you tonight," he said. "I am so tired that I will be at a handicap. But I think I will enjoy being thoroughly bested."

"You speak as though I have never bested you before," Dora said mildly. "I suppose I will concede to your weariness and pretend that you have ever had a victory, my lord."

Albert laughed now, too. "Why, now we have dinner *and* a show," he said. "Brilliant. I am of a mind for a bet. Does anyone dare lay odds on the Lord Sorcier in his currently weakened state?"

"Albert!" Lady Carroway scolded him. "I swear, I do not know who raised you! It cannot have been me."

"You raised him perfectly fine, Lady Carroway," Elias informed her. "I fear it was France, and possibly myself, which then corrupted him."

"You have admitted it yourself," Lady Carroway muttered, just low enough that Dora heard her and no one else.

"Put some food in your mouth, Elias, before my mother strangles you," Albert told him cheerfully. "I'd rather you not perish beneath this roof with an empty belly. It would reflect badly on our hospitality, I'm sure."

Elias seemed only too content to oblige – now that he had

taken a bit of soup, he had clearly realised just how famished he was. Dora frowned at him worriedly. Certainly, such exhaustion couldn't be good for Elias's health, and there were far more normal diseases to be caught than just the plague itself.

"Doesn't Mrs Dun feed you?" Dora asked him, when he'd finished the last dregs of the soup course.

Elias waved her off as though she were a gnat. "That woman has eighteen children to feed," he said. "I am not one of them, and I don't intend to be."

Lady Carroway frowned at that. "Mrs Dun?" she asked. "Surely not the same Mrs Dun who runs our orphanage?"

Albert coughed gently. Elias blinked, and then coloured. Dora found herself fascinated by the obvious blush of embarrassment on his face. She smiled suddenly.

"The Lord Sorcier donates a great deal of money to Mrs Dun's orphanage," Dora informed the viscountess. "I imagine that he sees her quite often as a consequence."

Elias shot Dora a piteous, betrayed sort of look.

"*Does* he?" Lady Carroway asked, narrowing her eyes at Elias. "How fascinating. One might have expected such a relevant topic to come up at dinner before now."

"I am not so often at dinner here," Elias said stiffly. But the very tips of his ears were red now too, and he seemed unable to look the viscountess in the eye.

"The Lord Sorcier is very fond of children," Dora added. "One of Mrs Dun's charges told me that he performs magic tricks for the orphanage when he visits."

Lady Carroway's eyes gleamed now with a mixture of triumph and fresh affection, and Dora knew that this information had mended whatever brief injury Elias's apparent courtship had caused to the lady's regard for him. "How charming," Lady Carroway said. "I seem to recall that our anonymous donor came forward not long after Albert asked to add three more children to the orphanage."

"I have been looking into historical curses!" Elias snapped at Dora, as though to cut the subject short. His ears were still red. "*Le Joyau* wrote a treatise on the subject, and I am far too tired to translate it on my own."

"You rarely translate anything yourself, even when you're fully awake," Albert observed wryly.

"I will be happy to take a look at the treatise after dinner, of course," Dora said pleasantly.

"You *will* stay seated until the main course comes, naturally," Lady Carroway said to Elias. The transformation in her behaviour was so sudden and magical that it might have been alchemy. "I have always said you do not take good enough care of yourself. You really *must* find a wife before you run yourself into the ground."

Elias pressed his face into his hands. "I far preferred it when you were upset with me, Lady Carroway," he said bluntly. "Your anger is at least more distant and less *nosy* than your affection."

Lady Carroway smiled brilliantly. "Then I am able to indulge my affection and my irritation all at once," she declared. "How pleasing!" She gestured at a footman, who headed over towards her. "Please fetch the Lord Sorcier a glass of wine."

Elias lifted his face from his hands and glared at the viscountess. Inspiration flickered in his tired mind, however, and he suddenly turned to Dora. "Miss Ettings," Elias said. "Have you plans to attend any more balls? I normally avoid them, but I shall endeavour to make my way to at least one if you will promise me a dance."

Dora blinked at Elias. She had been readying some witty insult to level his way – but the unexpected pleasantry rocked her back in her seat. Her mind blanked, and she found herself searching vainly for a proper reply as his hazy golden eyes focused intently upon her.

What is this? Dora wondered. The distant, fluttering feeling had returned to her stomach, now redoubled in strength. It was a lantern warmth, mixed with confusion and just a hint of nervousness. Was it a pleasant feeling, or was it uncomfortable? She could not seem to decide.

Elias was still looking at Dora, and she somehow did not want him to look away.

"Vanessa and I are going to Lady Cushing's ball," Dora said. "But I will save no dances for you, my lord, on the supposition that you will not show up. If you happen to venture into the jaws of high society after all, then I suppose I shall reward your unusual sociability with any two dances you like."

Elias smiled grimly. "The lady misjudges my determination," he said. But Dora saw that he had halfway directed the comment towards Lady Carroway, and she realised belatedly that the entire exchange had been meant simply to infuriate Albert's mother once again.

The flutterings turned ever more nervous, and Dora decided finally that they were *not* a pleasant feeling after all.

Lady Carroway had a slight frown upon her face now. But though Elias had clearly baited her, the expression was more uncertain than frustrated. Albert's mother glanced towards Dora, who dropped her eyes to her half-finished soup.

"Do you know," Lady Carroway said slowly, "I believe I have been deceived, Lord Sorcier." Her eyes flickered to Albert's silver right arm. "You are so *very* good at being temporarily unpleasant . . . somehow, you managed to convince me to forget what a generous, loyal man you can be, even with such a perfect physical reminder before me."

Elias shook his head. "I am unpleasant because I loathe expensive, superficial things, Lady Carroway," he said. "I assure you, it is not some intricate plan to deceive people. I have often thought I would be better served if I could keep my frustrations to myself." He gestured towards the table. "Everything I see here tempts me to bitterness. All of you – through only so much fault of your own – see only a normal dinner spread. Do you know what I see? Truly?"

Lady Carroway leaned forward slightly, now with genuine interest on her face. "Tell me, please," she said.

"You don't want to hear this," Albert warned his mother quietly. There was a resignation on his features that suggested he did not expect the conversation to go well.

"I do," Lady Carroway said. "Spare me no pleasantries, Lord Sorcier. My son is used to your sharp tongue, and Miss Ettings seems inured enough to its bite. This time, I will endure, and you may speak your mind."

"As you wish," Elias said. "I am sure I will remind you of your graciousness forthwith, Lady Carroway." He met her eyes directly. "When I look upon this table, I see all the people who might have starved to set it. I see a lavish meal painstakingly prepared by an entire staff, when half such lavishness would not have materially harmed anyone."

His fingers curled in front of him, and his jaw clenched. "Meanwhile, there are so many starving in the workhouses as we speak. Some children, innocent of wrongdoing. Some soldiers, just like your son – men who had no money or connections waiting for them when they came home, and no Lord Sorcier to mend their broken limbs. Their blood kept all these very fine tables safe from Napoleon . . . and now that they are home, it has earned them not one scrap of bread, nor even the consideration of being allowed polite discussion over dinner."

Lady Carroway did not respond to this immediately. Her face was so carefully composed that Dora could not eke out the slightest hint of what she might be thinking.

"Father has always supported your causes in the House of Lords," Albert said quietly. "And there are many charitable cases just like Mrs Dun's orphanage." It sounded like a rote response – an attempt at reasonable comfort which might have sometimes yielded fruit.

"No one gives what they *could*, Albert!" Elias hissed. "Everyone gives what they *please* – and certainly not without plenty of self-congratulations for their miserly gestures. With one hand, they raise grain tariffs, muster soldiers and create the workhouses. With the other, they deign to save a few poor souls from the very hell they made. This country is mad. It's rotten. It's unthinkable, and none of you can see it." Elias shook his head and shoved to his feet. There was a wild, frenetic despair in his manner that certainly had not been helped by his exhaustion. "I cannot eat a fine meal while some poor girl lies dying," he said. "It is not in me. But I suppose it is in *you*."

Albert widened his eyes. Dora saw a hint of real injury in his expression, and she thought this time that Elias must have gone further than he had ever gone before. The Lord Sorcier stormed for the door, his steps haunted by that horrible cloud of fury and self-loathing.

The other side of the table stared in their direction, shocked by the display. Auntie Frances shook her head in terrible disapproval and sniffed at Lord Carroway. Vanessa shot Dora a bewildered look.

Silence fell upon the foot of the table.

This is actually quite bad, Dora thought dimly. *Elias is losing his mind. He will drive off his only allies this way.*

Dora stood up from the table herself. "Lady Carroway," she said slowly. "I fear I require a chaperone. I would consider myself deeply in your debt if you would accompany me while I tell the Lord Sorcier what a fool he has made of himself."

Lady Carroway considered her with that carefully neutral expression. At first, Dora thought she might decline – such a request was terribly improper, especially given that the lady was still obliged to act as hostess. But the viscountess stood up a moment later and inclined her head. "You may have to catch him, Miss Ettings," she observed.

Dora nodded and started towards the door with determination.

It wasn't hard to figure out where Elias was headed. He had gone directly for the front door, sweeping past the butler in a dark mood. Dora headed out after him in her slippers, with a hard determination in her own stride. To her credit, Lady Carroway kept up, ignoring the slight drizzle of rain that covered the street.

As it turned out, they did not have very far to go at all.

Just out of sight of the stairs to the front door, Elias had leaned himself back against the wall of the house, breathing hard. He had his hands in his hair, and there was such a look on his face that Dora suspected he had realised, on some level, the extent of his decline.

In that light mist of rain, with his white-blond hair pinned to his face and his golden eyes ragged, he looked far less lordly and dangerous and far more . . . lost.

"You need food and sleep," Dora told him promptly as she approached. "And a dose of good sense – but food and sleep supply the latter, I am told."

Elias looked up at her sharply. He tensed his shoulders, and Dora saw the danger in his manner. She had cornered him just when he thought himself safe to drown in misery. Elias flicked his eyes to the viscountess behind Dora, and then back again. "I do not wish to speak to you, Miss Ettings," he said coldly. But there was a tremor in his voice, and it did not do much for his authority.

"Everyone does things sometimes which they do not wish to do," Dora told him evenly. "Even magicians." She closed much of the distance between them, standing very straight so that she could look him in the eyes. "I am not angry with you. You know that I am not."

Elias sucked in a breath. Dora saw him struggle for a long moment with his own irrational emotions. ". . . I believe you," he said finally. It was only the thinnest of acknowledgements – but it was something.

"You are angry, of course," Dora said. "And I think you have good reason. But you are also not in control of yourself – and you have said things now which I suspect you will regret."

Dora searched her thin array of emotions, trying to find some understanding which made sense. The idea that Elias was angry enough to lash out at Albert seemed incredible. She had *seen* the circumstances of their friendship! It was so very clear how much they loved one another.

. . . but I love Vanessa too, Dora realised. *And she has disappointed me all the same. I was so grieved, and she did not share the depths of that grief. Perhaps I might have also been angry with her if I were capable of such a thing.*

Dora reached out to touch Elias very carefully on the shoulder. "You do not have many friends, Elias," she said slowly. "I may be wrong about this – in fact, I am most likely wrong – but I think that you are grieving. And if you trusted your friends enough to show that grief instead of turning it to anger, you would not now be outside in the rain."

Elias stared at her. As Dora considered his face, she became convinced that there were tears there.

"Oh, bother," Dora sighed. "I am about to flout propriety, Lady Carroway. Do be kind to me, please."

She wrapped her arms tightly around the magician – and felt him crumble away against her.

Elias was not light; Dora found herself buckling more than a little bit beneath his weight. But she bore up as best she could as he pressed his face into her shoulder and sobbed.

The awkwardness of the situation was not lost on Dora. She could not help but notice it in her usual, detached way. But there was also a profound relief in the breaking of Elias's anger that she thought had affected them all. After a moment's hesitation, Lady Carroway stepped forward to press a hand to Dora's shoulders, helping to keep her upright – though the viscountess did not quite dare to touch Elias himself.

Many minutes later, Elias managed a hoarse, terrified whisper. "I am going to fail again," he said. "There is never anything that I can do. And the world will go on, just as it always has. There will be people at fine dinners, pretending . . . *believing* that nothing is wrong." The wretched, lonely grief that Dora had suspected in him was now absolutely obvious in his manner.

Lady Carroway took a slow breath. "You are wrong," she said. Her tone was kind and reassuring, rather than accusing. "My husband has wept and raged over the blindness of his peers. He has asked me before how the world can be so heartless. It is this dastardly need to remain calm and composed and polite that has left us all feeling so alone." She was very quiet for a moment. "I admit that we are better off than we could otherwise manage. It is a hard thing, giving up what is already had. But each time Lord Carroway vents his frustration, we find it in ourselves to give up a little bit more to those who need it more."

Elias shivered strangely at this. He held harder to Dora's shoulders. He took a few more deep breaths, and forced himself upright.

"I . . ." Elias swallowed hard. "I needed to hear that, Lady Carroway. I did not by any means *deserve* to hear it." He looked towards the viscountess, over Dora's shoulder. "I am terribly sorry. And I am grateful."

Lady Carroway smiled, but Dora saw that it was tremulous. "Your anger can be terrifying, Lord Sorcier," she told him. "Since we are being honest with one another, I must admit to being frightened by it. I cannot help but forgive such earnest grief, since it is caused by such earnest love. But I beg you to remember the effect you may have when you forget yourself." She drew in another breath. "And I . . . I will ask that you do not leave bridges unmended with my son. If you come inside now, I swear that all shall be forgotten on my side. Talk to Albert. You will have a hot meal and a warm bed tonight, instead of sitting in the dark in some wretched bachelor's lodging, thinking of terrible things."

Elias hesitated.

Dora surreptitiously kicked him in the shin, and he hissed in surprised pain. His eyes flickered back towards her, and Dora smiled serenely. "You must say yes, of course," she told him. "Because there is no other proper answer."

Elias sighed. Slowly, he removed his hands from Dora's shoulders. "I am scared of facing Albert," he admitted. "I would rather face a French firing line again. But since it was Albert who saved me from something of that sort in the first place, I suppose that would be a terrible waste."

"If you change your mind," Dora told him helpfully, "I will have my scissors on hand. You may borrow them whenever you like."

Elias coughed on a hazy laugh. "That is very dark humour, Miss Ettings," he managed. "I cannot help but approve."

They headed back inside, all three of them dripping on the floor in front of the quietly horrified butler. Lady Carroway sent a servant with Elias to find him a room. She turned to Dora then, and there was a fond, rueful smile on her face.

"I shall have to lend you a gown, Miss Ettings," she said. "And perhaps a set of slippers."

Chapter Eleven

*L*ady Carroway gave Dora one of her older gowns – it was a lovely mint-green silk that was so far beyond Dora's means that it looked somewhat ridiculous, especially with the bust so obviously fitted for another woman. Still, one of the maids helped Dora change in Lady Carroway's room, pinning back the extra material so that it looked nearly right. They eventually tracked down the matching slippers too, which fit her feet tolerably well.

"I will see how quickly I may return this to you," Dora promised the viscountess. "It is so expensive, I almost fear to wear it at all."

Lady Carroway shook her head. "I have not worn this dress in years," she said. "I still think fondly of it – but it is a style fit for a younger woman, and it is time I gave it up." She smiled at Dora. "I do not think that I have ever seen such grace and calm under pressure. I am suitably impressed with you tonight, Miss Ettings."

Dora blinked at that. Somewhere distant, the words gently nudged themselves against a pile of misery, knocking away a few of the other ugly words that had nested there.

"That is . . . most kind of you," Dora told her. "But I fear it is more of an affliction than a grace. I am often not emotional *enough*, my lady."

"You were quite emotional enough to calm an angry magician and drive him to tears," Lady Carroway said wryly. "I ought to have died of shock to hear an apology cross that man's lips, Miss Ettings. But he seems truly chastened tonight, and now in a more generous and contrite state of being than ever before. If you continue to perform such miracles, you may yet be in danger of being canonised."

Dora looked down at the green slippers on her feet. "I will ask the priest on Sunday," she said absently. "But I suspect I must be dead before I may be canonised, Lady Carroway. The thought does not immediately appeal, so I shall do my best to refrain from any further miracles."

The viscountess laughed at that. It was a warmer sound, now that they were away from dinner and behind closed doors. "Miss Ettings," she said, "it is a terrible shame that you will not marry Albert. I would have loved you as a daughter."

Dora froze in place. A warm, flustered confusion beat at the inside of her chest. "I . . . I don't know what you mean by that," she said.

Lady Carroway patted her shoulder. "Albert has set himself against the match," she said. "For the life of me, I could not understand why at first. But I have seen now what he must have seen from the beginning. You have a rare sorcery indeed to wring a few such smiles from the Lord Sorcier, Miss Ettings. And I think you must be nearly as taken with him as my son is."

Dora gave a few slow blinks. The hundred or so implications of this little speech moved like molasses through her head.

This is ideal, she thought. *Albert will be pleased that his mother has given up.*

But Elias was not *really* courting Dora, and obviously she was not taken with him. Dora could not really be *taken* with anyone, could she? She was almost certain one required a full soul for that sort of thing.

"I would have loved you as a daughter."

The words made her chest sore. Dora reached up to rub at it, confused.

"I am very mindful of the compliment you have paid me," she told Lady Carroway quietly. "I value it dearly, though I do not quite know how to express it."

"You may help me with a new project," Lady Carroway replied. "For after tonight, I feel it necessary that we must part with another sliver of our comfortable living, or else I will sleep restless." The viscountess reached out to tuck a strand of rust-coloured hair behind Dora's ear. "Mrs Dun is quite at her limit, as is the orphanage itself. Perhaps we could find another building and another administrator. But I will need more than one person keeping an eye out for the *right* building and the *right* administrator."

Dora considered that seriously. "My chaperone, Miss Jennings, is quite excellent with children," she said. "She is an ex-governess, and she can keep a sick room. She has been generous with her sentiment over the workhouses, and I think she would be very amenable to a permanent position."

Lady Carroway nodded thoughtfully at that. "I will see if I can engineer a chance to meet her," she said. "You must come here for tea one day and bring her along."

They went back down to dinner, though some of the courses had come and gone, and Albert had disappeared – called up to speak with Elias, one of the servants informed Lady Carroway quietly. Albert's mother had some food sent up to them both, after which time she settled both herself and Dora closer to the head of the table.

"It is raining dreadfully outside," Lady Carroway said cheerfully. "As we have accidentally discovered." *It is drizzling*, Dora thought with mild amusement. But she did not contradict their hostess. "I really must insist that you all stay the evening with us, Lady Lockheed," the viscountess continued. "It will be far more pleasant for you to stay inside where it is warm and dry, and to take off fresh in the morning."

Auntie Frances had been looking at Dora and her borrowed dress with a familiar, growing suspicion – the sort of expression that asked *what strange thing have you done now?* But at this invitation, Dora's aunt became all smiles and undying gratitude. "You are so gracious to offer," she cooed to Lady Carroway. "I would decline, but since it is so awful out, I will stay for the sake of the girls. I cannot bear the thought of them catching cold for such a small thing as my pride."

Lady Carroway sent a runner back to Hayworth House, informing the countess that they would be staying the evening. As dinner wound to a close, the gathering retired to a drawing room, whereupon Lord Carroway sneaked himself a brandy and Lady Carroway requested to hear Vanessa on the pianoforte. Dora settled herself on a sofa in the corner, sorting quietly through her strange piles of emotion as she listened. Dimly, she noticed Lady Carroway's oldest son, Edward, watching Vanessa with the same sort of stricken expression that Dora had seen so many times before on other suitors. *Even if I never marry Albert*, Dora thought, *I suspect the hens will have their true desire soon enough.*

Even as Dora thought this, Vanessa glanced over the piano at her with a desperately quizzical look. Dora realised that her cousin was far too preoccupied with the evening's earlier events to notice her lovelorn attendant. She rose to her feet and padded over towards the piano, settling herself onto the bench next to Vanessa.

"I will play the simple part of a duet if you like," Dora said.

Vanessa searched her eyes – for distress or confusion or fear, Dora was sure. As she found nothing immediately concerning, however, Vanessa forced a smile. "Yes, that would be lovely," she agreed.

"The situation has sorted itself," Dora said softly, beneath the strains of the piano. "Elias has calmed himself and made his apologies." *I am almost certain that he has apologised to Albert by now*, Dora thought.

"I did not realise the Lord Sorcier had such an awful temper," Vanessa murmured back. "I begin to think that you were right, Dora. We must find someone else to help you."

One of those flutters returned to Dora's stomach. "I do not want someone else to help me," she said. "Elias may have an awful temper, it is true. But he is angry about all the *right* things. It's so very strange, Vanessa. I cannot think of respecting anyone who does not feel at least a *little* angry at all of this injustice now. It is almost nonsensical to be calm about it."

Vanessa pursed her lips at that. At first, Dora thought she may have accidentally insulted her cousin. But then, Vanessa said, "You call him Elias?"

Dora missed a note on the piano, and promptly apologised.

I have used his name too much tonight, Dora thought. *When else did I use it? I have likely embarrassed myself without noticing.*

"I can forgive much," Vanessa said softly. "But if he should ever speak to you the way that he spoke to Lady Carroway, I will find a new pair of scissors, Dora."

Dora managed a smile at that. "You do not need to find a new pair of scissors, Vanessa," she said. "You gave me a pair of my own, and you taught me how to use them."

For just a few hours, the lantern warmth between them returned. Dora basked in its glow, letting the feeling soothe the long-tailed worries that had built up within her over the course of the evening.

—⁂—

It was another very different feeling, being bundled into a bed that wasn't even her *normal* borrowed bed. Dora tried to sleep, but she soon found herself pacing the bedroom in search of some feeling which she couldn't quite put her finger on.

The mirror, she thought after a few minutes, pausing her steps. Dora had not scryed on Elias more than a handful of times – but she had grown used to the idea of having the mirror nearby, so that she *could* do if she wanted to. Elias was under the very same roof tonight, and yet she found herself unsettled knowing that she could not speak to him to know whether he had ended the night in a less tortured frame of mind.

Dora chewed at her lip thoughtfully.

I could find a normal mirror, she thought. *Elias did say that perhaps I could manage, even without the spells.*

This seemed like a perfectly reasonable alternative somehow, and so Dora slipped out of her borrowed room and went off in search of a mirror.

She found one not far away, mounted upon one of the walls in the hallway. It was a burnished brass plate rather than a silver-backed mirror, but the reflection was clear enough to do. Dora focused upon it, trying to imagine Elias as she had last seen him – soaked and bedraggled and looking awfully miserable.

The strange, detached state of mind was easy to come by. But the image of Elias remained stubbornly stuck in Dora's head, unwilling to come out. She frowned and tried to focus on it harder – this time, Dora felt a distinct pressure against her mind, as though she were trying to press into molasses. The pressure became harder, and somehow more ominous, the more that she leaned into the effort. *Bother*, Dora thought. *Elias has protections, I'd forgotten. It was the mirror he gave me that could bypass them—*

"What *are* you doing, you twit?" Elias's voice hissed behind her, and Dora startled free of her trance. She saw him in the reflection of the brass mirror, standing just behind her in a loose cambric shirt and trousers. His hair was even more mussed than usual, and his eyes seemed raw and tired, but he was somehow more real than he had ever been before.

His hand closed on her shoulder, warm and very present, and Dora realised that he *was* quite real.

She turned around with a pleased, even smile. "I was trying to scry you," she said. "But here you are."

Elias pressed his fingers to his forehead. "You might have hurt yourself," he told her. "You're lucky I felt someone trying to barge through my wards. I had no way of knowing *who* it was, but I thought that there must only be one person foolish enough to try."

Dora smiled at him again. For some reason, the expression came much easier to her at the moment. It had something to do with his hand on her shoulder, she thought, or maybe the fact that he seemed closer to his normal self than he had been before.

"Are you much better?" she asked him.

Elias laughed softly — but it was the sort of tired laugh that suggested he had given up a fight. "We are both in the hallway, barely dressed better than our night clothes," he told her. "Naturally, you would like to have a heart-to-heart just now."

Dora's smile broadened. "Naturally," she said. "I am remembering now how strange that is. But I was worried. I hope you will indulge me somehow."

Elias sighed. "I will," he said. "That is the worst of it." He dropped his hand from her shoulder. "Stay here. I will go and find something to solve all of these silly, modest rules."

He disappeared down the hallway again, and Dora waited patiently. When Elias soon returned, he brought with him one of the lanterns from downstairs, which now gave off a watery, unearthly sort of blue light.

Dora gave the lantern a fascinated look. "What have you done to it?" she asked.

"I have thrown together the most hurried, slapdash spell of my career," Elias informed her dryly. "But it is something akin to one that I have used before. As long as the candle is still lit and we stay within the light, we will be difficult to notice. Not *impossible*, mind you, but . . . we will be considered relatively unimportant and uninteresting."

Dora nodded, fixated on the dancing flame inside. "I am sure that it must have better uses than avoiding nosy servants," she said. "But how novel!" Dora offered out her arm to Elias as though they were standing in a ballroom fully dressed instead of in a strange hallway looking far less than proper. Elias took her proffered arm, carrying the lantern in his other hand as they paced down the hallway.

"Are you much better?" Dora asked again, very quietly.

"I am better," Elias murmured. Shame and embarrassment coloured the words. "I have eaten. I have spoken to Albert. I have even had some modicum of real sleep. Now that I am more steady, I am frankly shocked to have been let back inside this house, let alone offered to stay the night."

Dora frowned at that, as they started wandering down the stairs. "You must give Albert and his family more credit," she said. "He loves you, and he must know how badly you have been driving yourself. He feels some measure of the same things – it is part of why you have remained friends."

"You could not have parroted him better if you had been in the room with him when I apologised," Elias observed dryly. He hesitated, then added, "Albert . . . has often suggested that I should take more pause, and feel less guilty for it. I have tried to listen to him this time. I am beginning to realise that I am no good for anyone this way. I am more apt to solve things when I am rested. I am more apt to rest if I am not alone with my thoughts."

Dora nodded. "I suspect that Mr Lowe has had occasion to take his own advice," she said. "I wondered at first how he could possibly go home at the end of the day and go to balls or dinners with his family. But he is not as haggard as you are, and he has kept his calm in the face of some very awful, bloody things each day." She paused. "Vanessa has kept me from losing myself, I think – though I cannot compare my difficulties to those that you and Mr Lowe have faced. And on those rare occasions when I have not had Vanessa, I have gone outside at night to look up at the stars. Or . . . I did such a thing back home in Lockheed. It is harder to do in London, I will admit."

"There are fewer stars to be had in London, it is true," Elias observed. He squeezed her arm – as much for his own comfort as for hers, Dora thought. They came to a door that led outside, and she saw that it was a way into the same garden where she had tried to wash her dress in a fountain. Clearly, one or both of them had started in that direction from sheer familiarity. Dora smiled and opened the door, stepping out into the night.

The slight drizzle had long since cleared up, though the grass was damp beneath their feet. There were still stars, Dora thought, as she craned her head to look upward. The stars were not as bright or as numerous here as they had been in Lockheed – though why that was, she couldn't be sure. Dora stumbled over her feet a few times, dizzy with the distance; Elias reached out to flick her sharply on the ear, but this didn't draw her attention in the way that he had probably hoped.

"I forget that you don't react as a normal person sometimes," Elias muttered. "At least keep your eyes on your feet while we walk. You might turn an ankle, and then where will we be? I know a great many spells, but fantastical healing is not among them."

Dora looked back down to keep track of her steps until they'd rounded the bench and settled safely onto it. "My apologies," she said, as Elias set the lantern onto the fountain in front of them and sat back down beside her.

Elias glanced sideways at her. There was a newly troubled expression on his face, and Dora pursed her lips. "You should simply say whatever you are worried about," she told him. "I will hardly mind it either way."

Elias sighed and reached up to run his fingers back through his messy hair. "I am not entirely certain myself," he admitted. "I think . . . I am worried that you think terrible things of me. And perhaps those things are right. I do not know any more."

Dora considered him with faint surprise. "I do not think terrible things of you," she said. "Though I am surprised that my opinion should worry you at all, you may safely cease any apprehension on that score."

Elias rubbed at his jaw uncomfortably. "Nevertheless, I . . . feel the need to explain certain things to you. I have never told another soul about them – but perhaps they have begun to eat at me too much."

Dora raised a brow at him. "If you insist on telling me tonight," she said, "then you will have only told *half* a soul. Perhaps that shall make it easier."

A ghost of a smile crossed Elias's face at that. "Perhaps," he said. "I suspect other reasons to be at play, however." Before Dora could ask him what he meant by that, he cleared his throat. "I am . . . not a magician, Dora. Or rather, I am not *just* a magician." His eyes flickered towards her chest, where the pair of scissors would normally lie – but Dora had taken them out and put them beneath her pillow, and they were not there. Elias frowned at their absence, but he did not otherwise remark on the circumstance. "I was born in faerie. Or else . . . perhaps the faerie that called me his son stole me before I could remember. I do not know exactly *what* I am, except that I am surely not all human, and surely not all faerie."

Dora considered this seriously. The revelation ought to have frightened her, she thought, given how much of her life had been altered by just *one* encounter with a faerie. But she could not bring herself to be even distantly afraid of Elias at this point. "That is why people say that your magic is impossible," she said slowly. "Because you are really capable of things similar to Lord Hollowvale." Dora paused. "But you and he are nothing alike, Elias. Lord Hollowvale was quite evil. He had no concept of mercy or pity. I cannot imagine him ever becoming anguished over another person's suffering."

Elias frowned at this. "But that is part of why I left," he said.

"The faeries there are all so cruel and thoughtless. I do not know that they *mean* to be, but it is what they are." He looked away from Dora uncomfortably. "I had hoped that England would be better. But it is so much worse in some respects. At least faeries have no sense of their own evil – but humans know quite what they are about, and this is still how they choose to arrange things."

"But if you grew up in faerie," Dora asked him, "then how did you end up in the war? You must not have had a concept of yourself as an Englishman . . . so why go fight the French?"

Elias smiled bitterly. "I was still young when I left faerie," he said. "I had no concept of England at all before I got here. I ended up in the workhouses, in fact. Everyone was starving because of the taxes from the war. I wasn't starving myself, mind you – I was quite good at stealing what I needed. But I heard so many people say that all this misery was because of the French – that they were simply evil, causing every awful thing that fell upon the English. I didn't know what lies were yet, since faeries cannot lie. I believed that if I vanquished the French, then perhaps everything would be better."

Dora sighed heavily. "Oh dear," she murmured. "I suppose I can see how all of that worked out."

"The French were never the problem," Elias agreed. "Or at least, they were not the whole of it. When I came back and got my title, I suddenly had access to an entirely different level of society. I thought that all of England had suffered from the French. But that was not true. The aristocrats never failed to thrive – and still, they continue to thrive. They are the native faeries of England, wreaking havoc where they go and always thinking worlds of themselves."

Dora considered that for a long moment. "I am one of them," she said. It was not a complaint, but an observation.

Elias glanced over at her. "You are," he said. "And now, so am I. I must stop thinking of myself apart from everyone else, as though I am watching you all make mistakes. I have made mistakes as well." He ran his fingers back through his hair. "You and Albert and his family give me hope, Dora. Perhaps things will not change as a whole . . . but at least I have finally found something better than the world with which I started."

Elias dropped his arm again – but his hand came to rest upon Dora's, instead of simply at his side. She blinked down at the unexpected contact. Both their hands were bare, and there was something instantly intimate about the gesture as a result. Dora had rarely had occasion to compare a man's hand to hers, but as Elias tangled their fingers, she could not help but notice how small she was compared to him. It was comforting rather than oppressive.

Dora tightened her fingers in return. The note of gratitude in Elias's voice made her feel off-balance. She was warm and fluttering again, and simultaneously worried that she did not quite deserve the compliment. *I have found nothing of use at the workhouses so far*, she thought. *He will be every bit as frustrated tomorrow as he has been these last few days.*

"If you give me the treatise before you leave," Dora said suddenly, "I will translate it tomorrow."

Elias shot her a sideways glance. "And you'll find time for that in between the workhouses and the ball you're slated to attend?" he asked. There was a gentle bemusement in his voice.

"I will find the time," Dora told him confidently.

Those golden eyes focused on her. For the second time since Dora had met him, Elias considered her so closely that she felt his gaze pierce beneath her skin.

". . . I shall leave it with you, then," he said finally.

Elias pulled his hand free of hers – and at first, Dora felt a low, empty disappointment. But shortly thereafter, he closed his arm around her shoulders, pulling her gently into his side.

The heat of his body soaked into her where they touched, sinking into her body with a hazy bliss. The ethereal blue lantern light flickered across Elias's features as he looked down at Dora, but she could not fully interpret his expression. It was more peaceful than most attitudes she had seen upon his face, but there was a hint of mild confusion mixed in as well.

"Elias?" Dora asked calmly. "What are you doing?"

Elias knit his brow. For a moment, Dora thought, *He doesn't know.* But he cleared his throat quietly and looked away again. "You have no sense of the cold, do you?" he said. "I remember you saying you do not feel things normally. Your clothing is damp. You really will catch sick this way."

Dora smiled at that. The cold really didn't bother her . . . but she couldn't have ignored his warmth, even if she had tried. She curled in closer towards Elias, leaning her cheek against his chest. There was that faint scent of myrrh again, trapped in his shirt, even perfuming his skin.

They didn't speak again for quite some time. It didn't feel quite necessary. Instead, Dora let her mind drift away as she listened to the steady beating of his heart.

Elias might well be a faerie, or part of one, she thought. *But his heart sounds just the same as anyone else's.*

Eventually, the lantern began to flicker unsteadily, and Elias sighed in annoyance. "I should help you back before we both become interesting to look at again," he murmured. Slowly, he released his grip on her shoulders. This time, when his heat departed, Dora thought she must have felt the cold – because the absence of him made her feel as though something crucial was missing.

Elias took her arm again and brought her back inside, up the stairs to her room. Dora found herself thinking of ways to hold him longer – topics of conversation which might seem too important to put off – but nothing came to mind. Instead, Elias released her arm and smiled in a way that suggested he'd been thinking similar thoughts.

"Goodnight, Dora," he said softly. "Do have sweet dreams."

Dora found it difficult to break his gaze. "And . . . you as well," she said, though the words felt lame and insufficient. *I am sure that I should have said something else*, she thought uncertainly. *That did not feel adequate. A normal person might have known what to say.*

Elias waited patiently – and Dora realised belatedly that she was supposed to go into her room. She turned to slip inside, aware of his eyes on her back.

As Dora burrowed underneath the covers of her bed, she closed her eyes and tried to think of sweet things to dream about. Strangely, her mind supplied only the warmth of Elias's hand and the sweet smell of myrrh.

Chapter Twelve

hatever had been told to Lady Hayworth regarding the hour of their return, they did not actually head back to Hayworth House the moment that they woke up. Instead, Lady Carroway insisted on having them downstairs for breakfast, where they lingered quite some time. Given the informal breakfast seating, perhaps it should not have surprised anyone that Albert's brother Edward had found his way over towards Vanessa – but this effectively blocked Dora from any substantial conversation with her cousin. She searched surreptitiously for Elias instead, but to her disappointment, he was nowhere to be found at all.

Albert had the treatise out before him, however, which suggested that Elias had already left. He was currently scribbling notes on a separate bit of parchment nearby while he took his coffee. To Dora's surprise, Miss Jennings had arrived at some point and settled herself next to Albert; the two of them occasionally spoke pleasantly to one another while Albert worked. Dora headed towards them both, settling herself on Albert's other side.

"Are you very far yet?" Dora asked him.

"Only a few pages in," Albert said, stifling a yawn. "I haven't been up long. Elias said you had volunteered to handle the rest, but I thought it best to start the matter, at least."

Dora searched for a hint of acrimony in Albert's voice or features as he spoke, but she could not find any. She smiled, feeling vaguely relieved. Since Miss Jennings was present, she phrased her next question as generally as possible. "He did apologise properly, then?"

Albert chuckled on his next yawn, which made it stutter. "Profusely," he managed. "Poor man. What *did* you say to him, Miss Ettings?"

Dora looked down at her plate as though she were very interested in the food there. "He would have apologised either way," she replied, rather than answer the question. "Eventually."

"Oh, I trust that," Albert said. "If nothing else, Elias would have eventually remembered how awful his French is, and how little he wishes to learn it better." He shot Dora an interested look. "I was planning on continuing to the workhouses today. I don't normally go so often, but with all circumstances considered . . ." Albert trailed off, far too polite to mention their deadline. He shook his head. "Will you still be joining me, or will you be staying in to finish with the treatise?"

Dora frowned. "I will come with you," she said. "I expect I will cry off sick from the ball this evening and finish the treatise then."

"Oh, please don't do so," Miss Jennings said. "I should be capable of asking a few questions at the workhouses without you, Miss Ettings."

Albert shot the chaperone a bewildered look. "If you have no one to chaperone, Miss Jennings," he said, "I must assume that you will not be paid for your time."

Miss Jennings shot him an offended look. "If Miss Ettings intends to spend the day indoors," she replied, "then I shall not be otherwise occupied today. I do not think it so outrageous that I should wish to see this matter through to the end, given the *circumstances*."

Dora straightened in her chair. "Miss Jennings?" she asked.

"Did you happen to speak to Lady Carroway this morning by any chance?"

Miss Jennings flushed at that. "Yes, I did," she said. "I walked over from Hayworth House when I was told you could be found here, since I thought it likely you would be out again today with Mr Lowe. Lady Carroway was kind enough to invite me to breakfast. She really ought not have, but it was very gracious of her."

Dora suspected that Lady Carroway had not communicated anything of her intentions to sponsor another orphanage, given the shyness with which Miss Jennings spoke of her. Still, Dora expected that the ex-governess must have impressed, given what she had seen of her for the last few days.

"Well, I will be glad for the help," Albert admitted. "I am not as accomplished at getting the children to speak to me. I expect the copious number of needles and recommendations for terrible-tasting medicine do not help my case."

"I will go as well," Vanessa said, from Dora's other side. The three already at the table turned to blink at her – for she had sneaked up on them most effectively, though probably not on purpose. "Dora has told me the sort of questions she has been asking with Miss Jennings. I believe I can stand in for her." Dora's cousin paused, with an uncertain look towards Albert. "If you are all right with having me along, that is."

Dora stared at Vanessa. *Edward is showing interest,* she thought. *Auntie Frances will not like Vanessa running off with Albert like this. It's sure to start a row with her.*

Vanessa flushed beneath Dora's gaze and looked towards the floor.

"I have ceased to question the fortitude of the young ladies in Miss Ettings' company," Albert told Vanessa ruefully. "If you are certain that you can handle it, I will bring you along, and Miss Jennings will have someone to chaperone after all."

"I am not certain," Vanessa admitted. "But it is important to Dora, and so I will do my very best."

Albert smiled at that. "Well, one cannot fault your reasons," he said. "I will finish my coffee, and then we may leave."

Auntie Frances was *not* well pleased with this situation. Not long after, Dora saw as Vanessa's mother dragged her out into the hallway with an angry, pinched expression on her face which she normally reserved for Dora. Vanessa came back in a few minutes later, looking flushed and upset. Still, she made her way over to Albert with determination and took Miss Jennings by the arm.

Dora felt a hint of guilt at this – but it was mostly overshadowed by an odd sort of relief. Just the thought that Vanessa might see and understand the same awful things that Dora had seen offered her comfort.

"It's past time we were leaving, Dora," Auntie Frances snapped, as she marched back inside herself. The dark expression on her face promised that her argument with Vanessa was far from settled. "We wouldn't wish to overstay our welcome."

Dora quickly snatched up the treatise on the table, along with its partial translation. "And what is *that*?" Auntie Frances asked her suspiciously.

"Just a bit of French poetry," Dora lied. "Lady Carroway loaned it to me from her library."

Thankfully, Auntie Frances did not look nearly close enough at the small book to catch any discrepancies in Dora's story. She grabbed Dora by her other arm, pulling her towards the door. They paused only to thank Lady Carroway for her hospitality before Auntie Frances had Dora in the carriage and on the way back to Hayworth House.

"You have had something to do with this silly behaviour from Vanessa," Auntie Frances said, as soon as they were in the carriage. "I know that you have."

Dora gave her aunt a blank look in return. She did, of course, have everything to do with Vanessa's behaviour this morning – but there were advantages, sometimes, to having only half a soul. "I do not know how I might have done," Dora said. "But I suppose that it is possible."

"The next Viscount of Carroway has just started setting his attentions upon Vanessa!" Auntie Frances hissed. "And now she is off in your place with his crippled brother, instead of with *him*!"

A cold, dull anger grew in Dora's stomach. Elias had once called Albert a cripple in front of her, but the word had not had such nasty connotations when he had said it. The way that her aunt said the word, it sounded dirty and shameful.

"Mr Lowe became as he is while protecting the rest of us off in France," Dora told her. She said it with perfect evenness, though she would have preferred otherwise. "He is a very good and charitable man. And if Vanessa *did* wish to marry him instead of his brother, I believe that he would treat her very well."

A crack sounded in Dora's ears. Her vision faltered. It took her a moment to realise that her aunt had struck her across the face. She blinked a few times, reaching up to press her palm against her cheek. The pain felt numb and distant – but the emotion behind the gesture dug more deeply into her, clenching itself slowly around her heart.

"Neither of you girls has thought for a single moment about *me* from the moment we first set foot in London," Auntie Frances cried, with her face all red and miserable. "You have no conception of what is at stake for me. If Lord Lockheed should die before me, his title will pass, and I will have only a pitiful income to my name! I shall be forced to survive on the generosity of my daughter's husband. Where will I live, Dora? Surely not with some physician! Perhaps that life will suffice for *you*, but you are barely a person at all!"

Dora did not react. It had occurred to her that she did not *need* to react. Rather, she could sit there like the doll that she was and let the awful moment wash over her without consequence.

She turned her eyes to the window of the carriage, thinking of Auntie Frances among the workhouses, tending to the children. It was such a dramatically unlikely vision that Dora managed a faint smile over it.

"– incapable even of paying attention for a single moment!" Auntie Frances raged. "It is no wonder Mr Lowe has yet to offer for you, you puppet!"

He will not offer, Dora thought. The idea satisfied her somewhat in the face of Auntie Frances's fury, but it also felt hollow and tired. *No one will offer.*

Their carriage came to a stop outside of the countess's residence. Auntie Frances was forced to calm herself somewhat, though her body still trembled as she wrenched Dora from the carriage.

"I do not wish to see your face today," Auntie Frances told her, as they swept through the door into Hayworth House. "Do not let me see you once until the ball, Dora, I warn you!"

Dora did not respond to this. But inwardly she thought, *That will be no problem. I do not wish to see you either.*

~~⚬⚬~~

Dora spent the rest of the day in her bedroom with the treatise open in front of her. Though it was short, it was also exceptionally dense, and it had many strange words which she assumed to be technical terms for magical things. Thankfully, Albert's partial translation had given Dora references for some of these words already; she left the remainder untranslated, with guesses from the surrounding context.

The majority of the treatise seemed to be a compilation of curses from different eras along with their supposed cures. Dora understood very little of the content – but she did see a reference to a sleeping curse, which she supposed must have been the main thing to catch Elias's interest. She spent extra time on this section, to be sure that it was painstakingly accurate. Unfortunately, the cure to that particular curse was true love's kiss, and Dora greatly suspected that such a cure was both very rare and not at all applicable to orphaned children.

The work was mentally taxing, which was just as well: it prevented Dora from dwelling on her aunt's words. The pile of ugliness at the bottom of her mind was bigger than it had ever been before, pressing dangerously at the surface of her conscious-ness. Dora knew it was becoming a problem, but she continued to ignore it mostly because she did not know what else to *do* with it. She could not sob on her pillow as Vanessa might have done, and there was no one about to whom she might turn for comfort – and so she continued her translation, vaguely aware the entire time of the sickness that pressed for her attention.

Dora had made her way through about three-quarters of the treatise when she heard a commotion downstairs. She padded over to the door, creaking it open to peer down the hallway. Voices filtered up towards her.

"– quite all right, Mr Lowe," Miss Jennings was saying breath-lessly. "A little bruise will not put me in a sickbed."

"You should hold a cool cloth against it, at least," Albert told her, with obvious worry in his voice. "You're not still bleeding?"

Dora headed out from her room, forgetting for the moment her aunt's order to stay out of sight. As she reached the stairs, she saw that Albert, Vanessa and Miss Jennings had returned – but Miss Jennings was leaning slightly on Vanessa's arm, and there was a slowly darkening purple bruise along her right eye. Albert had a deeply concerned look on his face, and Vanessa seemed to be in a similar fright.

"Please won't you sit down?" Vanessa asked Miss Jennings. "I will see if we can get you some tea."

"What on earth happened?" Dora asked from the top of the stairs.

Vanessa glanced up at Dora sharply. Her expression turned

even more distressed. "Oh, Dora," she said. "I . . . it's too terrible, I'm sorry. I think we will all need to have some tea before I'm even able to speak of it."

A few minutes later, once they had all settled into the morning room and had a pot brought out for them, Vanessa began to explain. "We went to the Cleveland Street Workhouse – the first one you had been to, I think?" she said. "Miss Jennings and I were asking questions of the children, and one of the boys told us—"

"That awful George Ricks creature!" Miss Jennings burst out, with a sudden, animated anger. "He threw that pregnant woman out on the street and pretended he'd never taken her in at all! He would have forced her to give birth out on the street if Mr Lowe hadn't been there to protest!"

Albert had settled directly next to Miss Jennings – he was still trying to convince her to press a wet cloth to the awful bruise along her eye, but she barely seemed to notice him. "I seem to recall you doing much of the protesting, Miss Jennings," Albert said dryly. "Though, to be sure, I would have done the job if you had let me."

"Miss Jennings confronted the workhouse master," Vanessa said quietly. Dora's cousin had curled into her chair with a pale face. Her fingers shook on her teacup. "He struck her for imper-tinence. I think his cuff-link might have caught her eye as well." Vanessa paused, and a fearful smile crossed her lips. "Mr Lowe struck him back – much harder, I would wager."

Dora frowned at Albert's silver right hand. She had at first assumed that the blood on it was from Miss Jennings's injury – but now that she looked, she saw that there was far too *much* blood for that.

"I wish I had been there to see it," Dora murmured. She could not imagine any greater satisfaction in that moment than seeing the pain that solid metal could inflict upon the workhouse master's face.

"That miserable excuse for a human being deserved far worse," Miss Jennings seethed. "He mustn't be allowed to remain in charge of that workhouse, Mr Lowe! Surely this sort of thing must be illegal – *oh!*" The ex-governess had gestured too violently at this and jolted the cloth so painfully against her eye that she had to let out a gasp.

"Please stay still, Miss Jennings," Albert begged her, reaching out to grab her chin and hold her in place. "You still have a cut near to your eye, and it will be most unpleasant when it swells up." He shook his head. "*Someone* will do something. But it will not be you. Any of you. Please, leave the man's fate up to me."

Dora expected that the workhouse master would not be getting off as easy as Miss Jennings clearly feared. There was a hard look in Albert's eyes which she had never seen before.

Albert pulled back from Miss Jennings, though he kept the cloth gingerly against her eye. "In the meantime, I will want your notes from the last few days, Miss Jennings," he addressed the ex-governess. "And Miss Ettings – whatever you have of that translation, I would like to take it with me."

Dora went upstairs to fetch the partial translation for Albert. He quickly put himself together to leave once more, but he insisted that Miss Jennings should come by Carroway House in the morning so that he could check on her eye again. When the two of them had both left, Dora turned her attention back to Vanessa, who had yet to move from the place where she huddled in her chair.

"You are upset," Dora said.

"Oh, Dora," Vanessa said, with a tremble in her voice. "How could I *not* be? I tried so hard not to be a bother while I was there, but it was just so awful!" Tears welled up in her eyes. "I cannot seem to forget any of it, no matter how hard I try. I cannot imagine going to some silly ball tonight!"

Dora settled into the chair next to her cousin, pulling her into an embrace. Vanessa held her back, sniffling into her shoulder. "I should not be so relieved to see you this upset," Dora said. "But I cannot help that I am. I wanted to believe that you would be of a mind with me on this matter, and you are."

Vanessa swallowed hard. "I do not even know what to do about it, Dora," she said. "It all seems so very overwhelming."

"We must choose little things to fix where we can," Dora told her, remembering what Elias had said about small evils. "I have decided to help Elias fix Jane, and maybe undo this awful plague. But perhaps you will pick something else."

Vanessa chewed at her lip, clearly thinking hard on the matter. But their conversation was cut short by Lady Hayworth, who swept into the room, clapping her hands.

"Look at the two of you!" the countess said, with a disapproving look. "There is barely time before the ball, and neither of you is properly dressed!"

Vanessa hesitated, tightening her arms on Dora. "I am . . . not feeling well," she said softly. "It might be best if I did not go, Lady Hayworth."

The countess laughed. Dora thought that was a strange response to Vanessa's obvious distress, but she was probably not the best person to judge. "Rumour has it that Lord Carroway's oldest son has suddenly decided to attend," Lady Hayworth said. "He intends almost certainly to spend more time with you. If you were dying in your bed, Miss Ettings, you would *still* be going."

Vanessa knit her brow. Auntie Frances had rarely crossed her daughter's moods – though to be fair, Dora thought, Vanessa rarely had *moods* at all. "Perhaps my mother—" she began tremulously.

"Your mother will agree with me," Lady Hayworth chastised Vanessa with a stern look. "I have told her that she is far too accommodating with the both of you. Perhaps that is how mothers treat their children in the country, but it is not proper *here*." The countess eyed them both in a most unfriendly manner.

"It is time that you both got dressed," she said, and there was an ominous note to her voice this time.

Vanessa pushed meekly up to her feet, unwilling to further protest. Dora considered the last part of the treatise upstairs – but the look on the countess's face was dark, and after her earlier carriage ride with Auntie Frances, Dora suspected there was little chance of victory in the matter. She rose quietly after Vanessa and followed her cousin up the stairs.

Only one of the maids had been sent to help Dora with her dress; now that Vanessa had caught Edward's attention, it was clear that Dora had become an afterthought once again. Since she had so few gowns with her, Dora put on the mint-green gown that Lady Carroway had given her, discreetly pinning it up along the sides once more. It was still quite clear that she was wearing a hand-me-down – however expensive – but the gown made Dora feel warm and comforted, rather like one of Vanessa's hugs. Part of her hoped that Lady Carroway would be at the ball with her son, and that she would be pleased to see Dora making use of her gift.

The maid styled Dora's hair as best she could in the time they had left. Dora had no jewellery to wear this time, but since she was unlikely to get much attention other than pitying looks, any further adornment was probably unnecessary.

Vanessa was in a new brown and gold gown, with her blonde hair done up in rubies. It was quite clear to Dora that the hens had pulled out all the stops to ensure that her cousin would be particularly eye-catching tonight. Vanessa looked calm and composed, but Dora could tell that she was still quietly upset over the day's events, beneath all the finery.

The countess was already waiting in the carriage by the time that Dora, Vanessa and Auntie Frances joined her. She was wearing a rich burgundy gown, along with an embarrassment of jewels – looking at her in that moment, Dora thought that she must surely be the epitome of everything that Elias so hated.

"There you are," Lady Hayworth cooed, as Vanessa settled into her seat. "Oh, just look at you! I cannot wait for you to walk into that ball. All of the other women will be just green with envy, won't they?" She shared a smug smile with Auntie Frances, who chuckled as though she'd heard a very fine joke.

"Thank you, Lady Hayworth," Vanessa said quietly. It was a polite rote response, however; she was already staring out the window of the carriage, and Dora suspected that her cousin's mind was very far away from anything like dresses and balls.

"You will keep Albert busy as much as possible, of course," Auntie Frances told Dora in a cool tone. "If he does still harbour an interest in Vanessa, he must not be allowed to show it too much, or else Edward might overthink his own attentions."

"I will do my best," Dora promised. But she was thinking about the ball nearly as little as Vanessa was doing; all of her thoughts were on the last quarter of the treatise, still sitting in her room.

Chapter Thirteen

*L*ady Cushing's ball was an even grander affair than the one they'd attended at Carroway House; the crowd seemed smaller and more choice, and the outfits correspondingly more expensive. There was a great chandelier on the ceiling with bits of dangling crystal which threw reflections all across the walls, and the entirety of the wooden floor had been chalked up with fanciful geometric designs.

To this affair, they had arrived fashionably late, after the dancing was in full swing. Predictably, Dora had ended up sitting with her aunt in the corner while Vanessa was politely swarmed with dance requests. Much later in the ball, however, Albert made his appearance, only slightly ruffled from whatever diversion had occupied him between the afternoon's events and the party. To the great satisfaction of Auntie Frances and the countess, he soon came over to ask Dora for her first dance.

"God willing, Master Ricks will not remain in his position for very much longer," Albert said, as soon as they had reached the dance floor. "My father has taken up the matter himself."

Dora frowned. "But Master Ricks is still in charge for the moment?" she asked.

"He is," Albert muttered distastefully. "I did what I could to dissuade him from further abuses this afternoon, but it is not so simple to remove him at a moment's notice. There is no exact law forbidding him from what he did, and there are not so many people willing to take his place. But it has occurred to me that Master Ricks looks much richer than his station should suggest. If I am right, and he has been embezzling from the workhouse, a short investigation into his thievery should accomplish what moral outrage would not."

Dora sighed. "I begin to wonder if moral outrage has ever accomplished anything," she murmured. "We do not seem to ever feel such outrage when it regards matters outside these ballrooms." Then, with a blink, she said, "Oh. I am sorry. That was a bit bleak."

Albert smiled wryly at her. "Just for tonight, I share the sentiment," he said. "With good luck and plenty of wine, I hope to recover my optimism again by tomorrow." His eyes focused over her shoulder, and Dora caught sight of Vanessa and his brother Edward dancing together, not far off from them. "You seem quite close to your cousin, Miss Ettings," Albert said distantly. "Would you do me the great favour of your honest opinion, and tell me the sort of wife you think she might make?"

Dora gave Albert an openly curious look, and he flushed. "Oh, not for me!" he assured her. "You must have noticed that Edward has shown an interest in her. He asked much earlier my opinion of your cousin, and I did not have an answer for him. After today, I believe she must be quite loyal, but I have realised that I otherwise know very little of her."

Dora smiled at Albert, bemused. "I am quite close to Vanessa," she said. "Surely you must know that I am likely to be biased."

Albert considered this. "You are right, of course," he acknowledged. "But somehow, in spite of that, I suspect your opinion to be more reliable than most. I do not think that I have ever seen you mince your words, Miss Ettings."

The dance ended. Dora kept her arm on Albert's, however, thinking to herself. "May we take a turn about the room while I think?" she asked. "I would rather not go back to my aunt just yet."

Albert obliged, and they walked off the dance floor. Dora spent another few moments putting her thoughts together. "I will tell you the truth, Mr Lowe," she said finally. "But only if you offer me the same privilege regarding your brother. I trust that is acceptable?"

"That is fair, of course," Albert agreed. "For my part, I have little to disparage. Edward has always done his best to be honourable and to see to both his duty and his family."

Dora frowned. "But is he a *good* man?" she asked. "I do not imply otherwise, of course, but I know similarly little of him."

Albert nodded, taking this in stride. "I think that Edward is a good man," he said. "But I have thought more than once that his goodness is untested. It is easy to be kind and generous and honourable when there is little to lose by it. Given his inheritance, however, I question whether he will ever be in a position to be tested at all. Perhaps it is a moot point."

Dora smiled ruefully at that. "I shall say something very similar to you in return, I think," she told Albert. "I love Vanessa dearly, and she has always been the kindest person in my life. I fear she can be callous with those things she does not see or understand directly. But to show her such things is a simple enough remedy, and the lack does not negate her other lovely qualities." Dora paused. "As to what sort of wife she would make . . . I could not know what a man looks for in a wife. But I take much comfort in her company, and I cannot imagine that her future husband would do otherwise."

Albert gave Dora a warm smile in return. "I am glad to know that," he said. "If I may say so, Miss Ettings . . . you have no lack of lovely qualities yourself. I am sure that I am not the only one to notice."

Dora blinked at the unexpected change in subject. "Mr Lowe," she said carefully, "I do not mean to get above myself. But if you have suddenly decided to court me in earnest, I am not certain I can recommend the idea."

Albert chuckled. "I would not dare," he told her softly. "Speaking of which . . . I believe I must relinquish you shortly. I hope you do not mind."

Dora had only the briefest moment to wonder at his statement before she heard someone behind her clear their throat. "Miss Ettings," Elias said. "I am here to call your bluff. I believe that I am owed two dances – any two that I like, in fact."

Dora turned to regard the magician. He was not dressed terribly well for the party – in fact, he stuck out like a sore thumb among those who had shown up in their very best attire. His face was obviously worn with weariness, but Dora thought there was an uncommon gentleness to his demeanour tonight, and he had a rare, tired smile on his features.

"You *were* invited, then?" Dora asked, before she could think better of the words. "I am surprised that Lady Cushing sent you an invitation."

Elias raised an eyebrow at her. "Most people simply assume that I will not come when they invite me to their parties," he said. "I am sure the lady will reconsider her approach after this terrible mistake." He held his hand out to her patiently. "I really will not take no for an answer, Miss Ettings. You would not wish to be known as a woman who ignores her gambling debts."

"I would not like to be known as a gambling woman in the first place," Dora said dryly. "But since I seem to have lost the same bet that Lady Cushing did, I suppose that it is supportable in this instance." She found herself smiling back at him though, and as she took his hand, the heaviness that had been in her chest all day lightened noticeably.

As Elias led her back onto the floor, his hand dropped to her waist, and a strange shiver went through her where he touched. At first blush, it should not have been a proper way to touch a lady in public – but as Dora glanced around at the other dancers, she realised that they were all engaged in similar positions. "Oh," she murmured. "We are waltzing, then?"

"Apparently so," said Elias. He turned fully towards her and lifted her hand to his arm. There was no looking away from him in such a position; his warmth was very close, even where they did not touch. The sweet scent of myrrh tickled at Dora's senses, and she found herself staring up at Elias in jumbled confusion.

"I do not have the translation with me, I'm afraid," Dora told him. "I gave it to Albert earlier. I should be able to finish the last quarter of it tonight, if I can borrow a candle."

Elias smiled at Dora again. "Albert gave me your work earlier today," he told her. "I am not here to bully more of it from you."

Dora considered this for a long moment. She could not help but be aware of his arm sliding around her back as they continued to prepare for the dance. "Is there some other help that I might offer, in that case?" she asked. "I cannot imagine you came to one of these parties you so hate in order to dance."

Elias had not looked away from her once as they talked. Tired as he was, there was no hint in him of the desperate anger she had seen only a day prior. There was still grief, Dora thought, but it was tempered with something softer and less violent. "You are correct, of course," Elias told her. "I despise these silly balls. I did not come here simply to dance." He cleared his throat slightly. "I have again had little success today. I found myself sitting alone in the dark, tired and bitter. And I suppose I could have stayed like that. But I promised Albert that I would be kinder to myself. And so I tried to think of where I would *want* to be if I were not so bound to this hopeless task."

Dora knit her brow. "You cannot have thought of Lady Cushing's ball," she said sceptically.

"I did not," Elias said. "I thought of you, Dora. But you are here, and so here I am." Those golden eyes held hers, and a flustered heat pooled against the surface of Dora's skin. "I did not come here only to dance. I came here only to dance with *you*. It is quite a different thing."

The dancing began, and it was a good thing that it did – Dora was suddenly certain that she could not manage to stay still beneath those eyes for even a moment longer. Her head was swimming and her breath was oddly short. Elias had a reassuring hold on her, and she found herself wondering whether she would still be able to stand upright once he finally let her go.

"You are very quiet," Elias said, after they had taken a few rotations around the floor. His gaze did not waver from her face. Dora thought he might be searching for something in her expression.

"I do not know what to say," she admitted. "I think I am deeply touched. But if I am supposed to react in some particular way, I should warn you that I do not know it. My condition confounds me." Dora found herself looking at his chin now instead of into his eyes. "I am a doll sometimes, and not a human being at all."

Elias pressed gently at her back, leading them aside from the other dancers. He paused there for a moment, and Dora felt his gaze hot on her face. "Surely you cannot think that of yourself," he murmured. "Or has someone else said it to you, perhaps?"

Dora stayed very silent. She did not want to admit that she had accidentally plucked the words from that pile of misery at the bottom of her mind. It would be too much like admitting that Auntie Frances had won some battle over her.

Elias leaned down towards her, probably closer than was proper. "It may be true that you only have half a soul, Dora," he whispered, with a surprising abundance of empathy in his voice. "But that does not make you half a *person*."

Dora trembled at that without quite knowing why. She felt the words all the way to her bones – deeper and more piercing than anything that Auntie Frances had ever said to her. The rare sincerity in his voice struck her squarely in what remained of her heart, somehow painful and relieving all at once.

Wet tears trickled down her cheeks. Too late, Dora reached up to wipe at them, bewildered.

Elias blinked. "Are you – are you all right?" he asked softly.

Dora nodded slowly. "It must be all this candle smoke," she lied evenly. "It always does make my eyes water."

Elias squeezed her hand. "There are better ways to light a room," he said. "Perhaps I might help." He released her hand to reach into his jacket, from which he withdrew a wand of twisted glass.

The candles in the room all snuffed out in the space of an instant. Gasps and whispers rippled among the crowd – but they soon transformed into awed murmurs. Wavering pinprick lights kindled in the air, scattered like faerie dust across the ballroom. One floated just past Dora, and she reached out to touch it with rapt fascination. The light flickered against her skin, but it neither burned nor cooled where it touched. Instead, it caught briefly upon her fingers and then fluttered away again like a floating ember.

"Are they stars?" she whispered in wonder.

"I am flattered by your wild estimation of my abilities," Elias said, with a hint of pleasant mirth. "I should lie and say that I have indeed brought down the stars for your amusement. But it's a simple magic trick and nothing more." He flicked a finger, and a haze of twinkling lights swept towards her, settling into the fabric of her dress and the strands of her hair.

A few of those gathered in the ballroom began to turn their attention towards Dora at that. If she had been anyone other than herself, she might have been embarrassed at the sudden attention. But Elias was smiling at her with a whimsical pleasure, and she was swimming in stars – and as the musicians slowly found their beat again and he took her back into his arms to dance, Dora could only feel the brightest, most wonderful lantern warmth she had ever known before.

The atmosphere until that moment had been tense and

somewhat smothering, as many balls were. But without the heat of all those candles, in the gentle light of those calm, floating faerie lights, there was suddenly a hushed sort of reverence; no one wanted to be the first to break the lovely spell that had come upon them all.

Looking up at Elias in the flickering starlight, Dora found herself utterly arrested. There was an ethereal, otherworldly beauty to him just now that made her think he must *surely* be at least part faerie. Dora imagined his skin like moonlight, his hair like white silk, his eyes like banked embers. He was looking at her, incredibly, and not at the stars around them. The soft atmosphere made her feel even more than usual that she was dreaming. But it was the sort of lovely dream that one dwelled purposely upon, unwilling to wake too soon.

A scattering of stars swept up as Elias turned Dora past the corner of the dance floor, and she glanced behind them, watching with awe. When she looked back at him, there was a new warmth in his expression. "You are smiling," Elias said softly.

Dora blinked slowly. "I suppose I am," she murmured, dimly surprised. And in fact, she could feel a distant, serene sort of smile on her face. "This is very nice, isn't it? Just for the moment."

A similar, contented smile blossomed across the magician's lips, and the warmth in Dora's chest grew with it. "It is very nice," Elias told her. He searched her face with a gently curious expression. "Are you happy just now, Dora?"

Dora blinked slowly, thinking on the question. "I am . . . very content," she said. But the trickling warmth in her chest increased as she continued to look at his smile, and she sighed suddenly. "No," she said. "I think I *am* happy. What a lovely feeling. I am dreaming, and I don't want to wake up."

The music fell, and they came to a pause along with the other dancers. Elias leaned closer towards her under cover of the dim starlight. Dora stared at him, entranced, as his forehead pressed lightly to hers.

"I don't want to wake up either," he whispered.

She felt his breath along her cheek as he said the words. The whisper shivered its way into her heart, and Dora thought, *Oh dear.* Because she was now quite sure that she was in love. Every remaining ragged fibre of her half-soul shivered with the awareness of it.

"You will have to dance another time with me," Elias murmured. "You did promise."

"I could not imagine dancing with anyone else," Dora said honestly.

She did not, however, keep very good track of just how many times they *did* dance, as the night went on. Dora knew that it was far more than was proper. But as the stars scattered away, she could only hope that everyone had quite lost track of who was dancing with whom at any given time.

It was supper that finally interrupted them, somewhere just after midnight. By the regretful look on Elias's face, Dora surmised that he had not intended to stay quite so late. As he released her reluctantly, she found herself feeling decidedly cold for the first time in years.

"Thank you very much for the diversion," Elias said quietly. "I fear I must now return to more unpleasant tasks."

Dora's smile wavered at that. *I do not want you to go*, she thought. But that was very selfish of her, especially as she knew how little Elias wished to confront his hopeless endeavours again.

"I was pleased to see you," she said instead. "I am glad that you came."

Elias stepped back – but he took her hand in his and leaned down to kiss the air just over her glove. For once, the gesture did not seem ironic in the least. "I will call on you again as soon as I might," he said. "If you could endeavour to be at home, of course."

Dora laughed quietly at that. "I will endeavour," she said. "But I do not know how successful I might be. Wherever your dragon-slaying accoutrements are, I suspect that you must bring them again."

Elias shot her a tired smile. "We shall muddle through together somehow, I suppose."

He let go of Dora's hand and gave her one last nod, before turning to leave.

Dora found herself next to Vanessa for supper, during which time exclamations abounded over the magical evening. Clearly, the Lord Sorcier had stopped by and personally conducted the display – a most uncharacteristic whimsy, someone assured the gathering, since he had once put Lady Rhine in fear for her life after being asked to perform "some magical party trick". No indeed – the conversation supposed that the Lord Sorcier must have attended in order to impress some lady in particular . . . and as ladies and gentlemen both compared recollections, Dora slowly found herself the object of much attention at the table.

"Surely not!" one of the ladies said in astonishment. "The *older* Miss Ettings? Don't you mean the younger one?"

"There is an older Miss Ettings?" a gentleman murmured in confusion.

"She danced with him all night!" a younger woman cooed. "How romantic! Are there no other magicians in London this Season? I really must find one for myself!"

Vanessa smiled at Dora, squeezing her hand beneath the table.

"Is it true?" asked the girl on Dora's other side. "*Did* you dance with the Lord Sorcier all night long?"

Dora gave her a look of mild interest. "I danced with him twice," she lied, with utmost serenity. "Anything else would surely be too much."

This lie was accepted with more or less scepticism by different people at the table. But as for Lady Cushing, she could not possibly have been happier – she was loudly telling anyone who would listen at the foot of the table how fond she was of the

Lord Sorcier in spite of his unconventional personality, and how she had always made a point of sending him an invitation out of sheer good manners. Dora privately thought that poor Elias might have resuscitated his reputation by mistake with his little bit of magic – for his flight of fancy had instantly made Lady Cushing's ball the most exciting event of the Season, and now every party in the city was certain to hope for his unexpected attendance.

The stars in the ballroom lingered through dinner and even into the early hours of the morning – whereupon they began to fade with the encroaching dawn. Dora had halfway expected to hear some recriminations from either her aunt or the countess in the carriage on their way back – but to her surprise, none were forthcoming at all. They rode back to Hayworth House in sleepy silence instead – and as Dora clambered into bed and closed her eyes, the stars from the ballroom twinkled in her dreams.

Chapter Fourteen

*D*ora slept quite late the morning after the ball. When she did finally awaken, she found herself wondering whether she had dreamed the whole thing. Surely, Dora thought, Vanessa would be able to tell her what was real and what was false – but when Dora went downstairs, her cousin was nowhere to be found.

"Miss Vanessa has stepped out with Mr Edward Lowe," the butler told Dora, when she asked after her cousin.

Dora considered this curiously. "With a chaperone, of course?" she asked. "Did Miss Jennings go with them, perhaps?"

"No, Miss Ettings," the butler replied politely. "Mr Lowe requested a private audience with Miss Vanessa, and Lady Lockheed granted her permission."

Dora blinked slowly. She was not by any stretch the most socially astute woman. But even she understood what such a private audience must mean.

Edward Lowe is proposing to Vanessa, Dora thought. The idea seemed even more unreal than the long, surreal evening which she had spent with Elias. After all of the hens' scheming and gnashing of teeth, they had finally succeeded in their aim: any moment now, Vanessa would be engaged to a viscount-in-waiting. Surely, within just a few short weeks, she would be married.

And Dora would be alone.

It was so difficult even to envision the idea that Dora brushed it away in confusion. *Perhaps not*, she thought. *Vanessa said that she would want me to stay with her after she is married. I am sure she will not change her mind.*

But . . . no. Dora was *not* sure. There was no reason to expect that Vanessa had changed her mind – but what if she *had*? Either way, everything would change completely as soon as Vanessa reappeared through that door.

"Dora!" Auntie Frances snapped from the top of the stairs. "You are finally awake, I see. Good. I will have the maids begin packing immediately."

Dora frowned distractedly. She wasn't sure, suddenly, just how long she had been standing there staring at the door. "Packing?" she asked. "What are we packing, Auntie Frances?"

"Your things, of course," Auntie Frances said in exasperation. "Vanessa will be back with a ring at any moment. The church will begin reading the banns this week, I am sure. The very last thing we need is for you to do something silly to upset the engagement before Vanessa and the viscount are safely married!"

Dora laughed with a hint of dazed confusion. "Edward is not a viscount yet," she told Auntie Frances. "His father is still viscount. What a strange idea that would be, if Vanessa were to marry Albert's father. Lady Carroway is very generous, but I do not think that she is quite *that* generous—"

Auntie Frances marched down the stairs and grabbed her by the arm. "This is *exactly* the sort of nonsense I am talking about!" she said, with a hard edge in her voice. "You simply cannot say such things in public. It will be far better to have you in Lockheed."

Dora struggled against Auntie Frances's grip, wriggling halfway free from her bony fingers. "I cannot go back to Lockheed," she said, in a voice far more reasonable than she would have preferred. "Vanessa asked me to be at her wedding. And I must find a husband, you said—"

"Vanessa does not need you at her wedding!" Auntie Frances interrupted in irritation. "And we both know that you will never be married, Dora. Mr Lowe has still shown no inclination to offer for you. We can hardly expect the countess to continue to house you here on a hopeless whim."

What is happening? Dora thought dimly. This was all far too quick. Vanessa was getting married. Jane was still dying. George Ricks was still a terrible villain. Dora could not possibly go back to Lockheed.

"The Lord Sorcier is courting me," Dora said evenly, though the words awoke a fresh confusion in her stomach. "He cannot have made his interest any more clear, Auntie Frances."

He is only courting me in order to keep the others away, Dora thought. *But his suit should be enough to keep me here as well, shouldn't it?*

Auntie Frances curled her lip, and she pinched Dora's arm sharply. "Do not speak to me of that magician!" she hissed. "You have made enough of a fool of yourself, Dora, taking up with him as though you are already engaged. Dancing all night together, really? All of that close waltzing! If the man truly wishes to offer for you, then he may do it in Lockheed – but I will not suffer him to tatter our family's reputation any further with his rude manners!"

What remained of Dora's heart sank horribly in her chest.

Auntie Frances hauled her back up the stairs and shoved her unceremoniously back into her bedroom. "Get dressed for the road, Dora," her aunt ordered her. "It is still morning yet. I shall have you safely on the road within the hour, by God."

Dora opened her mouth to respond – but before she could manage so much as another word, her aunt closed the door with a sharp *snap*.

The silence of the room deepened around her. Slowly, it pressed in, smothering her thoughts like a heavy blanket. Dora stood in place, trying to make her mind work – but even more than usual, it refused to focus. Somehow, the more effort she expended trying to anchor herself in the moment, the less Dora was able to concentrate at all.

She forced herself to take a few steps across the room, if only to make her body move. Inevitably, she found herself at the dresser, digging in the drawer where she had hidden the scrying mirror.

But the mirror was gone. So too, Dora realised, were the flowers that had been on that dresser.

The hens have thrown them both away, Dora thought with rising dread. *We came back so late last night, I did not even notice.*

Dora stepped back again, shivering with confusion.

I must do something, she thought. *This is not a dream, however much it feels that way. I cannot disappear back to Lockheed while all of this is going on.*

But the blanket over her mind grew heavier and heavier now, blanking out all reasonable consideration. Dora sat herself on the edge of the bed and pressed her face into her hands, trying to force away a sudden dizziness.

I am trapped, Dora thought. She needed air. She wanted to be somewhere else, anywhere else.

But . . . no. That was not it at all. This crushing weight on her chest was far more insidious and far more impossible to solve.

I want to be someone *else*, Dora thought.

The truth of the realisation sank into her gently, like most everything else in the world always did. This time, she felt quietly smothered – trapped in a dream with herself, unable to escape.

Dora wavered on the edge of the bed as the hopeless dizziness grew deeper. If she could have laid down on the pillows and simply disappeared, she was sure in that moment that she would have done it.

For years, Dora had not bothered to wonder why it was she

had been singled out – why she had been cursed instead of anyone else in the world. It had always seemed irrelevant, insubstantial, irreversible. But today, she felt the unfairness of it all like a corset laced too tightly.

What might Dora have been if she had not lost that half of her soul? Would Auntie Frances have loved her more if she could smile properly? Surely, Dora would have fallen in love more fully, with some man who loved her back exactly the same. She would not have needed to wear iron scissors around her neck, nor to hide from suitors for their own safety.

She would not now be going back to Lockheed all alone, to be safely forgotten in the country once more.

"I must not think this way," Dora whispered aloud. The words broke the uncanny silence in the room. They made the situation feel more real, more stable. The sound of her own voice, Dora thought, would help her focus again.

She sucked in a few deep breaths and began to count in French.

"*Un, deux, trois . . .*" Tears trickled down her face, and she blinked them away in confusion. ". . . *quatre, cinq, six . . .*" The sound of her aunt's voice hissed in her ear again, accusing her of being a puppet. ". . . *sept, huit, neuf . . .*"

Dora wiped unsteadily at her eyes. The mirror that stood upon the vanity in the corner drew her gaze, and she pressed her lips together. Before she knew it, Dora had risen to her feet and crossed the distance to that mirror, leaning in towards it. She stared intently into its silvery surface, reaching out for Elias.

His wards pressed back against her almost instantly, tingling against her skin with warning. Dora leaned her mind against them only gently. *I will continue until it becomes dangerous*, she thought. *Only until he has realised that someone is trying to find him.*

Ah, but even then, what will he do? A small, doubtful voice whispered from the bottom of her mind. Of what importance was it to Elias if Dora ended up in the country? He was dealing with far greater matters, to be sure. He had an entire plague to worry about. And, well – perhaps it was true that Dora had tried very hard to help him with that. But in the end, she had not helped all *that* much, had she?

Perhaps I would have been able to help better if I were not split in two. Dora could not stop the thought from bubbling up. It distracted the image of Elias that she had fixed in her mind, making it waver uncertainly.

The silver in the vanity mirror rippled as Dora grappled with her intentions. Slowly, it began to stain itself black. At first, Dora wondered if Elias had dismissed his wards – but the image that appeared in the darkness of the mirror was not his.

It was hers.

The Dora in the mirror was sitting at a pianoforte, wearing a gown of such fine white satin that it made her glow like moonlight. Her rust-red tresses were far longer than Dora was used to; her hair was braided elegantly down her back, with shining pearls worked into every twist.

The other Dora was crying. Really, she was sobbing – the sheer violence of emotion in her expression took the real Dora aback. But still, the other Dora played the pianoforte in front of her with a careful precision, unable or unwilling to break her performance.

"I don't understand," Dora whispered, as she stared at her own mirror image. "What is this?"

The other Dora's fingers slipped on the keys of the piano. She glanced up in shock, tears still wet upon her face.

Her left eye was grey.

"I don't understand," whispered the other Dora. "What is this?"

Footsteps sounded nearby. The real Dora whirled, and saw a finely carved door, with its edges gilded in gold. The door was of far higher quality than even those in Lady Hayworth's residence – as Dora looked more closely, she saw that the carvings upon it were of nymphs and satyrs, joyfully leading children by the hands in a sort of wild dance.

The door opened. Through it walked Lord Hollowvale, with his eyes of pale blue and his many layers of expensive jackets – limping only slightly with the use of a long, silver cane.

Dora met his gaze with horror.

It did not matter that Dora was only scrying and not actually there in person. Lord Hollowvale *looked* at her in the same clear way that Elias might have done. The marquess frowned at her curiously. "Why have you ceased your piano practice?" he asked Dora. "And whatever are you wearing?"

Lord Hollowvale's eyes shifted towards the other Dora, who was still at the piano, and he became even more confused.

"Oh, now *that* is interesting," the faerie mused. He said it with the same sentiment with which one might remark on a particularly pretty ribbon, or a rug of exotic origin.

Dora reached instinctively towards her chest, where the iron scissors *ought* to have been. But the sheath around her neck was inexplicably empty.

Iron and magic did not mix, Dora remembered with belated dread. Everything else seemed to have come with her in some fashion as she scryed this strange place, but the scissors had stayed behind with her body.

Lord Hollowvale smiled, and Dora knew that he had an inkling of her vulnerability. He took a few languid, graceful strides towards her, as Dora closed her eyes tightly and sucked in her breath.

Think of the vanity, she told herself. *Think of the wood beneath my hands. I must think of absolutely anything else but this.*

A cold hand settled upon Dora's shoulder. The slight touch drove all the air from her lungs in the space of an instant. Something very important snapped in Dora's chest, with the same terrible sort of finality as a piano wire being cut.

"How very good of you to visit, firstborn child of Georgina Ettings," said the marquess. "Please, allow me to welcome you to the Hollow House."

Chapter Fifteen

If Dora had been anyone else, she was certain that she would have been panicking. As it stood, there was a deep and terrible dread in her heart – but since she could not possibly react with anything other than calm, she opened her eyes on Lord Hollowvale and asked, "What have you done to me?"

Lord Hollowvale frowned at Dora consideringly. "I have taken the rest of my debt," he told her. "This half of your soul shall return to the mortal world no longer. But what a problem! I had imagined that you would be one person again, and that does not seem to be the case."

Dora looked towards the other version of her which still sat at the pianoforte. The other Dora leapt to her feet with a furious cry. "You must let her go at once, you monster!" she exclaimed. "Are you not content with what you have done to *me* already?"

Lord Hollowvale tsked at the other Dora. "Your manners!" he sighed. "How can they still be so awful, Theodora? After all my labour to increase your virtues, you remain incapable of maintaining a lady's composure." His pale blue eyes flickered back towards Dora, whom he still held in place with his hand on her shoulder. "But I see now! So long ago, I took the more passionate half of your soul. If I can knit the two of you together again, I shall have a proper English daughter for certain!"

Dora's stomach turned at that. "Daughter?" she whispered. "I am not your daughter. Surely not."

"Oh, but you are!" Lord Hollowvale told her pleasantly. "I make it a point to own at least one of every English thing. I told your mother that I wished to own an English child, and she sold you to me well before you were even born. As you grew, she insisted that you were of even more incalculable worth. Why, I must have given her a fortune in faerie gold! Before she died, she declared that a daughter was in fact a priceless thing to have." He laughed at this, as though it were a joke. "But now I have an English daughter, and I will be the subject of absolute jealousy! I was already much envied for owning only half of one."

Dora looked towards her other half. *I shall call her Theodora*, she thought. *For I must call her something other than "me" if I am to stay sane at all.* Theodora was indeed much more passionate than Dora was; even now, tears streamed down her face with ease, and she was flushed and trembling with anger. For just a moment, Dora envied her, before she realised how silly a notion that was.

"I cannot stay here," Dora informed Lord Hollowvale evenly. "This is not where I belong, and I have things which I must do. You must send me back at once."

Lord Hollowvale shook his head at her, bemused. "My dear Theodora," he said. "Both halves of you are impudent after all. But do not worry! I am an incredibly generous lord, as you will come to find. I will see that your virtues are increased a thousandfold! You shall be the most enviable English daughter that ever a faerie lord had – all patience and sweetness and discretion!" He patted her fondly on the cheek. "You may ask your other half. I have found her all of the very best lessons, have I not?"

"So many lessons!" Theodora sputtered. "And never any time for rest! You left me three days to play the piano once and forgot about me, and my fingers began to bleed!"

"And you are quite the accomplished pianist!" Lord Hollowvale sighed proudly. "I do hear that is a mark of virtue in an English daughter, and so you are even *more* virtuous now than when I first brought you here!" He turned Dora around by the shoulders to face her counterpart. "Alas," he said, "I must see to a previous appointment very shortly. But as soon as I return, I am sure that I shall find a way to make you a single person again. In the meantime, do become reacquainted with yourself, Theodora!"

Lord Hollowvale released Dora and turned back towards the door. Before she could protest, he had closed it behind him. There was the distinctive sound of a key turning in a lock – and then, the sound of retreating footsteps.

Dora tried the knob anyway, rattling it violently. She pushed her shoulder against the door, and even tried to kick at it with her foot. All of this accomplished less than nothing: the door refused to budge.

"It will not open," Theodora told her with a heavy, mournful sigh. "I have tried so many times." Dora glanced back and saw that Theodora's lower lip had begun to tremble. "Oh *no*, I am likely to cry again. Why am I like this all the time? Did I somehow leave all my patience with you when he tore me away?"

Dora turned to consider herself calmly. "I suppose that is possible," she said. "For my part, I seem to have left all of my short-tailed emotions with *you*. I have never been able to react to things in the way that normal people ought."

Theodora *did* begin to cry at this – she wiped at her face with her sleeve, shivering with sobs. "How awful!" she said. "Then neither of us has been quite right for years and years! Have we both been miserable in our own way?"

Dora thought on this. "Perhaps not," she said slowly. "I was very upset with my condition only minutes ago. But I was not nearly as trapped as you have been, and at least I have had some real company. Vanessa has been wonderful, and Elias—" Dora cut herself off, suddenly uncertain just what she ought to say.

Theodora stopped crying abruptly. She widened her eyes and clutched her hands to her chest. "Who is Elias?" she asked. "Oh dear. I feel so happy and so terrified all at once. Is that because you are in the room with me, and that is how we *ought* to feel?"

Dora looked down at her feet. "I am in love with him," she said, since it seemed silly to try and hide the truth from herself. "But I fear that he does not feel the same way." She frowned faintly at that. "I should have simply asked him. If I *do* manage to get back to England, I will surely do so."

Theodora wavered on her feet. She sat down on the piano bench quickly, blinking away some overwhelming feeling. "Oh," she said softly. "Oh, this is love then. How wonderful and terrible." She looked up at Dora and pressed her lips together. "I have tried to escape before, you know. But this time, I truly must. I cannot imagine never seeing Elias again!" Theodora paused in confusion. "I do not even know him. What a strange circumstance this is."

Dora nodded slowly. "I feel the same," she admitted. "On both counts. Though you and I are certainly still connected, or else I would not have had one foot in faerie, which made me able to scry. And . . . oh. I must have scryed upon *you* by accident just now. That is how I ended up here. I was looking at the mirror and thinking desperately how much I wished to be a whole person again."

"Yes, it *would* be lovely to be whole again!" Theodora sighed. "You have no idea how exhausting it is to always be emotional. I am always furious or heartbroken or terrified or . . . or *sometimes* I am joyful, but it is so rare to find anything to be joyful about here." Theodora pushed back to her feet and crossed the distance to Dora, taking her by the hands. It was a surreal experience, to be sure. There was a slight tingle between them, and Dora felt a distant echo of fear in her chest – but it did not quite take root. Instead, it slipped away like a ship without an anchor.

"There is something missing," Dora said. "I do not know

how to knit us back together. But if we can get back to England, then I am sure that Elias will know what to do. He is the most talented magician in the country."

She headed over towards a window on the far side of the piano and peered outside it. The view overlooked a sprawling garden of white roses, all smothered in a thick mist. Beyond the garden, a large, forbidding building loomed up from the fog – but from this distance, she could only make out its general shape.

"We could climb out the window," Dora suggested. "How far does Hollowvale extend through faerie? Do you know if there is some way back to England if we walk far enough?"

Theodora knit her brow with obvious irritation. "Climbing down was the very first thing that I tried!" she snipped. "I am *you*, after all. I walked to the very edge of Hollowvale – but by the time I had reached the borders, I was so weak that I couldn't go on. I do not have a body of my own, and it is only Lord Hollowvale's magic that sustains me."

Dora blinked slowly. "No body?" she murmured. "But does that mean that I have no body either? Have I left mine behind in Hayworth House?" Now that Dora thought further on the matter, that only made sense. She had never brought her body with her when she'd scryed before, so why should now be any different? A new thought occurred to her as she considered this. "Perhaps if I were to scry upon myself again, I could get back into my body," she said. "Does that sound reasonable?"

Theodora crossed her arms. "I know nothing about scrying," she said tartly. "It was never touched upon in my lessons. If you think that it is reasonable, however, then I suppose that *I* think it is reasonable."

Dora nodded at that. "Then all I should require is a mirror," she said. "Do you know of any here?"

Theodora scowled. "I do not," she said. "And isn't that strange? You would think with how the marquess goes on and on about having one of every English thing, he would have at least *one* mirror here."

Dora sighed. "Well," she said. "We shall have to see what we can find. At the very least, I have no intention of waiting here until the marquess returns from his appointment."

She began to search the window for a way of opening it – but before she could look very hard at all, Theodora picked up the piano bench and slammed it against the window glass with all her might, shattering the fine glazing into a thousand little pieces.

Mist trickled into the room like an exhaled breath. Dora expected it to feel wet, but instead it seemed to numb her slightly wherever it touched her skin. This did not alarm Theodora, who was already climbing outside the window and grabbing a nearby tree branch – so Dora followed calmly after her.

There was something both familiar and comforting about climbing down a tree again, though Dora had not done anything of the sort since that fateful day when she had first met Lord Hollowvale. Below her, Theodora snagged her fine dress upon the tree branches and tore at her silken slippers, but there was a joyful smile on her face that suggested she was having fun.

"How long do you think the marquess shall be at his appointment?" Dora called down to her other half, as she navigated her way carefully down.

"Not for long, I fear!" Theodora responded. "He is careless with his bargains, and he always gladly overpays. He will be back with another child soon enough, I am sure."

Dora's foot missed the next branch, and she found herself sliding down the last bit of the tree until her feet hit the ground with a hard *thud*. Theodora, still a few feet up the tree, looked down at her with concern. "Is there something the matter?" Dora's other half asked her.

"You mean to say that the marquess has been buying children?" Dora said. Her tone was level, but even as she spoke, she saw the horror in her heart reflected in Theodora's eyes.

"Oh!" said Theodora. She hopped down the rest of the way and covered her mouth. "That *is* awful, isn't it? I've grown so used to terrible things here, since the faeries are all so casual about it."

"Are those children like us – I mean, like *me*?" Dora asked her. "Trapped in Hollowvale, I mean? Where has the marquess put them?" A dreadful suspicion had arisen at the back of her mind, and she knew she would have no rest until she confirmed it.

Theodora gave her a wary look. "He keeps them all at Charity House," she said. "It is a foolish name, by the way. There is nothing charitable about it at all." Theodora pointed across the misty garden before them, towards the tall, foreboding building on the other side.

Dora started in that direction immediately, pushing her way through the garden's brambles. She had expected the thorns to be sharp and wicked, given the wild look of the roses – but they were nearly insubstantial, the way that Elias had felt when she'd tried to touch him while scrying. The white rose petals wavered beneath her fingers like the mist that surrounded them.

"Faerie stuff isn't very certain of itself," Theodora said from behind her. "It's why the marquess prefers his English trophies, I think."

Dora was about to respond to this – but she found herself brought up short as Charity House finally came fully into view. A faint nausea tingled in her stomach, tinged with familiar recognition.

"I have seen this place before," Dora said. "Charity House looks just like the Cleveland Street Workhouse back in England."

"I have never seen the Cleveland Street Workhouse," Theodora said. "But I am sure that the marquess has twisted up its purpose entirely. I managed to get a peek inside just the other day. It's *terrible*! Only a faerie could engineer something so awful and bizarre!"

Dora tried the door out front and found it unlocked. As she

pushed it open, she was assaulted by the sharp, familiar stench of lye. The workhouse inside was a facsimile of the one she had visited in England; the hallways were cleaner and quieter, but the air was still laden with that acrid steam.

As Dora crept towards the place where she remembered the mess hall, she saw inside perhaps twenty children of varying ages, all sitting down at a long table. Those on one side of the table were twisting up a rough hemp rope with their little hands; those on the other side seemed to be *un*twisting the very same rope with quiet, fanatical concentration, much as the people at the Cleveland Street Workhouse had been doing.

"Half of them seem to be picking oakum," Dora whispered in puzzlement. "But the other half are reknitting the strands again. Why?"

Theodora sighed heavily. "You must cease asking *why* when it comes to faeries," she said. "I am sure there is an explanation, but it will not make any more sense than you expect."

Dora's eyes caught on a particular little girl with straw-like hair and a pockmarked face, who was currently working at unpicking her bit of rope. A burst of surprise rippled through her, and though Dora made no sound herself, Theodora let out a loud gasp next to her without quite knowing what it was she was gasping at.

A few of the children at the table glanced up at them in curiosity – but none of them stopped working, even for a moment. Jane shot Theodora only the briefest of annoyed glances before returning her concentration to the task before her. Closer up, Dora could see that the little girl's hands were scarred and bleeding from the rough hemp.

Dora stepped forward, unable to help herself. "Jane?" she asked. When the girl failed to respond, Dora remembered belatedly that *Jane* was simply the name that they had given her. She took a few more quick strides across the room and brought her hand down on the girl's shoulder.

Jane flinched at first – then she scowled, and tried to slip Dora's grasp. "What d'you want?" she asked in a rough voice. "I'm goin' as fast as I can."

"And what would it matter if you went any faster?" Theodora asked as she came up behind them. "The other children will only undo it all!"

Jane narrowed her eyes at the rope in front of her. "You don't have to rub it in," she said sourly. "I couldn't stop if I wanted to, anyway."

"You were at the Cleveland Street Workhouse in England," Dora said. "I saw you asleep in the corner. The Lord Sorcier has spent days now trying to figure out what's wrong with you." She wanted to sound more urgent, more relieved, more tearful – but as usual, the words came out with unnatural calmness instead.

At this, Jane *did* turn to look at Dora. "He what?" the little girl said. "You're jokin'. This is some other faerie trick, isn't it?"

"Not at all," Dora assured her. "I was trying to help him, before the lord of this place stole me away." She squeezed the girl's shoulder. "We have been calling you 'Jane', since we do not know your name. But what *should* I be calling you?"

The little girl bit her lip uncertainly. But she must have been convinced that there was little she could do to worsen her situation, because she eventually decided to reply. "I'm Abigail," she said reluctantly.

Dora nodded. "I'm Dora," she responded. "And this is . . . well, also me. But you can call her Theodora, I suppose."

Theodora blinked at that. "I hate the name Theodora!" she protested. "Why can't *you* be Theodora?"

"I could call you Charity instead," Dora observed dryly. "It *is* one of my middle names."

Theodora made a face at that. "Oh, fine," she muttered. "Theodora it is. But I still don't like it."

"Would you stop arguin' with . . . yourself?" Abigail asked.

The little girl glanced between the two versions of Dora, briefly confused. "Do either of you or . . . or your hob-nob magician have a way out of here?"

Dora frowned at that. "He's not a hob-nob," she mumbled. But it wasn't the time for that discussion, and so she shelved it for later. "Now that I think of it, I am not even sure that Elias knows we're here—"

A surge of strange heat made Dora waver on her feet. Theodora swayed next to her, and she realised that it had affected them both.

"*. . . I'm so sorry, Dora*," whispered Elias's voice. "*This is all my fault.*" There was a hideous anguish in his tone, though the words seemed to come from very far away. "*Wake up, please. What must I do for you to wake up?*"

Theodora pressed a hand to her chest. Her face was pale. "That was his voice, wasn't it?" she murmured, with obvious distress. "He sounds so upset."

Dora leaned heavily against the table in front of her. "Elias?" she asked softly. "Can you hear me?"

The sudden heat in Dora's body began to ebb away. But for just a moment, she was convinced she could feel a spot of warmth on her lips.

"Is he doing something?" Theodora asked urgently.

Dora bit at her lip. "He is *trying* something," she said softly. "And it is failing, just as it has always failed before." The realisation made her stomach sink all the way to her toes.

Abigail was not enough, Dora thought. *Now Elias is convinced that I've caught the sleeping plague, too.* She stared down at her hands on the table. *He must think I contracted the illness from the workhouses. That is the more logical assumption, even if it is wrong.*

Elias was not going to realise that Dora had been spirited away to faerie. He would work desperately against her illness . . . and in the end, he would watch her slowly fade away.

"I must find a way to tell Elias what is going on," Dora said. "Now more than ever." She turned towards Abigail. "Do you happen to know where I can find a mirror?"

Abigail shook her head. "Nothin' like that," she said. "I did look at myself in a wash tub downstairs once, just to see if I'd changed since comin' here."

Dora nodded at that. "Looking into water might suffice," she said. "I have never tried it before, but we are low on options."

She meant to reiterate to Abigail that someone was trying to save them – that none of them were alone in the world, and that they had not been forgotten. But she was cut off as the door to the workhouse opened, and Theodora dragged her quickly down to the floor to hide beneath the table.

"How fine you all look today!" Lord Hollowvale declared with a charming smile. "I declare, all of your virtues continue to increase by the day!"

The faerie had returned from his appointment; in his arms, he held a small bundle which even then began to cry.

Chapter Sixteen

"And what virtue is that?" Abigail demanded loudly. "We're just twistin' and untwistin' a bunch of hemp!" The little girl nudged at Dora with her foot, clearly intending that she and Theodora should sneak their way to the other end of the table.

Lord Hollowvale did not seem at all fazed by this belligerent response. He smiled patronisingly. "Hard work and suffering will improve your virtue," he told Abigail. "You do not realise it because you are low-born and prone to laziness. But I was born to a higher station, and so I know what is best for you."

"Accordin' to *who?*" Abigail asked, and she now seemed genuinely flustered.

"Why, according to the English!" Lord Hollowvale said. "Is that not why you were put in a workhouse in the first place? But I can increase your virtue even faster here at Charity House, for you need not even sleep!" Another soft whimper came from the bundle in his arms, and he shifted it absently onto his shoulder. "I do not expect you to thank me, of course, since you are low-born. But generosity should be given without expectation of gratitude, and I must improve my own virtue as much as I can!"

Dora and Theodora crept their way breathlessly towards the other end of the table as he spoke, hiding behind the other children's feet.

"You're mad!" Abigail declared.

"Oh, maybe so," laughed the marquess. "But if I am, then all your nobles and your king must be mad as well!"

"The king *is* mad, though," Theodora muttered under her breath. Her face was red and furious. Dora quickly brought her finger to her lips, though she didn't dare to shush her other half. *She is too emotional*, Dora thought. *We must get out of here before she loses control.*

"On that note," Lord Hollowvale mused, "I have bought a brand-new inmate! The price was very dear – Master Ricks assures me that it is difficult to come by newborns – but now I realise that I do not know what to do with it. How *does* one increase a newborn baby's virtue? Perhaps it must be taught to be quieter and less needy?" His steps approached the table.

Oh no. It couldn't possibly be, could it?

But the baby in Lord Hollowvale's arms cried again, and Dora knew with certainty that George Ricks had sold the faerie the very same unwanted child whose mother he had tried to leave out on the street before.

Theodora's mouth dropped open. Her mismatched eyes blazed with unspeakable anger. Dora knew that it was really *her* anger, but she also knew that it was likely to get them both into terrible trouble.

Dora reached out to press her palms firmly to either side of Theodora's face. Slowly, she shook her head and focused keenly on that faint connection between them. *Patience*, she thought. *We have to be patient. Both George Ricks and that awful faerie will pay, but we cannot confront Lord Hollowvale now.*

Theodora clenched her fists and gritted her teeth. Dora could tell that she was struggling to control herself in much the same way that Dora sometimes struggled to focus on the matter at hand. But something about Dora's physical presence must have helped – because Theodora began to breathe in and out very carefully, and she closed her eyes and started counting to ten in French.

Lord Hollowvale's steps began to take him closer to their side of the table.

"I'll take the kid!" Abigail blurted out.

Lord Hollowvale's steps paused. "Whatever do you mean?" he asked curiously.

"I'll teach 'em virtue and such," Abigail said. "Stayin' quiet, smilin' at strangers. That's hard work, so it'll make me better too, right?"

The marquess considered this for a long moment.

"What an idea!" Abigail laughed nervously. "Me, proposin' nice things. Guess all this hemp pickin' really is workin' on my soul, isn't it?"

"How delightful!" Lord Hollowvale said finally. And he *did* sound delighted this time. "Yes, your charity becomes you, little girl! I knew that all my efforts were not in vain."

He snapped his fingers, and Abigail's hands stopped their work. She blinked down at them in bewilderment, even as the faerie placed the crying bundle into her little arms.

Abigail quickly shushed at the baby, rocking it in her arms. The motion did little to calm the poor thing, but Dora thought that the newborn must have at least been more comforted in the arms of a human than being carried by a mad faerie.

"Since you have the creature well in hand, I must be off," Lord Hollowvale said. "I have my own daughter with which to deal."

He turned on his feet and strode back for the entrance. As the door closed behind him once more, Theodora let out a ferocious hiss.

"I hate that creature!" she said. "I hate, hate, hate him! Stealing babies, now, what *won't* he do?"

Dora pushed back up to her feet. "The marquess did not steal the baby," she sighed. "I fear that he bought it. As awful as he is, all of his evils would not have been possible without Englishmen willing to indulge him."

Theodora hesitated. ". . . and Englishwomen, too," she said slowly. "Isn't that right?"

Dora didn't need to parse Theodora's meaning. It was *her* thought, after all.

"Mother sold me," Dora said softly. "I think that she must have regretted it eventually. But that is not the greatest comfort in the world." A dull sadness settled into her chest.

Tears gathered in Theodora's eyes – but this time, she wiped at them and pressed her lips together. "Nevertheless," she said. "We must undo what we can of this. If you need a washing tub for whatever you are doing, then we will find one for you."

Dora glanced towards Abigail, who was staring down at the newborn in her arms in abject confusion.

"Thank you for holding off the marquess for us," Dora told her. And now she *did* reach out to hug the little girl gently, careful of the baby between them. "I will not give up until you are home, I promise."

Abigail smiled ruefully at that. There was a chip off of one of her front teeth. "Closest thing I've got to home is with Master Ricks," she said. "And isn't he the one that sold me off?"

Dora set her jaw. "George Ricks will not see you again," she said. "You are sleeping in a clean, cosy bed, with a lovely woman named Mrs Dun looking in on you. I cannot believe that Elias would send you back to the workhouse after going to so much trouble to save you. But if he does, then . . . then we will find you a new home."

Abigail shrugged, and Dora knew that the little girl didn't believe her. But Lord Hollowvale had to be searching for her and Theodora even now, and there was no time to insist. Dora released the little girl again reluctantly.

Dora had visited the laundry room once or twice with Miss Jennings – the way there was the same as it had been in the Cleveland Street Workhouse. As she and Theodora descended the stairs, the scent of lye grew overwhelming, and they both began to cough.

The tubs downstairs were full of fresh, soapy water, though there was no laundry to do and no one there to perform the washing. Perhaps, Dora thought, Lord Hollowvale had simply wished to recreate the atmosphere of a real, true workhouse as closely as he was able.

Pale, wavery light streamed into the semi-basement from barred windows near the top of the walls, barely bright enough to light their way. Dora headed to the tub closest to one of those windows and settled down onto her knees before it.

"This is far from ideal," she sighed, as she looked into the soapy water. But she could see a faint, distorted reflection in the water nonetheless, and Dora knew that it was the closest she was going to find to a proper mirror on such short notice. "It will simply have to do."

"You'll be able to talk to Elias this way?" Theodora asked urgently.

"I don't know," Dora admitted. "He has wards against such intrusions, and I have never found my way past them before. I was thinking that I might scry on *myself* and hope that he is nearby, but I'm not certain if that would allow me to speak to him in the same way."

"Well, we surely do not have much time," Theodora said. "Do your best, and I shall watch at the door."

Dora looked back down into the soapy water and tried to concentrate. It was harder than ever before – even the vanity mirror in her room at Hayworth House had been more yielding. But with Theodora nearby, it was a simpler matter to imagine herself in detail, only with shorter hair and less emotion on her face. Surely, Dora thought, she would be asleep somewhere, with her hair down.

The image slipped away, again and again. Having both her halves in faerie at once was helping, Dora thought, but the soapy water was a miserable substitute for a helpfully enchanted mirror. Still . . . after a few careful tries, she began to see black tendrils in the water, bleeding in at the edges. Slowly, a familiar image asserted itself before her: a sunny, upstairs room with two small, clean beds.

Jane – or rather, *Abigail* – still slept in the far bed, though her body looked more pale and haggard than ever. Dora saw herself tucked into the other bed. Compared to Abigail, Dora looked as though she had just gone to sleep for a midday nap; her face was arranged in peaceful repose.

If anything, the man who had settled himself into the chair next to Dora looked far worse than she did. Elias's face was worn and drawn, and he had great black circles beneath his eyes. He was holding Dora's hand in his, but he must have fallen asleep in spite of himself; he was slumped in a terribly uncomfortable-looking position in the chair.

The sight of him sent a confused relief through Dora. Simply seeing Elias again was a kind of proof that she had not dreamed him up. But the idea that Dora had now contributed to his grief with her foolishness made her sad.

Dora took a few steps closer and reached out to brush one of those wild, white-blond locks of hair from his face. Her fingers passed right through him, of course, and she sighed.

"Elias?" she whispered softly. "Can you hear me? You must wake up. You would be very upset with yourself if you did not wake up right now."

His eyes slitted open blearily, and Dora's heart jumped in her chest. "This is why I never give anyone a key to my room," Elias mumbled. "Curse you, what hour is it . . . ?"

"Elias, you must listen to me," Dora told him sternly. "I have been stuck in Hollowvale, along with my other half. The marquess has been buying children from the workhouse masters – from George Ricks, for certain, but probably from the others, as well. I have seen Jane in Hollowvale too, though her name is really Abigail."

Elias blinked a few times, and Dora saw his golden eyes begin to clear of sleep. "Dora?" he murmured. He sat up sharply, now fully awake. He reached out for her with his hand, but the gesture went through her just as her fingers had done with him before. His brow knit, and he looked back towards Dora's body, which was still asleep in the bed next to him.

A wash of emotion played over his face, so immediate and intense that Dora could not make heads or tails of it. "I'm not going mad," Elias said hoarsely. "You're here. I thought . . . with the plague . . ." He couldn't seem to bring himself to finish the thought aloud. Exhausted tears threatened at his eyes.

Dora looked down. "I thought as much," she said softly. "I heard you talking, at least a little bit. I would have said something sooner, but it has been very difficult to find a mirror."

Elias reached out for her again from instinct, but Dora was still less solid than he was. He glanced towards her sleeping body, then shoved violently to his feet, reaching into his jacket to pull the same glass wand he had used to make the stars in the ballroom. As he passed the wand over Dora, a fresh heat came over her, and she shivered. For just a moment, she thought she could feel the bedsheets against her skin, and the pillow against her cheek.

The sensations of the bed disappeared almost immediately, however. The heat drained away like water through a sieve. Elias hissed out a soft curse to himself and ran his hands back through his tangled hair.

"The marquess has bound you to him instead of to your body," he said. "I do not think that I can put you back until I sever that connection."

Dora nodded patiently, though the revelation was greatly disappointing. She had hoped that finding Elias would solve everything at once, but that was clearly not the case.

Even as she finished the thought, a strange weakness began to overcome her. Dora sat down quickly on the side of the bed next to her body.

"Oh dear," she murmured. "So I am bound to Hollowvale now, just like my other half. It might not be safe for me to stay for too long, lest I fade away entirely."

Elias stowed his glass wand again. His eyes flashed in alarm, and again he moved his hand to steady Dora – but the gesture was still useless, however well-intentioned it might be. He let out a frustrated growl.

"Faerie," Elias muttered incredulously. "You have been in *faerie*. And all the others too. No wonder I have not been able to cure you, since you aren't even here to be cured!" He kicked at the chair next to him. "I'll kill that damned creature, see if I don't!"

Dora blinked. "But you never go to faerie," she said. "I was going to ask if you could draw us back from here, or ask your advice on escaping. I didn't mean to imply that you should—"

"Of course I am coming for you!" Elias told her hotly. His gold eyes burned at her. "I have tried everything, Dora. *Everything*. When I had no ideas left, I even *prayed*, for God's sake. You have slept for a full day and a half since your cousin found you, and I have counted every awful second of it!"

Dora found herself momentarily speechless. There was something intimidating about Elias's fury, but she could not quite bring herself to be afraid given that so much of it was on her behalf.

". . . everything?" Dora asked, before she could stop herself. Elias froze.

"Did you try *every* potential cure from the treatise I translated?" Dora asked him. "One of the few applicable bits for sleeping curses was true love's kiss, if I recall."

A bright flush spread along Elias's cheeks. "I did say everything," he muttered. "Useless as it all was."

Dora smiled. "I do not think that true love's kiss can bring a soul back from faerie," she said. "But even if it could, you would have to love me, Elias."

Dora had expected him to snap at her over the ridiculousness of the idea. But there was an odd silence instead – and the longer it went on, the more her heart began to turn over in her chest.

"I will bring you back," Elias said finally, in a far more subdued tone. He seemed suddenly unable to meet her eyes. "You and all the rest of the children. It's clearly within the scope of my duties now either way, so there's no use complaining at me."

"Oh," said Dora. She smiled dimly. "I am in love with *you*, just so you know. I had some trouble realising it, because I did not think that I could fall in love at all. But I am quite certain of it now."

Elias looked up at her with such a shocked expression that Dora immediately knew she had said something unconventional again. She pressed her lips together. "I see," she sighed. "People do not normally say that, I suppose. You must pretend that I was much more elegant and indirect about the matter."

Elias swallowed. "You are perfect as you are, Dora," he said softly. "And . . . and there are things which I should tell you—"

What he meant to tell her, however, Dora did not have the chance to find out. For she felt a cold hand on her shoulder, and the feeling of being pulled sharply back from a great distance.

"My wayward daughter," Lord Hollowvale sighed at her, as she opened her eyes back in the laundry room at Charity House. "This half of you is even more belligerent than the first!" His pale blue eyes looked down at her with recrimination. "Clearly, we must put you back together soon."

Chapter Seventeen

ora looked around for Theodora. She found her other
half just past Lord Hollowvale, staring blankly into the
distance. Her hair was tussled and her dress torn, and Dora
knew that Theodora had tried to fight the faerie off.

"You have agitated yourself, dear," Lord Hollowvale said
lightly. "In the most literal way, I fear. You were so well-behaved
until you showed up!"

Dora stared at him calmly. Logic would not get her anywhere,
she thought, unless she played along somewhat with the creature's own delusions. "I am Lord Lockheed's ward," Dora told
him. "And he put me into the care of my aunt. It is only virtuous
that I do my best to return to her."

Lord Hollowvale frowned at that. "I see your error," he said.
"But Lord Lockheed is *not* your caretaker, Theodora. Your mother
made me your guardian, and I take that duty quite seriously."

Dora smiled at him. "But you have no paperwork to that
effect?" she asked. "How must I believe you, then?"

The marquess drew himself up in a cold fury, and Dora
realised that she had misstepped. "You are fortunate to be my
daughter," he informed her in a chill tone. "For I would be
otherwise obliged to avenge such a slight to my honour. I am
the Marquess of Hollowvale, and I would not tell a lie even if
it were in my power to do so!"

The cold power that he held pressed down upon Dora like a smothering blanket, chilling her bones and crawling through her veins. Her knees buckled, and she managed only barely to keep herself upright.

"I am sorry," Dora gasped out. "I should have known better, of course. You are generous not to punish me for my error."

The marquess frowned at that. The overwhelming power that hovered in the air around him receded slowly. Eventually, Dora managed to catch her breath.

"It is true," Lord Hollowvale said. "I am the *most* generous of any faerie lord that you shall ever meet."

"You are, of course," Dora said. And for the moment, it was true – for she had never met any other faerie lord in her life, and so Lord Hollowvale was by necessity the most generous of them.

The marquess continued to frown at her, and Dora found herself shrinking beneath his pale gaze. Eventually, he spoke again. "I do not like having two daughters," he said. "One was the very perfect amount. I must find a way to put you back together with yourself, or else I shall be obliged to remove one of you."

Dora swallowed slowly. "I would be pleased to be a single person again, my lord," she said carefully.

Lord Hollowvale snapped his fingers, and Theodora came back to herself with a start. "Dora!" she gasped. "Lord Hollowvale is—"

"Yes, so I see," Dora replied evenly. "He was just now observing that we would be better as a single person." Dora knew that she needed to change the subject, lest Theodora become overwrought again and trigger one of the faerie's mercurial moods.

"But *how* to put you back together?" Lord Hollowvale mused. He looked them both over, and Dora got the distinct impression that he was looking at something she could not see herself. "Ah!"

he exclaimed. "Yes, there is something tying you together still. A trickle of emotion. If I were to stimulate *that*, then perhaps you would come together naturally." He beamed at his own genius. "I must simply make you very emotional while you are near to yourself, Theodora!"

Dora saw the terrible thoughts already whirling in his head. She knew suddenly that she needed to say something before the mad faerie decided to torture her for her own good. "A party!" she said quickly. "The last time I felt a very strong emotion was at a party, dancing with a handsome man. And it is the season for balls in London right now, so you really must have one."

Lord Hollowvale nodded sagely at this, as though he had been about to suggest the very same thing – though Dora was quite certain that his mind had been trending in a much darker direction. "A fantastic ball!" he said. "Yes, that is the only reasonable answer. I shall throw such a party as would make the *ton* unbearably jealous!"

He turned for the laundry room's exit, clearly expecting that the two of them should follow. Dora did not feel optimistic that disobeying him again so soon would do her any good, and so she went after him, gesturing for Theodora to do the same.

Neither of them dared to look at Abigail as they headed out of the mess hall. But Dora reached out to squeeze the little girl's shoulder as they passed.

All of us will find a way out of here, Dora thought with determination.

***

As Dora had hoped, the marquess wasted little time haring off to plan his perfect English ball. Unfortunately, he did not make the mistake of leaving Dora to her own devices for a second time. Instead, she found herself dragged away from Theodora and put into the care of a faerie tutor in etiquette – "to perfect your skill for the ball, of course!" Lord Hollowvale told her cheerfully.

To Dora's great surprise, the tutor – an unnaturally tall elfin woman with eyes of purest coal – was introduced to her as the Baroness of Mourningwood. Dora recognised the title, though it took her a few minutes to remember from where; it eventually occurred to her that she had seen Lady Mourningwood listed in the peerage of faeries which she had perused at the magic shop. "Surely a baroness must be too busy to teach me how to behave at a ball," Dora protested to the faeric woman. "And I have been to many so far, so my manners must be tolerable, at least."

"Tolerable will not do for Lord Hollowvale's daughter," Lady Mourningwood informed her in a voice like a deep, dark well. Her black eyes bore into Dora discomfortingly. "You are only human, of course, and so we must make do with you."

Lady Mourningwood first instructed Dora on the importance of supper. She was to eat the dishes in precisely the correct order. Furthermore, said Lady Mourningwood, Dora must always keep one eye on Lord Hollowvale himself, and drink a sip of her wine whenever he raised his own glass to his lips, or else she might be forced to leave the ball in shame.

"And if you look at one of the servants," said Lady Mourningwood, "you must be sure to scowl at them, just so." Her features took on an expression of faint disgust, as though she had eaten something which disagreed with her.

Dora tried to mimic the baroness, but she was very bad at showing any emotion at all, and she knew that she probably looked faintly puzzled instead.

Dora was not certain just how long her lessons went on. Time seemed to be of no particular consequence in the Hollow House. It occurred to her belatedly that she could not possibly have been there for more than a few hours before scrying upon her sleeping body – and yet Elias had said that a full day and a half had passed.

That is no good, Dora thought warily. *For all I know, my funeral might be any moment.* But there was no way for her to know what day it was in England, and no way for her to escape Lady Mourningwood's doom-filled gaze, and so she resigned herself to trying to seem obedient for the moment.

Eventually, the baroness brought Dora into another room of the Hollow House and told her to stand very still and close her eyes. "Since you cannot seem to use the proper expression with servants," Lady Mourningwood said, "you must not look at them at all."

A soft skittering noise surrounded Dora, and she frowned to herself, unnerved. "Am I allowed to inquire as to what they are, and what we are doing here?" she asked the baroness.

"They are brownies," Lady Mourningwood informed her. "And they shall be dressing you for the ball." She clucked her tongue at something which Dora could not see, and turned to address the faeries that surrounded them. "We will not be making her a gown from moonlight, you cretins!" the baroness said sternly. "That has not been popular since last week at least! Do you want Lord Hollowvale's daughter to be laughed from his own ballroom? Today's style is to be clad in forgotten memories!"

Dora really did want to open her eyes at that, but she stopped herself just in time. She did not want to learn what sort of punishments a faerie called Mourningwood might perpetrate upon her for ignoring instructions.

Dora was expecting the brownies to take her measure as the woman at the dress shop in London had done. But instead, while they continued to skitter about, she felt a light whisper against her skin as the gown was woven *around* her. Each touch of the strange material seemed to come with a distant, absent memory, so that Dora was quickly overwhelmed by the whole of it.

There was the scent of fresh-baked bread, wafting over a

summer breeze; the taste of bland, boring gruel, served over and over again; the sigh of a gentleman asking a lady to dance. The rain drizzled outside yet again, and a priest droned on about which biblical figure begat which *other* biblical figure for what seemed like ages on end.

"*I have been so silly, my little Theodora,*" a woman whispered softly. "*I thought I needed money in order to marry the man I loved. But now I have you, and I know the awfulness of what I have done.*"

The memory passed in such a blur that Dora nearly missed it among the others. She tried to find it again, but it was lost among the rest of the gown. *I am sure that was my mother*, Dora thought. Had that been Dora's own forgotten memory from when she was very young?

"*I do not believe in such a thing as love,*" Elias scoffed. "*Perhaps attraction, or companionship, or friendship. But so many men act as though love is a special sort of magic. I feel that I am qualified to say it isn't so.*"

"*Well, but you have just described love, I think,*" Albert replied in bemusement. "*Attraction and companionship and friendship. Is there nothing special about those things, especially if they are all together at once?*"

The sound of the faerie servants ceased, and Lady Mourningwood instructed Dora to open her eyes. She glanced down and saw a dress of tattered grey gossamer that shimmered in the misty light of the window. The gown was more unnerving than it was beautiful – but there was still something rare about it that made it seem more dignified than its ragged layers should have suggested.

As Dora looked over the dress, the baroness draped a long strand of oily, iridescent pearls around her neck. They felt unnaturally chill against Dora's skin, and she shivered. "Er," she said. "Are these normal pearls?"

"Heavens no," Lady Mourningwood said evenly. "These are

children's tears. They are a bit common, I suppose, but we have
them in special abundance here due to Charity House."

Dora's stomach twisted. She had to fight the instinct to tear
the pearls from her neck. "I see," she said instead, unable to
formulate anything more polite in the moment. "Could I perhaps
look at myself in a mirror? I would like to know that I am
properly dressed."

Lady Mourningwood shook her head in displeasure. "Mirrors
are a dangerous thing in faerie," she said. "They are not for
looking at oneself."

But that is exactly what mirrors are for, Dora thought. She
kept the words to herself, though, and changed her tack. "Then
perhaps I might see Theodora—"

The door behind them opened, interrupting her, and Dora
heard the distinctive uneven click-clack of Lord Hollowvale's
cane against the floor.

"Marvellous!" said the marquess. "You are ready, then. We
must go to the ball so that you may be happier than ever before."

Dora glanced back towards him with faint alarm. "Already?"
she asked. "But a proper ball takes weeks to prepare, back in
London."

Lord Hollowvale laughed. "Ah, back in London perhaps!" he
said. "But in faerie, balls happen all of the time, whenever we
please!" He offered out an arm towards Dora, as though to escort
her. She did not dare refuse – but something shivered inside her
as she placed her hand on his sleeve. As she did, she noticed
that Lord Hollowvale was now wearing at least one more jacket
than he had been wearing before.

"How *many* jackets are you wearing?" Dora asked him, before
she could stop herself.

"Five in total!" the marquess beamed, clearly pleased that she
had noticed. "One in each of the latest styles, you know. I have it
on very good authority that wealth improves a man's virtue, especially if it is visible – and they are all quite obviously expensive."

"Oh," Dora managed. "Then you must be very virtuous indeed."

"Everyone agrees as much," Lord Hollowvale said cheerfully.

"Wealth does not improve a lady's virtue, of course," Lady Mourningwood informed Dora from her other side, as they headed out into the halls of the Hollow House. "But a good chaperone is essential to her reputation. Naturally, I will be your chaperone – and if you look any men in the eyes, I shall be sure to pluck your own eyes from your head in turn."

Lord Hollowvale nodded in approval at this as though it were completely normal. "Lady Mourningwood is the very best of chaperones," he said. "None would dare to impugn her honour!"

How on earth has Theodora managed to stay in one piece for so long? Dora thought. *I would close my eyes for the entire ball, except that I must be sure to sip my wine whenever Lord Hollowvale does.*

Dora had not seen the ballroom before, but it was every bit as ridiculous as she might have expected of a faerie's residence. A great domed ceiling rose above the impossibly sized room, which was surely as large as five of Lady Cushing's ballrooms all put together. The floors were an uncanny black and white marble that looked more like a chess board than a dance floor. White candles burned upon every surface with an eerie blue light which reminded Dora of the lantern that Elias had carried at Carroway House.

There were tables of finger food set up along the walls, with bizarre centrepieces on display. One of them had what looked like a single black Hessian boot covered with impressive ribbons – Lord Hollowvale proudly told Dora that this was one of Lord Wellington's very own boots. Another had a very large porcelain gravy bowl which he said had once belonged to Queen Elizabeth, and one had an actual pillory, prominently surrounded by a whole pile of pineapples – this one, he said, had once been used in the Tower of London. There was no rhyme or reason to any of it, but the faerie seemed inordinately pleased with every display regardless.

Phantom strings floated upon the air, but Dora could not see any orchestra, nor any dancers or attendees. She frowned dimly. "Has the ball not started yet?" she asked Lord Hollowvale next to her.

"Of course it has started!" the marquess replied with enthusiasm. "But you have not been formally introduced to any of the attendees. It would not do for you to see them until you have formally made their acquaintance."

Some unseen person stepped on Dora's foot then, and she jerked back abruptly, blinking. "You mean to say that the entire room is invisible to me?" she asked in puzzlement. "But I shall be running into people by mistake all evening!"

"A small price to pay for the sake of propriety, of course," Lady Mourningwood said with absolute seriousness.

Dora caught sight of Theodora heading into the room from the other side then, on the arm of some invisible person. She wanted to go over so that she could cling to her own company at least, but Lord Hollowvale directed her instead towards the dance floor. "I will have your first dance," he told her. "But I am sure that there are many handsome elves who shall wish to have your acquaintance soon enough."

The dance that he performed was far from anything that Dora had ever learned in England, and she struggled to follow his lead. It was something like a minuet, but there seemed to be another dignified bow every few steps, so that it was barely a dance at all.

But the worst part by far was when Lord Hollowvale switched partners in the middle. Dora found herself trying to dance with some invisible faerie, unaware even of the make-up of the crowd. There was absolutely no use to it – someone bumped into her every other second, and she found herself reflexively apologising with each new misstep.

Dora was only too relieved when the music finally changed, signalling a brand-new dance. She tried to stumble her way towards a chair near the wall, but Lady Mourningwood caught her by the arm instead and marched her towards an unseen elven gentleman. "This is Miss Theodora, Lord Hollowvale's English daughter," the baroness informed the air in front of them. "Miss Theodora, this is the viscount, Lord Blackthorn."

The air in front of Dora rippled – and then there was a tall, lithe figure standing before her. Lord Blackthorn was an elf of long fingers and very pale skin. He was dressed in a very fine black velvet jacket, and he had a long, winding rose vine twined about his body which blossomed into a single yellow rose at his throat. His posture had a cheerful cast to it, but Dora remembered just in time to look down at her feet before she could catch sight of his eyes; she had no doubt that Lady Mourningwood would make good on her promise to remove her eyes if she slipped up and met the elf's gaze.

"How charming!" Lord Blackthorn enthused in a melodic voice. "Oh, she is very pretty for a human! And what a lovely gown of forgotten memories!"

"You must not be so free with your compliments, Lord Blackthorn," Lady Mourningwood said severely. "The English generally talk about the weather instead."

"Oh yes, where is my mind at?" Lord Blackthorn agreed cheerfully. "It is very misty out, is it not, Miss Theodora?"

"Is it not always misty in Hollowvale?" Dora asked distantly.

"It is!" Lord Blackthorn said, in exactly the same enthusiastic tone of voice. "Oh, you are very good at English conversation, Miss Theodora. I suppose it is to be expected." He offered out his gloved hand. "May I have this dance with you?"

"You may," Lady Mourningwood told him, before Dora could open her mouth to respond. "But you must bring Miss Theodora right back to me when you are done, or else you will be obliged to marry her."

"Oh yes, of course," Lord Blackthorn said, as though there were nothing strange about this at all. "I do love these authentic English balls. Their etiquette is so delightfully odd!"

"That is not how English etiquette works at all," Dora said. But Lord Blackthorn took her by the hand and led her back out onto the dance floor, and she sighed heavily.

"The weather is still quite misty," Lord Blackthorn told her helpfully, as they bowed to one another in that endlessly tedious sequence.

"Yes," Dora told him. "You have said as much already."

"It would be nicer if it were sunny, perhaps," Lord Blackthorn said, and they bowed to each other yet again. "Do you like sunny weather, Miss Theodora?"

"English people *do* speak of more than just the weather," Dora told him flatly.

"Do they?" Lord Blackthorn asked curiously. "Well what else *do* they talk about?"

Dora thought back on all the garden parties and balls that she had attended over the years. She was embarrassed to realise that indeed, nearly half of her interactions with strangers had been about the weather after all. Thankfully, she had many other interactions to call upon. "If one were to breed a dolphin with a horse," Dora said ponderously, "would the resulting creature have a dolphin's head and a horse's end, or would it be the other way around?"

"Oh!" Lord Blackthorn said. "Well, clearly the creature would have a dolphin's head. For dolphins must stay in the ocean, and horses are very terrible at holding their breath."

"That is a more sensible answer than I was expecting," Dora admitted to him. She bowed a bit more deeply this time. "It is another English tradition to trade information about one's culture," she lied. "I will answer another of your questions about England if you will answer me one question about faerie in return."

"How novel!" Lord Blackthorn said. "Yes, of course. Then

let me ask you, Miss Theodora: who do *you* consider to be the most virtuous person in all of England?"

Dora blinked at that. "I . . . I have never thought about it before," she admitted. "I suppose that it would be most proper for me to say it is the king, or the Prince Regent, or some figure who is otherwise above reproach, like the Duke of Wellington."

"Ah," said Lord Blackthorn. "But that is not what I asked at all! Lord Hollowvale keeps going on and on about his English virtue, you see, but I find myself wondering just who it is that *you* consider to be most virtuous."

Dora pressed her lips together. She probably could have lied again, and the faerie would not have known the difference. But the question *had* made her think, and she found herself startled by the answer that suddenly came to mind.

"I think that it is the Lord Sorcier," Dora said.

Lord Blackthorn made a thoughtful "hm" at that answer. "I thought that only France had a Lord Sorcier," he said.

"There is an English one now as well," said Dora. "And yes, I . . . I think that he is the most virtuous man that I have met." She found herself unaccountably shy on the words.

"But why is that?" Lord Blackthorn asked. "What makes him virtuous?"

Dora smiled distantly at her feet. "I think that he is virtuous because he is kind to the powerless and cruel to the powerful," she said.

"But is he wealthy?" Lord Blackthorn asked curiously. "Does he have five jackets like Lord Hollowvale, or a manor full of servants?"

"I do not think that he is wealthy," Dora said. "In fact, I suspect that he has given away most of his money."

"How puzzling!" Lord Blackthorn said. "I was sure that money had something to do with English virtue. All of the most respected men in England become even better respected as they gain more money, do they not?"

"They do," Dora admitted. "But respect is not equivalent to virtue. And you specifically asked me whom it was that *I* believed to be most virtuous in England."

"So I did," Lord Blackthorn mused. "And what a confusing answer. But now you must ask me *your* question, Miss Theodora."

Dora paused long enough to circle the tall faerie and bow to him again, as she phrased her question very carefully in her mind. "I would like to know all of the most reasonable ways for a mortal to defeat a powerful faerie," she said.

She was expecting Lord Blackthorn to be offended at this – but he laughed instead, as though they were playing a game. "Oh, but that is simple!" he said. "Iron is always best – for it will end our magic in a hurry, and it is terrible poison to us. If you do not have iron, then powerful magic might do, though most of us are far more practised than even the greatest of mortal magicians." He considered for a moment longer, then added, "Some mortals have managed to defeat us through trickery and careful wording, but we almost always get the better end of every deal we make."

Dora smiled vaguely at that. "How interesting," she said. "I have so many more questions about faerie. Would you like to exchange another set of queries?"

"I would love to!" Lord Blackthorn declared. "But alas – the dance is close to ending, and I must return you to your chaperone, or else we must get married."

Dora hid a sigh as the viscount led her back towards Lady Mourningwood. The dark-eyed faerie woman took her by the arm again and turned towards another man – but this time, Dora was surprised to realise that she could *already* see him. She did not dare to look up at the faerie gentleman, but she saw that his boots were more worn than Lord Blackthorn's had been. *Whoever it is*, Dora thought, *we have already been introduced somehow.*

"This is Miss Theodora, Lord Hollowvale's English daughter," the baroness said again. "Miss Theodora, this is the earl, Lord Longshadow."

"How charming," said Elias, in exactly the same tone that Lord Blackthorn had used before – and he offered out a hand. "May I have this dance, Miss Theodora?"

Chapter Eighteen

*I*t took all of Dora's willpower not to look up at Elias as he spoke. Thankfully, Lady Mourningwood replied as she had done before: "You may. But you must bring Miss Theodora right back to me when you are done, or else you will be obliged to marry her."

"How terrible," Elias said. "I shall keep the punishment in mind."

He took Dora by the hand, and some subtle tension she had been holding inside herself melted away in abject relief. Elias's hand was warm and familiar, and she was suddenly so glad to see him that a hint of real joy sparked inside her chest.

Elias led her out onto the floor, and Dora took a deep breath. "I will find it difficult to follow your lead," she told him. "I cannot see anyone here unless I have been formally introduced to them. I would not even know if someone were listening over my shoulder." She tightened her fingers on his, hoping that Elias would understand the hint.

"I will keep us away from the others as much as I can, then," Elias murmured quietly. "And I shall hold your hand more tightly if someone should come too close." He squeezed her fingers once in demonstration, then loosened his grip again. "They have placed many silly rules upon this party, I am sure. Is that why you will not look at me?"

"Lady Mourningwood will pluck out my eyes if I look at a man directly," Dora told him evenly. "She is a very good chaperone, you see."

Elias let out a soft sound of disgust. "I thought it would be too soon if I ever attended one of these ridiculous balls again," he muttered. "Thankfully, faeries do not expect each other to lie. I am wearing Lord Longshadow's face right now, since it is one of the few that I know well. I claimed to be him, and they let me right through the door."

"So you are *not* Lord Longshadow," Dora said. "I wondered for a moment, I admit."

"I am not," Elias said in a low voice. "I have no title. I killed my father, and so I might have inherited his – but I left faerie, and someone else claimed it in my place."

"You *killed*—" Elias squeezed her hand, and Dora cut herself off abruptly. He took them a few long paces forward, and his fingers loosened again.

"It is a common method of inheritance in faerie," Elias said, and there was a sadness in his voice now. "I did not *want* to kill him. But he left me rather no choice in the matter. His successor would not be happy to see me return, in case I should decide to overthrow him as well."

They bowed to one another again, and Elias shook his head. "There are even more bows to this dance since I was last here," he added, and Dora knew that he was hoping she would drop the subject.

Dora was beginning to feel oddly dizzy, though she had done little for the last few minutes other than walk and bow. She caught sight of Theodora on the other side of the room, dancing with an invisible partner – her other half seemed similarly off-balance, and she sucked in her breath.

"Lord Hollowvale believes that I will come back together with my other half if we are in the same room and I am very emotional," Dora said. "I think that he was right. I am growing faint. The children are in Charity House, across the gardens from here. I asked Lord Blackthorn how one might go about defeating a faerie – he told me that iron, magic and trickery are best. We do not have any iron, and Lord Hollowvale's magic is very powerful indeed, so perhaps trickery— "

Elias pulled something from his jacket pocket then and slipped it into Dora's hand. His fingers shook as he did so . . . and she knew before looking down just what it was she would see.

"My scissors," Dora whispered. "You brought them all the way here?"

"Iron is very powerful against faeries and their spells," Elias said. "Even more so when it has tasted their blood once before. Lord Hollowvale has attached you and the children to himself with strings of fate – I can just barely see them myself. If you cut those strings, you should all return to your proper bodies. He will notice what is happening immediately, which is why I will distract him while you work."

Dora pressed her lips together. "That sounds very dangerous for you," she said. "And what will happen to the children whose bodies have already died, Elias? They have nowhere to return to." The thought struck Dora with another wave of awful worry, and she had to lean heavily upon his arm.

"They will go wherever it is they were meant to go when they died," Elias said quietly. His hand hovered at her back. "I do not like it either, Dora. But it is better than being trapped here for an eternity, unable to move on."

Tears pricked at her eyes. For an instant, Dora felt more like Theodora than she did herself – overwhelmed by a riot of confusing emotions all at once. "I do not want something terrible to happen to them – or to you," she said. "There must be some other way."

Elias reached up to brush his thumb over her cheek. "There is only so much time," he said softly. "And I will not let you die. You once told me that your cousin was a warm lantern to you,

Dora. I know what you mean by that now. Of all things, you have become my lantern too – and I cannot bring myself to let you go out."

Dora's heart twisted in her chest. She wavered on her feet, and this time Elias had to catch her entirely before she could hit the floor. More than ever, she wished that she could look into his eyes. But he drew a bit of glittering dust from his jacket pocket and breathed it over her head – and suddenly she saw a hundred blurry silhouettes surrounding them, each in the dim shape of another faerie noble.

Footsteps came quickly towards them, and Dora heard Lady Mourningwood's stern voice. "You must give her back to me immediately," the baroness said. "The dance is over, Lord Longshadow."

"I must not," said Elias whimsically. "You said that I must give her back promptly or *else* I should be forced to marry her. I choose the latter option, Lady Mourningwood."

Dora blinked in confusion.

Shocked gasps went through the dark shadows surrounding them. Lady Mourningwood stared at Elias, uncomprehending. "But that is not done," she said. "No one ever chooses the latter option."

"Then why give two options at all?" Elias asked mildly. "Surely you did not lie to me when you offered them both."

This stymied the baroness as nothing else had managed to do yet. She stood there for a moment in consternation – but eventually, Lord Hollowvale approached with his brow knitted.

"What is the meaning of this?" the marquess demanded. "Why will you not release my daughter, Lord Longshadow?"

"I was told that I must marry her," Elias said cheerfully. "And I now accept that fate."

"You do?" Dora mumbled at him dimly.

"Well, why shouldn't I?" Elias asked her. "I sent a letter to

Lord Lockheed asking for your hand in marriage a few days ago. I was quite reasonable about your dowry, and so he gave me his immediate consent. I meant to tell you earlier, but you disappeared before I could." His hand tightened at her waist. "I would ask if you are amenable to the idea yourself, but Lady Mourningwood was very clear on her ultimatum. And I do not intend to hand you back to her."

"Oh," said Dora, and she was suddenly so dizzy that she found it hard to breathe. "But I *am* amenable."

"But I am *not* amenable!" Lord Hollowvale declared furiously. "You may not marry my English daughter." He narrowed his pale blue eyes. "And you are not Lord Longshadow at all, are you? You do not sound like him in the least."

The marquess gestured violently at Elias, and Dora felt something snap in the air between them. Dora still could not look up at Elias, but she suspected that his disguise had been unceremoniously torn away.

"I am Elias Wilder, His Majesty's court magician and Lord Sorcier of England," Elias said in a grim tone. "You have stolen several citizens of England, and it is my duty to take them back from you."

"How dare you!" Lord Hollowvale said, and the air grew chilly with his power. "I have stolen nothing and no one! I have paid fairly for every English citizen that I have taken!"

"It is illegal to buy and sell human beings in England," Elias said. "It has been against the law since 1807, in fact."

"The creatures that I have bought do nothing here that they would not be doing in England!" Lord Hollowvale hissed stubbornly. "I have been nothing but charitable to the ungrateful wretches. You shall not come into my home and impugn my virtue, you mongrel changeling creature!"

"Oh!" Lord Blackthorn's voice rang out with amusement, and Dora saw him standing very close by within the crowd, with Theodora leaning faintly on his shoulder. "But Lord Hollowvale

– you are addressing the most virtuous man in all of England! I have heard it most reliably!"

This only made the marquess's face grow darker and more forbidding. "I do not believe it for a moment!" he said. "What a preposterous idea! Look at the sorry state of his boots! And he is wearing only one jacket, you see!"

Dora's other half was flickering in and out of view in a very strange way. Dora saw a frayed red thread extending between Theodora and herself, and she realised that whatever Elias had done to her sight, it had shown her more than just the invisible faeries around her. Even as Dora watched, the red thread began to strengthen and contract.

She glanced back towards Lord Hollowvale and saw more than a dozen red threads tied about his arms and fingers. *I must cut those threads*, Dora realised. *I cannot wait until I am whole again, or it will be too late.*

Dora forced herself to stand on her own two feet, though the effort was extreme. She clutched in her hand the leather sheath which Elias had given her, feeling the cold touch of the iron scissors against her palm.

Elias released her. "I suppose that we must duel then," he supplied helpfully. "For I intend to marry Dora and take her and those children home. And you must protect your honour, for I have accused you of the crime of slavery."

"How exciting!" Lord Blackthorn said. "I have always wanted to see an English duel. I shall play second for the Lord Sorcier, then!"

Lord Hollowvale's pale eyes flickered with rage. "I need no second," he declared. "For this duel will be over in only a moment."

Dora slipped her way back through the shadows of the crowd, trying to angle herself around Lord Hollowvale's back. There was a burst of arctic chill, and she ducked her head with a gasp. Frost crackled its way along the marble floor, curling in fanciful designs beneath her feet. Her slippers gave her little traction, and she was forced to drop to her knees to keep from falling on her face.

A hand grasped tightly at her arm, and Dora glanced back in surprise. Lady Mourningwood had followed to try and seize her; the baroness's coal-black eyes seethed with alien fury.

But Dora had begun to remember a hundred lessons with the awful faerie woman, and her emotions were now so keen that she could *feel* Theodora nearby, staggering to her feet. Her other half leapt forward onto Lady Mourningwood's back with a furious cry.

"I will tear out *your* eyes, you evil creature!" Theodora yelled.

Dora wrenched her arm free of the baroness, just as a hiss of blistering heat threw back the unnatural frost. It was the brilliant fire that Elias had wielded upon the battlefield in France – and as dreadful as the marquess's power was, Dora thought that the faerie had never dared to take on whole armies of men, nor had he fought through the sting of such terrible injuries as Elias had felt.

Perhaps Elias will win, Dora thought hopefully. *He has killed one faerie lord already, after all.*

She crawled her way free of the crowd, just behind Lord Hollowvale. The crimson strands that surrounded him were taut with power; Dora knew that it would take barely a snip from her scissors to set them loose. He would notice her then, of course, but he would have to turn his attention from the duel in order to do anything about it.

Dora pulled the cold iron scissors from their sheathe . . . but as she approached the first red strand, she found herself hesitating.

No, she thought sadly. *This will not do.*

You are right. She felt Theodora agree with her weakly. *We must be better than this, for everyone's sake.*

Dora lifted the scissors between both hands – and stabbed them down into Lord Hollowvale's back, just over his heart.

The faerie staggered forward in shock. Bright red blood began to dribble from the injury, much faster than Dora had anticipated. An awful nausea rose within her stomach, but she held onto the scissors and dug them in more deeply still.

The unnatural chill that had surrounded him began to fade. Dora looked up and met Elias's eyes for the first time since he had entered. There was a stricken expression on his face, and she wondered if he suspected the full consequences of what she had done.

"I am not well-versed in English duels," Lord Blackthorn observed. "But I am sure that young ladies are not supposed to stab the participants!"

Lord Hollowvale collapsed to the floor, clutching uselessly at his chest. Dora stared down at him with a mixture of grief and sadness and disgust at her own actions. Thick, sticky blood covered her hands, and the texture of it was very different from punch indeed.

"I did not agree to any duels," Dora said softly.

Lord Hollowvale stared up at her with trembling, blood-flecked lips. "I have . . . only ever . . . been charitable to you," he whispered.

Dora blinked back hideous tears. "I am sure that every evil man believes himself to be charitable," she told him. "In that respect, at least, you are a true Englishman."

The marquess shuddered once . . . and then went still.

Very slowly, his body began to dissipate into a calm, cold mist. The crimson strings that had attached themselves to him began to waver dangerously.

Theodora struggled towards Dora, staggering into her arms. "I have killed my father," Dora's other half declared to the gathering in a shaky voice. "From this point forward, you shall call me Lady Hollowvale!"

Theodora reached her hands into the mist and grasped at it with her fingers.

"Don't!" Elias said quickly. He leapt forward to try and stop her – but he was far too late.

The crimson strands that had been wavering before suddenly attached themselves to Theodora's arms and fingers. Her form, which had been halfway insubstantial, strengthened and solidified. Fearful power wove its way through her soul and crossed the strand that still connected her to Dora, who felt it like a cold, wet mist upon her heart.

Dora hit her knees with a gasp. The memories of Hollowvale and the bright, vivid emotions that had only just begun to bubble up within her were abruptly torn away again. The sharp fear and ugly horror at her own actions faded away into a dull, distant sadness.

"I will release your strand," Theodora said to Dora. Great tears trickled down her face, displaying the grief that Dora knew she truly felt. "And all of the children who still live. The others shall be loved and taken care of for as long as they desire to stay."

Dora nodded listlessly. "You have taken the harder path," she said softly. "Thank you."

"It is not so hard," Theodora said with a sob. "We are closer than ever. As long as you are content, I shall be happy too. So you must do your best on that score, please."

Elias hurried towards them both with horror still evident on his face. He grabbed at Dora, who was still covered in blood. "What have you done?" he whispered to her. "What have you done, Dora? You will never be whole again."

Dora smiled wanly at him. "You spent so long trying to save all those children," she said, "only to feel like you were killing them yourself. Neither of us could bear that thought. Just this once, you must let me help you, since it was in my power to do so." She met his eyes again. "This is my small evil to vanquish, Elias."

Dora became aware of the feeling of warm sunlight and cotton against her skin. Elias held her close, and she caught the brief scent of sweet myrrh – before her eyes opened once more, and she found herself in a bed at Mrs Dun's orphanage.

Chapter Nineteen

*ora was not alone.

"Miss Ettings! You're awake!" Albert's bewildered voice came from her left-hand side, where Elias had been sitting before. He reached out to help her sit upright. "Has Elias succeeded, then?"

Dora blinked slowly. She had a headache, and her stomach felt mostly empty, but she did not feel in terrible health otherwise. "He has," she said dimly. She glanced towards the other bed, where Abigail had begun to stir. "But you must help Abigail, please. She is probably far weaker than I am."

Albert hastened towards the girl's bed with a gasp. Abigail mumbled in confusion, but she accepted the water that he offered her and submitted tiredly to his check-up. Dora found some water of her own, then stumbled her way down the stairs towards the kitchen in her nightgown. There she found Mrs Dun, who was even now rocking a freshly woken newborn in her arms.

"Mrs Dun?" Dora asked calmly. "I don't mean to trouble you, but could we have a bit to eat when you are able?"

It was a good hour before the resulting furore died down at all. Dora found herself plied with plenty of food and liquids and then shoved unceremoniously back into bed "to rest".

"But I have already been sleeping, haven't I?" she asked.

"You have been sleeping without proper fuel," Albert told her seriously. "Now you must give your body a chance to use what you have given it." Abigail, for her part, had already fallen right back asleep, and Dora had to admit that there was some small amount of logic to the idea.

Whatever Albert's intentions, he was not to have his wish – for Vanessa showed up soon enough, and Dora's cousin insisted on seeing her immediately.

"Oh, you are well!" Vanessa sobbed, as she launched herself at Dora and dragged her into an embrace. "I was so worried, but they would not let me near you at all once they took you away!"

"Miss Ettings was under quarantine," Albert told Vanessa seriously. "It would hardly do for you to get engaged to my brother and then fall asleep for ever, Miss Vanessa."

"So you *are* engaged?" Dora asked distantly. "How wonderful, Vanessa. I hope I will be able to come to your wedding."

"Why shouldn't you be able to?" Vanessa asked, bewildered. "I wrote your invitation to the wedding feast first of all, Dora! Oh – don't tell Mother that: she will be upset that she was not first, I am sure."

Dora frowned. "The countess will not give me a room any more," she said. "And Auntie Frances would like me to return to the country, she said."

Vanessa gasped. "Those awful women!" she said – and it was such an uncharacteristic exclamation from Dora's sweet cousin that even Albert shot her a bewildered look. "They will not dare!" Vanessa declared. "I am sure that Lady Carroway would let you stay with *her*, at least until the wedding."

Dora could not help but smile at that. "Engagement has made you bold," she said. "It suits you very well, Vanessa."

"I will ask Miss Jennings if she would be kind enough to keep Miss Ettings company while she is in residence with my mother," Albert said.

Dora glanced his way. "Your mother shall more than suffice as a chaperone, Mr Lowe," she said slowly.

Albert blinked, and Dora could swear that there was suddenly a faint flush to his cheeks. "Oh," he said. "Yes, I suppose that is so."

Dora raised an eyebrow at him. ". . . but I would be more comfortable with Miss Jennings about, of course. I have grown very fond of her company, and your mother cannot be about at all hours. I am sure that Lady Carroway has a wedding to help plan."

Albert laughed sheepishly. "How generous of you, Miss Ettings," he murmured.

So Albert has fallen for my chaperone, Dora thought with bemusement. *That shall be the scandal of the Season, I am sure.* Somehow, she doubted that either party would much care about the scandal involved.

"You really must leave Miss Ettings to rest," Albert told Vanessa with a slight cough. "I promise I will see her back to Carroway House as soon as Miss Jennings is able to arrive."

Vanessa took her leave only reluctantly. Once she had gone, Dora found herself blinking back sleep.

"Elias is not back, then," she observed wearily. "I suppose that makes sense. I came straight back, but he must leave faerie by a longer road."

"You really were in faerie?" Albert asked softly. "How strange that must have been."

"No," Dora murmured. "It was terribly familiar, in fact. I think that must have been the worst part, Mr Lowe." But Dora laid her head back down upon the pillow and suddenly could not stay awake for even a moment longer – she fell into a deep sleep once again.

As she slept, she dreamed of Hollowvale, with its broad ballrooms and misty gardens. Dora wandered the halls of Charity House and found them much changed; the few children who remained there ran about shrieking with cheerful laughter, building forts from the furniture and playing hide-and-seek.

A bubble of joy grew within her chest as she watched them, and she knew that she had no regrets.

When Dora woke in the middle of the night, she found Abigail to be somewhat more lucid. The little girl had sat herself up in bed with her arms around her legs; she was staring out the window with great concentration.

"Abigail," Dora said. "Are you feeling better?"

The little girl turned her head and blinked. "Better'n ever," she said. "Can't remember the last time someone let me sleep as much as I liked." She hesitated, then added, "Mrs Dun says it won't be for ever. She said I'll have chores eventually, an' lessons."

Dora smiled at that. "A *few* chores and lessons are not so bad," she said. "At the very least, there will be no picking oakum."

Abigail was silent for a long moment. ". . . is Lord Hollowvale dead?" she asked quietly.

Dora blinked slowly. "Yes," she said. "But how did you know?"

"I felt him die, I think," Abigail said. "It's the only reason I've been sleepin' all right."

Dora looked down at her hands in her lap. They were quite clean, though they did not feel that way. There had been no blood on them even when she first awoke. "I killed him," she admitted softly. "I did not know that I was capable of such a thing. And now I do not know if I will ever be able to cry over it."

Abigail swung herself down from her bed and headed over towards Dora. She climbed into her lap and hugged her tightly.

"I'd have killed Master Ricks if I could," Abigail offered quietly. "I'll never get the chance to try, I figure. Mr Lowe says he was arrested for black magic."

Dora nodded dully. "I know that I would regret it even more if I had *not* killed Lord Hollowvale," she said. "But either way, it still feels very awful."

Abigail had nothing to say to that. She stayed with Dora for the rest of the night, though, and eventually they both fell asleep once more.

⁂

Miss Jennings was overjoyed to see Dora when she next awoke, though the ex-governess managed to be somewhat more sombre about the entire affair than Vanessa had been. Dora learned that Miss Jennings had volunteered to help keep watch over her in spite of the quarantine, but Albert had shooed her sternly away instead.

"But I do not understand why it is you need me at Carroway House," Miss Jennings admitted in puzzlement, during the carriage ride back. "Surely no one could think that Lady Carroway is an unsuitable chaperone?"

Dora glanced towards Albert, still sitting on the other side of the carriage, and she smiled serenely. "I may yet have someone come courting," she said. "But until then, I suppose that we shall just be enjoying your company." She paused. "Though interested parties had better make themselves known in a hurry, I would say."

"Indeed," Albert mumbled, shaking his head. "Your point is well taken, Miss Ettings."

Miss Jennings knit her brow, but did not inquire further.

Lady Carroway was there to greet them when they arrived. The older woman insisted on seeing Dora directly to her room and tucking her into bed, in spite of Dora's protests that she had slept and slept already.

"You must not come down ill again!" Lady Carroway told her sternly. "You may do as you like — you may even have visitors – but you must do it from your bed for at least a while yet!"

Dora could not bring herself to protest overmuch. There was something comforting about being so worried over, and the maids had put warm bricks in the bed to heat it up for her feet. Eventually, it occurred to her that someone must have brought over her things from Hayworth House, for her gowns were hanging in the closet very neatly.

"I wrestled them away from Mother," Vanessa told Dora, when she inevitably came to visit. "I can see it now, how guilty she is feeling. It's why she would not come to see you, though I know that she wanted to."

Dora found herself oddly unconcerned by the idea of Auntie Frances and her guilt. *Perhaps she will come and try to mend fences*, Dora thought. *But perhaps she will not. Either way, I have so many more important things to worry about.*

"The plague is broken," Vanessa said. "Does that mean that the Lord Sorcier can fix your condition when he returns?"

Dora shook her head slowly. "My other half shall remain in faerie for evermore," she told her cousin. "I made the choice to leave her there, and I do not regret it."

Vanessa looked stricken at that. "But after all of that, Dora!" she said. "Was there no point at all in bringing you to London?"

Dora smiled calmly at her cousin. "I am very glad that I came to London," she said. "And I will not regret that either, whatever else happens. But are you happy to be engaged, Vanessa? Is Edward the husband that you would have wanted?"

Vanessa hesitated. "He is very handsome," she said. "And he seems very kind. And that night that we danced with all those stars surrounding us, it was quite romantic." She looked down at her lap. "I now realise that I do not know him very well. But I suppose that I was never to know my husband very well. I hope that he is truly everything he seems."

"Albert believes that his brother is a good man," Dora said. "And I trust that he is truthful on the matter."

Vanessa chewed at her lip. "Has the marquess ceased to be a problem, Dora?" she asked. "Do you think that you would marry Albert *now*? The two of you do seem to get along, and we would see so much more of one another that way."

Dora shot her cousin a bemused look. "The marquess is no more," she said. "And I may marry whom I like, as long as they do not mind marrying only half of me. I admit that I would consider marrying anyone if it gave me the chance to stay near you. But I am already in love, and I suppose that I have already promised to marry someone else."

Vanessa's eyes widened. "You *suppose*?" she said. "And you are in love! Dora, why did you not say anything?"

"I did not know myself until most recently," Dora said. "But perhaps it has all worked out for the best." She paused uncertainly. "That is assuming that the man in question ever returns—"

A knock at the door interrupted that train of thought. Lady Carroway headed in looking very flustered, holding a vase of fresh white roses in her arms. There was something distinctly different about these flowers, however – and after a moment of looking at them, Dora realised that they sometimes looked more like mist than like roses. *Those are from Hollowvale's gardens*, she thought.

"These are for you, Miss Ettings," Lady Carroway told Dora. "I think they are meant to entice you downstairs." She settled the flowers onto the dresser and shook her head with a smile. "The Lord Sorcier would like a private audience with you. We all know he is not here to ask about French translations. Should I have him wait downstairs while you dress, or turn him away in order to save his pride?"

Vanessa caught the implication in a moment, having just finished her own private audience with Edward only a few days prior. She let out a delighted little gasp and clapped her hands over her mouth.

For once, Dora felt a real smile spread across her face. "I will be down to see him as soon as I can," she said.

Lady Carroway sighed at that, but there was a fondness in her expression. "We shall all depend on you to keep him in hand, Miss Ettings," she said.

Vanessa hurried to help Dora get dressed. "We must have a maid do your hair and make-up—" she started, but Dora shook her head.

"I do not need either," Dora said. "I know I do not seem happy, but I am. I would like to see him as soon as possible." If she were truly honest with herself, there was still a hint of irrational dread in her heart in spite of it all. What if Elias had changed his mind now that Dora would never be cured? Surely he had thought quite a lot about matters on his way back from faerie, and if there were any doubts in his mind at all, they must have come to the forefront.

It was not her imagination, Dora thought, that Lady Carroway's servants were all watching her keenly as she headed down the stairs. One of the maids led her to a side room; Dora opened the door, and the last of her lingering worries instantly dissipated.

Elias glanced towards Dora as she headed inside. He had been pacing, but the moment that she came into view, he stopped himself abruptly. The shadows under his eyes had nearly gone now, though a faint memory of darkness still hovered there. He was dressed more finely than usual, and his neck cloth was neatly tied – and while this made him look quite handsome, he was also clearly unused to it.

Dora closed the door gently behind her, and Elias straightened with an awkward cough. He seemed uncertain just what to do with his arms, and so he settled for clasping them behind his back.

"I was beginning to think you had been waylaid by brownies," Dora told him with a smile.

Elias blinked. "By *brownies?*" he said in a flustered tone.

"Well, that would explain your attire," Dora pointed out. "You are looking nearly like a gentleman today, and we both know that is not your preference."

Elias's mouth dropped. "I am *not*—" he started. "I have *never* been—" But he was still so muddled that he couldn't seem to settle on a single retort.

Dora threw her arms around him.

Elias stiffened for only a moment. In short order, however, his rigid posture relaxed and he tightened his grip on Dora with an audible sigh of relief. She pressed her cheek against his chest and closed her eyes, taking in the now familiar scent of myrrh which he always carried with him.

"It's good to see you well," he murmured. "I could not help but worry that perhaps you hadn't woken up."

"I am very well," Dora told him softly. "I have not been allowed to exert myself at all, you know. If plenty of rest makes for good health, then I must be the healthiest woman in the country."

Elias brought his hand up to run his fingers through her hair, and Dora found herself very glad that she had not paused to pin it up. "I did bring flowers this time," he murmured.

Dora opened her eyes and saw him looking down at her with a strange intensity. The gold of his eyes mesmerised her in a brand-new way, and she tightened her fingers in his jacket.

"I am not certain what to say," Elias admitted. "I am sure that I had words in mind, but they suddenly escape me." His tone was nervous now, and Dora thought that very odd indeed for a man who had just faced down the Marquess of Hollowvale in his own realm.

"You should say whatever you like," Dora told him. "I am happy to see you. Surely you know that the rest does not matter."

Elias narrowed his eyes. "I do *feel* that it matters," he said, and there was suddenly a note of contrariness to his voice. "One does not simply say *let us go and get married, if you are amenable.*"

"But you did say that." Dora beamed gently at him. "And I *was* amenable. I still am."

"Would you not argue with me for once?" Elias said with a flush. "Listen here, Miss Ettings! I am in love with you. You deserve to hear that. I love your wit and cleverness. I love that you are kind but almost never nice. I love your eyes and your hair and your freckles, and the fact that you smell like some monstrous floral perfume all of the time." He paused, now looking somewhat offended at himself. "And I love to dance with you. That is the worst of it by far."

Dora blinked slowly. Each word heated up her heart bit by bit until it was a bewildering bonfire. That fire burned its way down into her mind, consuming all the ugly things that still lingered beneath its surface. When she was alone or tired or uncertain, Dora knew that these would be the words that came to her now instead of all those others, and she could not help but smile in a silly, dreamy way.

"And obviously," Elias said with a huff, "I would like to marry you. I cannot say that I recommend myself very fondly, but I make the offer all the same."

Dora reached up to pat at his cheek. "Then I shall recommend you instead," she told him. "I already have, you know. I told Lord Blackthorn that I thought you were the most virtuous man in all of England." She considered for a moment. "I should rather ask if you are sure you will be pleased with me like this for ever. I will never feel things quite as other people do."

"Dora," said Elias. "I am sure that your other half is very lovely. But I fell in love with you exactly as you are. And perhaps that is for the best – if you were suddenly twice as charming, then I should be utterly overwhelmed." He curled his hand around hers, and she felt a pleasant tingle against her skin.

Dora looked down and saw that there was a silver ring against her finger, set with a single glimmering *star.*

Elias slid his fingers just beneath her chin and lifted her eyes to look at him. "You have yet to say *yes*, you frustrating woman," he breathed. "Do not leave me in anticipation."

Dora felt his breath along her cheek as he said the words. The whisper burrowed down beneath her skin, making her shiver.

Dora's heart did a little flip. "Yes," she whispered back softly.

Elias leaned down towards her. His lips brushed hers. The touch was so light, so painfully gentle, that Dora might not have believed it had happened at all except for the cascade of dizzying tingles it sent down her spine.

His thumb stroked down her jaw. His lips pressed just a bit harder, as though to test her reaction. Dora wound her arms around his neck in response, leaning up towards him. His body was warm; the heat of him melted through her completely, washing away any other awareness of the world around them.

For the rest of my life, Dora thought, *this will be the dream in which I live.* It was a blissful thought indeed.

Epilogue

$\mathcal{D}$ora had the distinct pleasure of attending her cousin's wedding feast with her fiancé on her arm. It was everything that a proper wedding feast ought to be – and more besides. Elias had been in an unusually pleasant mood for weeks by then, and he was feeling so whimsical that he made the swan-folded napkins get up and flutter around for everyone's entertainment. Vanessa's resulting smile was nearly a magic spell all on its own.

Dora's own wedding was small, but Lady Carroway insisted on hosting a feast at Carroway House for her as well. Albert's mother had not forgotten her plans to open another orphanage, and much of the morning's conversation ended up scandalously centred around those plans, rather than around the weather or the wedding. Dora thought it was the perfect sort of feast.

Life after marriage was much different than Dora might ever have imagined. In fact, it was much better in nearly every possible way – but she suspected that had much to do with her choice of husband. As a married woman, she was far more free to spend her time as she pleased; and since she was of a mind with Elias on most things, he was only too happy to let her roll up her sleeves to help both Mrs Dun and the new orphanage. Most women of the nobility had only a few children, Dora liked to say – but she had very many, and she loved them all the same.

And though it was rare for Dora to feel any sense of breathless joy, she carried with her always a soft, contented glow, rather like the star upon her finger.

The *ton* soon began to murmur that married life quite agreed with the Lord Sorcier; for while Elias would never be *well-mannered*, he was certainly distinctly happier. There were times, of course, when dark things threatened and great evils endangered his rest – but if he sometimes came home to sit awake in the dark, Dora always insisted at least on staying up with him.

Miss Jennings never did quite return to her previous employer. In fact, the lady was astonished to receive a quiet offer of marriage from a very respectable physician. She and Mr Albert Lowe had a wedding in the country, far away from sharp tongues and miffed matrons who gasped over the indiscretion of a well-bred gentleman marrying the chaperone of the woman he was meant to be courting. Mr and Mrs Albert Lowe were not ever invited to any respectable parties outside those thrown by Lady Carroway, which did not seem to dim their happiness even by a bit. Mrs Henrietta Lowe did spend quite some time helping with the new orphanage, however, which meant that Dora had the pleasure of spending far more time with her as the years went on.

England did not, alas, become a better place for the orphaned, the poor or the infirm. In fact, contrary to all protests by Lord Carroway and the Lord Sorcier, laws were passed to make the workhouses more punishing than ever, on the assumption that the poor were naturally lacking in virtue. But there were two orphanages in London, at least, which solved some of the small evils – and as the workhouse masters grew ever more cruel and punishing, children began to murmur that a faerie lady with two mismatched eyes sometimes came to steal away the worst offenders, who were never seen again.

One day far in the future, Elias and Dora visited their closest friends and family in the manner of a final farewell. The next morning, England discovered that the Lord Sorcier and his wife had both quite disappeared, never to be seen again.

But somewhere off in faerie, it is said that Lady Hollowvale finally fixed her mismatched eyes – and she and her husband rule there to this day, from their place in the Hollow House.

Read on for a special bonus prequel
novella by Olivia Atwater:

The Lord Sorcier

THE
LORD
SORCIER

Chapter One

ike any good English army man, Albert preferred to avoid complaining. It had been a long week of trudging on mountain roads, of course – in bitter winter weather, no less – but this, he decided, was simply to be borne. His sturdy, more expensive boots were holding up much better than those of the other men at least, and he decided he ought to thank his mother in his next letter home for insisting on their purchase.

"Bollocks," cursed Gillett next to him. "Didn't seem so bloody far when we was headed *to* Spain."

"Didn't seem so bloody far because we was *winnin'* then," groused Baxter on Albert's other side. "That smug French git's goin' to take back everything we left behind, too."

"Stiff upper lip, chaps," Albert reminded them helpfully. "Napoleon has his own troubles, I'm sure. Besides, just think of the French that are chasing us. Every misery we endure, they're forced to share alike."

Gillett spat onto the ground at the mention of the French. "Least there's that," he muttered. "Keeps me a little warmer, thinkin' of them frogs shiverin'."

Baxter groaned. "Most of them's just like us, I bet – bein' marched by their officers, just killin' 'cause they're told. I'd be happier, me, if they left us alone and went off to one of their colonies for the holidays. Hear it's nice in the Indies this time of year."

"The French are not *really* like us, though, are they?"

This observation came from a man just behind Gillett, surprising the lot of them. Albert turned his head and frowned as he focused on the speaker.

It was Wilder – or at least, Albert *thought* that was the man's surname. The soldier had joined their regiment only recently, after one of the more devastating attacks on the army's retreating flank. Wilder was easily the most peculiar among their current ranks; though he was probably around Albert's age, his face had a young, ageless quality to it which never seemed diminished by the cold and misery. Wilder's once-red coat was just as stained and battered as everyone else's, but he wore it with a strange nobility which made him seem more like an officer than the run-of-the-mill grunt he really was.

"What do you mean by that exactly?" Albert asked him curiously. "How are the French not like us? I mean . . . other than the obvious, that is."

Wilder turned his head to consider Albert. "Why, they are evil, of course," he replied. He said it so simply and so naturally that Albert couldn't help but pause. The statement was no exaggeration – rather, Wilder spoke the words with utter seriousness, as though he were discussing some mythical monster from a faerie tale. "Perhaps the French do not *look* evil," Wilder added. "But many terrible things in this world take on fair or mundane forms. Faeries, for instance."

Baxter shivered and crossed himself at the mention. Even Gillett slowed his pace for a moment, with discomfort showing on his features.

"I . . ." Albert started. He blinked slowly. "I don't know that I ought to say this. But I fear that you are incorrect on this account, Wilder. The French are no more good or evil than we are, at least on a cosmic scale. God loves all his children, after all."

Wilder narrowed his gaze at the words. This close, Albert saw that the man's eyes were a peculiar molten reddish-gold that didn't seem quite natural. Albert nearly followed Baxter's lead and crossed himself at that uncanny stare – but he resisted the urge, just barely.

"I have heard it told over and over that the French are evil," Wilder informed Albert coolly. "That they are in fact the cause of everything terrible in England. Now, you insist that they are *not* evil. I admit, Mr Lowe – that does seem strange to me."

Albert reached up to rub at his forehead. Wilder, he thought, was an odd one. Albert was beginning to suspect that the poor man was ever so slightly touched in the head. "It is not so strange for human beings to search for an easy villain to blame for all their troubles," Albert told him. "We often lie to ourselves every bit as much as we lie to each other, in order to feel some comfort in hard times." He paused. "Do not mistake me – the French are a danger to everything we hold dear. But their defeat will not solve every English woe overnight."

Wilder's stare grew ever darker at the words, and Albert shifted uncomfortably on his feet. "Lie?" Wilder asked. "What do you mean by *lie*, Mr Lowe?"

Baxter snorted. "What's this new joke?" he asked. "Are you havin' us on, Wilder?"

A look of consternation crossed Wilder's face at this. Albert suspected that Wilder was not, in fact, having them on.

"To lie is . . ." Albert trailed off, blinking quickly. He struggled to put together an explanation of the simple concept. "It is to say something untrue," he said finally. "For instance, er . . . I could say that the sky is green today." Albert gestured up towards the pale, wintery sky.

Wilder glanced up sharply, and Albert got the strangest feeling that the man truly expected to see a green sky. As his eyes focused upwards, however, he frowned with sudden uncertainty.

". . . but the sky is not green, Mr Lowe," Wilder said slowly. The man's voice now held a thread of underlying fear.

Gillett guffawed. "No, no, Wilder," he assured the other man. "The sky's green, all right. You're just not seein' it proper – isn't that right, Bax?"

Albert shot Gillett a disapproving look. "The sky is *not* green, Wilder," he said reassuringly. "And neither are the French pure evil."

"Elias," Wilder corrected him. Those molten gold eyes searched the sky – vainly, desperately hoping, Albert thought, to catch a glimpse of green. "My name is *Elias*, Mr Lowe. Wilder is simply the surname they gave me at the workhouse."

Albert sighed heavily. "Elias," he corrected himself. "You need not look so distressed. The French are not pure evil, but they are still our enemy. You need feel no guilt for killing them, for they would surely do the same to you if they could."

Albert would later reflect that he should have known better than to utter such prophetic words in the same conversation as the fickle Fair Folk. Surely, some nasty member of the Gentry had been listening in and had decided to fulfil his fateful observation.

The first shouts went up from behind them, further down the mountain trail. Shots rang out in quick succession – screams followed in the wake of each thundering echo.

Chaos erupted, as it always had done during the skirmishes at their back lines. Men fumbled for their muskets, loading up their ammunition. There was no room here for a proper firing line; Albert was not even certain he knew where to find the nearest superior officer, spread out as they were along the trail.

Baxter cursed. "An' still no ammo, me!" he hissed. "Bloody stupid supply lines!"

Albert cringed. "I'm out as well," he said. "I suppose they'd look down on us shooting off our ramrods, wouldn't they?"

"Blow my arm off that way anyway," Baxter muttered. But

there was a hint of panic in his tone now, and Albert thought the man might be seriously considering the possibility.

Wilder – *Elias*, Albert corrected himself dimly – pulled out a pouch and tossed it towards Baxter. The other soldier blinked and caught it with a dull clinking of lead. Baxter widened his eyes. The pouch must have been nearly full – but surely Elias had been shooting Frenchmen with the rest of them until now?

"Have mine," Elias offered Baxter gravely. "And start loading your weapon." He grabbed Albert by the arm, dragging him back. "Head further up, Mr Lowe," Elias said. "We cannot have our surgeon taking a lead ball to the face."

Albert flushed at the suggestion. He did not like the way the other men protected him during danger – it made him feel cowardly, and he could not help but feel that his noble father would disapprove. Nonetheless, he stumbled up the trail, pulling his musket from his back in case of danger.

The French were growing talented at harrying their back lines. Much sooner than Albert would have liked, he heard the gunfire draw closer and saw the dirty blue of French uniforms flashing among the smoke. A musket ball whizzed past his shoulder, thudding into the rocks with a faint puff of dirt.

Elias kept a few paces behind Albert, with his posture straight and his uncanny golden eyes staring down through the smoke. Albert briefly fancied that the man really *could* see everything that was happening, despite the haze. The other man's lips moved, but Albert could not quite make out the words that he murmured to himself.

Another *crack* sounded from below – and Elias staggered back, collapsing to the ground.

Albert rushed towards him, dropping to his knees. "Where are you hit?" he yelled urgently. The ruckus was now deafening; and at first, he thought that Elias might not have heard him, judging from the glazed look on his face. But Elias merely shook his head and muttered something.

"Louder!" Albert urged him. "Where. Are. You. Hit?"

Elias blinked at him slowly. "I was not hit," he said. This time, when he spoke, it was soft, and calm and measured – but somehow, the words wove their way perfectly through the din to settle next to Albert's ear.

Albert knit his brow. *He's in shock*, he thought. He started pulling at Elias's jacket, searching for spots of blood.

Elias tugged himself away from Albert's hands, struggling to rise to his feet. "I was not hit," he repeated in that soft, eerie tone. "And the sky is not green, Mr Lowe. I do not know how to lie – do you understand?"

A cry went up nearby, and Elias jerked his gaze before them. A figure resolved from out of the smoke – blue-jacketed, and not red-. Albert had only long enough to note the musket in the Frenchman's hands, pointed directly at them, before the gun went off.

What happened next he later found very difficult to explain.

Elias threw up his arm and breathed out a word. It was not a word that Albert had ever heard before – and he counted himself a very fine linguist indeed, with an ability in French, Latin and Spanish at least. It was a word that made the world around them tremble; it somehow made the rocks *clitter-clack* in fear.

The smoky haze before them solidified into a serpentine form, which opened now its reddish-gold eyes and hissed at the Frenchman. The musket ball which should have found its way to Elias and Albert had thudded instead into the serpent; now, it clattered uselessly to the ground. The smoky creature struck at the French soldier with alarming speed, snapping its jaws closed upon his shoulder.

The Frenchman screamed – in mortal terror as much as in pain, Albert was sure. The serpent reared up, dragging the enemy soldier up off his feet and tossing him away down the mountainside like rubbish.

Elias looked away uncomfortably.

The serpent in the smoke roiled and hissed again – and then it darted away, searching for new French prey.

Albert stared at Elias, his mouth agape. He knew that he needed to get up – that there were surely injured men he needed to see – but the sheer unreality of the situation had yet to wear off.

Elias reached down to grasp Albert's arm, tugging him back up to his feet.

"You are a magician," Albert whispered.

Elias did not reply. It occurred to Albert that if Elias *did* reply, he might be forced to admit the truth. *I do not know how to lie*, he had said.

But soon, Elias too had disappeared into the smoke, following in the wake of his unearthly serpent.

"Surgeon!" a man screamed from below. "Find the surgeon!"

Albert did not have time to ponder further.

⁓᷍⟋ᔕᕯᕤᕯᔕ⟍᷍⁓

The butcher's bill was smaller than it ought to have been.

Albert knew it, even as he rushed to treat what injured came his way. Baxter had taken a ball to the leg; thankfully, it hadn't hit anything vital, but the man was going to be limping even more slowly than usual from now on. Albert did not voice aloud his real worry: if the wound became infected, the leg would almost surely need to come off.

"Mr Lowe!" Lieutenant Banks barked at Albert as he approached. "Any casualties this time?" There was a weary note beneath the question.

"There were a few, I hear," Albert admitted. "I have not been to the back yet. But I know that one or two men fell in the initial ambush."

Lieutenant Banks grimaced. "More than that, I'd expect," he said.

"Maybe not," Albert replied slowly. "The French retreated quite abruptly this time." He was just considering how to broach the subject of strange Elias Wilder and his magic when he heard Gillett exclaiming on his way up the trail towards them.

". . . wanderin' around without your gun out!" Gillett spat. "Next time, mark my words, the rest of us won't save your miserable arse!"

Gillett's features twisted with incredulous rage as he berated Elias, who was next to him. Elias, for his part, did not seem inclined to take the matter seriously. Indeed, Albert had begun to suspect that Elias did not require the gun that he had been given, and that he had not, in fact, been using it at all.

Lieutenant Banks straightened sharply. "What's this, now?" he demanded.

Gillett froze. Angry as he was, Albert suspected that he did not intend to get his fellow soldier punished. "Small misunderstandin', sir," Gillett stammered. "We'll handle it, sir, don't you worry. Plenty else to worry about, I'd bet."

Lieutenant Banks narrowed his eyes. "Have you been derelict of duty, Wilder?" he asked archly.

Elias glanced up at the lieutenant. His golden eyes were hard and unimpressed. "I have killed at least three Frenchmen today, sir," he informed Lieutenant Banks.

Gillett whirled on Elias. "The hell you have!" he said. "Can't kill a man without your gun out, Wilder!" Whatever mild generosity Gillett had been clinging to before now disappeared like smoke on the battlefield.

"He has killed many men, I am sure," Albert interjected abruptly. He glanced over towards the lieutenant. "I saw it with my own eyes, sir. Elias – I mean, Wilder – he used some dire magic to drive away the French. It is because of him that they fled."

Lieutenant Banks blinked slowly at this. Albert could tell that the lieutenant was fighting against the urge to call him a liar, and so he added, "On my word, and on my family's honour. I am Lord Carroway's son, as well you know. I swear to you, Elias Wilder is a magician, and he has saved more than one of us today."

Elias turned those golden eyes upon Albert now, and the look within them was not friendly. Rather, there was a hint of betrayal and a sense of tired resignation.

Lieutenant Banks let out a long breath. He settled his hard gaze upon Elias. "Well," he said. Then, with another breath: "*Well.*"

Gillett also stared at Elias. Slowly, he took a step back from the other man.

"I shall have to report this up the chain," said Lieutenant Banks. He jerked his chin at Elias. "Come with me, Wilder."

Elias climbed the trail in silence, keeping his eyes to the ground. Albert felt a mild stab of guilt as Elias passed him, though he wasn't sure just why he ought to feel that way. *Surely*, Albert thought, *they'll give him a commendation for this.*

"Thank you," Albert murmured to Elias before he had gone too far ahead.

Elias said nothing in return – but Albert thought, perhaps, that he saw the man nod.

Chapter Two

*E*lias did not return to the back lines that evening. Nor, in fact, did Albert see him at all for the next few weeks.

It was only once they had reached Portugal and settled in for the winter that Albert heard the rumours.

"The regiment's magician took on an assistant magician," Baxter muttered to Albert one evening as a few of them sat down to mend their coats. "Some raw talent from the common recruits. Wonder who *that* might be?"

"I cannot imagine that magicians are so common on the ground," Albert admitted. "Still . . . it has occurred to me that Elias must have been hiding his magic for a purpose. I begin to fear that I repaid his help with a poor turn."

"Poor turn for him, maybe," Baxter snorted. "Better for us. We need more magicians, an' that's a fact. I heard Napoleon's Lord Sorcier is skulkin' around battlefields again. You know what they say happened in Corunna."

Albert considered this grimly. The Battle of Corunna had been before his deployment. By all accounts, it had been an utter rout for the English. Surely, there were other factors at work than just Napoleon's infamous Lord Sorcier . . . but some said that the French magician had whipped up a literal hurricane to chase the English out of Spain. It was rare that the Lord Sorcier took a direct hand in things – but the knowledge of his presence hung persistently upon them all like a heavy, ominous cloak.

"I very much doubt they will set our assistant magician against the Lord Sorcier himself," Albert observed. "But perhaps Elias will free up Magician Lilley to focus more upon the matter."

Baxter shook his head at that. "*Lilley,*" he muttered. "Not sure whether he's more a threat to us than the Lord Sorcier sometimes."

Albert decided it was best if he pretended not to hear this comment.

The next time Albert saw Elias Wilder, it was at a dinner table, surrounded by officers. Albert's family connections and his status as a gentleman often resulted in dinner invitations when the fighting was less pressing. So it was that he found himself in a local mansion in Lisbon, which had been politely co-opted for the housing of several English officers.

Elias was not himself commissioned, but he seemed to have been assigned as Magician Lilley's constant shadow. Next to the older, more distinguished gentleman, Elias could not help but appear shabby, and Albert marvelled at the change this comparison made in his estimation of Elias's bearing. Where once Albert had thought the man strangely dignified, he now saw only a tired young man in a messy, patched-up uniform.

Elias did, however, know precisely how to follow proper table manners. Even as Albert headed in to find a seat, he saw the new assistant magician select the proper fork for the current course. *Perhaps Magician Lilley has been teaching Elias things other than magic*, Albert thought idly.

"Ah, lieutenant!" Magician Lilley greeted them, as Lieutenant Banks strode ahead of Albert. "Sit down, sit down. We were just discussing Spain. I hazard we'll be returning right to it in the spring, won't we? What do you think?"

Lieutenant Banks settled in at the table, and Albert quietly followed suit. "I think I dare not speculate," the lieutenant said with a stony face. "For every time I have tried, I have ended up wildly mistaken."

Magician Lilley chortled at this and pounded his palm on the table. "Good man," he said. "Leave the planning to the upper ranks. More trouble for them and less for us."

"Better to speculate on one's own area of expertise, isn't it?" asked a captain down the table. "What odds would you put on yourself against the Lord Sorcier if he should show up at the next battle, magician?"

Perhaps it was only Albert's imagination, but he thought he saw Magician Lilley pale at the suggestion. The magician forced a smile, even as Elias cast him a sideways glance from the chair next to him. "Stories of the Lord Sorcier are overblown, most certainly," Lilley assured the table. "No magician on this earth could call up a proper hurricane. It's all poppycock and exaggeration. The troops gossip as badly as a bunch of housewives."

"I beg your pardon," Elias cut in suddenly. "But you are incorrect, Magician Lilley."

Heads turned up and down the table. Lilley blinked at his assistant magician, briefly stunned by the lapse in decorum. "Excuse me, Wilder," he said. "I could swear I just heard you evince a magical opinion. You *are* aware that you're not even a full magician?"

Elias arched one contemptuous eyebrow. "A superior rank does not give one licence to lie outrageously," he said. Elias fixed his golden eyes upon Albert as he said the words, and Albert wondered if the strange man had finally figured out the nature of a lie. "A powerful enough magician *could* call up a hurricane," Elias continued. "Rather, they would summon up a dangerous creature – an elemental, or a member of the Gentry – and request the favour in return for some dreadful payment."

Lilley's face went beet red. He sputtered soundlessly for a moment, grasping for a response. It was clear that he could not deny the accuracy of the statement, however – for when he finally settled on an answer, it was merely this: *"Insubordinate! Out! Get out, I mean to say!"*

Elias pushed out his chair and rose to his feet. He bowed stiffly to the gathering and headed for the door.

There was a hard tension in Elias's manner that Albert could not quite interpret. So it was that after a few minutes of eating, Albert rose and politely excused himself, claiming some minute duty to attend.

Albert caught up with the assistant magician only by pure luck on his way back to their temporary barracks. Elias had paused in the street, staring up at the sky in the same way that he had done in the mountains. As Albert caught up to him, the assistant magician spoke with his eyes still cast towards the heavens.

"The sky is green today, Mr Lowe," Elias said. "At least as far as Magician Lilley is concerned."

Albert startled at that. "I'm not sure that I understand," he said.

Elias turned to face him directly. "Magician Lilley is a hack," he informed Albert. "I am not sure whether he truly believes himself to be better than he is, or whether he is putting on a conscious show for everyone else. Either way, he is lying to *someone.*"

Albert shivered. Though he had just heard Elias tell an outright lie about a green sky, he did not suppose that the man was lying about *this.* "I have seen Magician Lilley doing magic before," Albert said weakly. "He must have *some* skill."

Elias shook his head. "Some skill," he agreed. "Parlour tricks, cleverly inflated to seem more useful and more powerful than they are. His practical knowledge is lacking. The Lord Sorcier would murder him in a heartbeat."

Albert took a deep breath. "I am not sure what there is to do about the matter," he said. "Magician Lilley was properly commissioned. As far as the regiment is concerned, he is our authority on magic. Worse – we have so few magicians at all, the other regiments probably ask his advice as well."

Elias pressed his fingers to his forehead. Somewhere in between the dinner and their meeting on the street, the assistant magician had regained his otherworldly dignity. Perhaps it was simply that he no longer stood in comparison to all those officers in their neat neck cloths and clean clothing. Perhaps it was a trick of the light. Or perhaps, Albert thought, it was something purposeful.

"I am no longer sure that this is my fight," Elias admitted softly.

Albert blinked. "Is it not?" he asked. "You are an Englishman, and you have taken the king's shilling."

Elias frowned. "I am not *sure* that I am an Englishman," he said. "No one has ever told me as much. And certainly, all of the workhouse masters were in a hurry to be rid of me. If I do not have a home anywhere in England, Mr Lowe, does that still make me an Englishman?"

Albert shifted his posture uncomfortably. "I am sorry that you were ever in the workhouses," he said. "I volunteered among them before I left. They are a dirty shame upon our country, to be sure."

Elias pressed his arms behind his back, contemplating. "I asked why the workhouses were so terrible, Mr Lowe," he said. "I was told that it was all to do with the taxes, and the war, and the evil French behind it all. But even if I killed the Lord Sorcier himself tomorrow, none of it would change, would it? The French are not evil. That was a lie. I am not sure that I can see the point in all of this now."

Albert hesitated. "I do not know that I have any right to dissuade you," he admitted, "though desertion is indeed a terrible crime. But there is a point to all of this, at least for me." He smiled helplessly. "I send letters back home to my mother as often as I might. I think of her, and of my father and my brothers, and how desperately I wish to keep them safe. I fear what things Napoleon and his empire might do to them if we cannot stem this tide."

Elias's features clouded with puzzlement as Albert spoke.

"You love your family, then?" Elias asked. He seemed confused by the idea – as confused as he had been by the very concept of lying.

"Of course I love my family," Albert said with astonishment. "They are the very best people that I know. I'm surprised that you – ah." He coloured with embarrassment. "I am so sorry. You were in the workhouses. You do not have a family, then?"

Elias frowned darkly. "I had one once, I suppose," he said. "There was no love there. Dare I ask . . . is it *normal* to love one's family?"

Albert cringed. "I daresay that it is," he told the assistant magician, with a hint of apology in his tone.

Elias nodded brusquely. "I see," he said. "I shall have to take this all in mind, Mr Lowe. Thank you for your input."

Albert sighed. "You may call me Albert if you like," he said. "For however long you remain, that is."

Elias smiled at this. It was the first time Albert had seen the expression on his face. The change it made in him was something to behold; Albert was sorry that he was the only one present to see it.

"Thank you, Albert," Elias said.

He turned back down the street again and continued walking. As Elias disappeared around a corner, Albert wondered dimly if he would ever see the man again.

Chapter Three

Albert did not hear any rumours that the assistant magician had deserted in the night, which he hoped to be a good sign. Nonetheless, he had little time to worry over the matter. As spring made itself known, the English army did indeed make its way back past the Lines of Torres Vedras, into Spain and towards Vitoria.

It was no leap of logic to assume that there would be a terrible battle at Vitoria. The French were attempting to pull themselves back to France; Wellington, of course, did not intend to let them get there.

Albert's regiment was assigned to a column of *many* regiments meant to cut across Monte Arrato and strike the river to the east. He would later remember that the bridge fell much too easily to their advance. He remembered very clearly pushing his way across the bridge with his fellows – and then, for a moment, he looked out over the river in instinctive dread.

Water hissed and roared . . . and then, the Zadorra River overran its banks.

Albert had only the briefest impression of a white, frothing bull charging out from the river rapids before the torrent rose up to greet them. He was swept so instantly off the bridge that he lost all sense of place or direction, dragged beneath the surface of the water.

There was no help for it, really – that was the worst part. As frantically as he kicked and swam, the river itself seemed to churn against him, pressing its weight upon his efforts. Albert struggled against the current, searching for something solid to grasp. At one point, he found another man's hand and tried to hold on; but whoever it was, they were swept away from one another in short order, pulled back into the deliberate chaos of the river.

If these are my last moments, Albert thought distantly, *I should spend them thinking of something pleasant at least.*

He thought of his mother, sitting back at home with her embroidery, sipping tea and thinking of him back. Lady Carroway had a terrible singing voice, much to her chagrin – but Albert had always loved to listen to her hum.

He was just trying to call to mind the last tune he had heard from her when the river suddenly spat him back up.

Albert blinked away the murk in his eyes, coughing up water roughly. All around him, he heard others doing the same as they crawled across the shore.

The rest of the regiment – those who had not been caught by the strange torrent – remained upon the foot of the bridge, holding their position. The frothing water-bull seethed upon the other side of the bridge, staring down some unseen figure within the regiment. For a moment longer, it twisted and writhed, straining against the unseen power which had caught it. Then, with a last loud roar – it winked away entirely.

Bright golden fire kindled upon the bridge. Albert could not see the source – but he greatly suspected that the figure beneath the flames was a dirty, ragged-looking assistant magician.

Albert struggled quickly back to his feet, gauging the distance back to the bridge. The bull's charge had scattered more than half the regiment; some of them now staggered back the way they'd come, hurrying to rejoin their fellows. Albert followed them in a cloudy haze.

The vision that swam into view as he approached the bridge was both breathtaking and terrible to behold. The rest of the soldiers had given Elias a wide, respectful berth as he lit into the enemy. French soldiers screamed and burned, backpedalling helplessly from the threat. The assistant magician wore a grim, methodical expression which Albert knew quite well; it was the expression Albert normally wore himself when he cut away another man's limb. The horror before them was absolutely, surgically necessary . . . and also deeply ugly.

Thunder rolled across the battlefield. At first, Albert thought a storm had come from the clear blue sky – but as dirt flew and men cried out, he realised that the French had opened cannon fire on the bridge.

The golden beacon of fire winked out, just as abruptly as it had appeared.

Albert rushed the rest of the way up towards the bridge. "Surgeon!" someone yelled in a familiar refrain. "Someone save the damned magician!"

"Surgeon!" Albert yelled back, shoving his way through the panicking soldiers. "I mean – I *am* a surgeon! Move, you lot!"

Someone grabbed him by the elbow, dragging him along. Another soldier shoved him forward, nearly banging his nose against another man's back. Finally, Albert found himself ejected into the centre of a defensive circle, where men had formed up to protect one injured man in particular.

Elias was on his back, screaming like the furies themselves had come to claim his soul.

Albert fell to his knees, scrambling to grab hold of the other man. Elias barely seemed to notice Albert's presence – his golden eyes were wide and dazed with agony, and his back was arched in pain. The assistant magician could not seem to halt his thrashing, even as Albert begged him to hold still and let him work.

"Grab him!" Albert snapped to the others. "Someone hold him down, for God's sake!"

A few of the nearby soldiers complied. Two fully grown men grabbed each of his arms, while another sat heavily upon his legs. At first, Albert wasn't certain what had caused the ugly screaming. But soon, his eyes alighted upon two spots of blood: one on the magician's right arm and one at his shoulder. Even as he watched, the blood began to spread like water – but worse by far was the way the injuries seemed to *burn*.

Albert stared in horrified fascination. *Is this some spell?* he wondered. *Will it hurt me too, if I try to pull the pieces out?*

He knew he had no time to consider the consequences. In the end, it was barely a choice at all.

Albert pulled his surgeon's knife and dug it into Elias's shoulder where the bigger piece of shrapnel had lodged. So agonised was the magician that he barely screamed any louder at all as Albert dug the twisted piece of iron from his shoulder.

It's only grapeshot, Albert thought in astonishment. *But this isn't magical at all!*

Albert moved quickly to the shrapnel in the magician's arm, prying it loose with an embarrassing lack of delicacy. As the other barb came free, Elias choked off his last scream . . . and his eyes began to roll back into his head.

Albert slapped him urgently across the cheek. "Don't faint!" he yelled. "Not now, *certainly* not now!"

Elias focused hazily upon Albert. His body still trembled and his breathing was laboured. "It's gone?" he asked hoarsely. He sounded bewildered.

"The grapeshot?" Albert asked, as he bandaged up the magician's injuries. "All that I could find. You're not burning any more, at least."

Elias grasped at Albert's arm and struggled back to his feet. He had to lean for a long moment upon the surgeon in order to steady himself. Men cheered around them even as the ghastly sound of cannon fire continued.

"Iron," Elias rasped at Albert, in a voice so low that it was nearly lost among the din of the battle. "Magic cannot block iron, Albert – and I must not be pierced by it. Do you understand?"

Albert nodded, though he wasn't entirely sure how he might prevent the matter. *I suppose I must simply dig the iron out again, if it happens once more*, he thought.

The French had rushed in to take advantage of the confusion; Albert saw their firing line on the other side of the bridge. But that golden bonfire reasserted itself soon enough . . . and the French soon had cause to regret their eager approach.

Albert cringed away from the sight. It was cowardly of him, he knew. But men were not meant to burn.

He stood as part of the defensive circle around their assistant magician, and selfishly hoped that no one would call upon him to kill any more men.

◦~∞◦

It didn't take long for them to retake the bridge, with their assistant magician recovered.

"We must find the Lord Sorcier," Elias ground out in a hoarse voice, once they had solidified their position. "It was he who sent the water elemental. Now he knows where I am, but I do not know where *he* is."

Albert startled at this. After that horrid display of sorcerous might, it had been easy to forget that there was a man of flesh and blood at the centre of it all. He turned towards Elias, knowing that his face was pale and his features uncertain.

Some part of him had expected to see a monster where the assistant magician once stood. But there was only Elias, with his beaten, bloodstained uniform and his strange, weary dignity.

Albert's mind caught up to the magician's words belatedly. "If the Lord Sorcier was the one who sent the water elemental," he said slowly, "then wouldn't the *elemental* know where he is?"

Elias blinked hazily. "Quite right, Albert," he mumbled. "Why did I not think of that?"

Albert considered the injuries that still bled sluggishly through the bandages on Elias's arm. "I suspect you could claim mitigating circumstances," he observed.

Elias raised his good arm again and flung his palm out towards the river. Men jumped and cried out as the water-bull rose sulkily from the depths. It was a dirty, growling beast of brown water and surging debris. It stretched and groaned, rising into the sky above them, as though to assert its power.

It had no eyes, Albert noted distantly. Where a normal bull might have had a head, there was only a round, churning void of water.

"Your summoner," Elias ground out. "Take me to him."

The water-bull twisted and burbled, thrashing against the magician's control. The Zadorra River seethed with such obvious hatred that Albert wondered if it knew the foreign nature of its assailant. But presently, the beast settled into a reluctant sort of submission – and, in a whirl of frothy water, it turned upon the shore.

Elias started after the elemental. Albert made to join him, and the magician paused in confusion. "What are you doing?" Elias asked.

"I am coming with you," Albert said helpfully. "To be sure you are not pierced by you-know-what."

Elias quirked his lips into a distant sort of grin. "Ah yes," he said. "Well. Do me a favour and don't get killed, Albert."

"I had not planned to die, Elias," Albert told him mildly. "But I shall do you the favour regardless, I suppose." He pulled his musket off his shoulder, surprised that it had survived his sojourn in the water. The whole of the gun was doused, though, and Albert stopped to switch with another soldier for a properly dry weapon. Since he was walking in the company of the regiment's assistant magician, the gun's true owner did not protest the matter.

"Dare I ask what happened to our fully ranked magician, Elias?" Albert asked as they shoved their way through the ranks towards the far shore.

"Magician Lilley awoke quite mad today," Elias said. "He was stomping and neighing like a pony. In fact, I believe he may have tried to steal oats from the lieutenant's horse."

Albert blinked in alarm. "What on earth could cause such an affliction?" he asked.

Elias considered this. "Many things," he said. "Many things *could* cause such an affliction. But perhaps it is most closely related to the gentleman magician's insistence that I be whipped and discharged for my latest insolence."

Albert gaped at him. "Did we not need him for the battle, Elias?" he asked.

"I daresay not," Elias replied. "Perhaps if the Lord Sorcier is vulnerable to card tricks." He paused. "In any event, I suspect that Magician Lilley's case shall miraculously resolve itself upon the morning. These things do tend to cure themselves with the next rising of the sun."

The giant, watery elemental waited for them at the far end of the shore. As they came to face it, Albert lost what little humour he'd regained. The faceless thing still frothed like an angry cauldron – and this time, Albert swore that it had looked his way with the eyes that it did not have. He became keenly aware that the only thing which stood between him and another mortal encounter with the Zadorra River was whatever invisible magic Elias had employed to stay the creature's temper.

Elias made another sharp gesture, however – and the elemental sloshed away from the river like a great wave, rushing along the trampled green fields beyond.

Albert and Elias had to hurry to keep up with it. More than once, Albert saw the assistant magician exert his control to slow the creature's impatient speed. A not-insignificant chunk of the regiment cheered and followed along after them when it was realised that the magician had stolen the enemy's unearthly ally.

"The French are pulling back," Elias observed breathlessly, as they stumbled along. "Where do you think they are going?"

Albert frowned. "I heard the lieutenant mention a village in that direction," he said. "Perhaps the French are hoping to set up defences there. Do you think the Lord Sorcier is with that contingent?"

"The elemental seems to be taking us in that direction," Elias said. He drew in a few more ragged breaths before he could continue. "I think I know how we might draw him out."

The elemental sped up suddenly, as though taking some silent cue. As it ran ahead of them towards the French lines, the enemy soldiers yelled and fired upon it. Their ammunition did nothing to slow the creature, however, and it soon became clear that it would wash over the hapless French like a tidal wave.

Just as the elemental rose to crash upon their ranks, it seized up and wavered in place.

At the same moment, Elias stumbled, and Albert had to reach out to catch him.

A single figure stepped forth from among the French soldiers to confront the water-bull. Albert presumed this to be the Lord Sorcier – and indeed, the man was wearing a French officer's uniform, with gold epaulettes upon his shoulders.

The French paused their withdrawal, unwilling to abandon their magician. But Albert and Elias had caught up to their retreat, and the English soldiers with them ran ahead to engage the enemy army. Musket fire popped unevenly across the battlefield, and smoke rose up around them.

Elias had begun to struggle. Albert felt it in his slowed movement; he saw it in the assistant magician's flickering golden eyes. Elias kept his gaze fixed upon the elemental as he stumbled across the battlefield on Albert's shoulder. His body trembled with some heavy struggle, and Albert realised that the Lord Sorcier was contesting his grip upon the elemental.

Albert hauled Elias through the thick, confusing smoke, following his mumbled directions. Though the way was unclear, Elias always seemed to know the direction of the creature he controlled. Ragged soldiers stumbled through the smoke like ghosts – more than once, Albert lifted his musket to shoot at a phantom in a blue uniform, before he remembered how badly he needed to hold his shot for the magician they had come to confront. Thankfully, the confusion was absolute, and none of the French ever came close enough to see them pass.

And then, they emerged from the smoke – so close to the elemental that muddy water spattered upon Albert's face.

There, on the other side of the water-bull, stood the Lord Sorcier himself.

Albert stared at him, suddenly taken aback.

The Lord Sorcier was wearing a fine officer's uniform. That much, Albert had expected. But the enemy magician was a very young man indeed – much younger than Albert himself. His long brown hair was pulled back into a ponytail, but the ends of it had been badly singed. Dirt and weariness and misery marred his smooth features.

Is this the man who brought a hurricane down upon Corunna? Albert wondered. *Is this the man who commanded the Zadorra River to kill me?*

He could not fathom it, suddenly. The Lord Sorcier could not possibly have been older than his youngest brother.

Shouts cut through the haze of Albert's surprise – and he realised belatedly that the French had left soldiers on guard for the Lord Sorcier, just as Albert had taken it upon himself to guard Elias. One of the French soldiers brought up his gun. Albert followed suit before he could think better of it. Both muskets fired – but only Albert's found its mark. The French soldier toppled over like a rag doll.

A few of the nearby English soldiers noticed the altercation, even among the smoke. Men shouted and ran – and a dangerous battle soon began around the two magicians.

Albert fumbled to reload his musket, cursing himself for the impulsive shot. The Lord Sorcier looked sharply over towards him – or rather, Albert thought, towards *Elias*. The French magician widened his eyes with a strange sort of horror, and he let out an exclamation in French.

"*Sainte mère de Dieu!*" the young man cried out. "*Les Anglais ont pactisé avec un être féerique!*"

Mother of God, Albert translated in his head. *The English have bargained with a faerie.*

Surely, he had heard the man incorrectly?

But no. The Lord Sorcier's features now revealed a fear that transcended all language.

Elias leaned heavily upon Albert's shoulder, groaning with exertion as he fought against the elemental's fury. "What . . . what has he said?" Elias asked. "Do you know, Albert? I am terrible at French."

Albert stared at him, unable to speak.

Have we really bargained with a faerie? Albert thought. *Is that what we have done?*

"It probably doesn't matter," Elias mumbled.

The assistant magician was flagging dangerously. He had lost more blood in their advance; Albert could see it staining through the bandages more and more. Elias's grip on the elemental wavered, and it turned slowly in place, looming ominously over them. Albert felt its seething, furious glee as it became aware of its impending freedom.

Another musket ball whizzed past his ear; the wind of it cut him so that he wondered for a moment whether it had actually hit him. The urgency of the situation flooded back full force, and Albert made a fateful decision all at once.

"Elias," Albert said. "Are all magicians vulnerable to iron?"

Elias gave a rattling breath. "Yes," he managed. "All."

Albert abandoned his attempt to reload his musket. Instead, he left the iron ramrod inside the barrel, and he pushed Elias away from himself.

This, he thought, *is a terrible idea. But at least it is an idea.*

Albert lifted his musket up to his shoulder. He took aim at the young Lord Sorcier – and he pulled the trigger.

There was a hot flash, and a loud bang. Fiery agony lanced through Albert's arm. In the next moment, he realised that he was on the ground, on his back, staring up at the sky.

There was a ringing in his ears – so loud that he was not sure any more whether the surrounding screams came from the English or the French. A roar of water echoed through the air . . .

. . . but the water did not crash down upon the English.

Albert rolled his neck to stare dazedly at his hand, even as a small voice in his head advised that he should not. There were fingers missing, he saw, and the whole of his forearm looked simply mangled.

The sight of it overcame him – not because he had never seen anything like it before, but because it was his *own* hand and his *own* arm.

Just before he passed out, he thought he might have heard Elias calling his name.

Chapter Four

lbert swam in and out of consciousness several times. It was hard to keep the time, of course, but it felt something like an eternity. If Albert had been aware enough to think coherent thoughts, he might have found this to be a good sign; after all, if the English had lost, he probably would not have lived long enough to suffer.

". . . very best surgeon?" he thought he heard Elias demand. "Go and get him, by God!"

"That'd be Guthrie, sir!" a voice responded, with a surprising amount of respect. "I'll go and fetch him, sir!"

Time was strange and distended – but the next that Albert knew, there was a fresh, horrendous pain in his arm, even worse than the pain that had gone before. Surely, it was the *worst* pain that he had ever suffered in his life, and he would later be ashamed to admit how much he screamed.

"You are not allowed to die, Mr Lowe," he heard Elias say. "I only stayed in this awful mire in order to send you home safely to your family, do you understand? If you spoil that for me, then I shall be very cross indeed!"

Is that the terrible bargain which I made with a faerie? Albert wondered dimly. *How very strange.*

But somehow, the knowledge that Albert must not cross the

faerie who had saved him kept him stubbornly clinging to life and awareness.

It was an interminable aeon of pain and delirium before Albert finally came back to full consciousness. When he did, he was surprised to find himself in a proper bed, in a proper little house. Sunlight poured in through a nearby window; one of the young boys who served as an officer's aide sat next to his bed, staring down at him with curiosity.

"Did—?" Albert coughed on the words, feeling dazed. "Did we win, then?"

The boy laughed. "Was a total rout, sir!" he said. "For the French, I mean! They couldn't run themselves back to France nearly fast enough once their Lord Sorcier died!"

Albert blinked slowly. He glanced instinctively down at his arm and winced as he saw only a bandaged stump.

Ah well, Albert thought. *I have cut away so many other men's limbs that perhaps I deserve it done to me.*

The boy shoved a flask towards him with a sympathetic look in his eyes. "Magician-general's orders, sir," he said. "You're to have a victory drink."

Albert took the flask with his good hand and choked down a swallow. The alcohol burned pleasantly as it went down. A moment later, he processed the boy's words.

"The magician-general?" Albert asked, bewildered. "Do we have one of those?"

"We do now, by God!" the boy said proudly. "Wellington created him an office on the spot after he put down the dread Lord Sorcier!"

Albert's mind slowly formed connections. "You mean to say that . . . Elias Wilder is now our ranking magician?" he asked.

"Yes, sir!" the aide told him. "The rest of the army's gone on, but the magician-general left me with orders to see to you. You're headed home, a'course, as soon as you can travel."

"Ah," Albert said. The suggestion seemed unreal somehow.

After all of the cold nights and trudging misery, Albert should have been thrilled at the prospect of returning to a safe home and a regular bed. But though he had apparently helped to turn the tide of battle, he could not help the stab of deep, dark shame that occurred at the idea that he'd lost the ability to fight.

"Would you tell me all about the battle?" the boy asked eagerly. "You was there, right next to that Lord Sorcier, wasn't you?"

Albert coughed. "If you'll search me out another drink," he said, "I will be happy to tell you what I can."

Chapter Five

*N*othing at home felt as real as it once had.

Albert had expected that the world would slide back into place as soon as he set foot back in England. Surely, he thought, the sight of his family would soothe him, and his old familiar bed at Carroway House in London would give him leave to dream away the horrors of war.

But though Albert's mother cried joyful tears to see him and his father held him close while his youngest brother hurried over with a great big smile on his face, Albert became aware of a sick, hollow place in his chest that he knew no bed could ever fill.

Of all things, Elias Wilder should have been the thing that he forgot. Compared to the blood and the surgeries and the awful cries of the dying, the assistant magician felt less consequential and more unreal, the longer that Albert tarried in England. But every once in a while, Albert would hear the maids gossiping about the magician-general, still fighting in France, and he would pause and remember that a very real faerie had saved his life, on the condition that he should come back to his family.

At those times, Albert wondered whether he had actually fulfilled his promise. *Perhaps I will wake upon the battlefield at any moment*, he thought idly. *Perhaps I am still in Vitoria, drowning in the Zadorra River.*

But one could not live one's life expecting to wake at any moment.

And so, Albert shoved these thoughts aside and smiled at his mother and allowed himself to enjoy the awful sound of her off-key humming.

The dream did not end, somehow, until that fateful day one year later, when Elias Wilder finally reappeared.

He did so in his usual unusual manner, of course: Carroway House's butler hurried into the morning room one day, sputtering that a man without a calling card had shown up at the door, insisting to see Albert. "He is not even dressed to call!" the butler fumed. "He said that he served with you in the war, Mr Albert, and that if I did not fetch you, he would turn me into a frog!"

Albert considered this statement carefully, turning it around in his mind and examining it from several angles.

Ah, he thought suddenly. *This is real. I am in England, and Elias Wilder has come to call.*

Albert broke out into a smile. "Please show him in," he said. "And . . . could I trouble you for a fresh pot of tea?"

The butler shot Albert an odd look at that – but he nodded once and hurried off to fulfil the request. Soon, he returned to let a man into the morning room – a familiar fellow in sturdy, unremarkable dress and very comfortable-looking boots.

It only made sense that Albert's world had changed so greatly, while Elias Wilder had not changed at all. Another full year of war had somehow failed to etch a single line upon the other man's face. Still, Albert thought, there was a heaviness about the pale man's shoulders which had not been there before, and now that Elias's hair was not so dirty, Albert could see that it was a very fine white-blond that did not seem quite natural.

Elias paused in the doorway. A frown flickered across his delicate features as Albert stood up slowly to greet him.

And these were the first words that the magician said, after an entire year of absence:

"You are still missing an arm?"

Albert smiled. The ridiculous statement felt warm and familiar, somehow. It was entirely too strange to be a dream.

"Hello to you as well," he said cheerfully. Albert offered out his remaining arm to shake hands. "I hear that you have earned yourself some commendations."

Elias scowled at this and allowed the matter of Albert's missing arm to pass. "Commendations are cheap," he said. "It is a simple matter to give a man a medal and tell him he has done a good job." Still, he sat down when Albert indicated a chair. "I must apologise," the magician added briskly. "You should have had a commendation yourself. I allowed a great many people to believe that it was I who killed the Lord Sorcier. I hoped that it would put them into such a fear that they would listen to me when I forced them to attend to your injuries in a hurry."

Albert broadened his smile. "I am sure that you did not *lie* to anyone about it," he said. "Not directly, at least."

He paused as a maid came in to refresh the tea and pour them both a cup. She edged towards the wall as though to stay and serve, but Albert shooed her gently away. The maids in his mother's household had signed on to serve idle nobles and not faeries – he was sure that the woman would be horrified if she'd known his visitor's true identity.

The maid departed, and the room fell once more into silence. Finally, Albert cleared his throat. "You have nothing to apologise for, of course," he told Elias. "You surely saved my life."

Elias glanced away uncomfortably at this. "Have we not saved each other's lives?" he asked. "I admit, I have lost track of the tally. That would be a deadly mistake if I were . . . elsewhere."

In faerie, Albert thought silently. But he had learned his lesson since the day that he had first outed Elias as a magician – it was clear that the man did not wish to discuss his heritage, and so Albert pretended to overlook the lapse.

"When you lose track of the tally," Albert told Elias gravely, "I suspect that means that you have become friends."

Elias blinked at this. "Oh," he said. A thoughtful look flickered across his face. "Are we friends then, Albert?"

"I am certainly *your* friend," Albert replied. "I suppose you must decide if you are mine, since I cannot decide the matter for you."

Elias smiled. It was one of those oddly enchanting smiles which so rarely graced his features. "I am your friend, then," he said softly. "And I am so very pleased to see you at home with your family."

Albert nodded at this. It seemed only natural, somehow, that they should come back to the matter of that bargain. "I am pleased to *be* home," he said. "Though . . . I must admit to some distress."

Elias raised an eyebrow, and Albert frowned, trying to piece his thoughts together.

"I have found it . . . difficult to believe that I am truly back home," Albert said. "Though seeing you has done me good. And . . . I have had a shame which I cannot throw off, ever since I woke without my arm. But that makes even less sense. Somehow, I am ashamed that I had to stop the fighting . . . but I am *also* ashamed that I killed so many men. How I can be ashamed about them both at once, I do not rightly know."

The weight upon Elias's shoulders grew heavier, and Albert saw a knowing look in the man's uncanny eyes.

"I understand your meaning," Elias said. "But this, at least, I can answer for you. Humans do not grasp the matter for some reason – but it is quite normal to feel many contradictory things at once. Emotions need not make sense, Albert. They are there so that *we* might make sense of them. It is your job to choose the shame that you prefer, though the ghost of the other one might remain."

Albert nodded slowly. He decided to politely overlook the reference to *humans*. He took a long sip of his tea, savouring the taste as he worked through the idea in his head.

He wasn't sure which shame he preferred, now that he

thought on the matter. Neither one was very appealing.

I am sure that I shall need to spend another full year deciding, Albert thought with a sigh.

Elias interrupted his musings. "The Prince Regent has asked me to be his court magician," he said. He had a sour note in his voice. "He has offered to give me the title of 'Lord Sorcier', since that is the man I supposedly killed. He seems quite taken with the idea, in fact."

Albert frowned. "The Prince Regent has *offered*?" he asked. "Do you mean to say that you have not yet taken him up on that offer?"

Elias shot him a dry look, and Albert remembered belatedly that he was talking to a man – or perhaps a faerie – who had little natural respect for English royalty. "I see," Albert said. "But should you not consider the offer? I mean to say . . . I *hope* you will be staying. And it is quite something to be offered a court position *and* a title."

Elias grew even more troubled at this suggestion. "I am not sure that I wish to serve England in any further capacity," he said. "I was right, Albert – though the French are defeated, the workhouses are worse than ever. I asked the Prince Regent if he intended to do anything about them, and he looked at me as though I was mad." He stared down into his teacup as though it had tried to conceal a terrible secret from him.

"It pleased me to protect the men I served with in France, as I had learned to like them," Elias said. "But I do not wish to serve a creature like the Prince Regent – nor to become a silly noble like the other useless ones I've met."

Albert chuckled. "I see your concern," he said. "I like to believe that not all nobles are silly and useless, given that my father and my brother are two of those. But if it worries you, Elias, I would like to point out that *you* would not need to be a silly, useless noble. In fact, if you are elevated as Lord Wellington has been, you would have a seat in the House of Lords and a voice in exactly those matters which distress you." He paused. "My father has helped draft several reforms for the workhouses. They have never passed, of course – but you would have an ally in him, if you so wished."

Elias knit his brow. Albert saw him turn the matter over in his head.

". . . I shall take this all in mind," Elias said finally. He said it in the exact same tone he had used so long ago when Albert had asked if he intended to leave the army. The magician cleared his throat. "But in the meantime . . . do you *enjoy* not having an arm, Albert?"

Albert blinked. "What an odd question," he said. "Of course I do not enjoy it, Elias."

Elias frowned. "Well, why then has no one made you a new one?" he asked with a hint of tetchiness.

Albert raised his eyebrows. "I do not know anyone who is capable of *making* arms, Elias," he replied.

The magician flushed. "I was not aware that it was so uncommon," he said. "But you are incorrect, Albert – you know at least *one* man who is capable of making arms." He downed the contents of his teacup in one inelegant swallow. "It will take some time, of course. But I very much doubt you will be able to volunteer in the workhouses without one. And of course – if I am injured again, I should prefer to have you with two working arms."

Albert stared at the other man. He searched his mind for the proper sort of reply to something which was at once so generous and so outlandish. "I do not know what to say," he admitted finally. "Other than . . . well, what on earth will you make the arm *from*?"

Elias considered this seriously. "Out of silver, I should think," he said. "It's quite traditional, where I come from. Why, you'll be after the style of a famous king." The heaviness upon his shoulders lightened at the thought, and another smile came across his face. "Yes. I think that is what we will do."

A few days later – after Albert had requested a bed and a sort of workroom for their strange visitor – wild gossip went up among the *ton* of London.

There was now a court magician in England, they said. A powerful magician – one who routinely performed three impossible things before breakfast.

The Prince Regent had named him Lord Elias Wilder – England's first and only Lord Sorcier.

Afterword

There is an apocryphal story about fish on the beach that has stayed with me my entire life. I do not remember where I first heard it, but I have always been able to recall it to mind with absolute clarity. It goes like this:

A great number of fish had washed up on the beach; there, they flip-flopped, gasping for breath. A little girl had taken it upon herself to walk up and down the beach, however, picking up fish and throwing them back into the ocean. A bystander marvelled at this, and headed out to talk to her.

"Why are you throwing these fish back into the ocean?" he asked the little girl. "It won't even matter in the end. There are so many of them! You cannot possibly hope to save them all!"

The little girl frowned at the bystander and held up the fish that she currently had in her hands. "It matters to *this* fish," she told him. And then she turned herself back down the beach and stubbornly continued throwing fish back into the ocean.

The story normally ends there – but I like to think that the bystander then joined the little girl, and that a great deal *more* fish were saved as a result.

I have often found myself in despair at how nonsensically awful other human beings can be. As much as we like to believe that we are capable of learning from history, I'm afraid that we are very prone to repeating the exact same mistakes as a society, time and time again. But every time I am confronted by some inescapable proof of the lowness of human nature, I am *also* reminded that I have within me the power to improve my *own* nature. There are plenty of fish upon the beach who would be grateful for a bit of kindness – and if you take the time to rescue even one, then perhaps you may even convince a bystander to join you and rescue another.

I do not mean to say that we should ever stop trying to solve the big problems in the world. But – as Elias would say – sometimes, when you cannot force the world to come to its senses, you must settle only for wiping away some of the small evils in front of you.

Every fish you throw back into the ocean is a triumph of the idea that human beings can be better. I do my best, every day, to throw at least one fish back into the ocean. I hope that you will join me.

With regard to this particular book, I must thank my husband for his constant love and support – and most especially for the coffee. I would like to thank my alpha readers, Laura Elizabeth and Julie Golick, for their boundless enthusiasm and occasional nitpicks. I must surely thank Sophie Ricard for her help with the French in this book, however few the phrases might have been – truly, Sophie, you are the Albert to my Elias when it comes to French grammar. I must give heartfelt thanks to Tamlin Thomas for numerous historical corrections. Without any one of them, this book would not have been nearly as good as it is.

I owe further thanks to Dr Kevin Linch of the University of Leeds for his answers to several incredibly niche questions on the Napoleonic-era British military, as used in *The Lord Sorcier*. Any remaining historical errors in the story are purely my own.

Last of all, I would like to thank you, dear reader, for coming this far with me. I hope you enjoyed this book as much as I enjoyed writing it.

Lord Elias Wilder, Regency England's court
magician, regularly performs three impossible things
before breakfast – but the one thing he cannot do
is raise a daughter. As Theodora Wilder continues
taking children under their roof, however, Elias
is finally forced to confront his dark familial past
and the matter of his dubious faerie father.

This short, exclusive novella, written from Lord
Elias Wilder's perspective, takes place just after
the events of *Half a Soul* and includes glimpses
of the Lord Sorcier's childhood in faerie. Visit the
link below to subscribe to *The Atwater Scandal
Sheets*, and read *The Latch Key* today!

https://oliviaatwater.com/newsletter

extras

orbit

meet the author

OLIVIA ATWATER writes whimsical historical fantasy with a hint of satire. She lives in Montreal, Quebec, with her fantastic, prose-inspiring husband and her two cats. When she told her second-grade history teacher that she wanted to work with history someday, she is fairly certain this isn't what either party had in mind. She has been, at various times, a historical re-enactor, a professional witch at a metaphysical supply store, a web developer and a vending machine repairperson.

Find out more about Olivia Atwater and other Orbit authors by registering for the free monthly newsletter at orbitbooks.net.

if you enjoyed
HALF A SOUL

look out for

TEN THOUSAND STITCHES

Regency Faerie Tales: Book Two

by

Olivia Atwater

Regency housemaid Euphemia Reeves has acquired a faerie godfather. Unfortunately, he has no idea what he's doing.

Effie has most inconveniently fallen in love with the dashing Mr. Benedict Ashbrooke. There's only one problem: Effie is a housemaid, and a housemaid cannot marry a gentleman. It seems that Effie is out of luck until she stumbles into the faerie realm of Lord Blackthorn, who is only too eager to help her win

Mr. Ashbrooke's heart. All he asks in return is that Effie sew ten thousand stitches into his favorite jacket.

Effie has heard rumors about what happens to those who accept magical bargains. But life as a maid at Hartfield is so awful that she is willing to risk even her immortal soul for a chance at something better. Now she has one hundred days—and ten thousand stitches—to make Mr. Ashbrooke fall in love and propose... if Lord Blackthorn doesn't wreck things by accident, that is. For Effie's greatest obstacle might well be Lord Blackthorn's overwhelmingly good intentions.

Prologue

Euphemia Reeves was a very irritable young woman.

This would have surprised most of the other servants at Hartfield – in fact, if you had asked the esteemed housekeeper, Mrs Sedgewick, she might have told you that Effie was nearly the *ideal* sort of chambermaid. As far as Mrs Sedgewick was aware, Effie never shirked her duties and always conducted herself with perfect composure.

Mrs Sedgewick would have been shocked to hear the words that currently spilled from Effie's lips.

"... no consideration whatsoever, *none!*" Effie hissed to herself, as she scrubbed down the wooden floors of the entryway for the third time that day. Mud caked the floorboards once again, as the men of the Family had come tromping inside one by one from the nasty winter weather outside. "Ought to be against the law to go out ridin' when there's mud an' snow!"

extras

Lord Culver and his younger brother, Mr Edmund Ash-brooke, had little awareness of the spectacular messes that they left behind. Effie would have received quite the tongue-lashing for leaving her boots on back home, but Lord Culver – more than fifteen years her senior! – was so used to messes magically disappearing behind him that he saw little use in peeling off his own boots until he'd already tramped up to his room. Some poor laundry maid would soon have to scrub his entire outfit once he'd pulled it off.

"*There's no use gettin' angry,*" Effie's mother used to chide her. "*It'll just get you into trouble. You can think all of the angry thoughts you want, but they've got to stay inside your head!*"

"Muddy, puffed-up popinjays, the lot of 'em!" Effie muttered at her brush. "Well, birds are smarter, aren't they? At least they clean their own feathers!" The words tumbled out beneath her breath today, instead of staying in her head. *Sorry, Mum*, she thought apologetically. *I've run out of patience again.*

Normally, when Effie became this cross, she went to find some convenient mending – she'd always found needlework to be remarkably soothing. But the Ashbrookes were hosting yet *another* ball tomorrow evening, and the staff was running about like mad trying to prepare for it once again. Lady Culver had only married Lord Culver last year in London, and ever since he'd returned with her, she'd been determined to take charge of the household to run things *her* way.

Unfortunately, Lady Culver's way mostly seemed to involve dismissing any servant who happened to displease her and refusing ever to replace them.

The way Lady Culver goes on, she must think she's hired a bunch of magicians instead of a bunch of servants, Effie thought tiredly. *She ought to put that in her next advertisement – maybe England's court magician will show up and do her laundry!*

This thought, of course, only made Effie even more cross than ever. She sighed and dug into her memory, searching for a nursery rhyme. The cook used nursery rhymes to time her preparations, and Effie had taken to using them as a method of last resort to calm her nerves. She narrowed her eyes and carefully recited at the floor:

> "Wind the bobbin up,
> Wind the bobbin up,
> Pull, pull, clap, clap, clap.
> Wind it back again . . . "

The long frustration of the day dimmed a bit beneath the monotonous rhyme, and Effie relaxed her shoulders minutely. She had just started the verse again, leaning back into the cleaning, when she was interrupted.

"Lydia! Are you about, Lydia?" Mrs Sedgewick's thin, reedy voice snapped through the air in the hallway behind Effie. "For goodness' sake – has anyone seen Lydia? I haven't the time to be tracking down every maid in this household!"

Effie took a deep, steadying breath and tried to erase the scowl from her face as Mrs Sedgewick came around the corner. The stern old housekeeper strode out towards Effie; the wooden soles of her half-boots made a neat clipping noise as she went. Mrs Sedgewick was in particularly immaculate form today, with her dark hair pulled back into a tight bun upon her head. She was dressed in her black silk housekeeper's gown, of course – for she was inordinately proud of the thing, and she preferred never to be seen in any other clothing.

"Effie!" Mrs Sedgewick said. "Have you seen Lydia? Her Ladyship would like the piano in the ballroom dusted again. She says she can still hear the dust in it."

Effie flinched at the suggestion. *We've already dusted that dratted piano twice!* she thought crossly. *Perhaps someone ought to test Her Ladyship's hearing, in case she's going deaf.* But what Effie actually said aloud was, "Mr Allen sent Lydia to air out another of the guest rooms, Mrs Sedgewick."

The housekeeper's eyes flared with irritation. "Mr Allen did?" she observed icily. "Well, well. And since when did the maids of the house start taking orders from the *butler*?"

Effie swallowed down a frustrated sigh. Mrs Sedgewick had been at odds with their new butler, Mr Allen, ever since he'd been hired on at Hartfield. Lady Culver had dismissed the old butler, Mr Simmons – but since Hartfield really could not get by without a butler, Lady Culver's family had insisted on sending Mr Allen to take over the job. He had been a very well-regarded butler in London, before he'd deigned to take over Hartfield. Everyone knew that he was only there by some noble relative's earnest request. Unfortunately, Mr Allen's immediate reorganisation of the household had infuriated Mrs Sedgewick, who was quite used to working with Mr Simmons and not at all fond of this newer, more refined interloper.

Lord only knew who was originally to blame for the initial spat between the butler and the housekeeper – but the rivalry had grown worse and worse as the weeks went by, until even the stable hands found themselves forced to choose an allegiance to one or the other.

"I don't know much more than that, Mrs Sedgewick," Effie said. "But Lydia should be upstairs if you're lookin' for her." Effie scrubbed at a patch of mud on the floor, keeping her eyes carefully on the ground.

"Ordering around the maids!" Mrs Sedgewick huffed again. "Oh, that nasty man, getting above himself! Lady Culver will hear about this – see if she doesn't!"

Effie did not respond this time, though she was sure that Mrs Sedgewick *wanted* her to do so. She had learned that if she did not react to the housekeeper's dramatic pronouncements, Mrs Sedgewick would eventually give up and go seek out one of the more gossip-friendly maids.

"Mr Allen might well spoil the ball at this rate," Mrs Sedgewick added insistently. "I tell you, I shall not hesitate to lay the blame upon him if he does."

"Yes, Mrs Sedgewick," Effie murmured obediently.

The housekeeper thinned her lips to a neat line. "Well," she said. "I am *buried* in work. I cannot simply stand here gabbing at housemaids all day." Mrs Sedgewick said this as though it were *Effie* who had started their conversation, and not her at all.

"Yes, Mrs Sedgewick," Effie repeated carefully. But her mouth had begun to twitch in annoyance, and she knew that she didn't dare look up for fear of showing her irritation on her face.

Mrs Sedgewick turned on her heel and started for the hallway again, the wooden *clip-clop* of her boots slowly fading behind her. As soon as she had gone, Effie let out a long, weary breath.

"None of us has time to gab, of course," Effie muttered at her brush. "Just imagine that! *Time!*" She glanced at the bucket of water next to her and sighed, shoving to her feet. She was going to have to spread fresh sand over the entryway all over again—

The front door opened abruptly.

Effie staggered back with a surprised shriek. Her foot caught on the bucket of water, and she found herself toppling backwards.

"Good God!" a man exclaimed. A strong, sturdy arm snaked around Effie's waist just in time to keep her from plummeting downwards.

Two warm brown eyes blinked down at her. A pleasant,

sturdy scent engulfed her – sandalwood, Effie thought, and just a hint of the outside. She coloured as she recognised Mr Benedict Ashbrooke's strong, handsome features.

"Ah!" Effie squeaked. "I . . . I'm so sorry!"

Benedict blinked again. His dark hair was pleasantly mussed and scattered with melting snow. Benedict was the youngest brother of the Ashbrooke family. Effie had always said that he was also the most *handsome* brother – or at least, she had quietly *thought* as much, before he had left a few years ago to travel the Continent. Now that he stared down at her with that sheepish smile, holding her in his strong, warm arms, Effie found herself struck utterly dumb.

"Nothing to worry about," Benedict assured her. "I should be the one apologising, I'm sure." He set Effie carefully back onto her feet – though his hands lingered on her shoulders with a hint of concern. He knit his brow at her. "I swear I know your face, miss. Have we met before? Are you staying here for one of Lady Culver's balls, perchance?"

Effie blinked dazedly. *For the ball?* she thought. *What on earth does he mean by that?*

"I should think you *do* know me, yes!" Effie said. She shouldn't have dared to be so pert – but her heart was still racing in her chest, and her head felt warm and muddled from his nearness.

"I knew I must have," Benedict said ruefully. "Do you know, I am terrible with names – but I normally remember far better when there's such a pretty face attached."

Effie widened her eyes. *I don't know what's going on at all any more*, she thought.

"Benedict, good heavens!" Lady Culver's voice called down from the stairs, and Effie glanced up towards her. The matron of the household was barely older than Effie herself – but the terrible scowl which currently lay upon her fine, aristocratic features made her seem more like old Mrs Sedgewick. "You're back from your tour, then?" Lady Culver asked impatiently. "Why did no one tell me to expect you? And for that matter – why are you exchanging pleasantries with the help?"

Benedict knit his brow again. He glanced back towards Effie, who shrank with embarrassment beneath his gaze. As she did, she caught sight of the old, fraying lace attached to the neckline of her gown.

I am wearing one of Lady Culver's old hand-me-down gowns, Effie realised belatedly. *But really, no one with half a brain ought to mistake me for a lady.*

"Oh," Benedict said. "I see." He managed another helpless smile at Effie. "Well," he told her. "I suppose I have made fools of us both. Do forgive me, miss."

"You're forgiven, of course," Effie mumbled out. It was the only thing she could think to say in the moment.

Benedict cleared his throat and looked back up the stairs towards Lady Culver. "I sent a letter to Thomas," he told her. "But I suppose he forgot to pass it on, did he?"

Lady Culver narrowed her eyes. "So he did," she said. "Well, Benedict – you are lucky that we have aired out the rooms. The lodge is uninhabitable at the moment, but there may yet be an extra room for you at Hartfield in spite of my husband's oversight." She paused. "There is a ball tomorrow evening, however. You will have to make yourself available to the young ladies for dancing, or else we shall never hear the end of it."

Benedict chuckled at that. There was a warm, earthy sound to his laugh which Effie suddenly found very difficult to ignore. "I enjoy dancing," he told Lady Culver. "So that is no imposition at all."

Benedict nearly took off up the stairs – but he paused

thoughtfully and glanced down at his feet. He took one careful step back and pried his muddy boots from them, one after the other.

"There's really no need to make *extra* work for you, is there?" he said to Effie apologetically. He headed up the stairs before she could find the wherewithal to respond.

As his figure disappeared, Effie was struck by a horrified realisation.

"Oh, bother," she said. "I think I've just fallen in love."

Follow us:

f **/orbitbooksUS**

y **/orbitbooks**

▶ **/orbitbooks**

Join our mailing list
to receive alerts on our
latest releases and deals.

orbitbooks.net

Enter our monthly
giveaway for the chance
to win some epic prizes.

orbitloot.com